EVEN LOVERS DROWN

R. Walker

EVEN LOVERS DROWN

A. M. Walker

Felix Publishing

FIRST EDITION

ISBNs:
978-1-80541-600-5 Paperback
978-1-80541-601-2 Hardback
978-1-80541-599-2 eBook

A mermaid found a swimming lad,
Picked him for her own,
Pressed her body to his body,
Laughed: and plunging down
Forgot in cruel happiness
That even lovers drown.

The Mermaid W. B. YEATS

I had long known the diverse tastes of the wood,
Each leaf, each bark, rank earth from every hollow;
Knew the smells of bird's breath and of bat's wing;
Yet sight I lacked: until you stole upon me,
Touching my eyelids with light fingertips.
`Open one eye at first; only one eye!'
The trees blazed out, their colours whirled together,
Nor ever before had I been aware of sky.

Gift of Sight ROBERT GRAVES

Canberra, July 1961

Dear Laurel,

If I were granted three wishes by your fairy godmother, I would wish firstly that my actions and decisions caused no harm, as I fear they have already.

My second wish is for you. That you find yourself a young man, a loving man, a man who makes you laugh and dance but does not in any way prevent you becoming... I cannot imagine what you will become. It has something to do with remaining a free spirit and yet still able to love him and the children you will have one day.

My third wish is my most constant wish and selfish desire. That you will (but not too late for my beard grows grey) having found Dr. Walter Solomon's London address, and thus mine, perhaps in Tanganyika or Patagonia ... appear at my threshold barefoot: the same and more.

Oh God how I miss you, you who made me a willow cabin at your gate and called upon my soul and showed me that love looks not with the eyes nor with the mind but with the soul. And now it looks and looks and waits and waits … listening to something you would like, a refrain from a musical: a woman is singing about spreading her wings to take to the sky. She's singing about Summertime.

We had a Summertime, didn't we? and a Midsummer Night's Dream as well. *Tous les deux*! What a feast!

My third wish compels me to post this letter, to post it from here, with my address, now, this moment.

My second wish cautions me to tear this letter up immediately.

My first wish will help me to decide. So, I reflect, with love,

Tom

PS It was you, more than the doctor, who restored my mind.

CHAPTER 1

1951 – THE BEGINNING

It began with a man being rowed across a lake. Sitting up in the stern of the boat, not completely centred. His hands were tucked in between his knees, his neck and shoulders rigid. He looks as if he's been dropped there, *thought Corporal Griffiths who was wondering if it was going to be as tricky getting his strange cargo out of the boat as it had been getting him in.*

It was summer and very early in the morning. Mist still hung round the tops of the trees on the distant shore of the lake. Fish broke the surface here and there. Two ducks took off squawking. Then a sudden beating and crashing of huge wings as a heron burst out of the woods and flapped overhead.

Any observer might have wondered if the passenger in the stern was asleep. He did not look around or seem to notice anything. He didn't move or speak. But there was nobody else about, just the two men making their way silently across a quarter of a mile of water towards a small wooden hut half hidden in bushes on the other side. Just the clunk-thud of the rowlocks and the little splash of the oars.

Corporal Griffiths was relieved at the silence. There was something odd about a man whose eyelids didn't blink. He tried not to look at him.

At least he wouldn't have to work with him or take orders from him or even talk to him much, just row his provisions over twice a week and get him across to the big house every Thursday for the meetings with the Doctor. He wouldn't need any looking after, they'd said. The Captain could look after himself. Well, as to that, the Captain had set out just now to walk through the shallows with his boots on. Griffiths had stopped him and unlaced them and now watched him sitting motionless with damp trousers rolled up over pale bare feet. Deep pink-brown scars were visible… it looked like they went right round his ankles. At the other side, he left the boat too soon, walking into knee-deep water. Griffiths handed him his boots to carry.

He watched him tread unsteadily through the reeds to the shore, and he watched as one boot dropped into the water, toppled over and floated back towards the boat.

The man didn't pause or look round. He went up and sat on the grass with his back against the hut, still holding one boot.

After putting the box of provisions down on the table and deciding not to stay and unpack it, Griffiths laid the sodden boot on the grass in the weak sunshine. The sock inside it had gone, floated off somewhere. He couldn't help that.

He shrugged at the silent figure on the ground and hurried off to row back to the house. As he sat down in the boat and reached for the oars, he was surprised to hear a soft, courteous voice: 'Thank you, Corporal.'

***

'He should have went on' the man wrote on the large pad he had requested. Sitting in his wooden hut at the table by the window which looked onto the lake he was aware of the powerful presence of the forest behind him.

He looked at the words, at the pen in his hand, and shook his head. Drops of water fell on the page. He was soaking wet having walked slowly naked into a sudden fierce shower just after dawn. Now he sat wearing only the trousers he had arrived in and which he did not recognize. They were also wet as he hadn't looked for a towel.

'Try to write,' Solomon had said.

'Not in a diary!' the man surprised himself by replying.

'Why not?' the doctor cajoled, waiting for a response which would provide a clue, waiting patiently. 'What is a diary?' Solomon asked.

'Something we don't keep.'

'We don't keep?' the doctor repeated.

'Daren't keep. Not allowed to keep. Bad practice. Dangerous. Do you remember why this might be so, Captain?' The man had no idea. The doctor waited then said, 'I will give you a large pad to write in each day. It will help you to assemble your thoughts. It will be easier for you, perhaps, than talking.'

'What is tucking?' the man asked, wondering why he was amused at the doctor's accent.

'Talking. Talking is what we are doing now and will continue to do. This will not be our last meeting.'

'I should never have come back' the man now wrote, correcting his first sentence which felt as if it was the first sentence he had written in a long time. But he left 'He should have went on' as evidence for Solomon of how his mind was working in the written mode.

'Everything is a clue' was one of the doctor's gentle and encouraging refrains. 'But where have I come back to?' the writing now continued, 'Is this back? What trousers are these? What trees?' He began to feel a measure of comfort as his coordination started to return and he asked himself *on paper: 'and what am I writing to find out?... too many questions...I have walked a little on the shore of this lake but not into these trees that surround this hut.'*

He began to write of the fear with some pleasure as a sense of control came to him for the first time in a long while.

'I can walk along the shore but not into the forest yet' he wrote, enjoying the changing of the form of words. Although I think I can list the trees.'

He found his right wrist was aching so put down the pen and watched the shadow from a small cloud move across the lake.

***

'To say I'm disappointed in you, Laurel, is an understatement. I'm shocked, saddened, but most of all I'm disgusted. I never thought I would be standing here with one of my girls who could have produced filth like this ... you presume to call it 'The Flowers of the Forest'... devious too. Hiding your smut behind a fancy title.' She barely touched the red exercise book lying on her desk. 'And a scholarship girl at that. I shall write to the Trust of course, cancelling the remainder of your scholarship. You must pack at once and stay in the dormitory until the taxi arrives.

You are leaving this school immediately. I have the moral welfare of the other girls to think of. And I forbid you to see or talk to Olivia Hobbs.'

A lump came to Laurel's throat at this mention of her best and only friend. So she was too infectious even to say goodbye. How ridiculous. It wasn't Olly's fault of course, but WHY had she insisted on reading that stupid story out loud just before the Latin lesson? Why had she begged Laurel to write it in the first place? No, don't blame Olly. She had agreed and taken up the dare.

'I can only say it's a mercy your poor mother is still away on tour. I gather you will be going to stay with your aunt in Wales. She will put you to school down there.'

***

I don't want to write syntax, *he thought and then wrote 'I want to list words only'. He closed his eyes.* I want to list what is in the hut but not what is in my head. *'There is no mirror in this cabin', he wrote and looked away from the reflection of his face in the window as the sun changed its angle. 'The light keeps changing. I am used to constant light then constant dark. The phenomenon of evening feels puzzling. I look away from my reflection so I do not know the colour of my eyes. It is easy to tell, however, that I am thin, too thin; not tall, dark haired. I can feel my beard, can feel the itch of scars as they stretch and heal.'*

***

'I'm sorry to have to say this but I have noticed that girls whose fathers have been sadly taken away by the war do seem to lack somewhat in the area of moral guidance.' The headmistress was still steaming on, her left hand rhythmically squeezing a large India rubber in the pen tray on her desk.

'And you had the effrontery to tell Miss Weatherby that this was a piece of 'creative writing' for the school magazine. It's beyond contemplation – or comprehension. That magazine bears the school motto –' Her voice was shaking. 'Do you honestly think that this unspeakable besmirchment is in any conceivable way 'Ad Majorem Gloriam…' I can't bring myself to say 'Dei'… I just hope that He will forgive you, that's all. Because I can't.

***

The relief of sleep… the thin dark man opened his eyes to observe that the door to the hut was open. He was pleased to find himself on a bed. I requested a desk and a table with paper and a book to read… and there they are, there in the light by the window. The light has returned again. I have slept all night, he thought. How strange to sleep all night. It must be peaceful here.

How strange to recognise night. And now day. And bird song. Solomon told me what I would be doing here but I have forgotten.

'Try to remember why you are here at this secluded spot,' Solomon had said. 'There is a fishing rod and equipment.' And so there was, placed neatly in the corner of the hut. There was this bed and a chair, a carpet, a curtain, food, even fruit, and drink, and what looked like sweets. He had forgotten sweets. The man moved to the desk to sit, to see if writing his observations stirred his memory.

***

Laurel had always prided herself on not getting caught. This was the first and the worst, she reflected as she pushed a remaining stray green sock into her bulging suitcase.

All her earlier misdemeanours, and they were many, had involved pinching marbles from the toyshop and loose change from the bottom of her mother's handbag or pretending to have a crippled leg and to have lost her bus fare so as to elicit sixpence from a passer-by to play the slot machines on the pier.

This was back in the seaside town of her early childhood, which was where, the day after her sixth birthday, she had discovered men.

***

He could not remember his name. He wanted to write his name as second entry, but nothing came to mind except the knowledge that he could not yet walk into the woods.

I passed along the water's edge

Beneath the humid trees

He wrote these words but felt they were not his. I know what's in the woods, he thought. I can make a list.

My list: Lowland oaks

beech

ash

alder, elder, guelder

poplar

hawthorn, blackthorn

11

rowan, holly
cherry, hornbeam
ivy, bramble, deep soil
bluebell, primrose, wild rose
wood sage, wood anemone, woodpigeon
He could hear the birdcall now and was impressed. He felt impressed by his list, wondered where it had come from and wanted to tell Solomon.

***

It wasn't her fault she had left it so late, with men. Her father had been killed in the war, or so she had been told. Anyway, she had no memory of him. Her mother had not provided her with any brothers or even a useful godfather, just Grandfather Lloyd who had a white beard and was very old.

As far as the men of the family went, she had to fill in the blanks herself. Her thick unruly hair was worn in an urchin cut. Skirts were a nuisance. When women in shops asked her 'are you a little boy or a little girl?' as if they really needed the information, she would vary her answers at random.

The truth was, she didn't realize that these were two separate categories of being.

Laurel had passed through her childhood up to now in the warm delusion that people were basically identical, that humanity was interchangeable and that someday, when she was grown up, she might just grow a beard herself if she felt like it.

All she knew was that some of her young companions could run faster, could ride bikes with no hands before she could, could whistle, which she tried and failed to do. And that some of the ones in frilly dresses would scream unaccountably – a revolting noise – if you put a spider down their necks or even an innocent earthworm into their hands.

***

This is day three, night four, I believe. I want to write Lindenbaum. I will write it though it is not English. Lindenbaum

> *Not English*
> *Enough trees*
> *Still the urge to list*
> *Eyes closed*
> *Sounds of water and birdsong*
> *Eyes open*
> *Woodpigeon*

Stockdove
Willow warbler
Garden warbler
Crow or jay

Small achievement. I ran to the little pier where the boat arrives. Ran quite smoothly. Felt quite strong so entered the wood backwards, passing several trees before the panic returned. Approached the lake and felt that I remember how to dive and to swim. But didn't. Desire to fish. Could list fishing terms. Slight desire for physical contact as bare feet entered water. Sexual feeling.

Vixen heard last night. Sign of dog fox this morning. The wind sometimes carries a bell from somewhere but no rain. I think it is Sunday and it sounds like a Protestant bell. The month is clear in my mind June – but I shall lose the month if I don't hold on to the day. The impulse therefore is to list days of the week, months of the year, to list in the most primitive and arithmetic way which will get me nowhere.

You, doctor, have urged me to 'write freely, not formally'. The contemplation of such amorphousness is tantamount to what I'm doing now: holding my breath.

Nice contradiction. Clue: FEAR. Syntax flowing remains alarming. Perhaps I can enter it backwoods.

***

On the day after her sixth birthday, as she boarded a bus into town with her mother to go and spend her birthday money on a real four-bladed penknife, her state of pre-lapsarian innocence came to an abrupt end. She bounded upstairs to sit on the top deck and there He was, her first real Man.

He had dark gingery hair curling up at the back of his neck. Laurel could see a beard which, on closer inspection, was thick and whorled with orange and grey like some jungle animal. He sat by the window at the front of the bus; alone, peaceful, looking out at the trees. The top of the bus was half-empty but she walked straight down to the front and sat herself down beside him. He was dressed in honey-coloured corduroy and wore a scarf of soft material round his neck instead of a collar and tie. The slight, heady aroma surrounding him was, she discovered much later, pipe tobacco.

***

Day Four.

A list of people I remember would be helpful in some way. Who do I remember? I think I see a boy writing at a table not unlike this one only he appears to be sitting at a window which looks not onto water but a large bare hill. No one else in the room where the boy writes. Someone in the house perhaps. The smell of... wood-smoke? Concentrate. Do I want to remember?

I want to make a garden, flowers and weeds, wildflowers... I can bore you doctor with their names, but a garden could be an informal expression of nature, not me. I will walk along the lake again. Try to run. Run into the edge of the trees looking, naming. Oak. English Oak. Pendunculate Oak. I could identify the birds that favour lowland woods and tangle...

Redstart
Nuthatch
Chaffinch,
Blue Tit,
Black Cap
Pipit
Robin,
Wren

***

Laurel gazed up at his beard, at his green eyes which crinkled into a silent smile when they saw this open-mouthed child staring up at him, and she was lost. It was an epiphany. This was something different. She could never grow up to become one of these.

Grow up. Grow UP. What did it mean? She was afraid it must involve a considerable loss of freedom. You didn't see adult women climbing trees or hurling themselves in a gate-vault over a fence, the only intelligent way to get across such barriers. There would be holes in nylon stockings to worry about and handbags and lipstick and 'keeping your knees together'.

Well, she just didn't seem to have the right sort of knees.

She closed her eyes and inhaled, pushing to the back of her mind the thought that she would most probably have to turn into a woman one day.

***

I begin another paragraph later this day which I want to call Monday. But I cannot concentrate and don't want to

17

think, so I permit a body feeling, not sexual. I am hungry. I want to prepare food. I desire something called soda bread. It is not here. I want to remember how to make it:

List:
Soda
Flour
Not enough

If you practice forgetting, they cannot reach you, or your name; only your body. Who said that?

***

One of the seaside towns where they were staying in digs had a big wheel which made her feel big not only because it took her up so high but also because her mother had let her ride it on her own, right to the top and round again.

'Look out for France! Look out for Paris! Try to spot Deauville while you're going round!' her mother shouted as Laurel swung off in her brightly painted seat.

These were the occasions, sudden and rare, when Laurel remembered being happy with her mother.

'Did you see anything?' came the question, almost lost in the whoosh as the seat swung down and swung off again. Laurel shook her head, grinning.

'Never mind, dear,' her mother took her hand and helped her down at the end of the ride; 'It was just the houses in between.'

'Sing it, mother, please!' Laurel begged.

'Wiv a ladder an' some glasses

You could see to 'ackney marshes

If it wasn't for the 'ouses in between!' Laurel's childish voice joined in.

'Your eyes are too young, dear. One day they'll penetrate the fog and you'll see France… oh dear!' Much laughter, from the child too, though she didn't quite see the joke beyond it sounding funny. 'I nearly said 'penetrate the Frog!' Moira's laugh was ringing. 'You know, the biggest Ferris wheel in the world is in Vienna, in Austria. And Ronald Coleman is the handsomest man in the world.'

Laurel observed that her mother behaved differently from other women, and perhaps from other mothers, though she did not know other mothers. It was confirmed by her being told, 'If you find me at all exaggerated you must understand that an actor is exaggerated by nature. It is what the French call 'deformation professionelle.' But I think it is thrust on us almost from birth. As a child I overdid the part.'

Laurel at once turned her face, opening her eyes wide, her best 'audience face', in the hope of hearing more about her mother's childhood. She'd had snippets, half-stories, usually when she'd been half-asleep, too tired to listen. She was hungry for information. Her mother had been abandoned by her own mother; she'd tried to run off with the gypsies aged seven, but they'd brought her back; grandmother had drowned; grandfather Lloyd nearly died of a broken heart. Maybe none of this was true. Maybe Laurel had only dreamed it. But they had walked out of the fairground now and Moira was not attending. She had stopped as she often did, almost in mid-thought, leaving her daughter puzzled and eager for more. She always stopped when starting to talk about her own childhood. Laurel felt frustrated. They waited at a bus stop to return to their digs. Moira had to get ready for her matinee. Laurel was aware of having had no lunch.

'And something else:' Moira lit a cigarette as they waited. 'I think that the role of mother that I play with you is also sometimes *over-produced* and I wonder if perhaps the time has come for us to make an adjustment… I wonder if the time has come for you to call me Moira rather than Mummy? All right? And I'll introduce you as my favourite niece.

***

Concentration works.

My completed list: *Flour Currants*
Baking soda Buttermilk
Salt Carraway seeds
Butter(Optional) Bran

Where does this come from? Are you listening, Solomon? Do you know?

***

It was usually fun, when not in a hotel room, playing this new role with Moira when they were out together 'on the town' as her mother called it, which often involved meeting up with men who paid a lot of attention to the little girl. The adjustment worked for Laurel, so that she stopped expecting the behaviour of a mother, which was vague in her yearning in any

21

case. She began quite naturally to take on the pretence that Moira was indeed her aunt. In one of the seaside towns, Cromer, which she remembered because it was where she was introduced to the taste of sweet stout, Laurel said boldly, 'Moira is my favourite Aunt, you know!'

Silence. But mother beamed and then the men friends uttered in theatrical voices with their hands making shapes in the air, 'Oh, isn't she a sweetie' or 'Ah, *très gentille*!' as one of the lovers would often say, his long coat always over his shoulders, one eyebrow always cocked.

It wasn't even true. Auntie Bron whom she'd only met twice, when four and five, was really her favourite aunt.

But Laurel had learned how to please her itinerant mother with sudden modest bursts of performance to delight the friends. And she had learned over six travelling years how to displease her mother too. Talking too much could not be borne, and worse... silence. The mother hated silence. She felt it personally. She called it revenge. 'Unwarranted revenge.'

So, the challenge to the child was to get the balance right. She felt, obscurely, that it was very important. A choice interjection, even a made-up story from time to time, set against a willingness to listen and not question whatever her mother had to say, had Moira beaming, almost purring... depending on the interaction with the alcohol.

Because by the age of six, what Laurel had begun to fear was becoming true: that Moira had tired somewhat of having to take her young co-star everywhere along with her.

***

There's something different stirring now, Doctor. There was a nurse... busy but she would stop, take my wrist, take my temperature, look at my face, feel my forehead. Pull the screens round, close them tight, discreet, hold my cock, clean my bum. Bed-wash me, brush my hair, shave my beard. Make my bed. Did she talk at all? I can hear her legs, her stockings. Thermometer in my mouth, scented fingers, scented hair when tucking me in, like mother... what was mother's name'? What was her face like... voice calling to boy sitting at desk. Temperature is an arbitrary measurement of an observable phenomenon such as the expansion of mercury... that's what the boy remembers. The man remembers the ice in the bath to reduce hotness or madness. Torture.

***

Since that day on the bus, though, Laurel had been secretly researching her new hobby of Men. The library provided her with The Origins of Man, on the whole a disappointment except for the suggestion of hairiness in unexpected places and an interesting parsnip-like protuberance that unfortunately was not named. When she did discover the name in an anatomy book, she decided 'parsnip' was better.

'She gazed at his parsnip as it emerged from the shimmering folds of his green silk dressing gown,' was to be one of the prime passages in the disastrous 'Flowers of the Forest' that she was later to write for a dare at her boarding school. But apart from 'emerge' there was little else she knew it could do, except wee.

She realized that her mother, too, was interested in men, very interested in men, but knew that she wouldn't talk about them in any way that provided useful information.

***

In this wood are indigenous trees. I recognize them and can name them. In this wood are woodlarks. I can name the bird and recognize his love song. Love song? 'Lulula arborea'. Did I know a woman named Lulu or Lalla? How do I know it is not a song thrush? The boy at the desk laughed at the Latin name 'Turdus philomelos.' Who did he laugh with, surely another boy.

There is another boy in this wood. It is not the boy at the desk, working, in my memory. It is not me. I have seen him twice. I was told there is no one in the wood, no entrance this side of the lake, that it is completely walled, that the wall is in good repair. I was told it is a thick wood and that it will hide me. The woodlark is only found in thin wood, and in the south mostly, yet the train went west, the train that brought me here.

I can't remember who picked me up at which station in which county. I can't remember the drive to the wood. Did I cross the lake if the wood is walled? I remember a boat, a rowboat, and an instruction.

Yet I can remember the difference – slight – between the song of the woodlark and that of the songthrush, whose clear bell-like whistle echoes for much of the year. These woodlarks add trills with long and short pauses like the nightingale held in such reverence by poets. John Keats. And Shelley celebrates the skylark who trills without breaks. No breaths.

The woodlark sings on the wing, away from the tree, but away from the water. The thrush would never do that.

In this wood when I am ready, I will follow this boy and frighten him off. I will continue to write this evening and report back from the recent past…

The boy was not tracked down today. A dog was heard barking, quite near the lake, quite near the shack but within the trees as I returned from a long walk round the edge of the forest near the wall, looking for the boy's entry point. Circumnavigation of trees. Good for the nerves.

Tired myself today. Need to eat. Hard to eat. Tack is finished. Must fish.

I seem to pine for a hill, for hills. Can't wait for soda bread.

***

Laurel's admiration for men did not extend to boys. When she was four-and-a-half she'd spent a first bewildered term at school. They were touring, her mother playing mostly in village halls around Wolverhampton, and the council primary school was in one of the rougher parts of town. There they all had a nit inspection each morning. She sat next to Arthur Briggs, the first real boy she had known. From being the only one, the centre of the universe, she was suddenly adrift amongst nudging, snuffling, nose-picking, open-mouth-eating hordes of her equals and she didn't like it. Her first school report summed up her social achievements of that first term thus: 'Laurel eats slowly due to her interest in watching the other children eat'.

She tried to stay back from the crowd but Arthur Briggs, a quick-witted, ferret-faced son of a merchant seaman who had a monkey at home for a pet and dropped his aitches, had marked her out for special attention. Perhaps because she'd misheard his name as 'Arf a brick'.

He sat next to her in their first lesson of reading round the class and shared his book. He could read, it seemed. At least he muttered under his breath as his grubby finger moved rapidly from word to word.

When the teacher came to her and asked, 'What's the next word Laurel?' His finger had whizzed on ahead and she had lost her place. It was possibly that longish word beginning with 'w', maybe wheelbarrow? She could see a picture of one. But Arthur had now moved his finger back to the previous word which she didn't recognise at all. It began with 'b'. She was dismayed. The teacher asked her again. She hissed to Arthur, 'What is it?'

'It's bugger,' he whispered. 'Just tell her that.'

Laurel had never heard that word before but at least it began with a 'b'. So, in a loud confident voice she said, 'Bugger, Miss Broomhead.'

'I beg your pardon, girl. What did you say?'

'I said, Bugger, miss,' a little less confidently now as the teacher's face reddened and her eyes enlarging like tenpenny marbles. Then followed a mysterious sequence of events which just confirmed Laurel's suspicions that she had been enrolled in another world, a different planet possibly, where all the rules were strange and you could never know what to expect. She was seized by the earlobe and pulled roughly out of the class. Miss Broomhead was clearly very cross. But however many adjectives she heaped upon her head, Laurel was still completely mystified as to what she had done, and concerned that she was picking up no clues to stop her doing it again. They went into the washrooms where the teacher put a bar of green soap into a cup and produced a cupful of very soapy water which she forced Laurel to rinse around inside her mouth.

That evening her mother asked her what she had learnt at school. She said, very carefully, 'I have learned that not everybody is your friend.'

At the end of that term they moved on, and Laurel, to her great relief, appeared to have finished her formal education.

***

This afternoon I saw this boy sitting on a log staring at a twig for at least half an hour. The dog's bark led me to him. He didn't see me. What was it? A beetle? A spider making his web? He looked completely absorbed, beautiful. The boy has given me the motivation to penetrate the trees.

***

Summertime: with her mother to rehearsals every day. Summer heat – Laurel's bare feet up on the plush red upholstery at the back of the Garrick Theatre, Southport.

Reading comics, colouring her picture books, making model aeroplanes, learning to play chess with the assistant stage manager, practicing headstands in the aisle, and, more secretly, teaching herself to read.

The Lady's Not For Burning. Moira had wanted to play the witch, Jennet:

'Lovers in a deep and safe place,
And never lonely any more.'

But Moira was the understudy. Laurel could follow most of it, though it went on too long. Four days here, ordering strawberry and banana sandwiches for supper from room service in the hotel, then up the coast by train to Morecombe. Here Moira was playing a silly girl in Charlie's Aunt for the hundredth time.

Mornings on the beach.

'She'll be jailbait by the time she's thirteen.'

This from the leading man, the one Moira had hoped to end up 'in a deep and safe place' with. Moira rubbing suncream into her daughter's slender, golden-skinned back. Replying sharply, 'She needs to go to school. She hangs around too much.'

Laurel was not surprised that her mother seemed less than pleased. 'Jailbait' certainly didn't sound a pleasant thing to aim for at any age.

Given a choice, she thought she would rather be a schoolgirl. She shuddered.

'Would you like to hear some of my tables?' she'd said brightly, hoping they wouldn't because they were far from known and the shallows of the ebbtide were already drawing her away.

Today she knew – as she ran and jumped into the cold shining water, that she would find a special shell.

***

The memory of the boy pondering the hills pulls harder than the recent past, but it throws up no names or faces. Facts, shapes, collocations come through my filter, and I want to give definitions to such things as temperature curves, temperature scales, temperature waves, temperature coefficients. I am guessing that the boy at the desk was me, though I recognize him not one jot.

When a word like 'jot' crops up, pops off the pen onto paper, I want to pursue it. To list its similarities, or synonyms. That seems a way of keeping track. Jot cot lot scot. I don't know what it means but am I writing freely, doctor?... dot, dab, spot, chip, speck, fleck, flake, rack... leave not a rack...

Our revels now are ended, these our actors,
As I foretold you, were all spirits and
Are melted into air, into thin air...
These are not my words.
'And, like this insubstantial pageant faded,
Leave not a rack behind.'

They are a writer's words. They are Shakespeare's words and when I write Shakespeare, or his words, I almost see a visage… hear a voice.

Was I an actor? What is an actor doing wearing these boots and trousers? In this shack? In this wood? With these hands and damaged wrists. And all these scars.

***

She made a friend, briefly, of a little dark-haired French Jewish girl her own age. Moira was 'resting' and took Laurel to the beach with the grey-haired man who had played the Dame in the pantomime at Scarborough. Probably in love with her, thought Laurel. They always were. Then they would buy the seven-year-old Laurel illicit sweets or really good presents. This one had bought her a red swimsuit and had earlier been tickling her tummy as she lay on the sand though she didn't want him to. So she rolled over suddenly which squashed his hand, and then raced down to the water's edge to hunt for baby crabs with her new friend.

She learned to say *'Cochon!'* and *'Merde alors!'*

She longed to stay in one place and have a friend that stayed around for more than a week or so; she dreamed of it.

'Why is your Papa old?' the new friend asked.

'He's not my Papa. My Daddy is away, doing something secret. Do you understand 'secret'?'

'Oh yes.'

'I asked Mama why she has such old boyfriends who always wear their coats over their shoulders and walk like this…' Laurel handed Rachel a little red bucket, swayed her shoulders slightly and tilted her head. 'Because there's a war going on, you silly girl!'

The two girls strutted around, both imitating with increasing excess the walks of all the adults they knew.

***

Dr. Solomon wants to see me. The boat comes tomorrow to fetch me. The boatman's name is Griffith. I'll tell Solomon that I have entered the forest, can sleep with the door shut; am sleeping, eating, running more smoothly, swimming a little, not listing so much, have a face or two in recall but not a name, and that I heard the boy talking to his dog. In a girl's voice. He can't whistle properly. This child is a girl.

It is mid-afternoon. I'm writing to you, Doctor, from well inside the forest, my pad on my knee waiting for something, looking at the way the leaves are arranged, how tall and smooth and unalarming beeches are, and cool. This canopy is so thick the light is held out. There are orchids in the darkness of this shade and somewhere on the fringes of the cool patch I can hear a warbler's short rising melodious song. A tack-tack then silence, then a warble. I think it's a blackcap. My memory for this – SYLVIS ATRICAPILLA – may be a clue, Doctor. Distraction. That's the clue. My memory is distracting me from remembering who I am, what happened to me, what I did.

***

Moira Sherborne, her stage name, was what Laurel loved to print at the top of billings she made up for imaginary plays. 'Moira Sherborne in *The Frantic Marchioness*' or 'Moira Sherborne stars in *The Hidden Garden of Wonderment*'. For Laurel thought that though her mother always looked startlingly beautiful on the stage, she had to do silly things in silly plays.

'Yes, they might well be silly plays, girl, but what does a seven-year-old know about what constitutes good theatre. Really?'

'I know a lot because I help you learn your lines, so I know all the other parts as well.' This was how Laurel learned to read.

Then Moira told her about a play she was going to be in to please a friend, and perhaps for no money at all and only one performance, 'And perhaps a reading performance only so I won't have to learn my lines.' Laurel liked the title though she didn't understand the play at all, but she loved the names in it: Mrs. Hushabye, Lady Utterword, Captain Shotover, and even her mother's role, Ellie. She sensed that Ellie was a part that somehow complemented Moira in a way neither could explain, and although rehearsals in a house in Chelsea during the blackout only two days and there were to be only two reading performances. Moira stayed sober and said she would introduce Laurel to the writer 'who is the most famous playwright living.'

'What's his name?'

'And he likes leading ladies. Why else would he call a piece 'Heartbreak House'? I'm going to lead him the giddy limit. Only he is aged, and we must play our cards carefully. He might like little girls, but he never lets a sip pass between cup and lip so… he's got a home in Hertfordshire and he probably likes Italy and takes his leading ladies to places like Ravello. Only I hear he's very chaste as well.'

'Chased?'

'Like Ellie in this play.'

'I'd like to play Ellie.'

'You make sure I play her well. We'll keep us off the Gin.'

'Yes, Moira. Are there real men in this play?'

'Yes dear, *some* of them will be real men.'

But, come the day, come the disaster, and the child Laurel found it hard to work out or to remember exactly just what went so wrong. So wrong that the second reading was minus Moira Sherborne who had thrown away, with a tot too many, not only any possible trip to Ravello but also her first chance of being a serious actress. A return to rep and revue and ugly boarding houses without food. A decrease in the energy required to attend, even a little, to a child who by now needed consistent schooling, friends, and something to replace the diet of adult fun.

Moira's younger sister Bronwyn was the answer, as she had been in occasional early crises. So, Aunt Bron, a real aunt, widowed and living in Wales, started investigating schools that did not penalise bright and unusual children.

***

Now here she was, somewhere near Hereford, right out in the country. Aunt Bronwyn had come from her house in Wales to stay in their hotel, and to take Laurel to see the school they had chosen. She'd been too excited to eat breakfast. Her favourite Auntie; a boarding school! And she had a new pleated kilt to wear – a novelty after shorts all summer. Aunt and niece walked slowly down the long drive, enjoying the trees, the smell of cut grass, the sight of tennis courts.

'Look, there's six of each!' Aunt Bron sounded amazed. 'Each what?'

'Courts. Grass, grey and red.'

For once Laurel had nothing to say. She was overwhelmed by her surroundings, by the big pink and yellow stone mansion they were approaching with its bell tower and tall chimneys like twisted barley sugar sticks. There was a stone porch above the great double doorway, decorated with shields and lions and a carved Latin motto.

'Grass, grey and red!' she said to herself wonderingly as Aunt Bron knocked on a door marked 'Mrs Evans, Deputy Headmistress', and a woman's deep voice called, 'Enter!'

The room was full of the scent of roses and honeysuckle. A window was open with creeper outside, and a big vase of blooms stood on the polished desk. Laurel felt faint and dizzy from the heat, the perfume and not having had any breakfast. Somebody spoke to her and shook her hand.

'This is my niece, Laurel.' Aunt Bron was talking to a short, elegant woman with friendly brown eyes and a big tortoiseshell comb holding up her thick auburn hair. 'I really *am* her niece!' said Laurel. Mrs Evans looked surprised. 'My sister is an actress Mrs Evans, often away, often touring. Moving around a lot unfortunately. So Laurel has not yet had any… formal schooling… Which is why we thought a boarding school would well…'

'Would provide some stability… '

'Of course her mother – we – were very well aware of the law. The requirement…'

'Ah yes, under the Education Act…'

'To send her to school…' Aunt Bron tailed off, embarrassed.

'Or to provide 'education otherwise',' said Mrs Evans, rescuing her, 'and perhaps you have.'

'Oh yes. She can read perfectly. And she writes quite well. But, perhaps… other things might be lacking.'

'Cherchez la mère,' the deputy headmistress said quietly to Bronwyn in that private tone of voice that

Laurel, who had spent so much time around adults, immediately recognised.

'I can speak a little French, you know.' She tried to sound casual and grown-up. 'And I know you are talking about the sea.'

'Perhaps.' The tortoiseshell comb was fingered and pushed more firmly into the hair.

'Well, I can see we must not underestimate you, my dear. So, you've had some French lessons?'

'Not really. Just conversations with a French friend. I sort of picked it up.'

'The best way to learn, Laurel. I expect you will get on well here.'

Mrs Evans started looking at the entrance exam papers Laurel had attempted the previous day.

'Well, the maths we can easily sort out. You didn't complete any of your maths paper, it seems – ah yes… she flipped through the pages. You wrote a story instead about three men looking for something in a desert, Miss Sowerby notes here. She's the head of mathematics.'

'Did she like my story?'

'Possibly…' Mrs Evans gave a slight cough. 'She hasn't commented on it except for the spelling.'

A bell rang. Bronwyn could see Laurel looking with great interest out of the window as a troop of small girls with tennis rackets ran past. The deputy headmistress beamed. 'Rudolf Steiner would have approved of you Laurel. He believed children should do drama, dance and art, and be taught only languages and a musical instrument before the age of seven. No spellings or tables. Do you have a musical instrument?'

'I would like to play the trombone,' said Laurel, 'but I've only got this.' And she produced from her pocket her precious miniature Hohner mouth organ, originally attached to a keyring, a present from the theatre pianist who'd been hopelessly in love with her mother last year. Bronwyn's eyes closed for a moment in anticipation. 'Does it work?' Mrs Evans asked. In answer Laurel put the tiny thing – only an inch long – to her mouth and started to play, with beautiful timing and phrasing, Brother James's Air. It all worked perfectly except for one low note which Laurel had to hum. Mrs Evans sat back in her chair smiling in delight. Two small faces peered in through the window, watching and listening.

'Well Laurel: you're musical and enterprising. You can play chess and speak a little French. Even if you don't know your seven times table, I expect the school will be able to absorb and to teach you. Would you like to come?'

'Yes please' said Laurel, who had caught the eye of one of the watching girls who had the longest blond hair she'd ever seen, and who had hastily squashed her school boater up to look like a battered fedora and was now giving Laurel an inspired imitation of a Harpo Marx grin, beckoning and miming and whispering to her through the window: 'Mrs Evans is a pushover but the headmistress is horrid.'

This was to be her very best friend Olivia.

***

The evening meeting with the psychiatrist had not gone well but he could not remember why. The journey across the lake in the dark with the corporal who rowed him so silently had stirred a fear, a dread, which made it very difficult to talk at all.

And he had forgotten to take his diary, he couldn't remember why. He'd forgotten what day it was.

His mind was hiding things, this he knew now. But Dr. Solomon was his usual reassuring self and they had walked around the grounds of the mansion and down the terraces and seen someone on a horse who had waved to them. He had watched Dr. Solomon's face and found himself wondering about his accent, his life. This felt like a relief. Then they had drunk coffee which tasted good. This day felt different.

***

Laurel , almost nine-years-old now, had been picked up from school for an exeat by Aunt Bron and a new puppy in the little black Morris 8. The car aimed towards the fields and trees, half a mile beyond the school grounds, for a picnic. The puppy had decided to impress Lauren and was leaping and sniffing and tail wagging her way into the child's affections. Laurel sat in the back, cradling the excited little animal on her lap.

'Mrs. Evans wants you to talk to me, doesn't she?

'She does, cariad. She's a good woman, I knew her sister, and she is Welsh remember.' New sentence 'I know. She's nice to me, smiles, if I'm not with the other girls.'

'That's just it.

She says she thinks you won't make friends.'

'I do. I do. I'm friends with the English teacher who does plays, and the Latin teacher, who taught us a pure love poem in Latin and—

'That's just it!'

'Cat… What was his name… Catullus. Isn't that a good name?'

'She says you don't make friends with people, your own age.'

'Don't I?'

'You only have one friend.'

'Olly. But Moira's friends were my friends, most of them'

'But they were her age or older'

'I think I like Miss Walsh, because she reminds me of one of mummy's friends we called Bunny, though he was really old. He was in her last play. You know, I think he introduced her to the director as if she was a serious actress, she knew how to look serious, especially if she wasn't on the gin. She did try.' Laurel sat on the picnic rug, stroking the little dog, while Bron unwrapped hard-boiled eggs and tomatoes.

'She said she let Bunny down it was so hot that day. Perhaps she thought she was drinking water. You know what vodka looks like actually, Mrs Evans is a much more motherly sort of person, and Miss Wetherby is horrid.

Bronwynn smiled, feeling something maternal stirring in herself which warmer her but dismayed her, for it reminded her of what she had lost – her son. 'Is it true that the whole of your life passes before your eyes if you nearly die?' Laurel asked suddenly.

'I don't know, my duck!'

'Well once I nearly drowned at Morecambe, because it was so cold.'

'And you were so small, your mother told me.'

'Did she? Did she tell you that nothing passed before my eyes as I was going down for the second time, before they hauled me out turning blue?'

'Well, you were so young.'

'Yes, but I had a life. It could have passed before my eyes. They said I'd nearly drowned, but nothing really happened except I ended up in a big hospital in a room all by myself.'

'And your mother gave up the tipple. Briefly.'

'That's right.'

'Have we had enough to eat?'

'Let's ask Muffin.'

'Oh, Auntie is she really to be my dog?'

'She certainly doesn't think she's mine. Look how she keeps running back to you.'

'Is this Wales or England?'

'Neither and both. We are right on the border.'

'Say something in Welsh Aunt Bron, see if I can guess it.'

'Mai hen wlad fyn haddai.'

'I know that: my hen made a haddock, it's the national anthem. Let's not go back yet.'

'Soon. But let's talk about your school.'

'Aunt Bron,' Laurel began to ask, searching for a question, 'How have you got all this petrol to take me out? The other parents can't get it.'

'Shhh!' said her aunt with a smile, finger to lips, knowing that Laurel was not really interested in the complications of the black market. 'I have a friend called Connor. He's a bit of a magician.'

'Do you believe in witches, in wood witches, Aunt Bron?'

They sat and threw pieces of sandwich and sponge cake for Muffin.

'Oh, I'm so glad you came to be with me my Cariad. And I'll be glad when it's holidays and you can stay at home.'

'Me too. Muffin too.

'Are you really going to call her Muffin?'

'Yes.'

***

'Try to write freely and informally, Tom,' Solomon had *insisted.* So, my name is Tom? *The naming of himself he found more frightening than exciting.* Why am I constantly afraid?

There is a menace in the forest, *he thought, fighting down a darker thought.* There is in all the rustling dry greenness an evil spirit. This is a primeval forest. Here in this place I will meet, face to face, not death but the force of darkness.

Why am I here? he asked himself. *What happened? And why can't I stay in this hut? Why am I scared to close the door? Satan does not come inside the cabin, he occupies the forest. Yet I have to get out. I have to get out, he repeated to himself. Asphyxiation is a greater fear than confrontation. The devil is the devil, suffocation has no shape, it descends like a formless shroud that cannot be shaken off. The devil has arms and legs and eyes and teeth and a tail and I have a knife. Choking for want of breath is…* 'It's a memory!' he shouted, standing in the doorway, *holding high onto the doorframe.* 'But I have no memory!'

'I can't be in the woods!' he told the forest. 'I can't be within walls,' he told the cabin. 'I'll move into the water.'

The water was cold, for the sun was yet behind the trees, mist across the lake, the dawn chorus drowning his voice as he called, 'Help me Lord!' He had rushed into the water still wearing the clothes he had collapsed in the night before, to toss and turn and dream in his narrow creaking bed.

Now he swam out, his boots pulling him down, trying to keep afloat, more, trying to swim to the other side of the lake where he knew there were gardens, low hedges, the large mansion, a friendly face and mind.

'Now Tom,' he said to himself, 'this is cold, this is cramp, nice and numb, time to go, just arch your head, just follow your boots that pull you down, choose your own choking, just let yourself drown. Lord, Lord! methought what pleasure it was to drown… to cease upon the midnight… twilight, daylight, daybreak, with no pain. Inestimable stone. Too much suffering makes the something stone deferred, maketh the something sick.

Why search for words? – they're not my own words – at a time like this?

For God's sake shut the language door, lie back, float off, observe the sky a blank and let your feet pull you down like a stone. 'I have no news of the world!' he called across the lake. 'I have no knowledge of my life!' his voice rang out. *'I don't know what I am! I doubt I am a man! I am not a boy! '*

The boat that picked him out of the water to take him to the mansion for a checkup had a leak, a bailing cup and a thin faced corporal who rowed in taciturn silence as if he knew and disapproved of Tom's story.

The girl watched from her hiding place in the shadow of a yew tree, perplexed, drawn by the shouting. 'It shouldn't be here, this yew,' the man had roared, angrily.

He meant I shouldn't be here, *the girl thought.* Now I've got the place all to myself.

CHAPTER 2

On market day the little town slackened its pace back a few centuries to something like the mediaeval hamlet it once was, and the women slipped easily into the rituals of meeting and circulating and slowly laying out their cakes and chutneys on trestle tables while catching up with the gossip of everyone else's lives. Somehow, the men returned from the war found it harder to fit in with this familiar slow waltz and were noisy and impatient. One had brought in a portable radio to listen to the rugby, despite the cold-shouldering of the wives.

Bronwyn Williams usually took her time moving across the market square with its new granite obelisk to the dead of the Great War and the open-sided market hall, packed now with stalls and chatter. Today though, several of the women noticed her hurrying, as if they were on the lookout. Elspeth Pugh remarked crisply to Mary the postmaster's wife that Mrs. Williams wasn't quite herself since that telegram didn't she think? Knowing that Mary, who was almost the soul of discretion, surely held the answer to the mystery.

'It's not as bad as that news of her son, though.' Mary revealed suddenly. 'Lord knows she's been through enough. Cheerful too, in spite of it all.'

'Into each life …' muttered Mrs. Pugh.

'But look at the rain that's poured into hers, Elspeth. And you wouldn't know, to look at her.' Mary Davis sounded uncertain about whether this was a good thing.

'Well, there's Mrs. Brian Jenkins, lost her husband and son in the same month – all the rest of her hair's fallen out now.' They stopped talking as Bronwyn stepped across the cobbles' on the far side of the War Memorial, wearing a full, swinging coat in a rusty orange with a long emerald green scarf tying back her greying chestnut hair. They fell silent with who knows what private thoughts under their tightly permed hairdos.

'It's her niece,' said Mary abruptly breaking the silence. 'Her godchild with the funny name, Laurel. Her sister's little girl.'

'Not so little now, Elspeth. She's coming down here from London.'

'To live, is it?' Mrs Pugh asked.

'It was a most peculiar telegram,' Mary went on, 'from that school she's at. Something not very pleasant at all.'

By the time Bronwyn entered the Dragon's Head through the door marked Lounge Bar, half the women in the market had picked up something or other about Laurel's arrival the next day. Luckily her childhood friend Mavis Preston was there with her dark hair as untidy as ever, sitting in her usual market day seat with her basket of shopping and Gareth, her grown up son. Gareth often had a vacant look, or else he was being bouncy like a puppy. Bronwyn gratefully registered that today the puppy was not around, and only a small part of Gareth was. She squeezed her well-fleshed rear between the wooden bench and the table until she was practically sitting in her friend's lap and sank back breathless and strangely out of sorts.

'Get us two rum and blackcurrants, Gareth, there's a dear. And something for yourself.' Mavis pulled a ten-shilling note from her purse and Gareth wandered over to the bar where he would probably become becalmed for quite a while.

'What's up, love?' They'd known each other since their early schooldays, with a gap when Bron's family had been off living in Egypt. They'd both had one son, and although Gareth's disability had at spared him from the fate of so many of the young men of the village, including Bronwyn's boy, his mother often wickedly wondered if she could have persuaded her doctor to have signed him A1 and then at least she'd have had a break. Now she sensed that Bronwyn was troubled, so she stroked the warm plump hand with its startlingly azure ring, willing her friend to share with her.

'Where's Connor?' Bronwyn looked round the bar. 'Do you think he's gone already? Been down to Zelda's maybe?' Bronwyn's voice sounded tense. Mavis absently continued her stroking.

'Nobody's seen Zelda for a while. Since the fire. She's lying doggo. Maybe she frightened herself this time.'

Bronwyn pushed back her hair, irritated as ever over the way Connor, that wise, tough man, allowed so much of his time and attention to be sucked away by that awful sister of his. Zelda treated him like a puppet. Or like one of those little metal children's toys shaped like a tortoise or a beetle on an unwinding string which came rolling along quickly towards you when you tugged sharply at the string. That was Connor with that hopeless sister of his, she thought uncharitably. A little bright red metal beetle on a string, with a rubber-band pulley inside him. He allowed no-one else, certainly not Bronwyn, to treat him this way. She needed to talk to him.

'Laurel's been expelled. For "indecency". She's arriving on the four -o'-clock tomorrow.' A big sigh. Mavis sighed too.

Bronwyn blinked rapidly, shifting her buttocks on the bench. She noticed two women talking across the bar. They had just looked at her twice. She didn't care about gossip. She was just worried about Laurel.

'However will she get on? What about the school? The kids will never accept her. And the teachers … you know what happens if you stick your head above the parapet around here?' Mavis agreed. They both knew. Things hadn't changed much. 'You got it used as target practice.' Mavis concurred.

Bronwyn sniffed. 'I won't be feeling like this by tomorrow, I expect. We'll just get on with it. Oh, why isn't Connor here? He's always propping up the bar at lunchtime. Specially on market day.'

'Oh yes – he's had a wisdom tooth out, I remember now. Heard Mary Davies telling everyone. She didn't think we'd be seeing him in the pub, she said.'

'How the hell does she know! Best place to be, to dull the pain' said Bronwyn with unusual asperity.

'And her mother?'

'Whose?'

'Laurel's … Moira.'

'Oh. I haven't had a letter for weeks.' Bronwyn was surprised at her white lie: in fact, she'd only ever had one postcard from her sister, more than ten years ago. 'She's still convalescing – drying out. I think.' 'On tour' and 'resting' were the usual public euphemisms for Moira's frequent attempts to get sober. 'Don't expect to see her this side of Christmas. Which, by the way, you're both invited to.'

Bronwyn always seemed to change the subject when her sister was mentioned, Mavis noticed. The truth was that Moira had become a myth. Nobody in Penforth had seen her now for almost fifteen years. No doubt she still existed, but you wouldn't know. That poor kid.

'Here's the man at last!' And Connor could be seen making his way through the smoky haze of the bar which was now filling up with market day customers.

Connor and Gareth reached the table together. Gareth was concentrating fiercely on not spilling the two overfull wineglasses of rum and blackcurrant.

'Take a sip, man!' roared Connor, nearly startling poor Gareth right out of his fragile concentration. He gazed pleadingly at his mother. Mavis waited. It was easy enough to answer for him. Sometimes she had to bite her tongue.

'No thanks. Connor. Don't like rum and black.'

He was scared of Connor, noted Bronwyn, amused. For the older man was a bit of a jungle-scarred lion with a great mane and ferocious eyebrows, but his paws were velvet when you got to know him, and Bronwyn enjoyed this secret.

'What's all this about a telegram? Bush telegraph's really buzzing out there. I tried half a crown, double or quits, that it wasn't a win on the football pools. No takers. So it's not whisky all round. Are you communicating, Bron?' He spoke gently now, noticing Bronwyn's flushed cheeks. His voice, deep with the distant burr of a brogue, still sounded attractive thought Mavis. Not at all Welsh. She then promptly reined her thoughts back. He was Bronwyn's man, though they'd never talked about it. But you could sense something when they were around together. She watched him offer a Woodbine to Bron who shook her head and he lit one up for Mavis then himself.

'How's Zelda?' Bronwyn made herself ask.

'How's Bronwyn, I want to know.' Connor replied, using half a smile.

'Well where did your sister get a name in the shape of Zelda?' Mavis joined in to the amusement of her friend, if not Connor.

'Zelda sounds to my ears like an American or a Hungarian or something way off these islands.' She gave her son Gareth another instruction and, when he went off cheerfully to the bar, continued to prod a little further. It reminded Bron of when they were at school together in this very town and they had enjoyed teasing the older boys who fancied themselves. She joined in, to forget the news about Laurel.

'So, how come you're not called Boris?'

'Or Horace?'

'Who's Irish then, in your family?'

'And how come you never bring her in here?' 'That's what we want know, Mr. Walsh.'

'She goes to Mass,' Connor offered reluctantly. She has to travel to do it.'

'She certainly doesn't go to Chapel,' said Mavis, who didn't go to Chapel herself.

'She's a very private person,' Connor sounded cornered, which was unusual for him.

'She's certainly not like her brother. Who's she like, Con?'

'Questions – I can't hear myself think in this place.' He felt for his cigarettes.

'You should be used to the noise level by now, *bach.*'

'He doesn't like questions at all, Mavis. He never has.'

'I'll ask you one and I hope it seeps through – where are those drinks? What's a man got to do to get a pint of stout?'

'Tell us something, boyo!'

'She's a prolific reader, is Zelda. A very big reader. Books are as important as her dogs'.

'What kind of books – astrology and suchlike? Penny Dreadfuls?'

'No, Mavis Preston,' Connor objected, annoyed but amused to find he was defending the woman whom he constantly berated.

'Bronwyn will tell you, and the Tudor Jones woman at the library, there is nothing vapid in her reading. All the great writers, and you'll know that we've turned out a few, from O'Driscoll to Synge, and the author she returns to again and again, Fitzgerald, Scott Fitzgerald.

'Aha,' Mavis began and then she paused, noticing that her friend was wearing an uncharacteristically anxious look.

'Go on, darling,' she said to Bron, 'we've teased him enough, poor boy. Tell him what you wanted to tell him.'

'Laurel's in trouble, Connor, she's in disgrace' Bron blurted out. 'Moira's daughter, you know.'

'Ah.' Connor registered. 'Trouble… how old is she?'

'She's only seventeen… almost eighteen, in fact.'

'Her mother was at it early, I recall.'

'Come off it, Paddy. We aren't in your peat bogs now.'

'It's the same the whole world over, don't you know the song?'

'Sing for us, Mavis.' Connor was easing up now.

'I would, for a pint.' They laughed.

'And I'll thank you, Miss Princess and the Pea,' he winked at Bron, 'to leave my home turf alone … and my sister. No more cod.'

'Moira treated her like… well, not like a child, anyway. She wasn't allowed to be just a child.'

'But now she's not one —'

'I know love, and isn't it about time she was allowed to be herself, at least.'

Connor nodded and under the table he slithered his big arm with its greying fuzz of hair along behind her back and round the side to fondle her waist as far down as he could reach.

Gareth now returned with two pints of beer and a big grin. Connor smoothly took his with his damaged left hand with the sheared off finger, and thanked him warmly for keeping a good head on it.

'She's behaved indecently, apparently, "to the detriment of the moral tone of the school",' Bronwyn blithely talked openly in front of Gareth although his mother often suspected that this was a mistake, that the dull boy did in fact understand more than he let on. Connor spluttered into his beer, blowing foam onto the table.

'What the hell is "indecent" in a girls' boarding school?' he asked, bushy eyebrows shooting up.

Mavis giggled. 'Dancing naked on the lawn at midnight. Tanya, our Russian refugee at school, remember?'

'I do.' Bronwyn relaxed with her second drink and smiled at Mavis. 'She was an aristocrat or something.

Danced like Isadora Duncan and had a wonderful slender figure.'

Connor squeezed Bronwyn's satisfyingly rounded thigh. She purred. The rum had done its work. Male cuddles plus alcohol. Perfection. Blue skies over. Pack up your troubles. In your old kit bag. Oops, she'd better watch it or she'd start singing, right here. And then they would have something to gossip about.

She found that Gareth had been mysteriously sent and had returned with another rum and black. Was this the third? It felt like the third. She was slipping them back like Moira…

Oh Laurel, you little darling; what did she do to you? she asked herself, sobering quickly.

'We'll find a way of making that girl happy, Connor; you'll see,' she said with conviction.

***

'This has been a long silence,' Dr. Solomon eventually said, softly. 'I was waiting for you to break it.'

Tom said indistinctly, clearing his throat. 'You were waiting for me?'

'Yes.'

Tom, without effort, allowed another peaceful silence.

'You don't want to talk… How can I help you Tom? '

'Ask me a question perhaps. '

'Like…?'

'What happened?'

'The corporal reports via one of our guards that you were trying to drown yourself… very noisily.'

'I want you to ask me what happened… and then tell me what happened.'

'I blame myself considerably!' The doctor rose, came round his desk, rang a bell, stood quite near where Tom was lying back.

'I think the isolation has been too extreme, perhaps too much like your imprisonment previously.'

'Ah, we haven't used that word before. You haven't.'

'You look angry Tom.'

'Why haven't you, doctor? You know more about me than I do.'

Doctor Solomon sat back in his chair by the window and put both hands on his knees, leaning forward to see Tom's face.

'I am not here to tell you your story, Tom. Even the parts of it that I know. Forgetting has a healing function. Think of it as scar formation. We don't want to rip off a scab before the skin is ready underneath.'

Tom's eyes had closed though his body remained tense as he lay on the couch.

'Tell me more,' he whispered, 'just talk to me.'

Doctor Solomon allowed another shorter silence.

'Your body is strong, Tom. You can see and feel the signs of the suffering it has survived. Atrocities.' Solomon sighed at this word and Tom opened his eyes, looking over at the doctor who was gazing down at his own hands. For the first time the thought came in, fully formed, of what this kind, clever man with a soft German accent must also have suffered.

'Were you interned? Did we lock you up?'

'You said "we", Tom; interesting.'

Tom sat up.

'Ah yes – that's it, isn't it? Whose side was I on? An English Army Captain, an Irish patriot with a Republican father. Enough to bring on fits of confusion, or worse.'

'Good, Tom.'

'You know what we called the war over in Ireland, Doctor?'

'I do. It was "the Emergency", wasn't it?'

'It certainly wasn't our war. "England's embarrassment is Ireland's opportunity." But why have I been forgetting so much?'

'Imagine if we couldn't forget. Anything at all. Imagine what hell it would be to remember every mistake or failure or hurt. Or betrayal. The regret, the shame, the pain; it would overwhelm us.'

Tom stood up as the clock struck and the adjutant's knock came on the door, indicating that coffee had arrived and the session was almost over.

'Yes. That word struck home. I'm afraid all this has something to do with betrayal.'

They both allowed another long silence.

CHAPTER 3

Two long hours had passed already in this stuffy third-class carriage full of dark brown wood and brown scratchy upholstery which she could feel even through her school skirt. Opposite her, a faded print of rolling hills in various shades of brown with a beige sky, and a man sitting on the seat below it wearing a thick brown tweed suit and a brown knitted waistcoat. A brown study, thought Laurel. Victorians would fall into them. She knew just what they meant.

The backs of houses with their narrow yards and dried-up mingy gardens showered with years of railway soot seemed to go on for miles as they clattered and puffed out of London. Scraps of washing hanging up, a child's swing so close to the railway line oppressed her with feelings of helplessness. These people had surely not chosen to live and breathe their years away in that exact spot with steam trains whizzing past all day and half the night. How easy it must be to get trapped. She had not chosen to be sent away in disgrace from school and Ollie, yet here she was. What other choices would be made for her?

Once they were well out of London the neat hamlets, the soft hills and woods they were passing through lightened her mood. Laurel was never able to remain gloomy for long. Even though she felt that this occasion demanded some grand, tragic emotion, she didn't have the energy or conviction to keep it up. The oddity of the lone man opposite took her attention. He had two large fleshy lumps growing from his nose and his cheek which were now wobbling like jellies with a rhythm of their own as he chewed his way slowly through a huge chunk of white bread and cheese. Also, she guessed from the sound of it, false teeth.

She looked around wildly, trying to conceal her rising laughter. But there was nobody else in the carriage to distract her. Suddenly, the light went out. The train roared into a dark tunnel. Total darkness. This must be the river separating England from Wales, she registered. The Severn Tunnel. It was quite long.

She'd made this journey as a young child with her mother (who was nervous of dark tunnels) on their way to spend holidays with her beloved Aunt Bron, who was the only good thing about this whole dismal episode.

Under cover of darkness and with the noise of the train magnified in her ears, she could let loose her laughter, and soon she was shaking and laughing out loud, though she could hardly hear herself above the tunnel's roar. But the laughter kept coming – for no reason, it didn't matter. It felt good. And she was crying as well. Alone in the dark in this train hurtling her into exile she sobbed and laughed herself free. Until, when the tunnel ended at last and the brown suited man came back into view again, she looked up – feeling weak, dishevelled but relaxed – and found he was staring at her with half-open mouth and a strange, fixed expression. Weird. Maybe he was one of those... keep your eyes up, Laurel. And get out. Luckily, they pulled into a station almost immediately, although it wasn't the one where she was supposed to change. But she hauled her two suitcases quickly from the rack, standing on the upholstery in her shoes regardless, and jumped down from the carriage. Ran along the platform. Two doors along, a soldier's kitbag was just disappearing inside. The sound of young men laughing. She dived in breathless, hurled her cases on the seat and the floor and two cheerful Army cadets leapt up to help her.

There were five of them, they were Welsh. They shared their chocolate with her. And their fizzy pop. She passed round her big box of shortbread biscuits. Got rid of them all. They told her a wonderful joke, involving a hedgehog, which she didn't quite understand though she guessed it was a dirty joke but she felt just fine. And she told them she'd been expelled from school, though not why, even though they were curious and insisted on knowing. So she fell back on a Moira technique. Each time they asked or guessed she replied 'Aha!' with a sweeping, upward inflection. She didn't feel eighteen.

And when the train finally pulled into Penforth station, they all managed to lean out of the one window and were blowing her kisses and she was laughing and blowing kisses back as Aunt Bron appeared and engulfed her in a big-bosomed hug – and then she burst into tears.

Nothing had changed. Maybe the railings beside the station yard had been repainted the same green, that was all. It was the same atmosphere, same smell, same odd absence of traffic sounds as the first day of the summer holidays aged six, seven, ten, when time to do as you pleased for almost an eternity was your birthright. And this weighed most positively in the scales against the promised grown-up delights of having your own glass of gin and tonic and maybe getting married; and having to go to work.

Mr. Rees's big black taxi was waiting for them as ever. The same square upright Austin with brown leather upholstery through whose cracks you could pull up little wiry bits of brown and black horsehair from some pre-war horse. Auntie Bron was handed up the step into the back of the taxi by Mr. Rees. He was older and stiffer, but a permanent feature of every holiday Laurel could remember. She must have known him all her life.

'I told Mrs. Rees I was bringing Laurel home; she gave me this for you, now. It's lovely to see you. Growing like a mushroom, you are girl! –Young lady, I should say.' He handed her a little square packet smelling sweetly of fresh lavender. She gave him a quick, speechless hug, feeling tears prick behind her eyes at the word 'home' and climbed into the taxi.

It might as well be home she thought as they started off sedately and turned out of Station Road and towards the hills. She'd been coming here longer than anywhere. And she'd apparently been born in the Nursing Home down the road which was now converted into apartments. Although the streets and shops and public buildings seemed meagre and dull after London, there was something about this little town that was right. Wherever you stood you could see hills. Whichever way you turned when you stood in the central market square it was clear you'd be able to walk out of it in about five minutes, in any direction. And be amongst trees and sheep. This place never seemed to grow at the edges, like London. Perhaps she minded that it seemed to resist change. Now she was coming to live here, it might worry her. There was the paper shop, the same sign outside it she remembered from before: 'Clothes Rationing to End.' Aunt Bronwyn noticed her glance.

'Oh Auntie; I'm all right. It's just strange. I expect I'll miss … things.'

'You're bound to. I've got one of my chicken casseroles on for you, I'm sure you won't miss school food.' Laurel squeezed her Aunt's hand and carried on looking out of the window.

They were now out of town and proceeding along the narrow twisty roads with their enormously tall hedges on either side which she remembered so well.

Through the occasional gate came a view of the hills. Mountains, as she used to imagine them. As she looked out of the back window, she could see the forest that stretched around a lake and didn't seem to end. It still looked as vast as it had when she was five and it still made her tingle with excitement. The road turned and climbed and twisted back on itself again. And set off in another direction. A wandering track it had been once, made by the feet of horsemen and farmers going to market, its surface of modern tarmac only inches deep over all that history. Drunken farmers, she thought, meandering back from market. Couldn't walk in a straight line. Good job she didn't get carsick.

Mr. Rees had told her how, years ago before you saw many cars, his dad had met up with an old farmer walking along with a pig on a rope, ten miles away from the town. 'Don't tell me you walk there and back every market day! How long does it take you?'

'Three hours there and four hours back,' said the farmer.

'Haven't you ever thought of getting a cart? Or a tractor?'

'And whyever should I do that now?' asked the old farmer.

'Well, apart from anything else, it would save time.'

The farmer thought about this for a while then scratched his head. 'What's time… to a pig?' he said eventually. Laurel loved this story. It said so much about this place and she didn't yet know what. She was coming home.

'Won't you tell me the story about the pig, Mr. Rees?' He told it again.

The taxi was driven like a hearse, with grand dignity and in the middle of the road. Woe betide, as her Aunt used to say, any milk lorry or tractor coming down the hill in front or up the hill behind him. They would just have to stop and wait or retreat to a gateway. Mr. Rees, invalided out of the Great War with three decorations for bravery, was not one for giving way.

Bronwyn waited for the story to end then put her hand on Laurel's arm. -' You don't have to tell me anything, Cariad. I probably know enough already.'

Cariad. She'd forgotten. They called her that when she was very small.

'But I can explain, Auntie…'

'Don't explain. Only explain what you've discovered – as my dear, dead love once said to me – not what you've done.'

Bronwyn suddenly wondered if she'd said the right thing. Would she be good as a parent to this one? *Bron, you spoil that boy*, her friends had said when she'd chuckled at her son's misdemeanours. *I will indulge her*, Bronwyn knew, and she smiled at Laurel and looked in the shopping bag for her favourite sweets. They sat sucking mints as the hedges lumbered past and a cottage or two.

She could see that her niece was exhausted so, with Laurel's head resting on her shoulder, they made the rest of the journey in silence, immersed in the perfume from Mrs. Rees's lavender bag mixed with the taste of mint humbugs.

'I'll manage this one, Mrs. Williams.'

'Oh no, Mr. Rees, let Laurel help. Young arms and legs.' They took a suitcase each, Auntie leaving the lightest one for Mr. Rees who was long past retiring age and was known to have been gassed in the trenches.

As Laurel stood with her case in her grey school uniform in the lane outside Bron's little cottage, 'Tan Hengoed', feeling shaky from the car journey, facing a future that couldn't even be guessed at, she caught a swift movement at the very edge of her field of vision and felt an impact, a sudden sharp pain in her shoulder. She heard mutterings in Welsh and saw two village boys walk past with their hands in their pockets, heads down, kicking pebbles. They were young. One was about four foot tall, aged about seven she guessed. The other was older. And one of them had just thrown a stone at her. She would look for it and pick it up later. Now she would stand there unmoving and stare at them until they passed from sight.

As they drew level, the tiny one looked up at her. She immediately contorted her face into one of her most ferocious grimaces, tongue lolling, mouth hideously distorted, eyes distended. For a moment he froze, then his friend pulled him along by the arm. The boys whistled and disappeared round a curve in the lane. You just wait, you boys, thought Laurel. She had not forgotten being shown by her cousin James years ago how to make a sharpshooter catapult. She would start in this village as she meant to go on. And that did not include having chunks of drystone wall hurled at her because she wasn't Welsh. Dammit, she was more Welsh than English. She had a right to be here. Confirmation of this came from the welcome she received when the front door was opened at last and Muffin ('Oh Muffin!' Did you think I'd forgotten you?

How could I?') leapt into her arms and licked her to kiss her. 'I bet you're a spoilt girl!'

There was a log fire in the sitting room. The smell of old wood and freshly roasting, spicy chicken. Aunt Bron had acquired some good cooking skills on her foreign travels and Laurel's nose told her that her aunt was still trying, single-handed, to introduce the garlic clove into North Wales. She inhaled, closed her eyes, picked up other familiar smells, then she looked for the familiar hand painted Ancient Irish Blessing in the hallway: 'May the road rise to meet you, may the sun be warm on your back...'

On the mantlepiece a photograph of her cousin James in his Air Force smiled as he always had. 'He was so happy,' she recalled, 'and I never heard Aunt Bron telling him what to do or not to do.'

Her shoulder twinged as she sat down to eat her chicken, slipping little warm slivers to an ecstatic, grinning dog. Delicious, yet her insides were too troubled to fully enjoy the meal. Those little boys and their stares. That man in the train. Jamie blown away by the war. Suddenly she felt a total physical draining weakness – and could hardly lift her fork or chew her potatoes. Energy seemed to be seeping out of her through the soles of her feet. A tear ran down her face. She stopped eating. Auntie Bron went silently into the kitchen leaving her gazing into the flames of the log fire.

'Take this up with you. Don't need to unpack, I've put one of my clean nightshirts on your pillow. Just climb in, love, and we'll meet for breakfast, whenever you wake.'

'Thank you, Auntie. Muffin will wake me,' she said, then whispered: 'I'm so sorry for all this…'

Bronwyn put her finger across Laurel's lips to stop her apology, gave her a hotwater bottle and a hug and unlatched the door to the staircase. 'Sweet dreams, Cariad. You can say your prayers tomorrow.'

'What prayers?' Laurel wondered, wiping her nose on her pillowcase and summoning up not just her best friend Olivia, lying beside her in the dormitory at school, but her little friend Rachel dancing beside her on the sands of Robin Hood Bay.

***

Tom had tried to camp in the woods. He lasted two nights and two days. Early on the third day two men, one the boatman, had found him lying back inside the larch and beech branch shelter he'd constructed with its loosely woven roof, right in the deepest part of the forest, in the cool and the dark with the rich scent of flowers in the air.

'I think I've cracked it he told the stranger dressed in boots and Norfolk jacket.

'Yes Sir. Let me help you up.' A hand was offered.

'The Doctor wants to see you, Sir,' the boatman added, also reaching his arm out for Tom. 'You were hard to find. We done a trip to Rhiwlas to find Doctor Prosser. He knows the woodlands well, Sir. He's a medic, Sir, but he's a kind of tracker, too.'

'Thank you, Corporal. I don't think I was lost this time.'

'We was afraid you hadn't taken food, Sir.'

'You're right. I hadn't. But I think I could survive in the forest now, gentlemen. '

'Your foreign Doctor was worried... he'll be pleased, Sir.'

'Next time I'll bring some food and a bottle. Preferably Bushmills.

'I have been planning some practical tasks. I want to make a better pier, a boat for myself, a cupboard, a small woodshed and a workbench. I shall need some tools.'

The two men were now dismantling Tom's construction and tucking leaves and branches into the thickets to leave no trace of his adventure. They worked around Tom who stopped divulging his plans.

'If you must do that please mind where you are treading,' Tom implored, *'there are orchids near the roots of these trees.'*

'Beg pardon, Sir. It's hard to see in here, Sir!'

'That's always the way with these branches,' said Prosser. *'Look at that!'* He pointed up towards the canopy and nothing of the upper reaches of the trees was visible, just faint shafts of light coming in from other levels of tree growth. Tom nodded.

'Are you ready, Sir? Feeling okay?'

'Yes. Lets' go! I feel like some coffee!

'Doctor Solomon has good coffee, Sir. So I'm told.'

***

Up in the attic room that used to belong to cousin James, there were balsa-wood planes hung up on wires from the picture rails. His own plane had exploded in a ball of fire over the English Channel, but he might have parachuted to safety, she was told at first. He'd never come home, though. Laurel turned off the light and climbed numbly into bed. The hot water bottle in its fleecy jacket she clamped between the insides of her knees where its warmth seemed to roar around her bloodstream, and her last conscious thought was about her mother, Moira. Laurel saw her standing in the wings checking her costume in a full-length mirror. I wish it were the other way round… I wish Auntie was my mum, she thought… she's standing in my wings, she thought, delighted by the idea, dressing her aunt in one of her Arabian robes. And fell asleep, almost. In her final moments of awareness, she heard a knock at the front door. A soft male voice. Then Bronwyn laughing. A quiet, contented buzz of talk from the sitting room. She fantasized it was her father, returned at last from who knows where; the grave, perhaps. But she had never known a father, she didn't know his voice and this one was slightly familiar. Then muffled laughter from downstairs. Comforted, she tipped into sleep.

***

'Come here woman, give us a kiss!'

'Hold your horses, boyo!'

'Want some ale? I'll get the glasses.' Bronwyn followed him into the kitchen though he knew his way around.

'Oh, she's lovely, Connor, is Laurel. A nice kid. Grown beautiful, too. She's a bit dazed at the moment and went to bed rather suddenly. She'll have her problems, settling in here. But I do so want her to be happy. I do want to get it right for her, not to spoil it for her.'

'Not to spoil her, you mean, you soft creature!' and he opened the bottle and poured out two generous glasses.

'And this sister of yours, is she turning up sometime to suit herself?'

'Moira; well, I hope not, in a way.'

'She's the bloody mother though, it has to be said. She's a fine example to a young girl. Wild creature – gallivanting all over the show like an overdressed film star, which she is not.'

'There goes your sharp tongue again!'

'And there goes the sweet head on the beer…' He drew the liquid in, raised his glass and said, 'Just a bit pale for me. What do you think?'

'It's a touch bitter, Con, to be truthful, but it's beer. What are you up to?'

'What do you think, woman?' He pulled her onto his lap and they sank into the old fireside chair together. Bron objected but felt cosy and she said, 'I'd like to talk, Connor.'

'You talk, my beauty. I'd like to hold you.'

CHAPTER 4

Walking was much preferred to studying for the exams she still had to take in the middle of that summer. She'd attended the village school for a couple of days; been stared at, noticed the ugly haircuts of the boys, felt taller than all the girls. The local library in town was suggested for her revision. It had arched windows set far too high to see anything but sky, and the smell of old books and old people. It made her fidget. So she walked, past the square chapel, past the clock tower, leaving the houses behind, and she would let her dog choose the route. She laughed to see the little brown shape leap away, tail and body wagging, to lead her always in the same direction: Forest Fawr. Perhaps Muffin could sniff rabbit or badger or knew their habitat. But she could not get near them for an old, well-kept wall travelling along the small road that skirted, for miles, the whole of the forest. Not deterred, each day, with great ardour, the little dog searched and burrowed to find a way through or under the wall.

There was no way over, Laurel had often glanced up in the hope herself of finding a weakness or a helpful branch. It was a thick wall, made from chunks of grey stone pitted with lichen, probably double layers filled with rubble. It gave no quarter if she tried shoving at a slightly crumbly bit. Both girl and dog had become fascinated by the great obstacle and Laurel had begun daydreaming of a door, a secret entrance, a way through to enchantment, fountains, both bears and tigers, a handsome prince, treasure. And sometimes she would just imagine the depth of the peace of a walk alone in an unspoiled forest.

Then one day a week after her arrival, Muffin found gold. Her system had always seemed random to Laurel. Rushing suddenly at the wall, sometimes through bush or hedgerow then running twenty yards, or five feet, and trying again. On one of these sorties the dog leapt with joy, wagging away, and abruptly disappeared into undergrowth and didn't return.

'Muffin!' Laurel called eventually, once a large Wolsey car had finished passing, driver and girl staring at each other – it wasn't often a car passed her on this road. *It isn't often I see a pretty girl on the road, in this part of the world*, Laurel thought on behalf of the driver. Muffin suddenly broke into a fit of quite frantic barking; scratching was heard, and she emerged from the bushes by the wall like a cork out of a bottle, leaping up at Laurel, triumphant, and determined to have Laurel confirm and praise her find.

Here at the base of the wall was a hole with eroded stone worn away at the edges, the ground beneath it hollowed and shaped into a channel by the frequent passings of some large animal – fox, badger? Something more exotic? All hidden from view behind quite thick foliage. 'We have Open Sesame, Myfanwy, you clever little dog!

Laurel proved bigger than the fox. Muffin, inside the forest, jumped around snorting and squealing with impatience. It took some work and some hammering with a stick and a fallen stone to loosen and then remove another piece of wall to make an entry large enough to squeeze her slim body through, and when she was there, with the excited dog sniffing and licking at her face, she closed her eyes so that she could first breathe in the deep greenery, and only then did she open them.

'Forest!' she gasped. 'Just trees... what trees! *our* trees!' she told Muffin who had already marked several of them and was now scampering off down her own chosen path.

'I'm now going to name this wood... The Beechwood.' Laurel proclaimed, but she could see that a variety of oaks rather than beeches prevailed.

'What a hide-out. I'll tell no one. We're sworn to secrecy, Muff.' A bark as a reply, and a charging back, a skidding on leaves, a quick turn, a quick departure down a newly discovered path. Both girls in delight, in their element.

'Where does it ever end? Where do you end a forest?'

***

Again – today: there is someone in this forest besides me. This morning, I saw a slight figure approach the water this side of the lake. I was told there was nobody here, yet I have seen a rider on a horse over the other side of the lake and now somebody walking near. I was just beginning to get used to the trees. Have you any idea, Doctor, how difficult it was talking to Griffith and Prosser that day they found me. Do you remember how difficult it was talking to you at first?

Let me start again: my calm is disturbed. Someone walks in this wood. A boy. Is it the same boy? A young forester, I am guessing from the way he looks at trees or places his hands on them and looks up the tree to the canopy. Today I watched him looking up into a vast tall straight elegant oak. He chose well.

I was impressed that I could still name the tree specifically: the Durmast as opposed to the English oak, grey-purple twigs which are on the leaf and not on the acorn. I listed, in my mind, as many names of oaks as I could. Perhaps because the stranger distracted me so. What can I tell you, Doctor? The stranger has a dog. Surely, I'm meant to be here on my own.

***

Tan Hengoed, Treforest, Penforth, Wales. 1st June 1951

Dear Ollie,

News of the exile: I feel so far away, like a convict transported to Australia without the kangaroos. These are the things I miss: you, first and always; London, the traffic sounds, the red buses, our walks on the Heath. Even the school, sometimes.

Mostly, I miss out on excitement and planning mischief and midnight secrets.

There are cows here which sort of roar and the sheep cough a bit and make their usual noises but otherwise it's so quiet you could hear a leaf drop if it wasn't Spring.

I'm living in the attic of Aunt Bron's house which I know because it used to be my grandad's. Tiny but what they call quaint, with a pointed porch and my little round porthole window above. It looks like a squirrel's rectory. And we're not even in the town but on the edge of a small village 3 miles away. It didn't seem to matter so much when I was here for holidays as a kid. But there's just one shop, a church and a chapel and a handful of small houses. And a school. Then there's the old Mansion, which is enormous, about 600 years old and partly fallen into the river. And another which I call the Big House which has its own lake and is set in the forest up the road, my dog Muffin's favourite place. It's something to do with the Army. Anyway, Muffin and I managed to find a way into it today.

Glorious. I will write you more of our explorations at a later date, or tomorrow, especially if we get into trouble which I'm hoping to avoid.

Love from Stan.

PS: Also, nobody here knows my nickname, not even Aunt Bron who seems to know more about me than my own mother and is about as good as an aunt can get. She never fusses, doesn't have any 'strictly forbidden' rules, likes to cook delicious meals, likes books, has a boyfriend, knows about the world and hardly mentions Moira.

***

4th June

Dear Ollie,

Did I ask about you: how are they treating you? How goes the dreadful witch Weatherby? And have they forgiven you for harbouring my 'filthy smut' inside your virginal desk? Wonder if old Weatherbelly is still secretly reading that story of mine or did she flush it away down the lav as she said it deserved? It was good though, wasn't it? 'Corrupting the girls' oho. Were you really corrupted, dear Ollie? And who's going to do it next? You'll have to find a boyfriend and go to the Heath on your own or have a good look at your Dad's naughty magazines.

I long to hear all your news. But first things first: the only decent MALE around here is living on the nearest farm; he's a sheepshearer called Mike who's about 6 foot tall and has dark hair growing all across his back. I've seen him in just boots and trousers in the farmyard, and he is certainly a beefcake – almost. You would approve.

He works for my friend Mr. Morgan the farmer and I go and talk to his horses. He's got a very musical accent but I think he prefers talking to animals than girls – a bit shy – so I've not made much headway there. I'm just hoping he'll let me have a ride on the little bay pony. Perhaps I'll have to change the way I talk.

But I'm saving the best till last: I'm now going to tell you about what I found in the Forest…

No, I'm not … because Aunt Bron and her friend called Connor are coming up the drive and they'll find me here in the sitting room, writing secrets to you. 'Bye.

False alarm. They are both checking that the front gate opens and shuts smoothly. Her sort-of-boyfriend was Irish once and has bushy eyebrows, a funny stare and an old van full of surprises. He'll pull a lawnmower out of it or a box of tools, once a new second-hand croquet set and yesterday two yappy dogs and a woman called Zelda jumped out and upset my friendly little friend Muffin, especially this woman Zelda who reminds me a bit of my mother because she thinks she's some sort of celebrity with masses of shiny make-up and a peevish expression. Then she's always looking at her shoes and straightening her stockings. By the way I've decided to keep my forest secret a secret for a while. I wonder if I can?

***

Diary

…Lists, becoming ever more complex, are the way my mind protects my – a difficult word because it feels as if it has been operated on yet this is one part of my body which has no visible line of stitches – heart. Syntax leads me to… sins of the flesh and to the feelings Dr. Solomon wanted me to disinter. In the hospital I was continually counting, that

is listing numbers. Tomorrow, Wednesday, I am going to
list birds – the names are coming back – but I'm not going
to bore my diary with it today. Where is the boy?

***

7th June

Dear Ollie,

Did you know I'm a quarter Welsh? It doesn't
really help. I've got the wrong voice and face and
restless spirit.

Some people here still break into Welsh in the
middle of a sentence when you go into a shop,
assuming you're English. A bit rude. But most folk
are friendly enough, and some are nosy. Aunt B. says
they're just shy and not to act superior because after
all it's their country and the English did conquer them
hundreds of years ago and they haven't forgotten it,
and that anyway I should be trying to speak their
lingo. Fat chance!

My head's too full of Latin and French to absorb
anything more. Though I wouldn't tell poor Auntie B
that, she's so amazing, and she's had me dumped on

her as it is. I doubt if she's got over my cousin Jamie's death yet. So, like Queen Victoria, I shall be Good.

Not much scope for mischief that I can see yet. But I resolve to work on it.

BOYS:

This was my total conversation the other day with the Almost Beefcake:

A.B: Um, how do you do.

Me: Hello there. What's your name? I'm Stan.

A.B: Stan? (Voice going up in that odd Welsh way at the end.)

Me: Though it's Laurel, really. What's your name?

A.B: (going red & fiddling with a rake he's holding) Michael, my name. Sorry: I have to be going. I daresay it's late by now.

I think I scared him away. Also, Ollie dear, he clearly hasn't heard of Laurel and Hardy so I couldn't even start to explain our nicknames. I don't think he's going to become a friend, just a distraction.

I felt sad thinking of you as I went to sleep in my little room with an owl hooting away outside somewhere in the forest. I think it's an owl – or a vixen.

I want to tell you about my trips to the forest. There have never been secrets between us: but it's late and I'm tired so I'll tell you tomorrow.

PS: People often say 'I daresay' round here when they dare not say or they can't think. Maybe I'll try it out.

***

Diary

I need to talk to you, Doctor. I'm going to light the beacon tonight. If I could row myself, if my wrists could take that action (strange I can chop wood without too much trouble) I would row across. But I'm not sure which days you are there.

There is progress with my thinking and the outline of a face or two, the frame of hair for example, in my memory, mostly female. And with the memories, a feeling of pain.

My fingers are getting back their feeling and a certain dexterity if not strength. I can open the lid on the honey if I don't tighten it too much. (I find I like honey and cheese) but I feel I want to carve sticks and my control is not quite fine enough. One day I'll carve a creature of the forest or the sea.

What I want to talk to you about is the stranger, the boy with the dog, and how I am now drawn to the woods as I was repelled. I'm drawn to the boy, to company. He has no idea I am here.

***

9th June

Dear Ollie,

Now I'm going to tell you about the forest, and then (if I know Aunt Bron isn't coming to my room) I'll give you my real news.

It's called Fforest Fawr which means Great Forest in Welsh. Apparently, it used to cover three quarters of the entire country and wild boars roamed around in it. Now it's just a biggish wood I suppose, and it's all enclosed inside a wall. I found a way in. I've been several times. Muffin and I both love it and want to live there.

We are not supposed to be there at all, Army property, all sorts of signs in English and Welsh saying

Keep Out. So I go in disguise: I wear my old black corduroys and a checked man's shirt from cousin Jamie's drawer and take my penknife and some bread and cheese and of course my compass. I sometimes wear my kilt: it's easier if I have to have a wee which I just love doing in those woods… I pretend I'm a forest ranger or an explorer with my Rhodesian ridgeback dog and I call Muffin 'Jock'. I'm tired of trying to act like a lady – I just haven't got the eyebrows or the knees for it. And anyway, Moira's not here and Aunt Bron isn't her.

I'm not scared of the forest: there may be foxes, but they're not around. I'd like to see a fox. But Ollie, I have seen something MUCH better than a fox in the Forest… This is it!

…Olivia my dear, you're not going to believe this, but there I was, right in the middle of this Woodland, miles from any house or road, no other human being in sight and I was innocently sitting on a log sharing some bread and cheese with Muffin, when what should I see just across the clearing but a MAN- peeing!

Out in the open. Right there in front of me. I could see his action and everything. He was peeing against a tree. I could even just hear the water splashing down and I saw the steam rising up from the grass.

He seemed to take his time, seemed to be enjoying it – which you do, sometimes, don't you? He didn't see me of course. I stayed as still as a rock, hardly breathing. I liked the way he shook it afterwards. That must be how they dry it. But I must tell you, innocent one, your friend Felicity was quite wrong about it sticking up like a candle – it was quite dangly, like a bit of garden hose. I have to say though, as the first real male protuberance I've seen this was slightly disappointing. I thought somehow they'd be bigger. But I think this man is probably a deserter and maybe he's wounded so that could have something to do with it. He's definitely hiding out, anyway. Perhaps he's an outlaw. Did I tell you what he looks like? Nice dark hair, not too short. Curly round his ears. A thick beard. Couldn't see the colour of his eyes but I guess they could be green with long, dark eyelashes. Reminds me of the man I saw on top of a bus years ago. But different coloured hair. He's slim, not very old, quite a find, and it's all very intriguing and definitely not to be divulged to your mother or even to my aunt because there's bound to be trouble and I've still more to learn. Also, I want you to come here as soon as can be. I want to share it with you.

I shall certainly go back and do a little stalking tomorrow and track him down to his lair. I think of him as a fox. Wild, but not really dangerous.

PS. To tell you the truth, Ollie, I did find it quite odd seeing him pee like that, and I don't understand, but a sort of strange sensation hit me inside my tummy, like when you go over a humpbacked bridge in a car. I'm going to start writing a dairy again and it will be private and profane. I shall call it my forest journal, and it's going to be quite something.

***

Monday

> *It's not a boy, it's a girl! Jesus Christ Almighty.*
> *DATA:*
> *She was wearing a shirt and a kilt today and she crossed her ankles when eating on a log. She fed her dog with great delicacy, very affectionate.*
> *I want to speak to her, but I must frighten her away. Strange tight feeling in chest area. Fear?*
> *I must try and remember why I am here, being hidden.*

***

Oh Ollie, I'm so disappointed. He's spotted me! I'm minding my own business looking at woodpeckers with Muffin when my man tramps up to me and asks me what I'm bloody well doing in this part of the wood. He says it's private. 'You're trespassing!' I couldn't believe it. Suddenly he's Mr. Stern, belligerent and nasty, like a schoolmaster.

'Listen,' I say to him, 'My family live around here. And anyway,' I add,' you're trespassing too. This forest belongs to Lord Crickadarn.' I made that up on the spot.

'I pay rent' he says in a smug tone, pointing at a tiny wooden hut.

'For that shack?' We're quite near the lake in this conversation.

'How much?' I hear myself ask, quite confidently really.

'Four pounds.'

'Four pounds!' I shrug. 'You've been rooked! Or you must be a very rich man,' I continue with just a slight hint of sarcasm.

The truth is, I daydreamed this entire conversation. (Did you like it?) In fact, I didn't say a word to him. Wish I had. But I was too astonished. He just spoke quite fiercely when I was snooping round his shack.

More coldly, it was. Or sadly, really, as if he just doesn't speak to people. He doesn't look at all dirty you know, he looks clean. I just stared at him, and I think he looked away and then I walked off slowly thinking: he's got a nice voice. Some sort of accent, not Welsh. I can't quite describe it. Quite deep and manly. A warm voice really, though the words, which I can't remember, were not very welcoming. Don't know why I minded when he shouted.

But he is a bit scruffy. Nice eyes though.

***

Tuesday.

I shouted at her today. Not sure what I said – not pleasant. But at least I got closer to her, or her to me – quite near the tree by the water. Her dog pissed there today, and I was close enough to see her eyes, though not the colour.

She stood her ground, defiant, until the dog was ready, then strode off, pulling a scarf from her head and beating her leg with it. Her hair is brown, red-brown. A Celt? Young, tempting…. so I shout her away like a bloody RSM.

Wednesday

She took action. She suddenly spoke to me today while I was fishing. I knew she was behind me – I'd summoned her up – I wish she was the boy I had imagined her to be – it would feel safer. Then she surprised me with the firm words, the light, clear voice,

'Are you a Scot?' she asked. She asked again when I turned and confirmed she was indeed female. I saw no detail, but form. I was shocked.

'Are you a Scot?'

'Why?'

'I know your name'

I turned away to the water. I cast out again, watched the float spinning. Fought off the wrench in the gut. Am I known?

'And you're a 'sir'. Or at least, a soldier.' I caught her saluting out of the corner of my eye. 'Maybe an officer; who knows, a gentleman! Ha! Unlikely.'

She must have overheard that idiot the General's man, Griffiths -'Captain Byrne, sir! '- he calls me, with the most correct salute, out here in the middle of nowhere. She must have crept up. I never heard her.

'I suppose you're a hero. I thought you were a deserter. I would desert if I were a man. Not because I wouldn't cast

the first stone but because I would hate being told what to do and who to kill 'She carried on like that then stopped suddenly. I thought she had gone. Then I saw she was in the water, leaning, looking at my face.

'Your name is Burns. You needn't tell me your first name'. Approaching me now. I told her to be quiet, that I need silence to fish, but she didn't pause, and her movement hardly stirred the water.

I also have to say that she was staring now at my trousers. Even at my fly.

'Is your name Burns?'

I muttered something about sound carrying across water.

'My name is… ' she began. I wanted to know. I think I had called her Alec in my head. Now I adjusted it to Alice. I think I had known an Alice, or Alice in Wonderland perhaps?

'You thought I was a boy, didn't you?' she declared – uncanny, very female. Then a perch struck. My hands went into their routine with the rod, the fish, the knife. Darkness was gathering. I think she saw me land it and gut it. Who knows where she lives and how she gets home when it's dark.

Suddenly she said to me, 'They are green! Your eyes.'

There was a good supper. The perch a bit muddy but my bread tastes like bread now. And I'm glad of the apples. My wine will soon be ready. Apple wine. The past has gone. Fuck the past. Girl has come. Alice through the Looking Glass. Spiegel im Spiegel .

Thursday.

She's here every day. She's young. What about school? What about her family? So free to roam. Is

this a trap? I want to attack something. Smash…. I'm glad I hold this pen.

Could I hurt her? Could I do what was done to me? What did I do to them? To other men? To women? To Sarah? Sarah who? Tomorrow I could go to the big house, speak to the General or stop his wife who might be his daughter who rides with long hair along the other side of the lake. I could list questions till the winter came. I could ask the girl about herself, tell her not to trap me. I could give up exploding on Thursdays.

***

Dear Ollie,

Have I told you about Romance around here? Well, the village boys and girls are always talking about it. At least the boys talk, in a coarse country way, and the girls giggle behind their hands and go red. They spy on each other, 'walking out' which just, seems to mean going along the road with a boy, alone.

'We know you now! Seen you behind the hedge!' they shout, whether they have or not. And then the boy and the girl become agitated – the boy throws a punch or even a piece of rock, and a fight starts. The girl looks a bit put out but pleased and rushes up to the other girls who comfort her and then they all stand and whisper as the boys try to hurt each other. It's very odd indeed and almost puts me off the human race, although of course dogs are even worse. I can't see what it has to do with love which I do still believe in.

One boy called Owen usually stands apart and looks as if he's embarrassed that he's a boy. Because I think they behave a lot more stupidly when the girls are around. Owen sometimes glances at me to see how I take this display. He seems the only intelligent one of the lot. Unfortunately, he's a bit on the short and wispy side, aged about fourteen, or I might take a distracting interest in him myself. I talk to him sometimes. He's a sort of friend. He's keen on poetry and fishing and wanted to know if I'd be going to the dance at the Young Farmer's Club. I want you to know, Ollie, that this YFC is the high point of the social whirl down here. I think I'm a bit of a snob and I don't know whether to blame Moira, our education or myself. It's me, I guess. Are you a snob too? I can't remember.

Aunt Bron says you must come to stay in the holidays, for as long as you like if that's what I want. It is. She'll put a mattress up in my attic for you.

We can take the dog out and tease the local youth and GO TO THE FOREST and I'll show you my Man. Wot larks, Pip old chap. I'd be thrilled if you could come.

Love from Stan.

PS. We haven't got a phone here you know – just a phone box down the lane. If you ever want to phone me, you ring Mary at the Post Office and leave a message and she gives it to her husband who cycles up the road to us. He gets a large cup of tea. They've got quite a nice daughter called Bethan and because they lived for a while in Cardiff, she seems different.

But no one could replace you, certainly not Bethan, not even my man in the forest.

***

Thursday, later.

My head is clear and holds a clear picture of her. Brown hair, brown eyes, white flesh, willowy walk, sudden runs, bare feet, shirts and trousers, jodhpurs, defiant, feminine. I could write all day this Thursday bloody Thursday, just about her. Sin and syntax. And food collocations too. Like oysters and brown bread and brown ale. Thirsty. Why do I think of Meister Eckart of all historical figures… I could make a list of poets philosophers politicians theologians. But I want to list all that I know about her – nothing, beyond her joke.

***

Journal. Laurel Williams Thursday.

It's an odd thing, but I realise that when a smoky mist like this morning comes down the valley it seems to float right inside me as well. It clouds up my head and makes me feel soppy and sleepy. But on days when the light is sparkling or the sun is bright, I feel alive and want to do things. And it feels that the world and I are turning into each other. I can't explain it any better, but I can't seem to look at the things in the forest without my mood changing them all. And when I take Muffin out there for an early morning walk in the mist, she catches my mood, and when she pees I want to pee too so we both do our squats together. Burns never appears at this hour. What's he up to? Would he peep at me as I did at him? Strange to look odd. Nobody say I miss it when I don't see him, if I've gone a day without catching a sight. Maybe it's just the forest and those awe-inspiring trees that I miss. I'm turning into a Naiad perhaps. I should like to be able to swing lightly through the branches – could the Naiads do that? Or were they too ethereal? I could practice a bit of ethereal swinging today. Get my clothes on. Forest, here I come.

***

Same day, later.

I broke off. A knock at the door which I shut when I write as that earlier boy did when he sat at his table attending to his diary. 'It's her,' I thought, shocked, caught out.

'Come in!' I said, breathless, instead of going to the door, hiding my new list which begins with Pindar.

'Morning Sir! '

'Morning.' I wanted to check, 'Is it Thursday?'

But General Ashworth's man looks so shell-shocked he might not know. Besides I want to hold onto time myself as I. did in hospital and in prison.

In what prison? What was my crime? Dr. Solomon said 'imprisoned'. That's different. I feel I have been imprisoned. Am still.

***

Journal. …Thursday, later.

I squashed two patterned snails by mistake on my way into the forest today. They had delicate brown and yellow stripy patterns and spirals on their shells. I did feel bad about that. I love snails. I like the shy way, when they think you're not looking they push their soft little horns out into the world, so carefully. And then they put them right up like radar aerials and tremble them about to see what the Universe is up to. I always feel like touching them then, so I pick a blade of grass and just gently give a tiny touch. Zuuut! In it goes, as fast as that. Inside its hard little shell, safe again. – I wasn't going to hurt you, little snail! But how was the poor snail to know?

But now I've gone and killed two of them just with one step. I think they were stuck together so at least they didn't die alone. Perhaps they were mating. Even better. Imagine dying making love? Imagine making love!

This forest seems to be watching me with all its eyes. I think I shall walk more gently, go barefoot; I'd better not upset it

I'd give anything to see a snake.

***

Thursday, still.

I knew the General was sending down to find out if I required anything. 'Books!' I heard myself say… 'Doctor Solomon will choose good books. And I want to see him'.

'Yes Sir!' Griffiths saluted and marched off. I watched him go, away, well away. My shack was mine again. Then as I turned, I saw the girl. No shoes. Sitting up in the great drooping main shoot of the cedar nearest the shack – some sixty feet off – a Deodar I recognised in its conical shape, low branches sweeping the ground. What's a Himalayan tree doing in a Welsh wood? And what's a bright-eyed girl barefoot in jodhpurs doing swinging on the lower branch?

I want to say 'she didn't bat an eyelid' but it's not what I would say. It comes from someone else. Or it comes from my shakiness.

'You're trespassing!' I shouted, quite fiercely, to send her off. 'Do you know what today is?' she shouted back.

'Don't tell me!

' She bloody knows it's Thursday.

'It's my birthday.'

'Oh. Well…' I was stumped, I didn't know what to say so I said 'Happy Birthday'

'Ha. Fooled you. If I'd kept it up for longer, would you have given me a present?

'I've got to go'.

'Fine. You've not got money for birthday presents or we haven't yet been formally introduced. It's not etiquette, and you're a gentleman.'

She was mocking me with such èlan .

'Go away, child!' I tried to look away, more than breathless and quite confused by what I was saying.

'Well, I can tell you a thing or three about etiquette. I am the possessor of a manual on etiquette, although it is rather old, and it's called 'DON'T' and by the way I'm not a child.'

She descended the branch.

'Shall I share a few choice 'DON'TS' with you?' she jumped to the ground. 'Don't eat anything with a spoon that could be eaten with a fork. School custard… you could have eaten that with a fork.

'Go away boy!' Exploding with fear.

'And gentlemen don't raise their voices when a lady is in the middle of explaining something… and by the way, if I was a boy I would… how do you know I'm a boy?'

'You behave like a boy, now bugger off!' I crouch down.

Aha, I know what bugger means, and a gentleman should – '

'Beat it!' I growl. She was getting nearer, angling her head to peer at me.

'I'm not scared of you,' she said.' I know you want to talk to me. We are both… we've both been landed here'.

'Now fuck off this instant or you'll feel this!' It was a fist I showed her. I was shaking with an inexplicable feeling of having been uncovered. Vulnerable is the word. And it was I who stalked off.

When I turned, having reached the edge of the lake, she was gone and I had to swim to cool off. Very distressed. What does she want? What does this mean? 'She had heard me talking to Griffiths. 'Who's Doctor Solomon when he's around and why do you want to see him?' I think she said as I was retreating. That's when I swore at her.

I wonder how long she hung around. A scent of woman in the air when I returned. I remember… enough.

Byrne was restless. He frowned at Solomon when he eventually entered the room. It had been a long wait between sessions.

'Please sit or lie, Tom. I'm sorry I have had to be away. Someone in trouble in London, intensive work. So…'

'Why don't you ask me questions?'

'But you sent for me, Tom… and that's not the way we work. '

'Ask me a question.'

Solomon's mouth twitched in what seemed to be the beginning of a smile. 'What sort of question?'

'The sort of questions psychiatrists ask.'

'Tell me some.'

'You know…. have I ever been violent? Do I want to get well? And what happens to people like me. '

'What question do you want to ask?' Solomon said in reply. Tom snorted with what seemed a mixture of anger and impatience.

'Why do I have to find my memory? Why do I have to wander about in my past? Can't you just heal me now, here, in the present?'

'What has happened, Tom?' Solomon's voice was neutral and gentle.

'You've got my words'.

'Yes.'

'Here…more …read them.' Tom handed over his latest sheaf of papers that he drew out of his belt.

'I haven't much time today, Tom.'

'Can we walk…'

'I can see you the day after tomorrow for a longer session.'

'Please. Read them while we walk.'

'Forgive me,' Solomon checked with his watch against -the time on the carriage clock that stood on the mantelpiece opposite him.

'I'd like to smash that clock.'

'Strong feelings, Tom. I'll read your piece. Come.'

They both stepped out of the French doors onto the verandah then down the path and Solomon let Tom choose the direction towards the maze with its topiary, change his mind, reverse direction towards a plantation that swept down to the lake.

There was silence except for leather on gravel while Tom scanned the sky for raptors and Solomon read, hoping to find in the diary notes some indication of what had happened to push his patient into turmoil.

Notes in the present tense for the Doctor:

Here I am in the hut. Darkness. Two candles. The door has to stay open. The sounds of owl and vixen, persistent, both hunting, she for a dog. Her cry is pleading like a wretched human child.. Midsummer courting, craving: do I crave anything? Slight hunger. Bread and cheese.

'An infant crying in the night,

An infant crying for the light,

And with no language but a cry… '

The lake laps against the pier and the shale. Bats are heard by their squeaks and their wings. Insects. The scratch of my pen as I sit at my desk reminds me of my task as I look down at my writing. Don't like it, the 'scrawl of it, the compulsion of it. What do I know about myself? My name is Tom. My mother's name was … Ruth. My *godmother's…Emer. Irish. My sister… nothing yet. Nor my father except…. he was a doctor, I think. A cat called… Tortie… tortoiseshell; a dog, a Sealyham. Tennyson wrote the above… In Memoriam.*

I was born in… twenty two. 1922… Good heavens.
It is now 1950 or 51. Soon I'll be thirty.
May 15th someone's birthday.
Place is vague, time more clear.
Hills and high moor.
Candles bring out memory of small altar, small church.
It feels quite comfortable with two persons either side of me.
May 15th is a woman's birthday.
Head of full hair. Full head of hair. Sarah somewhere.
What do I know about my body, concrete and present?
I feel quite separate from it. Long limbs, slight limp, ugly feet. Moustache, beard, curls in hair. Scars, recent scars, dry mouth. Body sweats, woody smell, not familiar. Genitals look redundant, not mine. Knees amusing, don't know why. Can't remember my face. Still distracted by thought of mirror.

Tonight, I shall venture into the trees again, right in. A test. I'll time how long I can endure. Want to watch, but not sure why, the light appear across the canopy at dawn.

Will need courage. Still need courage. I want not to write any more.

This will have to do for a while, Dr. S. Pen on strike.

CHAPTER 5

'Look, that's a March hare, in July'

'It's the first of the month – you saw the hare, Laurel, you'll be married before Michaelmas!' laughed Bethan, 'better get a move on, girl! Anyone asked you to the Young Farmers' dance yet?'

Laurel was walking home from the village on a hot afternoon after the rain with Bethan and Owen, who was Bethan's cousin and who was tagging along with them as he often did.

'You can take me to the dance, Owen.'

The boy looked wistfully through his spectacles at Laurel, whom he adored.

'No, he can't. Has to be a member of the YFC, and over sixteen.' Bethan was walking out with a Young Farmer, David Morgan, so she spoke with authority. David was at least nineteen, the son of Edwin the farmer, Laurel's friend. Bethan was a year older than

Laurel and Owen was almost two years younger which made him, at not quite sixteen, a complete baby in Bethan's eyes.

'Nobody's asked me,' said Laurel. 'I don't mind. Haven't got a dance dress anyhow.'

'My mam's making mine. What about your mam? Oh, sorry Laurel. She's ill, isn't she? Is she still in the hospital then?'

'Yes, well anyway – she's only ever made me one thing in my life: for a fancy dress competition. The White Rabbit in *Alice Through the Looking Glass*.'

'Get away!' Bethan looked impressed. 'Ears and all?'

'Oh Yes. A rabbit head and ears. And white furry legs and paws. And a blue velvet jacket and knee britches. And a silk embroidered waistcoat and a little tail here.' She bobbed her bottom and Owen blushed. 'I was about eight, I think.'

'Bet you won!'

'First prize. And a photo in the local paper. My mother loves winning things.'

'I wish mine did,' said Bethan.

'I don't know, it wasn't so good for me… she was very beautiful, you see. She was an actress. She still is. So of course, I didn't dare to just stand there as the white rabbit "like a lump of suet" as Moira would say. I trotted round getting out my big fob watch and going, "Oh, my fur and whiskers! I'm late!"'

'Fantastic, Laurel,' said Owen.

'No wonder I won. I had to work hard for that ten-shilling book token... The Duchess gets so savage if I'm not on time!' and Laurel mimed the rabbit pulling his watch from his waistcoat pocket, smoothing his ears, tweaking his whiskers.

Bethan looked at her friend thoughtfully. Village folklore still echoed with bits of stories about Moira, Laurel's mother, when she'd been young here. She had eloped to London with a visiting actor at the age of seventeen. Apparently she had a vile temper.

My mother didn't really make that costume,' Laurel suddenly confessed. 'She just altered it to fit. I think she pinched it from one of the plays she was in.'

'She'd have been savage if you hadn't won!' guessed Bethan, correctly. Laurel's eyes glistened for a moment. She nodded.

'She didn't much like me taking a dancing prize later, though. Sounds silly, but I think she was a bit... jealous. So.' Her voice was brisk now. 'I live with Auntie Bron now and she's my friend, *she* doesn't think I look like a beanpole.'

'You never look like a beanpole!' said Owen as they passed the gateway to Edwin Morgan's farm. Edwin was walking past with a pitchfork.

'Evening, Mr. Morgan!'

'Evening girls! And Owen... just the chap. You coming in to help me turn the hay? My tractor's up the spout.'

'We've to be home for tea now, sorry Mr. Morgan,' said Bethan.

'I'll help you,' said Laurel, wanting company.

'Come on then girl, you'll do fine. I'll get you a pitchfork.' So Laurel spent half an hour of the

fine warm evening forking over heaps of sweet-smelling grass, forgetting about her mother.

In the distance she could see Mike the sheep shearer coming down the hill with the two sheepdogs, herding the sheep into the lower field.

As she forked, a tiny fieldmouse raced out of the grass and practically fell onto her foot. 'That's a young 'un, said Edwin. 'There's a nest under there, I daresay.'

She felt easy with Edwin Morgan. He sang hymns on his tractor and folksongs like 'David of the White Rock', and sometimes his distant tenor was the first sound she heard in the morning. He teased her like a grandfather and taught her how to talk to lambs and how to pleach a hedge and always to greet a magpie, 'Hello, Mr. Magpie!' He watched her turning and forking the grass for a while.

'Now Laurel, I want you to tell me something; if someone young and handsome wanted to ask you to the dance next week but he was too shy, what advice would you give him?'

'...to ask me?' Laurel sounded shocked.

'And why not? A fine young lady like yourself... oho, here he comes now,' and Edwin started whistling as he moved deftly down the row, pitching and turning. Laurel watched Mike leap the gate, the two dogs flattening themselves to slide under it. She felt surprised, but willing to go along with the farmer's friendly expectations.

'Michael!' she called, stopping him in his stride. He came over to them.

Are you going to the Young Farmers' dance?' she asked boldly.

'No – well, yes, maybe – I'd like to...'

'So would I.'

'Oh right. That's good, then.' His voice died away.

'Aren't you going to ask me?' Edwin had stopped turning hay to watch this exchange with a wry smile, confirming his conviction that there were questions to be raised about who was the weaker sex, not that he needed to raise them with Mrs. Morgan.

'Oh – yes! Of course. Um, please would you come to the dance, Laurel, then. With me.'

'Since you ask…' she struck an elaborate thinking pose. Edwin nodded to himself.

'I haven't got my diary but, yes. I feel disposed to make myself free.' She curtsied and clumsily but willingly, he bowed. Edwin clapped. Laughter all round.

What am I doing? Who wants to go to a dance? I'm doing a Moira! …So what! she said to herself defiantly, the child checking the adult.

'So, what is it fashionable to wear this year?' More male laughter, delighted at this piece of feminine language amongst the pitchforks. 'I shall ask my Aunt Bron to make me a ball dress so Cinderella can go to the ball; do you do the tango, Michael?'

'No, I don't think so.'

'Good.'

'But I can do the foxtrot, after a fashion, and the slow waltz.'

***

Diary

Now it's Friday and I have done nothing. No girl. Yesterday, when she came I shouted at her again and I used up all my energy. This morning, I wandered about in desultory fashion trying to find a good fishing spot not knowing what I was looking for. Heard a gentle, unmistakable yelp. Her dog. Damn it, the dog even knows me now. There she is, the girl, in her boyish clothes looking at me, arms akimbo.

She's sticking her chin out aggressively, eyes flashing. Fierce. It must be a continuation of yesterday.

'Listen – what do -you mean 'what am I doing here? This is where I live!' she launches in. 'My mother was BORN in this village, I'll have you know, MISTER man, whoever you are when you're at home. So what the hell are you doing here anyway? With that hair and that beard ? And those clothes? Not doing any constructive work, I can see that. And you're trespassing, probably. Don't believe you even pay rent. You're just a tramp. '

'I do pay rent,' I say lamely. A feeling of being found out. She sniffs, runs her hand through her curly hair and returns to the attack, her face flushed.

'Well, where do you get your money from? You aren't earning it. Something odd's going on here.

'Are you planning to turn me in to the authorities?' I felt like smiling now, but must resist it. 'I haven't broken any laws.'

'What about poaching? That's a law,' she answered.

Then I played my trump card – 'Well, the law won't look kindly on a girl and a dog who've been breaking and entering Army property with a sentry on the gate and a fifty pound fine for trespassing.'

She glared at me and shrugged and turned towards the lake as a heron flew off.

'You don't seem to like me very much,' I said.

'Like you? What is there to like? I think you're peculiar. Where's your family anyway?'

Damn. That question caught me off guard. I turned to look at the lake. There was a loud splash, was it a perch jumping? No, it was that darn girl throwing a stick in for the dog. Upsetting the fish. But the little dog, rushing up excited tail wagging like mad, is too intelligent to go in. Must be ten or more feet deep just there. Who knows how deep in the centre.

As I stared into the depths, I heard a breathy little whistle and the dog rushed off. Good. That's one thing she doesn't have over me. She can't whistle. If I whistled now the dog would run back. But I want her to go. I can't cope.

***

Journal – At home. Saturday. 4th July.

Had a strange fainting fit at the dinner table yesterday. First my heart started pounding like mad for no reason in the middle of eating macaroni cheese. I went hot and flushed and then I passed out. Not my period time either. Though I have been having some odd fluttery twinges recently. Bloody growing pains, I expect they'll tell me.

Auntie phoned Doctor Prosser, really nervous, as if I'd had a heart attack. Poor man was having his supper too. Maybe it was a heart attack, and I shall soon die an interesting death. Hope Weatherby feels guilty when I do.

The doctor came round and asked me about my eating and drinking habits. Did I smoke! (I didn't tell him about the dried shredded banana skins Ollie and I made into cigars and sold last term. That was months ago.) He seemed interested that I'd been hungry and thirsty recently but seemed to be losing weight. The adults are now treating me with respect. They must think I've got something serious, but I feel fine. Just a bit fuzzy.

***

Diary, Saturday.

Didn't sleep. Numbers come to mind, but that way madness lies. Measuring was all I did in my cell. I measured everything, counted everything, kept loss at bay. Alphabetically.

Alice, Beth, Claire, Dora-Theodora, Eva, Felice – that's not English, Greta, nor's that, Saoirse… where the hell did that come from? Sarah – yes, Sarah: out of order. Lulu, Medea, Nina, Olivia. 'My best friend… Ollie…' the girl said that. The girl….

***

Dear Ollie,

Guess what? I've got a 'thyroid condition'. Just like Elizabeth Barrett Browning. I shall lie about on a chaise longue – well, the sofa – and receive young men bringing flowers.

Doctor Prosser thinks I've been under nervous strain which is apparently the only thing that brings it on suddenly like this. Can't imagine what nerves

I've been straining, apart from boredom... that's gone, anyway. I will now lie about a bit and enjoy my thyroid condition, get some attention and read Jane Eyre again. My heart keeps pounding oddly. I wish it would stop

I do get tired, so I'll keep this short. But please write me a long letter about anything, especially any film you've seen or tricks you've been up to, even if they're mild.

**

Diary. Day?

Why have I got no books? Knives, nails, pots, pans, hooks, brushes, bottles. But no books. Did I pack my bag? End of question. My boots and trousers are military. So is my bag. My shirts and jacket and coat seem new, or little worn. My underclothes and socks feel strange.

There is no looking glass in this shack. Dr. Solomon's prescription: look at your face. Know thyself. That's the cure. How can I see my face, Doctor? Lines, not mine, come into my head: like... when I spotted and named a willow yesterday, I heard a woman's cadence 'Willow cabin', then

'Make me a willow cabin', now 'Make me a willow cabin at your gate and call upon my soul'. I call upon my body.

I can smell mushrooms now in the wood, but it is too early for them. I shall want butter not oil to cook them. And lemon. Food comes to mind, yet I am not hungry, not quite. A muted stirring as with thoughts of spring. The girl with no clothes. It's more the spring of the flesh than the feeling or inhaling or... yes, inserting. Yes. The memory returns and the member re-members more than the mind but going in is the business and it goes into my hand... now ... too softly. I put down my pen to insert it in my other hand to see if it comes to life... no.

I call upon my body to heal my mind... How?

***

Journal Tuesday.

I've been in bed for THREE days. I'm getting better and I miss my forest. At least I have all James's books to look at, mostly scientific, and I've been reading a book about the solar system. When I get up I feel dizzy: but when you think that at this very moment I'm spinning at 800 miles an hour round the earth's axis, it's not surprising. And it's also not surprising that I return with relief to Charlotte Bronte and my big box of biscuits.

***

Diary

Oh, let me write a sentence now that flows with its own momentum because its source is the simple desire to say what I want to do in order to come fully alive again not just to my body but my mind which gives the thought to the feeling which makes a man human: I want the girl here now please. I want her eyes in my eyes.

***

Journal.

It's Wednesday apparently, or so they tell me. I've been here for four days now so I've lost four whole days of my life. Getting stronger though, less dizzy. But something has happened to my sleeping: I wake up after a few hours. Why? I wake up expecting something, or looking forward to something, and I can't get back to sleep. Perhaps it's just chocolate I'm

127

yearning for – or maybe a glass of Tizer. Perhaps I've lost weight and am really turning into a beanpole.

***

Diary

That was better. Yesterday. I don't care what day it was. It worked. The sentence came from the wish.

***

Journal.

Three lovely letters from Ollie. No visitors apart from dear Bron. Who else would there be? Owen would notice I'm not around but he's too shy to visit. I wonder what Mike thought about me asking him to the dance like that? Mr. Morgan seemed to be pleased. They both laughed anyway. I can't imagine Burns laughing. I can't imagine Mr. Rochester laughing either.

Can't keep up this jolliness, yet I'm not sad. Just tired. Got the sulks, a bit weak or something I can't quite describe in words. But I feel I'm getting stronger,

I think I'm feeling better. Maybe the diagnosis is very simple – too simple for doctors to understand – girl changing. Treatment – just keep reading.

I have discovered there are 228 separate and distinct muscles in the head of an ordinary caterpillar. Whatever for? It makes you exhausted just to think about it. If I was creating a caterpillar, I'd be a lot lazier.

I think the most disappointing thing in Jane Eyre is when the author says: 'Reader, I married him.' I just wanted her to love him.

***

Diary

A squirrel came to my water trough and I in my distraction have not thrown out kernels. Pen down. Nuts in hand. Cast! … come the squirrel come the jay. No more nuts. I throw a root. Two jays hoping to beat the squirrel to the task. The French word for root is racine. *But how do I know it's a jay? It hops like a chough or any crow… the French word for crow is* corneille. *The markings of jay are what I see: the grey plumage, flecks of white and brown on crown, moustache effect near bill, black tail, white rump, blue flash on wing.*

I see the eyes – I remember the eyes! A pale pink which I check now – pin down – with my field glasses which throw up a fragment of torn flesh, not the bird, a part of a man. And a muffled explosion in my cranium. Stop writing or start listing!

de Havilland

Gypsy

Rolls-Royce

Merlin… Alphabetical:

Alvis

Buick

Chevrolet

Dodge

Ford

My father had a Ford. My father was wounded. His war was Purgatory. He relied on me. That's it! I

must tell Solomon. I must not wish her here again.

That girl. I must wait. Not long. I'll wait till she's a woman.

***

Almost forest journal.

I've got to get OUT OF HERE! This room is too small, it's driving me crazy. Walls, ceiling, curtain rail, picture of Switzerland: give me a bigger view. But Auntie says I must stay in bed for one more day. The doctor comes tomorrow. I can hear Auntie watering the garden. She says there's a drought and the farmers are very worried. I told her the doctor's got ice-cold hands.

Maybe when she's asleep tonight I'll just sneak out for a walk, and I won't go too far. I'm strongly drawn to the trees. I may just go into the forest for a while. I'll pray for rain this evening. I'm not scared of the rain, or the dark. I'm only scared of suffocating in a small hot boring room.

CHAPTER 6

Diary Day?

I don't know what happened today. I lost it. I can't remember it. Just an echo in the forest like a shot gun both barrels going off in my head. Counting my extremities hands fingers feet genitals. Viscosity in my head in a soft flowing explosion like larva moving like contingency moving in my head. and confusion stemmed by counting the days I have lost. I count the entries. This is day twelve of entry. Entry... Into the deeper water. The colder water. Alone.... ah wilderness.

I want her here in my wilderness on the thirteenth day. Friday. I'll call it Friday. Good Friday. Girl Friday. Tomorrow.

Whoever Sarah was, she has gone. The echo in the forest is not the ghost rattling the machine but at least one woodpecker drumming in short bursts, loud and frequent, to call the girl to look at his scarlet undercarriage on her way to wake me from my nightmare, to scare me back to life, to start to be… listless… soft in the head, soft in the heart… countless… still … my engine only hers, her beat, her bare feet.

***

I take off my boots. No girl.

It is night.

But it's the thirteenth day, the thirteenth entry, and the girl should have come.

She was there. Out there in the dark. I walked to the door holding my boots and she ran away.

It has rained at last. All night and all day. No fishing, no books. A trip to the theatre of my mind where I see, in my right hemisphere and through the field glasses of my memory, someone on the stage playing the part of the General's wife or daughter, striding about with a riding crop in her hand, talking about vine leaves, walking off into the wings or the garden and shooting herself. I think I am regressing again, and Dr. Solomon is in London and this rain reminds me of imprisonment and my firewood is damp and where is she?… And then there she is, the girl is here, the girl is sitting, crouching in the wet forest watching me hunting in the dark for kindling. I want to take action but wait for her.

Except... I leave the door open when I return to try to light the fire.

I must take action and call to her then search for her and find her huddled, her head covered by her hands. No coat. Wet through.

She is light as kindling, she doesn't struggle. 'Dry your clothes' I tell her as she kneels at the fire. 'Here's a blanket!'

'Close the door!' she says almost crossly.

When I turn, I see a flash of flesh as she bends to remove her jodhpurs. She wears no underclothes or shoes. Her shirt she pulls over her head. On the stone she lays her two items to dry, huddles again and waits whilst I fold the blanket around her.

She is shaking. She is thin.

'I take two sugars' she says. To the kettle that is rumbling.

'I've no sugar,'

'Honey then.' Her head turns towards me. She takes the cup and drinks, sipping noisily and almost smiling. Watching me drink too, speaking when finished.

'I take sugar'

'I know. I have no sugar. '

'It was horrid.'

'Why'd you drink it?'

'I was cold. Why didn't you put brandy in it?'

'I only have wine.'

'I don't like wine.'

'I wasn't going to offer.'

'I would like some wine.'

'It's too young.'

'No it's not! Open it!'

Tempted, I respond. Open a bottle, allow it to settle while I wash the mugs. Pour carefully while

she turns her clothes on the stone. She feels the clothes and smells them. The blanket falls away to show her shoulders, but it is her hands that hold my eye, woman's hands. They take the mug, and the eyes look up at me as she sips the wine. The smile in her eyes that enters mine.

'This is good. Did you make it?'

'Let it settle.'

'My friend Olivia — '

How did I know her friend was named Olivia? She spoke on, telling me something, but I was

looking at her hands those slender fingers wrapped round the mug.

'— and our headmistress said we were behaving like drunks. We were. I was.'

She goes to school. Her eyes are very bright.

'Where have you been for the last few days?' I ask, 'I haven't seen you.

'Well, I've been ill, sort of,' she says it shyly.

'You don't get ill!' I tell her, as if I know.

'Well, it wasn't what you'd really call "ill".

'Where's your dog?'

'I didn't want to wake the house, so I crept out without her. Gave her a piece of chocolate.'

'Why did you come?'

'The summer is almost over'.

'What?'

'Almost gone. The holidays'

'How many days. Don't tell me. How many weeks?'

'Why don't you take your clothes off too. You're wet.'

'I only have one blanket.'

'You have an eiderdown.'

No movement. Move. I started with my boots.

'Are you going to watch?' I asked.

'I've seen you before anyway. How many women have you seen?'

'Where did you see me?'

'I want to see your scars.'

'How did you know?'

'Guessed. You don't want them touched, right?'

'Right.'

I have taken off shirt and then trousers and stand in awkwardness wrapping myself in the eiderdown. She can't see my scars. They are under my wrists, under my feet, across my back, between my legs.

'My friend Olivia I mentioned, she's really sweet. A sweet girl. You'll like her. Oh yes.'

'Why are we talking about Olivia?'

'She's coming to stay, soon.'

'So?'

'So. I'm bringing her to see you.'

'Do I want to be seen by Olivia? Am I a fairgound attraction?'

'Of course. The man in the forest. I've told her about you already. From the first time I saw you. '

'Oh yes?'

'You were peeing. Against a tree. '

Tom looked at Laurel as if she were a total stranger again. 'I'm not going to see your friend.'

'You don't have to pee for her.'

'I can't be seen, I'm being hidden here.'

'Well, I can see you all right. Loud and clear. Someone's hopeless at camouflage.' She laughed, spluttering into her *mug of wine. 'You do look silly in that eiderdown. What's your real name?'*

I hesitate. She shrugs and carries on.

'Mine's Laurel, but I think I've said that. Do you know Laurel and Hardy? Olivia and I are Stan and Olly. So, I'm Stan to you. Or Tom or Dick or Jack.'

She had moved to pick up her jodhpurs, dry now, and pushed her bare legs into them. Confused, I turned to the basin and poured out warm water from my kettle to wash out the mugs. Now she is dressed and looking like a boy again.

'Yes, Jack. Call me Jack, in case you get into trouble, except – ' she turned to me and smiled a smile. A flash of lightning. 'I'm going to a ball and I'm going to have a magnificent ball dress – I shall look like a mermaid under water. I'd like to bring it to show you. But I expect you don't dance, though.

'Not to music, any more.'

'So, you'll have to call me Laurel sometimes.' And she twirled about as if in her dress in the middle of my wooden hut. Looked around the walls. 'No mirror! You don't even have a mirror! Don't you ever want to see yourself? You're not that ugly.'

'Yes, ' I said, 'I'd forgotten. That I wasn't ugly. I should have a mirror. 'My mother insisted on calling it a 'looking glass'.

'Your mother?'

This is a very long wait, Dr. Solomon, not just for you and to show you these notes. This is a very long struggle with temptation, a tall dark temptation to take this girl, to lift her up, to sink myself into her defiance and disappear upon the midnight with no pain left whatsoever. No shame. 'Shade' you would say in your mother tongue. Yet it would be shame until she wants me too. Freud means joy. Girl means life. Life in me again. Life in my head. She is safe. I am impotent.

But am I safe? I shall not show you these pages. She is still twirling past.

'Yes,' I say, 'bring me your ball gown ! '

'Yes! She shouts and runs and is gone as surprisingly as she came, saying over her shoulder,

'It's a ball dress not a ball gown. '

Mind! Careful how you go in the dark! I want to shout and run after her, but I resist again. And I am left full of worried virtue, almost a joy. 'Jack' indeed.

CHAPTER 7

This was her favourite time of day at Auntie Bron's. The fire was lit and was beginning to warm her face as Laurel half lay on the floor propped up on cushions, with her mug of cocoa. Now the sky was turning a clear pink-yellow with a long wisp of bright coloured cloud floating above the dark silhouettes of trees on the skyline.

She had a pile of *Vogue* magazines and was flicking through them for inspiration for the ball dress. Bronwyn came in with a big brown paper package that rustled.

'Found it! I knew it was up there somewhere.' She pulled off the brown paper. 'I bought this in Paris, on my way back from Egypt.' There were several layers of tissue paper to unwrap before the thick folded rectangle of material was revealed.

'Meant to make an evening dress for myself – but coming back here – and then of course I was pregnant with James – so I put it off.' The last piece of tissue was unfolded.

'Good job I did. Look, Cariad, it's just your colour!' Laurel leapt up, almost spilling her cocoa. It was a deep, shimmering peacock blue. Taffeta brocade. In the firelight it flickered with greenish glints, like shot silk.

'It's stunning! It's glorious! It's exactly the colour I've been dreaming about only better!' Laurel ran her fingers over the texture of the brocade, put her head sideways to catch the greeny depths of it, stroked it with her cheek, then wrapped her arms round aunt, brocade and all and did a jig of delight.

'Careful! Don't get too carried away, Laurie. I haven't unwrapped it for over eighteen years…'

'My lifetime!'

'So it could have the moth.'

'Moths? No! But it isn't wool…'

'Doesn't need to be.'

Then Bron, as often happened, slipped softly into song.

'What are you singing, Auntie?'

'Nothing special… well,' she stroked the material. 'It's what we call a Cân Serch, a love song actually, I don't know why.'

Both women, the young and the older, carefully, eagerly held out the material between them, unfolded it in front of the fire, scrutinised it.

The folds were a little dusty but otherwise it was perfect. No moth holes. Bronwyn draped it round her niece's shoulders.

'How shall I make it? Strapless perhaps. Low back.'

'Oh yes. And tight down to here…' Laurel put both hands on her hips, 'then whoosh! Out in a full skirt so I can twirl. What a lot of material!''

'I got it before the war, remember. Let's see: you'll need plenty of petticoat.'

'Can we do that?'

'Oh yes. No problem about clothes coupons now – thank heavens.' Laurel opened the magazines again.

'I've seen just the thing, you see… here, can you do something like this, Auntie dear? don't they look silly with those gloves on!'

'You always had to wear gloves. Even in Alexandria. Young ladies weren't dressed properly without them.'

'Did you, too? It must have been hot.'

'No. Hardly ever, in fact. But then I was outside 'society'. I was living with an Arab.'

'And you worked too, didn't you? How outrageous!'

'I'd started my little restaurant. It was a bar really, with food. We called it 'Paradiso'.

'Paradiso: what a name!'

'That's a Persian word, you know. His choice. Oh, he had a way with words, that's how he charmed me. He loved words… and with his soft foreign accent. The language has produced some wonderful poets. Rashid would read to me. Persian, and Turkish. I couldn't understand a word, but, beautiful! Did you realise that the Turkish language is very highly regarded because it has some kind of internal harmony, something indefinable but good to the ear. Oh, we know so little, living on this little island!'

'I know, I know! But tell me!'

'You travel, girl, as soon as you're able.'

'Oh Auntie, tell me about how you met Uncle Rashid again, and how he charmed you.'

Both women looked at one another recognizing that they both knew something mysterious that went beyond all language.

'Not now, Laurel my pet.' Bronwyn looked away. 'Not now'.

'What is it, Aunt Bron, what is it?' Tears were not Bronwyn's currency.

'Silly it is,' Bron replied, using a small handkerchief from her apron. 'Goofy it is. Because I can't be unhappy when I'm talking to you; you being here and all. It's the remembering. It's just… that they too were here once upon a time. Oh, Jamie would have loved this colour! Blue was his favourite colour. Now let's talk about frivolous things…'

Laurel managed a small laugh.

'Yes, let's talk about clothes and dressing up and dancing and feasting. And the Paradiso!'

'Well, I wore a different outfit for each day of the week and changed the menu just as often. So the customers were always … surprised.'

'And you played the piano for them, in your lovely dresses – oh, Auntie, will I look even half as good as you did?'

'Even better. You'll look wonderful. Show me that picture, I can copy it easily from there. Or we'll design it ourselves.'

Laurel showed her a haughty model with a long cigarette holder and gloves, wearing a figure-hugging strapless ball gown which flared out below the waist in a great swirl of skirt and petticoat.

'Cut on the cross I'd say,' Bronwyn murmured looking at the picture carefully. 'Practically circular, that skirt. It will give a great whirl when your partner turns you around.'

'Oh. Michael! I'd forgotten about him…'

'Don't you like him, Laurie?'

'A bit. Not much. He's all right… is that wrong, Auntie?'

'Is what wrong?' her aunt smiled as she laid the material, folded inside out, flat on the dining room table.

'To go to the dance with him if I don't … if I don't really…' Laurel's voice faded out. Bronwyn laughed. 'It may be a bit of a problem if *he* does! … but you can manage, my dear, I'm sure. Just think of it like this – he's very lucky to be going with you. Lift your arms now…' Bronwyn was running the tape measure round Laurel's chest. 'Mmm. These have been quietly growing. We'll need some thin strips of whalebone to make this dress stay up, strapless. I've probably got some in an old dress of mine.'

'I don't have to *kiss* him just because he's taking me to the dance?'

'You just have to make it clear what you want. Or don't want. Let me get this round your hips now.'

'You'll come and fetch me? It's my first dance you know.'

'What in?'

'Jamie's car.'

'I'm not driving at night.'

'Connor's van, then? You and Con can come.'

'Won't Michael walk you home? No – I suppose – silly me, you don't want… that's why you're asking for a lift.' Bronwyn was now drawing the outline of the bodice onto the material with tailor's chalk.

'Oh Auntie, life is a bit complicated sometimes. That shape's looking good. Slinky!'

'Don't you worry, love. You're going to have a marvellous dress – not for Michael, it's for you. And for someone you'll really want to wear it for, one fine day.'

'It's funny how you can have really disgruntled feelings about someone and feel … fond of them too.'

'Disgruntled feelings?' Bron took a pin from her lips, pushed away falling hair from her forehead and looked carefully at her niece.

'You're not talking about your mother, girl?'

'No,' replied Laurel emphatically. 'Not really,' she added, wanting but not daring to talk about what was happening in the forest lest it be stopped. But Auntie doesn't forbid things, she said to herself. She would understand.

'My, my, you do want to talk, don't you Cariad? Well, I'll tell you this… boys aren't that difficult to manage, and that's a fact.' The doorbell rang and a knocking at the same time told them both that Connor Walsh had arrived.

'I think Connor wants to talk to you.'

'What about?' Laurel asked, indignant.

'How would I know, Cariad?'

'You know him!'

'I do and I don't!' The knocking persisted. 'We'll keep him waiting. He'll sit on the porch and open his beer. 'And you'll join him there.'

'I will. Now, let's look hard at this dress.'

While Aunt Bron, pins in her mouth, returned to the design and shape of the party dress, holding the material up against her niece's body, Laurel's thoughts returned to a scene and a conversation she had witnessed and overheard the week before. Her aunt was holding a piece of knitting against Connor's chest, and she'd seen him cunningly move his arms, held out at first, right round until he was hugging her hard. Bron had laughed and Laurel then saw Connor rub his body against her beloved, most beloved member of the family. She had closed her eyes and moved away. Then, when she returned, after going for a walk with Muffin, the beer was being poured out and the whisky too, and Connor was saying:

'You must never fock with a Scorpio, Bronwyn, do you know that?'

'Not, you mean,' her aunt had laughed, 'with an Irish Scorpio.'

'Not any Scorpio. Not anybody.'

'Oh, once a Catholic,' her aunt had said, shaking her head, 'always superstitious.'

'And jealous. You dance too close to other men.'

'We are not married, Mr. Walsh, thank the Lord!'

'I'm talking about respect. If I take you to a dance…'

'You've had too much, boyo.'

'I will drink till I am dry, Welsh woman.'

'Suit yourself.'

'Scorpio, I tell you, is the most powerful sign in the Zodiac.'

'Oh no! Has Zelda been doing your horrible-scope again, Bach? I thought she got up your nose with all that nonsense. Yes,yes, I know we're not supposed to criticise your precious sister, but just tell me will you how you can believe in Jesus and Mary and that mumbo jumbo at the same time.'

'As I was saying,' Connor persisted, eyebrows beginning to seesaw, 'Scorpios make great friends, but they also make great enemies.'

'You're really drunk. What's happened?'

'And they make great detectives too, and, easily hurt, they feel betrayal intensely. So, you don't fock with a Scorpio, ever! He might take years to sort out revenge, unlike the Aries, spontaneous attack... but when he strikes – what revenge. Joseph Stalin was a Scorpio.'

'So ... and when a Scorpio has got it wrong he turns upon himself and stings himself to death.'

'I never get it wrong, Cariad!'

***

Next day.

This thin girl with womanly hands and breasts, concave belly and wise eyes is now going to keep away again. Woe! She has no idea – or has she – how acutely I miss her when she goes about her life outside this forest. Is this missing her so intensely because I am so removed from the mainstream, removed from women, although I feel that separation has always been a part of my old life? Or is it that she has the remarkable gift of penetration? Is she a wood nymph who has invaded my bloodstream? For she courses through my mind, and despite arresting all other thoughts with the one thought, when will she arrive? I nevertheless feel that I am on the edge of being well. Missing her feels good.

The cobwebs of amnesia are drifting away, and I don't feel the need to spin them in and follow one straight strand. Perhaps her advent has given me a don't-care-ness. I like the focus, which is a feeling in that part of my heart that is well, on her mystery infinitely deeper and sweeter than mine. So, I shall sit and walk and fish and swim and hide and write and sleep and miss her till she returns. But I must watch myself.

CHAPTER 8

The dancing had started when she arrived with Mike. He had smoothed back his thick, straw-coloured hair with something that made it look darker and shiny. He wore a white shirt with a blue silky bow tie and a smart dark suit.

'Like your dress, Laurel,' he said, and gave a small self-conscious cough. They entered the hall as everyone was clapping after the band had played the first dance. So Laurel, holding her head high and taking Michael's arm, walked into her first ball in her first ball dress to a roomful of applause.

The next dance was a waltz. Laurel had waltzed plenty of times in the ballroom dancing class at school, but she'd been leading then. Usually with Ollie. She was taller – and bolder – than Ollie. And there were no boys. Now, as the band played 'Always' and couples started to move around the floor, this tall young man in a bow tie stood in front of her, smiled nervously, said: 'Okay?' and reached for her hand. She was confused for a moment – it seemed the wrong hand. But then she let him guide her with his other hand resting in the middle of her back, hers on his shoulder, and they started to dance.

It was fine. He smelled of soap and Brylcreem and she began to fit in with his steps, pleased to find that he was less hesitant that she had imagined. Her petticoat swished as they turned, her dress looked good. She was going to enjoy this. But then she became aware of his hand in her hand, and her body vividly remembered the touch – only the other day – of Burns' hand as he'd grumpily allowed her to follow him across the submerged logs to his hidden fishing hole. A few days before her drenching and the mug of wine.

'There's no room for two,' he'd practically snarled, walking stiffly, almost limping. He'd been in a particularly bad mood that day. So of course she pestered him.

'You'll disturb the fish.' He wouldn't even look at her. 'I won't breathe.'

'They'll see you anyway.'

'I'll sprinkle fern-seed on my head. It makes you invisible.'

He'd muttered something that sounded like 'damn!' so she'd pulled her most gruesome face and scowled at him. Stuck her tongue out as well. This made him laugh. And he reached for her hand to help her climb across the mossy boulders in the shallows of the lake.

His hand, with its scar at the base of the thumb and that strange ring-mark around his wrist. She had watched it, gutting fish, kindling the fire, even once in the distance shaking his cock after having a pee. Now it held hers, firmly, warmly, and it stayed holding for several moments after they reached dry land.

'You're far away, Laurel?' came a voice in her ear. Michael. 'Bit of a dreamer, aren't you?'

'Yes, well. It's a dreamy waltz.'

Girls needed conversation, thought Mike. Perhaps she was slipping out of his grasp. His hand on her back brought her body slightly closer as they danced. His other hand tightened round hers. She looked at it, remembering Burns that day and how their palms then had fused, standing close together in the long grass by the edge of the lake. His blood warmth connecting instantly with hers. But now, nothing. In her hand there was just another hand, big, sunburnt, young, slightly sweaty. Just flesh and bone.

Connor strode into the dance hall looking for Laurel. They were just finishing the last waltz. The balding band-leader was singing: *'I had the last dance with yooooo…*

Two dreamy people toge-e-ther…'

Laurel saw Connor watching her over Mike's shoulder. She'd had the Ladies' Excuse-Me with Dan Morgan the farmer's younger son but had otherwise been fairly stuck with Mike who was now dancing her round so close and so slowly that she was hardly shifting from foot to foot. Twice she had felt something move in his trousers against her stomach.

'This last dance will last for-ever!' crooned the singer who looked to be at least ten years older than Connor himself.

But it wasn't the last dance, which delighted Mike and irritated Laurel for she was ready to go; a plan for tomorrow was formulating in her head which her partner was trying to have rest on his shoulder, as others' girls did.

'I see you in my dreams,' came a Welsh-American croon,

'*Hold you in my arms…*' Connor stood with an expression on his face that Laurel couldn't read; something more than impatience, so she rested her head on Mike's tuxedo and let herself dream into the next last dance '*Goodnight Sweetheart.*'

But what she saw and what she imagined was Burns' eyes upon her back with herself lying on leaves, and then his hands, and then she heard the voice say softly almost inaudibly, 'This is my favourite part of your body.' She was shocked but smiled into the bend of her arm. 'This is the innocent part that nobody knows, and here' she shuddered at the imagining of his hands moving, bigger and warmer and more searching than Ollie's, 'this is where we find, even on the back and undiscovered… breasts… and sometimes wings… off you fly…'

And off she flew.

***

Diary. Two days later.

She does not return. Solomon also is away. He goes, I think, to London which is a long journey and he has other patients there to listen to.

He has concealed from me information about why I am hidden here, why I must see no-one. Is he waiting for me to ask? Or to discover the reason for myself?

I have concealed from him that I have a secret visitor. I am breaking his rules. Perhaps they are not his rules but the General's.

I have not told Solomon that my dreams have returned, not those violent dreams of gunfire but quiet, sad ones. I think they are dreams of loss. I have not told him that I fear I am no longer fully a man. I am frozen as a man. That I dare not touch my genitals expecting some pleasure to flow or that electric charge the boy at the desk or the younger man that I could experience so easily. There is no movement in my body, nothing to feel. It's all finished.

Why does he not ask? Why does he not know? How could he help me?

CHAPTER 9

'Go on. Say something else!'

Laurel was leaning against a low wall in the playground of the village school with seven of the local children forming an admiring audience in front of her. One small boy squatted on the wall beside her and gazed at her clothes. She was the only one not in green school uniform since she was not really a pupil there, just enrolling for her public exams. Her bare legs emerged from a short tartan kilt, and she wore white plimsolls, no socks, and a yellow poplin shirt she'd found in her cousin's wardrobe.

'Say something!' they begged. The single-decker buses had begun arriving in the schoolyard to take the children home to outlying farms and villages. Although she'd been wary at first after the stone-throwing incident, these older ones seemed to find her interestingly exotic and were friendly. They were still amazed by her accent and her turn of phrase.

'Go on, Laurel!' she was running out of ideas.

'Friends, Romans, Countrymen!' she declaimed.

'No. That's cheating. Say some real London.'

'You mean cockney?' she asked.

'Cockney, that's it.'

'Not posh.'

'How they talk in London.'

'Oh well…' she couldn't think. 'There's a song, a cockney song I know…'

'Teach us a song!'

'It's about winkles.'

Two boys giggled at this.

'Shellfish. You get them at the seaside: you eat them with a pin. I know the chorus anyway.' And she sang softly to her small group:

'All the big ones gorn!
It made me rage and shaht,
Cos my ole woman an 'er seven kids
Wos pickin all the big ones aht!'

'Again!'

They lapped it up. One or two began joining in the second time. The home buses had all come in now and a few children were getting on but not Laurel's lot.

'You said you knew some poetry; teach us a poem!' another said. At this, all the poems she'd ever remembered flew out of her brain. She was thinking 'I'm showing off…I like it. I like this village, and these people. That Burns man – why do I wish I was showing off to him?'

'A poem!' came a voice, interrupting her thoughts. Her mouth opened and she started one, coming up from who knows where:

'There was a young whore from Peru…' The words reached her ears just in time. Oh no.

'No. Sorry. That's just nonsense…'

'More!'

'I've forgotten the rest.' She found she was blushing, more in annoyance at herself than embarrassment. What a stupid thing to come out with! One of the smutty limericks she'd been taught by her mother's boyfriends.

'Do you speak Welsh?' she asked the boy standing next to her in an attempt to recover her balance.

'If you live north of the village, you speak Welsh,' said a freckled, auburn-haired girl. 'I speak Welsh. Do you want to hear it? I sing it too.'

'I don't!' said the boy with a basin-cut head of dark hair who was still dealing with the first line of the limerick.

'Well, you should do, Neville Lewis. Why do you think you have lessons?'

'Well, I live south of the village and you don't have to speak Welsh to grow potatoes. My Dad doesn't. Not one word.'

Mercifully, the buses were now filling up and her audience started to go home. But not before she thought she heard some boy in an older group behind them say something that sounded like 'her mother's a whore'. She couldn't be sure she'd heard it. Her mouth felt dry. She glanced at Bethan, one of the friends who had rescued her from her initial isolation.

Bethan stood protectively near her by the wall, but was now talking to her younger sister, pulling her skirt straight, making ready to walk home. Her other friend, Bethan's cousin Owen, was across the yard. Now, the buses had all gone. One of the bigger boys lingered. He came up beside her as she walked towards the gate with the bag of three rockcakes she'd made in an extremely boring domestic science lesson which all the girls were expected to attend.

'Give you sixpence for the rest of that poem.'

Laurel didn't like the look of him, instinctively. He had mean looking eyes. He was older than she was, but shorter and stocky.

'Can't remember it.'

'Sixpence says you can.'

'No, really. I can't, I told you.'

But he nudged closer, forcing her to walk with her shins almost banging against the wall. She was just getting ready to turn on him with an earful of swearwords when someone came up behind them.

'Hello, Laurel.' It was Owen.

'You walking home my way?' she asked. To his credit he quickly said, 'I am, yes!' even though he didn't know where she lived. The older boy clenched his jaw, kept up with them for a few paces then fell behind. When they were round the corner, Laurel broke into a run: 'Come on!'

Owen took off after her. 'Where are we going?'

'The old mansion' she said. 'I need some help.'

'You going in there?' he sounded impressed.

'Are you coming or not?'

'Of course. I know a way in through the back.'

'I have to look for some things.' She slowed down, out of danger now. 'For a friend of mine who hasn't got much furniture.' She knew the boys had been climbing in and out of the abandoned mansion and furnishing their dens with the loot.

'It's not stealing,' she told him. 'Anyway, property is theft. I know quite a famous actor who believed that.'

'I don't. But then I'm a farmer's son.'

'Well. Abandoned property is… carelessness.'

'That's true. Stuff could be getting mildewed in there.' She smiled at Owen and opened the bag of rockcakes. 'Take two. They're almost inedible.' Owen was pleased.

The mansion came into view with its yellowish stone, numerous chimneys and even more windows. It seemed huge from the front, behind its railings and curving drive. Tall pillars formed a shadowy veranda with French windows on the ground floor. Two big carriage lamps stood shattered beside the front door.

Owen led her past the chained and barbed wired front gate with 'Cadwych Draw!- Keep Out!' left there by the Army.

Round the side they went, down a little track where the railings ran out and an old ivy-covered wall began. It was cemented, which was unusual in this landscape of drystone walls. At the back, the character of the house changed abruptly. They passed a crumbling stone coach house with one huge door hanging loose and broken, the other missing. Derelict stable buildings stood around a courtyard. Outhouses had their heavy stone slates fallen off and smashed on the cobbles. They came to a low hanging roof which Owen grabbed onto with one hand and vaulted over the wall.

'Okay!' he called. 'It's safe. There's not much of a drop. I'll come and help you up.' But Laurel had found a toe-hole in the wall and was up already. He stretched out his hand for her to jump down. Then they realised there was a broken gate just a little further along the wall which had obviously been opened recently. The locals had used the courtyard as a rubbish dump. There was a pile of junk crowned with an old pram.

The kitchens were round this part of the house, a side window broken. Owen clambered through it and unbolted the scullery door. It was vast and dark and stone-flagged inside.

'I know about this place. It was a Tudor farmhouse. Then when the English took it over, they built the big house onto the front. Hundreds of years ago. So, all this stayed the servants' quarters.'

Laurel took in the massive oak shelves and built-in dresser the length of half a railway carriage and the deep stone sinks with their single cold tap and the great copper boiler in the corner with a brick oven below. Nothing here for her purposes.

'Let's find the smarter part.'

They opened a door with bells and wires suspended above it, went down a long corridor and up a dusty broken staircase. On a windowsill Owen found an old wooden rattle. Laurel looked puzzled.

'It's a clacker. You know, you hold the handle and swing it round and round. At football matches. Makes

a hell of a din.'

'Go on,' she said, 'show me.'

'Could have been used for a fire alarm,' said Owen. 'It's noisy enough.' He picked it up by the handle and started to swing it round. Klaack-klaack-klack-klack-klak-klak-ak-ak-ak-akak-ak..

'Wow! Impressive.'

'It's an ack-ack gun,' said Owen.

'Terrific. Let's take it.'

They opened another door at the top of the back stairs, and they were on a wide landing, in a different world. Ornate plaster work on the ceilings, wood panelling on the walls. At least six doors leading off. Huge fancy doorknobs.

The first room was empty except for a chair broken beyond saving. Large expanses of paler cream showed on the wallpaper where pictures had been removed from the walls. But in the second room, which had three sets of windows overlooking the front lawn, there was a big grey stone fireplace. Marble, Laurel guessed. And over it was exactly what she now knew they'd come for. A mirror. It was perfect. Curly golden bits around the edges. It was the width of the fireplace, but they could manage it. There was the pram to take it away in.

'That's it!'

Owen looked startled. 'How do we get it off, then?'

'See if it's screwed or nailed.'

He climbed up on the mantlepiece like a monkey. It was wide enough for him to sit or stand on in comfort. He knelt and inspected. 'Rusty screws. Wish I had my scout knife. Hold on, do you want this as well? We've got a fancy old clock up here, a real antique this is, Laurel. it's called a carriage clock, just like the one at my nan's.'

'The kitchen!' Laurel had opened a drawer and seen some ancient cutlery. 'Let's get a knife to screw it off with; we can take the clock another day.' So, with a good deal of chiselling and hacking at the plaster, the screws were released, several knives were demolished, and the big ormolu mirror was at last lifted down and carried out triumphantly to be wedged across the old pram and wheeled off. As an afterthought, Laurel dashed back for the clock and pushed it in beside the mirror though it rattled brokenly when she gave it a shake. They bumped carefully over the cobbled courtyard. Owen looked pleased with himself. He pushed the pram while Laurel walked beside him with the rattle and steadied the mirror. She was steering them away from the village. He was puzzled.

'You live with your Aunt, don't you?'

'Oh, it's not for her. It's this friend who's… setting up house. It's a sort of house-warming present.'

'Grand present all right.'

'This friend doesn't have any mirrors, anyway. Come on Owen.'

They had now left the village. The forest stretched beside them. They were approaching the secret hole in the wall. Laurel stopped.

'Phew. I'm hot. It's getting late, too. Maybe we'd better stop now.'

'And leave it all here? Somebody could find it.'

'Oh well, maybe hide it over the wall and I can come back another time.'

Owen looked at his watch. It was six o'clock. On Thursdays he usually helped his dad. He was confused by this strange instinct he felt to go along with Laurel's whims, even if it meant humping a valuable stolen mirror over somebody's wall into a wood in the middle of nowhere. She smiled encouragingly at him. He noticed her small white teeth, pointed chin, freckled nose, green eyes… he seized the mirror in his arms and heaved it onto the wall. It slid slowly down the other side into a bramble patch.

Finding a chunk of slate, he scratched a series of marks on the wall. 'So, you'll know. Now I'd better be off home. You all right, then, Laurel?' She leant over and kissed his cheek.

'Of course. I'll just have a rest here before I go. Thanks, Owen. Maybe just chuck the pram over too so nobody finds out.'

Looking dazed from the kiss he lifted the pram and with Laurel's help manoeuvred it over the wall. Then he ran home.

Laurel had soon climbed through her hole in the wall and rescued the mirror, picking up a vivid red bramble scratch on her leg in the process. She wheeled her cargo carefully through the trees. It was nearly dusk. Maybe Aunt Bron would be worried. But there was the shack and the lake. All thoughts of her aunt dissolved. She'd go and find Burns. He'd love his mirror. She would surprise him.

As she approached his hut, she saw the fishing rod still out over the lake, propped up on a forked stick. The little stool and a basket beside it. So he wasn't far away. Probably gone back into the hut for some more bait.

The door was open. This mirror was so grand, she thought, it really needed a fanfare to announce its arrival. She could do with a bugle right now. But she had the clacker!

She seized the heavy wooden rattle by the handle and raising her arm above her head, whirled it strongly around. Krack! klack-klack-ak-ak-ak-ak-ak! echoed loudly through the wood. Suddenly, there was a strange sound, half-shout, half-cry, which seemed to come from inside the hut. Then silence.

Her heart started to pound. She flung down the rattle and ran to the open doorway. No sign of Burns. He wasn't there. But then she saw him. He'd fallen down. Was lying in a strange, curled position on the rush matting beneath the window. Wearing only a pair of trousers, no socks or shoes, no shirt, His arms were clasped across his chest, his knees drawn up together.

His eyes were closed, and his face was deadly pale. Worst of all, he seemed to be convulsing with violent shaking tremors every few seconds. He was shaking and trembling and on his forehead and his upper lip were beads of sweat

Without stopping to think she kicked off her shoes and lay down behind him, enfolding his back in her arms, bending her knees in behind his trembling knees, touching his twitching feet gently with her toes.

She rested one arm behind his head, her fingers on his brow, and breathed slowly and softly into his neck.

Rocking him. Humming below her breath to him, calming him with her body. 'It's me,' she whispered.

Who knows how long they lay like that? Although it was growing dark outside, time had stopped. She didn't want to be anywhere else. She liked the smell of his sweat. She felt it dry. She didn't know that although what she smelt was man, was Tom, it was also fear. She would never know how much men fear.

After what felt like half the night but could have been half an hour, he gave a deep, shuddering sigh. He said a word. It sounded like the rattle sound 'Krack'. But it wasn't that. He said it again. Laurel could hear it now.

It was 'Jack'.

CHAPTER 10

Tom was amazed. Waking up on his bed, wearing just his trousers, aching all over, his vision blurred, yet there on the floor of his hut he could clearly see a magnificent ornate mirror leaning up against the rough planked wall. It was at least four feet wide. Beside it was a gilded clock. A mantelpiece mirror and a mantelpiece clock, looking like two aristocratic *emigrés* from the French Revolution fallen on hard times. No chance of a mantelpiece to put them on. He laughed aloud but it hurt his forehead. Remembering now that he'd blanked out the night before but had been stroked back to consciousness by a woman – by Sarah – by his mother – by the girl. Laurel. That was her name. He'd seen her leave the hut but was unable to speak to thank her. Somehow, she had brought him these gifts. He stepped carefully off the bed, his bottom half reflected in the glass. He could make some wooden brackets, fix up a shelf for the mirror. Secure it to the wall by those screwplates at the sides.

Now the old carriage clock caught his attention. It wasn't working, the winding key didn't respond yet he felt a flutter of excitement. Sitting at his desk he carefully opened the back and whilst removing the dust from the mechanism itself, blowing and flicking his handkerchief, he became aware of a long-closed mental door, something in a part of his mind that felt other than memory and that now was slowly starting to open.

He began by cautiously identifying a starting point whilst at the same time sensing a growing admiration for the beauty of machinery, the workmanship, the radiating, interlocking gearwheels. An image of the original maker came to mind, a German, a Swiss, surrounded in his workshop by watches and clocks and the different sounds of their workings. Then something more specific, a memory was released, of an engine sound, his father's Ford V8, open, the bonnet lifted, his father looking down with a grin of delight, and a full beard,… 'Listen to that, my boy! Feast your ears on the music of that engine!'…and he thought: He cannot see. My father is blind…

Tom felt an ache now for the fragmentation of his story, of his family.

He immediately switched his mind back to the task, and looked at the small brass plate he now wiped clean, to the craftsman – no name, but a date, 1829. He leaned back on his chair conjuring up the time and the place and without thinking he released his imagination to become the man, the clockmaker, and feel the pleasure as he locates the catchment, the beating heart, the muscular spring, the galaxy of wheels and bearings, the smell of old brass and oil still waiting for the movement.

A thin steel wire is his first applied tool and with it he gently prods the lightest gearwheels, willing them to turn. This something to do with his hands stirs something deeper than memory, a pleasure in the body, a trace of reconnection as if – like the clock – his body being used via his hands will prove the way to mending his mind.

He looks down at the cloth he has laid on his desk, he lays the clock face down on the cloth. He places the tool beside the clock. He places his hands on the desk.

He knows as he reaches for the other tool, knife, that he is going to dismantle the whole machine, clean it properly after his first probe and put it together again and just contemplating this at six in the morning, even before beginning the task of repairing and reassembly fills him with a tranquillity that he dare not name lest it fly away.

Tom closes his eyes and visualises the making of his new pier and his own boat, of collecting the tools to do so, polishing them, and the healing in the feeling in his body, plus the thought of no people there – no one. Just the business of working with his hands towards restoration and completion. Then his body sends a message to his head which says, soft and clear, You desire her. The girl Laurel. She will be here.

CHAPTER 11

His first narrow raft gave him a pleasure that surprised him. He was learning that making things either enhanced thinking or rested the mind and now as he lay on his raft and paddled with his hands, lying with his face near the water, he realised that one of the joys was the feeling after the making: 'This is mine! This is my boat.'

Slowly he was propelled towards the reeds that lay in the shadow of the forest. On the line that he cast and kept drawing in, instead of small wriggling roach, he had attached to the hook a fake fish made of silver wire and various coloured leaves. Pikes, he knew, in their green, mottled camouflage, with the canniness of all great predators, were best caught in late autumn or early winter when they were hungry, when they were not finding food on the bed of the lake but coming to the surface for warmth. They would sometimes then take a chance on an unfamiliar shape and movement.

Not so this glorious summer's day. Not a nibble, not a strike. He did however register and would report to Solomon that memory had not only provided him with information on a past pleasure but also... there was something else... someone else perhaps, that had flashed into his realisation. What was it?

Tom lay on his back, no longer fishing... floating into the reeds... warmth on his eyelids spreading down his body as he dozed... he felt his senses alive to more than bird-calls...the smell of the water turning, as memory stirred, to the smell of brine... the touch of an old man's gnarled hands, the sensation of a boat moving down the slipway, the sound of the hull hitting the water... the sight of this old man's ocean-beaten face, a fist, a knife... oysters being opened, searching for the pearl...

Then he recalled the journey to the sea, to visit... his grandparents? A winding walk down from the cliffs to the fishing village. The shrieks of gulls, Gaelic in the air, horses on the sands...

Back to the lake he was brought by the sound of the soft then loud churring call of a sedge-warbler in the reeds. On raising his head from his semi-sleep he caught sight of the girl. He gasped. She was looking for him. He waited to be found...

***

JOURNAL: L. Williams. Saturday.

What a day! Everything I started turned out different. I should have been reading *Paradise Lost* for my English exam, but it was far too hot. Bron had persuaded Muffin to accompany her on a visit to her friend Mavis, promising that Gareth would throw balls for her, so that I could work. But I couldn't settle. I was longing for an ice cream or a swim in the sea, so of course I took off for the forest, feeling impatient until I was in the deep shade of those big trees.

I made for the lake, not sure if I wanted to meet my man today. I didn't want to talk. Or for him to be moody, or, as I had found him last time, in a right old state. I thought I'd just spy on him, so I sneaked up slowly and quietly, keeping hidden, watching the open door of his hut. No sign. I went right to the edge where the bushes and tall reeds would hide me if he suddenly came out. I was the tracker, very still, waiting for a sight of him, to watch him unseen.

Secret watching is much the best. Then suddenly I looked down in the ripples amongst the reeds, thought it was a fish rising. But it was him! Floating asleep with one arm in the water, all stretched out on an arrangement of fence posts and boards fixed together, a primitive raft. I think James made me a better one when I was six.

He was there among the reeds by my feet.

I waded in, quiet as a heron. I stayed completely still and watched him, asleep like a baby but certainly not a baby. Just wearing khaki shorts.

His stomach has brown hair that seems to part in the middle. His ankles are bony. They have painful dark brown scars. His nipples are deep pink and delicate. The inside of his arm is white as white. His toes are long and pale. I couldn't stop looking. I couldn't move away. Watching him when he doesn't know is amazing, like a wild animal but better. Why was he wearing shorts? The raft wasn't watertight, they'd be soaked underneath.

I stood there hardly breathing by the reeds. He didn't move. My knees were trembling. I moved behind a tree then back one more, completely hidden now. What is it about this man?

I thought he'll probably wake up soon and perhaps feel hot and want a swim and take off his shorts or maybe he'd need a wee. I remembered watching him that first day. Then when he moves and does those things I'd watch some more and see if his bottom is as white and smooth as his inside arm – I'm sure it is. And he would never guess I was there – and then I'd slip away unseen.

It was boiling hot. I'd have liked to have plunged into the lake, pretending it was the sea. I love the sea, I remember the sea, the seaside.

But then he rolled over and sat up and rubbed his eyes and looked around – didn't see me – and he just flopped into the water, shorts and all – disappointment! – and swam towards the little beach and went back into his hut.

That was all. Nothing else to do but go home. Legs still trembling.

Confession: He's sort of seen me naked but not really looked. It was an accident, so don't be too shocked, journal. You can't explain a genuine accident, not even on paper, when John Milton's supposed to be occupying your higher mind.

Do boys get trembling legs, I wonder?

***

The sound of several pairs of shears clipping and the ornamental effect of topiary steered both Byrne and Solomon away from the lower terraced gardens and the gardeners on the neatly paved path. They headed towards the lake. The shack was not visible from this distance, but Byrne recognized the haze of reeds where he sometimes fished and half hoped to see a tiny figure walking by the edge a mile away, Laurel.

'Do memories of your childhood begin to stir?'

'Yes. I think I've seen my sister's face.'

'Tell me.'

'Listen doctor, is this between you and me?'

'As always, Tom.'

'I have fallen in love.'

Solomon glanced sideways at his patient as they continued slowly towards the lake. Tom stopped walking: the expression on his face was one of astonishment at what he'd just said.

'There's a girl in the forest, there, who is driving me mad with desire and delight.'

'There really is? This is not fantasy?'

'No! Look!'

Byrne handed Solomon a note from Laurel which read, in a bold hand:

THERE'S A MIDDLING-AGED MAN IN A
SHACK
WHO'S GOT BENT LEGS AND STRAIGHT
BACK
HE HAS OTHER THINGS
HARD HEART BUT SOFT WINGS
AND A SECRET HE'S KEEPING FROM JACK

'JACK?' Solomon always stroked his hair and pushed it flat when -seldom – taken by surprise.

'It's a joke. It's a girl.'

'Ah.' Solomon's voice was neutral as he walked beside Byrne, but his face carried a smile. 'I did think she was a boy. At first. But it's a girl.'

'I have a patient who enjoys the picture in his mind and the problem to the world had the angel said in Luke two, verse ten: *'Have no fear; for behold I bring you good news of great joy that will be for all people; for today there was born for you in the city of David a girl, a baby girl.'* The doctor laughed.

'I don't want the General to find out, or any of his gang.'

'Is she good for you?' Solomon asked, serious again.

'Yes. Oh Yes. Absolutely yes.'

There was a long pause. They watched each other's boots and shoes as they crunched on gravel towards a meadow with horses and sheep. 'Brogues' Byrne remembered, fascinated as ever by the quality of Solomon's shoes. He had always been attracted to women who wore elegant shoes. And gloves. Laurel wore no shoes. He tried to picture her in gloves. Why would she wear them? For communion? Had he seen her in shoes? In sandals. But now he visualized her feet with their well-shaped toes and high insteps. Small, neat. How clearly he could see them there in the shallows when they'd fished together. And when she'd danced they were dancer's feet and legs. He allowed himself to study her legs, her calves, her thighs. He felt them and felt her as a woman and suddenly was overwhelmed by her scent, her skin-smell.

He had kissed her wrist, she'd wrestled away. He realised that a musk flowed from that very spot, the inner wrist, where women applied perfume.

He wanted to inhale her there and in that other spot between her Laurel-like breasts where silken warmth drew his head and his unconsciousness.

He blanked. They were somewhere near a small plantation a good half mile beyond the horses, one neighing in the distance behind them, walking rhythmically, silently. Solomon always allowed silence. Byrne heard himself say: 'What are they going to do with me?'

'We'll see! What is your concern?'

'I don't want to leave her. I don't want to leave her yet!'

Footsteps some way behind them. It was the General. They stopped, Solomon with eyebrows raised, perhaps in irritation. Inscrutable as ever. Byrne liked that. As the General approached them, they were both looking down, observing leaves.

'Is Autumn on its way already?' Solomon asked wistfully. Byrne looked at the doctor and noted the suit, the shoes, the smoothed thin hair, guessed his age to be sixty something. A faint accent which could be Austrian or further East. He was dark enough and polite enough to be Indian. He had quoted from the Vedas and the Koran in their hospital meetings and even there they had walked and talked outside in all sorts of weather. 'It blows the cobwebs away. Nasty things get trapped in cobwebs.'

'You two making sure you're not overheard, hey?' The General spoke with his jaw. He was clipped, resonant.

'No, airing the demons' Tom said.

'Demons, huh! Fighting with demons, eh?'

'No: fighting is your job, Sir.'

'And have you finished your job, Doctor?'

'That's never finished, General.'

'Hmmm! No wonder you're expensive.'

'And in this case, in fact, no I haven't finished… *we* haven't finished.' Solomon sounded firm, almost fierce. And if the General was taking his tone to veil a hint of an accusation, then, thought Tom, inwardly applauding, he was probably right. The General personified Security. And Solomon knew just how disastrous had been his patient's betrayal by this most insecure and inefficient bunch.

'Well, you'd better just carry on. We've no plans for you yet, Captain, nothing that's materialising yet, but I've a notion we can use you back somewhere that you'll be safe, eventually. When we get the all-clear from Intelligence. Now the war's over, that only leaves us with your lot out to get you, eh?' Solomon frowned slightly and looked quickly at Tom's blank face.

'Got to look after you' General Ashworth had not noticed the look. 'You're a good man, Byrne. When you're completely fit again of course. You're looking more in fettle. Well done. Solomon will keep me posted on progress and then things can move on. I trust my man is looking after you. Food, booze, books, that sort of thing.'

'We'll make a list today, thank you Sir.' Solomon spoke in a flat, level tone, he sounded as if he was holding his breath.

'We don't want you seen; you know that Byrne.'

'I do, Sir.'

'Not by anyone. Course, my wife's constantly seeing you... likes the look of you, I think!' A big laugh which was not echoed even by a smile from the other two men.

'Well, I'm off. Take lunch at the house if you will. Alice is around somewhere. I'm sure she'll be pleased to see you both. I'm off to Whitehall. More tedium. I miss the war. Gentlemen.'

The General nodded to them abruptly, turned on his heel and strode off, almost marching, arms half swinging. Then he halted. Turned and spoke in a rush as he moved back.

'Listen man, you might be a wounded soldier, you might, for all I know, be a man on immense modesty. Well, I want to tell you what I do know and perhaps the good doctor too. You are a hero! A damned hero, Byrne! You have done this country proud, and this country will not forget. We know how to honour good soldiering, always have. We shall protect you, son. Mark my words. The whole damned army will. This is just a start. Carry on, Doctor.'

'Do you feel like a game of chess?' Solomon asked.

'Yes.' Tom was blinking rapidly. 'Will we talk?'

'Yes, Tom. Tell me what you want to know.'

'Did they get me?' asked Tom, moving his knight to threaten Solomon's bishop. 'My lot, as the General put it. He's not talking allegiance here, is he?' Solomon shook his head and smiled sadly as he moved a pawn out in defence.

'They got me and they hurt me and they wanted me dead. Still do, I guess. So I have to be hidden; by your lot, *Mein Doktor*!' he laughed, eyebrows raised at the surprise of his realisation and at his own effrontery. His black bishop moved in to the attack.

CHAPTER 12

Dear Ollie,

Since I wrote to you last, I have been thinking much about LOVE. It's an odd thing – but I must have had all these thoughts before, stored up somewhere inside. You remember that you and I used to talk about ways we could make our lives more beautiful? We'd say we were sure that love is an art, and that we'd pick up tips to be able to practice it one day. Not the slushy stuff in the flicks: not jealous husband/wife stuff either, always having rows. We wanted to re-discover it and get it right this time, didn't we? Well, the oddest thing is that after I found a little, ancient book on Aunt Bron's bookshelf, called *The Ring of the Dove*, she sort of broke down almost in tears and started telling me all about her Egyptian lover – imagine – my cousin

Jamie's father – and about her own ideas on love. And they're amazing, Ollie; they're just the same as ours!

This book is all about love and about some man's experiences with various women. It's written by a Persian and it's nearly a thousand years old. He says love is a sort of magic that transforms people into the best they can be. It makes stupid people clever, greedy ones generous, clumsy ones gracious and beautiful. It's the most important experience in life, he says in this book, and sex is a most important part of it all because it allows love to flow freely into the soul. I think that's pretty well what he said. What do you think of that?

I think it's beautiful, and true.

Auntie B saw me reading it and she gasped. I didn't know it had been the last present from her lover. I'd found a poem called 'Mine is the religion of Love' and there was an old, faded pale yellow flower pressed flat in between the pages. So, she told me about him. She has to be in the mood.

His name was Rashid. He had been the great love of her life.

'How romantic!' I said.

'No, Laurel dear. 'Romantic' is not the right word. This was a pure love, a passion, as the ancient Persians perfected it and wrote about it over a thousand years ago. Not possessive, not at all "romantic".'

'No jealousy?' I asked.

'He believed in independence, which is the opposite of jealousy.'

'So: you had affairs?' I had to ask her.

'I didn't need to. But I could have. He thought that giving love was always a good idea. The more you gave, the more you'd get back. Not necessarily from the same direction, but somehow the universe always returned your investment. With interest.'

'Okay: so he had affairs?'

'Maybe. Or not. I never asked. I don't think so. It didn't matter.'

Aunt B looked so different as she spoke. Her brown eyes which I had never noticed much before seemed darker than ever and I saw that her skin was hardly wrinkled even though she must be at least fifty, or even more.

She showed me a photo of Rashid, her lover. He'd been born in Alexandria where she went to live with her parents as a girl because her dad was an engineer. She was only seventeen when she met him. Our age Ollie, just think! She was his mistress for twenty years she says, and it was a dead secret even though they had a son, James. Then Rashid died suddenly just like that, without warning, some sort of cancer, aged fifty-five.

'I thought I would die too,' she said, and I could see she meant it.

'I read Cleopatra's last speech in Antony and Cleopatra – we lived only a few hundred yards from where her tomb is supposed to be buried.

'I dreamed there was an Emperor, Antony; Ah, such another sleep that I might see But such another man!'

But I never did.'

After a while I asked her, 'What happens, Auntie, when you lose a man like that? What happens to you?'

She thought for a while and then said, 'Alas my dear, you have to settle for second best.' Then, with her arms around me and with tears streaming down her face she actually started to laugh. I think she was thinking of Connor. So I laughed too though I felt sad as well, and we both laughed and laughed so much – I can't think what on earth we were laughing at – that our ribs ached with it and we had to lie back on the sofa to recover. But you know what I thought, Ollie? If he was fifty-five years old when he died, then he was twenty years older than she was. Old enough to be her father.

Talking about him really brought her to life. She's promised to read me some Arab love poems tomorrow. Says they're very EROTIC (nice new word, please note) and she'll cook me a tagine, which is a special Arabic stew with lamb and apricots and honey: 'the food of love', she said. I tell you what, Ollie, this place gets more interesting every day.

Longing to see you – Laurel.

By the way, there are plenty of horses here if you're losing interest in love.

***

Forest Journal: L.Williams.

I have some brilliant plans for Ollie. They'd better be secret plans for now. I plan to rescue Burns. I've decided he's like an animal who's been wounded and has crept away somewhere private to lick his wounds or to die. No sign of dying yet but you never know. He doesn't look at all cheerful. I think I've only seen him smile once and that was at some stupid remark of mine. He seems very sad in fact, and sort of bottled up. It can't be good for him to be like that. But maybe Ollie can be the bottle-opener.

She's so pretty – he couldn't find a prettier girl. He's not likely to find any girls at all, of course, stuck in the middle of that forest.

Bethan says it's not natural for a grown man to have no girlfriends at all – unless he's an 'unnatural man' and does it with sheep…. I can't even begin to think how that works out. Never mind – he looks perfectly natural to me. So Ollie will be perfect. She'll just not have to mind his rudeness, or his silences. Or his weird sense of humour. Or the odd facts he keeps on jumping out on you. Or the way he stares, and winces. I'm used to all that but she may be put off. He'll like her though, he's bound to. He'll probably fall head over heels in love with her because she looks more of a woman than me, with her shoulders and her breasts, and if that old Persian's right, love will transform him into a gentle, adorable sweetheart. So then she'll fall in love with him. Off into the sunset, happy ever after. And with a real man she'll never want to see her weedy boyfriend Alistair again. I wonder if Burns will find her more interesting than me?

Dearest Ollie,

I've found a new friend up by the lake – he's a buzzard. A beautiful soaring great bird with big dark wings and a white belly. He just zooms and hovers and sometimes seems to bounce across the sky like a slow-motion rubber ball. I know he's a male somehow. Seems to spend most of the day soaring and circling high above the trees. I've seen him do a spectacular dive straight downwards and come up with some small creature in his claws – a vole or one of these tiny, odd-looking elephant-nosed shrews. Such a lazy bird. He feels like me: just wandering around having a good time and not working and occasionally stopping for a bit of grub. Gives a ringing cry Kee...ow! over and over again.

I've asked Burns who seems to know a lot about birds and animals (wouldn't you guess!) and he says it's a buzzard all right, but a single male who ought to be in a pair. Must have lost its mate.

So a lot of this soaring is looking for her.

I've decided to adopt this buzzard. Think up a name for him and I will introduce you when you come to stay. I can't wait.. I've got so many plans for us, so many things to show you. Then there's Burns of course. I've told him about you. He's a bit gruff so didn't say much. But I am determined to get you two together so don't worry, he's certain to like you. Just don't expect any manners. See you soon, very soon I hope.

Love from Laurel.

PS: He tells me that the female is more beautiful than the male only in one species of bird – the lesser kestrel. He also told me that they will nest anywhere; he even saw them during the war in bombed-out houses. But the second piece of information is not as interesting as the first.

Also. he likes me to go barefoot but not to paint my toenails, which I like to do… so… compromise: I only do every other toe. And finally: he once let me paint his nails too… fooled you! Only kidding, as Ida Lupino says in 'Roadhouse'.

Tell me what you've seen on the silver screen lately, Miss Olivia Hobbes. I'd love to take Burns to the flicks to lighten him up, and he never seems to go out of his forest. He knows about the movies as he calls them. He says the directors like Alfred Hitchcock are more important than the star. He also says for me to tell you there are wonderful horses in Ireland. No, he didn't really, but it's true all the same even if it came from Aunt Bron's gentleman friend Connor who Auntie likes to call Mr. Blarney. He claims all the best actresses are Irish like Maureen O'Hara, Margaret O'Sullivan (who's she?) even Geer Garson who's never in anything anymore, but she was good wasn't she? My mother used to take me to her films 'to have a good weep' she said. Give me news, please, Ollie. What's on?

JOURNAL. L Williams.

This afternoon I watched Aunt Bron unbraid her hair, to wash it. It's that kind of hair you can sit on. I never saw anyone actually doing that, but Aunt Bron can. She rubs oil into it first, a perfumed oil, I had some too and she massaged it into my scalp while I lay by the fire and it felt marvellous.

'Shall I grow my hair?'

'It would suit you. But you like being a tomboy, Laurel. Stay with that as long as you need to. Then, grow your hair.'

The smell of the tagine cooking slowly on the stove combined with the perfumed oil: it was a fruity brown smell and when we ate it the feel and the taste of it were like nothing I had ever experienced.

'This is a dish I often cooked for Rashid.' I had a vivid image of them lying naked on a couch feeding each other with this delicious food. 'Or he would cook it for me. Never make love with a man who says he can't cook. He won't be much of a lover either.' We both laughed at that. I thought of the local boys, of Hywel who strutted around with his little moustache.

'There's a boy in the village who fancies himself a Casanova. He has the most awful way with girls. And at home, he claims his dad is always served food before anyone else in the family.'

'…And don't tell me – his mam will wait until he's finished before she eats, I can guess.'

'Yes! And Hywel boasts his dad never even puts a kettle on. Or applies heat to anything. So when his mam went to hospital they all had bread and dripping for a week, or chips from the chip shop. Oh, Auntie – are men all like that, apart from Arabs?' She laughed and hugged me. Her skin smelt of sandalwood.

'No – and yes, and it's not just men, Laurel. Don't you know about the lions? Well, you need to know.' I settled back luxuriously in the firelight, still with the taste of tagine on my tongue, meaty and spicy.

We sipped a warm red 'peasant' wine. She's saving the best bottle for my eighteenth birthday next week. Aunt B tied her hair back with a broad silky scarf.

'So… the lions. A lesson in life, my girl, and not just the jungle. The baby lions are hungry, the mother goes and hunts, brings back a dead animal. What happens next – well, the father wakes up, ambles over and eats his fill. The baby lions watch, getting hungrier. When he's finished, the little boy lions go up to eat. The girl lions wait with their mother. They watch their brothers eat; their little eyes getting round with hunger.'

'What!' I shrieked. 'That's not fair!'

'Then, and only then,' Bron went on with a wicked grin, 'when the boys have finished, the girls go and eat, and the mother too.'

'If there's anything left!' 'Quite. So you see, my dear, it's not just men. This is something about the world that women have to know.'

'But why do the female lions let it happen?'

'Because they know the males' terrible secret. They know they would not survive.' She poured me another glass of wine.

'Is that true?'

'It's true. The males would not survive. And it's in the interest of the race that they should. So now – who really is strongest, who really has the power, dear girl?'

'Ah. The women, I suppose.'

'Exactly. And don't forget it', she said. 'But watch out, because some men have never liked this situation and some women have had a hard time because of it.' I was enjoying my second glass of wine by now and the feel of it, and I thought to myself: 'No wonder Moira loves this stuff so much.'

Although I'd been surprised at Bron's story, I was completely at home with the conclusion. Had I known this all along? And what about my man in the forest? He's a male lion trying to buck the system, isn't he? Is he going to survive?

When I'm with Bron I feel like a grown-up; when I'm with Ollie I feel like a child, pretending. When I'm with Burns I feel both, sometimes one, sometimes the other, sometimes both at the same time. He's a lion, a wounded lion. I want to catch him his food.

CHAPTER 13

'Why do I have to do all the talking, Doctor?' Tom inquired.

'Well, Captain,' the psychiatrist replied, looking right at him, 'I am not the one whose story we are trying to work out.'

'But you know my story!' Tom looked round the wood-panelled room, leant back on the sofa and peered up at the ceiling.

'Of course I do. I know most of it, but…' the Doctor went on to explain once again in his slow and patient delivery the theory of trauma and its release whilst Tom, who usually listened carefully, now shut off, for he understood the mechanics of the task and wanted to be able to guess exactly where in Europe Dr. Solomon had once practiced. How deep and dark his eyes, Tom thought. And what large hands for such a small-boned man. 'How long have you been bald?' he wanted to ask, 'and do you mind?' 'Have you a wife and children? Do you know I like you and want to embrace you when we meet. Have you any idea how tasty this coffee is? Could it be Italian? Why do we work in this room? Is it work? Have you met Freud? How do I know what that word 'freud' means? Are you a practising Jew or an atheist like Freud? What do I think about atheism? Did I once know God?

'Where have you gone, Tom?' Solomon asked.

'Ah!'

'Are you back in the depths of your forest?'

'No!'

'Do you know what the forest means for you?'

'No. Not at all. But I've been in forests… haven't I?'

'Well, I'm not going to say too much, except to trust that what I do say could generate a memory, *causa causans*.'

'There were forests as well as hills in my childhood, and the sea too, I think.'

'That's what we want to retrieve. Starting from there. Every single bit you can. Tell me about your father.'

'Tell me first, did you ever meet Sigmund Freud?'

'I wonder Tom: was he a Republican, your father?'
Tom blinked.

'Did you meet Freud, Doctor?' His voice was harsh.

Solomon paused before replying, his voice formal.

'Oh yes; I did have that honour. Here in England. In London.'

'Tell me a little about him before I talk to you. His character?'

'Is this your bargain? I accept. Is it cool enough to walk and talk outside?'

***

JOURNAL. L.Williams.

To the forest again, but no sign of Burns today. Where is he? Is he okay? Muffin seemed happy enough so I took her word for it.

I found some red clay in the stream that feeds the lake. Quite a find. It was perfect, solid, slimy clay. I dug a chunk out with a stick. Enough to make a small bowl. It was such a slippery lump as I turned it around in my hands – much easier on a pottery wheel – but I managed to pinch the sides fairly evenly, pressing into it and pulling it up with my fingers and thumbs. It makes a clumpy, primitive looking bowl but it works and it doesn't look too bad. I expect it will take a couple of days to dry in the sun. Then I might leave it outside Burns' hut with some of that homemade fudge in it, he's not been well I think. That will cheer him up. I don't expect he's had fudge for ages.

CHAPTER 14

Diary. Saturday

Rain. I had been outside all morning, trying to repair and re-caulk the old wooden dinghy upturned in the grass outside my door. I went in, resting my limbs, watching through the door for the buzzard. Big drops of rain fell without warning on the newly scraped wooden planks. They have already taken several days to dry. Out again in the quickening downpour to cover it with an oilskin. Then a shout, quite nearby. I couldn't see anyone. I stand with face upturned for a few moments in the sweet rain like a thirsty tree.

'Mine, O thou Lord of Life,

Send my roots rain!'

That shout again. Closer. It's the girl. It's her. She's running towards me, laughing. Something jumps up inside me like a fish, striking my ribs. I can't resist smiling at her trying to avoid the rain,

zig-zagging in between the raindrops, little idiot. I put down my tools. Grasp her by the soaking shoulders – a thin cotton shirt, drenched – and hurry her inside the shack. (Why, whenever I ask for something, anything, she always appears?)

She's laughing and shaking herself like a wet dog. I throw her one of my clean shirts to change into and think about thanking her for the gift of fudge but don't speak. Remembering the white flesh she revealed carelessly a week ago. The boat! I'm distracted. I go out again while she changes and pull it in by the hawser. It slides easily enough inside the shack. I push it so that it sits like a sofa along one wall.

'Okay. You can talk to me now. You can stop working. I'm ready and decent. Any tea?' She has clambered astride the upturned dinghy and perches on the keel, covered to mid-thigh in my red tartan shirt, bare legs crossed. Holding her arms up, elbows bent, head high, in Egyptian Princess position. 'The barge she sat on…' I declaim, unable in my rush of feelings to use just my own words. '…like a burnished throne, Burned on the water…' Who said that?' I stop because she laughs at me. 'I've left school, Tom,' she says, 'and we don't need Shakespeare tests. And I'm eighteen next week.' She laughs again, a great delighted roar of girlish, womanly laughter, and I think that, at this moment, I love her. No reflection, a spontaneous thought at last. This princess, girl-child, woman-creature, is what I want to belong to. She catches my look and holds it and echoes it, she takes my hand and leads it, and what followed then has been consigned to that which some people call the Dream Time.

I cannot for all the joy in me retrieve in any detail or coherence the events that brought about our collision. All I can report to you, reader Solomon, is the feeling of having been earthed at last. In your terms, of having recovered my mind. But I want to assure you that I recovered it in my body, in her body.

I am now wedded to her, and I want to remain thus for as long as I breathe.

I don't question what she wants for she will always tell me. For the moment I know that what she wants is me, madness, oldness, scars and all.

I end by saying that I know there are grand words to describe this collision, and there are certainly better words than 'collision' which, despite the massive physical crash that occurred between us, was full of softness and sighing. But I refuse and have no skills to use the words and what is more, these notes I write now, weak with adoration, I shall tear up.

CHAPTER 15

The first sound in the morning was invariably the lapping of the lake as if it had a tide. But sometimes it was the sound of the trees if the lake was still, not necessarily wind, just trees creaking or rustling to such an extent that he thought it was raining again. He breathed in to check damp leaf, kernel, earth. Dry. Rustling. Trees.

Then there was the excitement of hearing footsteps, sometimes barefoot, her feet, if he was awake. Though she could come so early, he would wake on the hearing of her tapping at the open door, or, more recently the creaking of floorboard or springs as she sat or lay on the bed. He would close his eyes and hear her breathing beside him, smell her skin, her breath, her hair, pretend to sleep, or sleep in a state of delight at her soft silent fragrant presence and out of this blissful waiting surrender, he would come awake, in confusion.

'This feels like the sea.'

'Are you talking to me, Burns?' she chuckled, sitting up. He gazed past her.

'Are you cracking up, boy?' she asked seriously, stroking his temple.

'I'm remembering that I once expressed my feelings only through poetry: 'Oh that I was young again and held her in my arms.'

'Can't you do better than that?' She plucked a grey hair.

'Oh but there is wisdom
In what the sages said,
But stretch that body for a while
And lay down that head – '

'I wish it would rain again, Tom,' she leapt off the bed to the door. 'I loved it when it rained and rained…' She fell silent; they both knew and felt what she was talking about.

'Midnight rain, nothing but the wild rain
On the bleak hut, and me Remembering again – '

'And me!' She turned to show her nakedness again with a little inner smile that was now a tremor as she recalled her surprise and excitement that very first time; seeing and feeling and watching and sniffing and touching and caressing him in amazement and reverence and exuberant delight; wanting to proclaim him. Then accepting and receiving him with her body as if she had remembered long ago from a dream just what it would be like.

She marvelled now that the experience could come flooding back to her with such force – as if she had been unconscious at the time. But she wasn't. She had been powerfully aware of the expression on Tom's face as he had entered her; it was unforgettable. An expression of utter astonishment mingled with bliss.

'I'm remembering that I once expressed my feelings only through poetry.'

'You said that already.' She returned to the foot of the bed, knelt, peeped up his legs at his face, as active as his body was still.

'Yes, we did make love and you are here. I think I fell asleep.'

'Your eyes were open.' She held his feet, stroked his ankles.

'And when I woke, instead of here I found myself in immense confusion, somewhere between savannah and desert.'

'I love that word 'savannah''

'A scrub terrain I think, with a smell of brine and peat and smoke.'

'If I have a daughter I'll call her Savannah.'

***

'Let's pretend we're lying on the lake in our own boat, floating, floating, stroking the water, and our favourite fish, trout, coming up to touch our fingers and the rain beginning quietly … go on.'

'And we float in any direction the current takes us…'

'Current?'

'Our lake has a current which, taken at the flood leads on to…'

'Happiness ever after. What's it like to be in love with me, Mr. Burns?'

They were lying on leaves seeking cool beneath a great spreading wych elm, the trunk forking just above their heads, smooth to look at but rough to touch.

'It's just like you,' she had said, rubbing the tree and rubbing his cheek with the back of each hand.

'Does wych mean witch?' she asked.

'Wych means pliant.'

'It doesn't.

'Supple. Like you. And you pronounce wych to rhyme with tick.'

'You don't. You're so full of nonsense-knowledge, Mr. Readit-all-teach-the-girl Burns!'

'I'll tell you what it's like to be in love with a *vixen*.'

'Oh, has she been back, our little fox? Have you seen her?'

'I've heard her, and I've seen her. Rust brown.'

'Have you fed her?'

'She's coming closer.'

'How close?'

'To your tree.'

'I want to see…' she was up.

'You won't spot her now.'

'I just want to see where she comes. Do you know Tom —' she was trying to pull him up '—I've never seen a fox. Never. Not in all these years. Of course, I've been in towns most of my life but my first real school was in the country, just next door, in Herefordshire, and we were always slipping out at night and having feasts in the trees. I've seen badgers, stacks of them and they're even harder to see than foxes. They've got hardly any legs, so they waddle. What are you doing?'

Tom was pulling her back onto his lap.

'Listen!' he said, 'Shhh!'

'It's a woodpecker'

'What kind?'

'Shhh!'

The sound seemed to echo amongst the trees.

'It sounds like drumming. And it goes soft and then loud. What is it, what kind?'

'I don't know.'

'You do.'

'Shhh!' He held her till her energy subsided and they sat in the silence and the hammering on the hollow trunk until the bird moved on.

'What are you looking at, Tom?'

'I shot an arrow in the air. It fell to earth, I know not where.'

'Here. Here!' she exclaimed, holding her heart. He smiled. 'What's that then?'

'Henry Wadsworth Longfellow, I do believe. The Arrow and the Song.'

'He must be American. You remember so much and so little.'

'And the song, from beginning to end,
I found again in the heart of a friend.'

'Oh yes, Tom, let's play lines. Guess who said this:' She was up again, facing him, taking a stance, deepening her voice: *'All that we see or seem is but a dream within a dream...* go on... you know... you do know... American. Middle name Allan. First name Edgar... Poe. You great cuckoo! You great woodpecker! You great tit! You knew, didn't you?'

'Take thy beak from out my heart,' Tom clutched his heart and knelt. *'And take thy form from off the door! Quoth the Raven...'*

'Nevermore! ... No Tom, the raven is an omen of... the raven is bad luck like the magpie.'

Tom lay back, his head across her knees. She stroked his forehead.

'A pity beyond all telling, is hid in the heart of love.'

'Is that your Yeats? Or is it you? What is it? I don't agree.' They stayed silent.

'I sneezed a sneeze into the air,' Laurel suddenly declaimed, in perfect imitation of his 'serious' voice.

'"It fell to earth I know not where..." Can you carry on with this poem, Tom? It's by Laurel Longlegs Williams. Not American.'

She was sitting with her back against the tree, legs stretched out. Tom sank down against her, letting his head and shoulders collapse gently into her lap. He lay on her, his arms heavy, his mind and his body limp. Unprotected… He could do this now, be like this, in the hut, on his narrow bed, with another person, with her, at last. He could let her take his broken body completely, and more besides.

'Truth or Dare!' Her fingers were circling his temples, brushing across his closed eyes.

'Say Dare,' she added.

'I feel too lazy,' he said and buried his face and ears in her thighs. He didn't hear a faint distant splashing from across the lake.

'There's a boat!' she whispered Tom turned, at full stretch, raising his head to peer out through the foliage. Laurel ducked to look through the leaves beside him.

'There's the boatman!' she whispered.

'You must hide…'

'I know, I am, I'm covered in camouflage, look, you can't see me.' She bent a branch thick with overlapping leaves across her kneeling body.

'Good girl; don't let him spot you. I've got a note for him, well, a letter, a long letter.'

Laurel lay quietly down and curled up in the shade under her branch, next to the reeds at the edge of the lake, watching the finches chattering and squabbling, suddenly aware of her nakedness. A note for the boatman, she thought.

'Is it a letter for Doctor Solomon?' Then she saw a male bird, all red and black, strut pompously past.

'He looks like an archbishop!'

'Yes,' said Tom quietly, 'He does in a way. How did you know?' he kissed her bare ankle amongst the foliage. 'I'm leaving you for a moment. I want Corporal Griffiths to think I've emerged sleepy from my hut.'

'Don't let him in, Tom. He'll see I've been here with you and made love with you, and he gives reports on you, doesn't he?'

'Probably.'

'Right, Tom, this is the Dare: you must walk up to the boatman and say Good morning, just as you are, lock stock and bare arse.' Then Tom moved towards the front of the hut, kneeling, crawling, as the boat approached.

'Tom!' she hissed 'What's your favourite line from Romeo and Juliet?'

'Love is smoke!' he whispered, and was gone. 'Magnificent! I dare you...'

'Shhh!'

***

The boatman, Corporal Griffiths, revealed uncertainty at receiving an order from an unexpected quarter, and from a completely naked officer standing in the doorway of the wooden shack.

'A letter, Sir? For the General?'

'No, man. For Doctor Solomon. His name's on the envelope. "Brigadier Doctor Solomon". The General will not be pleased if you jump the chain of command.'

'Letter first to Docotr Brigadier Solomon, Sir, who in turn passes it to General Ashworth.' The Corporal studied the envelope which did not in fact say 'Brigadier'.

'Certainly, Sir.'

'That's it!' Tom smiled, pleased to have heard a whole sentence with its Welsh cadence coming forth from the very worried Corporal.

'Make haste before the tide turns.'

'Tide, Sir?'

'Just a saying, Griffiths.'

'Yes, Sir.'

'The fishing's good this side.'

'Yes, Sir!' He saluted, stepped back in the boat and prepared to turn and row off.

'Was there anything you brought for me, Corporal?'

Griffiths looked amazed. Especially since he had just seen, out of the corner of his eye, a nearby bush trembling and shaking though there was no wind. He'd forgotten to deliver the basket of provisions and the books. He lugged them out and passed them over to Tom.

There was beer and wine in the basket today, and some choice-looking food. A feast, and his girl to share it with.

Tucking the letter inside his tunic, Griffiths pushed the boat out and rowed away, trying not to look too hard at this strange Man Friday who now punched the air with delight imagining Solomon's face when addressed, uncertainly, as Dr. Brigadier, Sir.

'Where is my treasure?' he uttered in Long John Silver tones. She was crawling towards him, a few camouflage leaves arranged in her hair. Now she came sideways and fast, like a crab. He rushed towards the hut as if afraid. He heard her laugh.

'Breakfast!' Then he stopped, on the threshold of his hut and whispered urgently, 'Laurel, look! She's come. There she is!' Both stood transfixed. The third creature, the fox, curious, seemingly unafraid, stood in its sunlit deep brown beauty by Laurel's tree, watching them both naked as they stood, Laurel's hair trailing with willow leaves. And when the fox moved away with slow rhythmic lope, having stood her ground a full and vibrant minute, Laurel sighed. Then she said, 'Will you tell me your life, Burn-Burns?'

'If I can.'

***

'How do I save the girl?'

'From what?'

'My recovery. From whatever hovers over me, or hides within, which will presumably emerge from the depths one day and pounce.'

'Does she come to your cabin?'

'She does indeed.'

'Regularly?'

'Every day if she could.

Solomon allowed himself to show uncertainty in a silence that lasted until a clap of thunder, distant and moving on, seemed to prompt the reply:

'It would be wise not to let it be thought that you have a… relationship.'

'I'm well aware of that, Doctor. And I'm good at hiding … things. You don't have to worry about me in that respect at least. Do you do any other jobs here?'

'You are asking, do I see other patients here? Oh yes.' 'If the General requires it?'

'If the War Office requests it.'

'Can we go out? The storm is passing over. I like storms, and we need rain, they say. Though this is a good room as rooms go. And I can see the trees.'

'Did you get your books? Would you like Conrad next?'

'You know my taste in books, Doctor. Do you know my taste in women?' They both smiled and as if waiting, rose together to move across the room.

'Maybe one day I'll be able to write my own book.'
'About her?'

'About me, from these pieces I'm stringing together for you and … yes, about her.'

'She has been good for you.'

'Has been?'

'She is good for you!' Solomon was opening the French windows.

'I always wait for you to slip into jargon … but you don't.'

'Oedipal Reversal' is what I'm struggling not to utter,' Solomon offered, and they both broke into laughter as they stepped into the garden, down steps and onto another terrace and made their way across the lawns, the sky still heavy with cloud, and towards the lake.

'I want you to try and talk about this girl to me.'

'She plays something she calls a Truth Game,' Tom offered. 'Is she after your past?'

'No, my present.'

'Your present?'

'It's as if she's forgiven me my past.'

Solomon stopped walking to look up into Tom's face. 'As if there was much to forgive?'

'We make love with words. It's such a short cut, this game of hers.'

'Yes?'

'Look, there's our buzzard. We have a buzzard, we have a fox, we have a dog. Shall I give you a list?'

'Please.'

See how he dips like a sea eagle. We are looking for a name for this lake. It's very different on the other side over there. I'm going to make her a fishing rod. She likes to watch me casting. 'Fishing is silent poetry,' I say to her, distorting a famous line. 'What are you when you're at home?' she asks me when I'm quoting or instructing, 'A teacher?' And this almost rings a bell. Strange, Walter, it feels as if I'm being unfaithful to her, talking to you today.'

'Go on.'

'Listen, can you hear the call? There!' Both men peered towards the sun, covering their eyes, suddenly arrested by the buzzard hovering as if held in a thermal, its underpart startlingly white, its wings spread wide.

'Buteo buteo,' Tom uttered, remembering the boy sitting at a desk identifying birds in a large blue book.

'Can you consider what it is that birds and the naming of birds represent for you, Tom?' Solomon probed as their stride lengthened again.

'And trees,' Tom added. 'We make love under the trees. We take turns to look up at the canopy. Jaysus, the life feeling that comes when she lies on top of me, when I feel her eyes on me. I feel like a man. No… a human being… or, I feel like a woman with this wondrous weightless weight on me.'

This man is getting well, was the doctor's conviction.

'I don't know what this means, because I feel like a child also, Walter.'

'You mean?' Solomon coaxed him.

'Full of… a return to… it feels like…'

'What's the word?'

'*Kinderleicht*! Where's that come from? *Kinderleicht*.' They both laughed, nodding with delight at a common understanding, a shared mystery. And the buzzard flew off.

***

'Truth, Dare, Kiss, Promise or Kalamazoo?'

'That's new! What's Kalamazoo?'

'Wait and see.'

'Truth'

'You always say Truth.'

'Yes, but do I tell it?' They were fishing from their raft, relieved to be on water on this hot, airless day with the forest feeling oppressive. She was wearing his hat, tipped up in the front, for it fell over her ears and required frequent adjustment.

'Have you ever smuggled?'

'Yes.'

'What?' Such sparkle in her eyes, he observed, as she asked.

'That's another question,' he replied . 'That's not fair. You should include the "what" in the answer.'

'You should ask the question better.'

'How?'

'Just try.'

'Tell me what you've smuggled if you've smuggled anything ever?'

'Whisky. Rum.'

'Guns?' She held her fishing rod with both hands, concentrating on watching for fish.

'Dare!'

'Help!' There was a tug on her line. She took fright and involuntarily struck, too hard, the hook leaping out of the water into the air, minus the bait.

'I know, I know, I'm supposed to nudge it into his mouth. I know…' she deepened her voice and frowned in imitation of Tom, almost achieving the soft burr of his accent, '…perch have enormous mouths, and…'

'I dare you to be my bait.'

'What do I have to do?' excitement in her voice.

'You just do it.'

'Done.'

'Right!…. you know my mother thought I was a loafer. 'Thomas, you're a loafer!' she liked to say. My God, how did I remember that?'

'Oh yes, please tell me about your mother.'

'Right! You fell right in, didn't you? Bait indeed…'

'Oh, that's not a real dare. You're supposed to tell me to take my clothes off or something.'

'Kiss'

'No, it's my turn. Kiss!'

'I don't want you to kiss me.' He seized her by the shoulders, she dropped her fishing rod into the bottom of the boat.

'Kalamazoo!' she shouted, and standing up together in an embrace they both chorused, 'KALAMAZOO!'

They were laughing till the boat was rocking, each trying to get the kiss in first, so that the General's Lady, as Laurel liked to call her, could hear and see some strange unboatlike commotion as she rode along the other side of the lake.

Then splash, they fell in, gulping and gasping, then kissing in the water.

The silence and stillness suddenly returning had the horse reined in by the lady who rose in her saddle, peering, wishing she had brought field-glasses, determined to come across to the forest side to find out if trespassers, poachers, were invading her peaceful vistas; or to send the General's man.

***

Darkness came and the smell of wild garlic underfoot as he walked back towards the hut alone. He could smell the wet wood and brackish water round the little pier.

His supper was good. He could taste once again and he relished a good, strong Cheddar, the soda bread he baked and the blood red Bordeaux that the General seemed delighted to provide from his cellar. This is good food; it is good for me, like the girl is good for me; the feeling of her goodness going into me. 'You are inside me' he would feel, think, whisper when he was making love to her.

There was pleasure, too, physical pleasure, in using his hands, in remembering his skills, in recollecting and hearing the instructions given to him by his father, by a teacher, by a stableman. 'You can speed up the natural seasoning of timber by the process of kiln-drying,' someone is saying to him. 'Wood not seasoned will shrink, twist or split after it's been cut, shaped, made up.' He can hear the voice and see the hands.

'You must always allow for a certain amount of natural movement even with well-treated timber.'

Before he had received his box of tools, he had listed his basic requirements: Handsaw Hammer Plane Chisel Screwdriver

Now, whilst eating his lunch at his desk, he assembled all his tools before him: handsaw, hacksaw, clawhammer, Warrington hammer, side-cutting pliers, round-nosed pliers, large plane, small plane, four screwdrivers, four chisels, pincers, wrench, brace and bits, woodrasp, soldering iron, bradawl, nail punch, 'G' cramps, oilstone, slide rule, folding rule, marking gauge, trysquare, oil can, glue pot, assorted nails and screws.

Chewing on his bread and cheese he looked down at his 'toys' as Laurel called them and planned, vaguely, the size and shape of the workbench he would make, where he would position the vice, which joints to use.

He was aware of his obsessional behaviour and hoped it would not transfer into his relationship with Laurel.

He visualised and smiled with joy as he saw just how to cut and shape a dovetail joint, then a mortice and tenon, a tongue and groove, a dowelled joint, a mitre joint. 'I can play for ever with these,' he had told her, and then hurt her: 'I don't think women like working with wood.' She had been standing there watching him test the sharpness, grasp the handle of each item, and she had responded; 'I don't think men like playing with dogs,' for Muffin was standing up sniffing at the smell of oil on Tom's hands.

'It's not true!' came the reply, surprised that he too was hurt at this very small teasing counter-accusation. He kissed the dog.

'It's not true,' Laurel said, reaching across to lift and sniff at one of his carefully cut planks. She had then proceeded to talk non-stop as she did when caught off guard, about a balsawood aeroplane she'd once made, about local farmers complaining about the weather and the cost of diesel oil, and about herself avoiding Aunt Bron's desire to talk to her about her long walks and late returns.

'I know she won't reproach me or forbid me. She says she trusts me, and I believe her. She'd

just like to know. I can talk to her, can't I, Tom?'

But as she asked him, this man almost twice her age, gazing into his eyes past her own tiny reflection in his pupils, she perceived the answer. He could not be shared, or at least not yet.

Because of the pain that she has sensed in his body, felt in her own body. Because he was being hidden and had to heal. She was a mother eagle protecting her wounded, broken-winged chick… yet how she longed to be able to tell Aunt Bron, to be the chick herself, protected and comforted by this best kind of mother in the world.

'No,' she said as he didn't reply, 'Of course I can't talk to her…' She took his head between her hands for a slow, soft kiss, a benison before departing.

Later, as he sipped at his wine alone in his hut, he wished he had been able to reply, 'Bring your Aunt Bron to afternoon tea in our cabin one day.'

Then he began to count his nails and screws once again.

CHAPTER 16

The lantern is lit on the desk because I want to record a dream. I dreamt that I was taken to a hospital behind enemy lines where there was no problem entering, I was a VIP, people saluted, clicked heels, bowed heads, and the Commandant-Surgeon, greeting me in German took me through to a patient in a kind of tent, a kind of camouflage net but thin as a mosquito net covering a young patient, a girl. 'Tell us what is wrong with her, Doctor, they said. I moved in, moved close, quite clueless, confused, thinking her dead. But she opened her eyes and whispered, 'I have glass bones!'

'I must get a message to Doctor Solomon. I must tell him that my appetite has returned… that I have remembered a dream at last and have a symbol for him to relish… then I must give him my recipe for soda bread!'

'But you are here, Tom!' Doctor Solomon moved from behind the desk to the sofa where Tom lay.

'But I am here.'

'Yes, you are talking to me in a familiar room.'

'But my eyes are closed.'

'Yes. You might have fallen asleep.'

'No! No, Sir! Just misplaced... in another place... and the girl wasn't there, the real girl, the Laurel girl. Do you remember?'

'Yes, I do! The coffee is on its way.' Solomon returned towards his desk, glancing out at the sky, considering a walk.

'Did you give me an injection?'

'Don't you recall?'

'I remember a recipe for soda bread. I don't think they make it in Austria.'

'How do you know I'm Austrian?' Solomon turned, interested. 'Or Hungarian.'

'That is so. I am exactly both. Indeed.'

'And Jewish.'

'Yes, yes.'

'Then let me tell you. A pound of brown flour, stoneground flour, plus six ounces of white flour; baking powder... let me see... a good pinch of salt, two ounces of butter, one small egg, one pint of soured milk. These are the ingredients.'

'Thank you.'

'Do you like bread?'

'Not particularly.'

'In Ireland you have brown soda bread for everyday normal usage, white on special occasions.'

'I think this is the coffee arriving.' A sergeant knocked and entered.

'Do you want to know how to mix and bake the bread?'

'Open your eyes Tom, try to sit up and see where you are.' Tom sat up and observed the doctor and noticed the sergeant standing by the table.

'Good morning, Sergeant!' Tom said with careful courtesy. 'Good afternoon, Sir.'

'Are you Irish, Sergeant?'

'No Sir, I'm local Sir.' Tom helped himself to two sugar lumps, not entirely certain whether he liked his coffee sweet or not.

'Thank you, Sergeant.' Solomon ushered the man out then moved to the French windows, opening them wide.

'Drink up, Tom. The fresh air will be good. Don't be too worried, you said nothing startling whilst you were unconscious, nothing you haven't told under hypnosis before, and in any event your dream is of much more interest to me, if not to the army.'

'I have a memory of a love story,' Tom told Solomon, 'but it is not mine... I went boating-fishing for hours yesterday. Maybe I got sunstroke.

'Shall we walk towards the stables?'

'Yes. I have music in my mind, very pure. Piano. I have the feeling that my mother played the piano. *Kinderscenen.*'

'She did.' A gesture towards the gardens. They moved past the great rhododendron bushes which had no perfume.

'And the heroine in this story played the piano. Her name is Clara. She plays the piano for the man she loves. He writes for her. She is his muse, and he needs her because he is not strong nor balanced. Like me. Can I play the piano? Do you know?'

'We have a piano here, but I doubt if it is tuned.'

'Can we try?' Tom asks.

'The place is empty. Come!'

They walked, their shoes resounding on oak floorboards, across a wide hall into a library lined with books from floor to ceiling and with a black grand piano standing before an empty fireplace on a blue Eastern rug. Tom sat at the piano keyboard, knowing to lower the stool with his hands on the two wheels, not looking, opening the lid, stroking the keys, stretching his fingers, straightening his back, his eyes closed, his head raised.

'It's not tuned!'

'How do you know?'

'Can we have the piano tuned?'

'Do you want it in your cabin?' Laughter as they left the room and made their way outside.

'Laurel tells me that if I ever invite anyone to supper, I must tell her how to behave. 'I don't know how to behave!' she says. Tom noticed the doctor looking quickly behind them to ensure that they were alone on the path and could not be overheard.

'Do go on, Tom.'

'What do you mean,' I asked her, 'You don't know how to behave?'

'You know what behave means,' she tells me, this adult child, 'Ways of doing things when others are around, ways of following rules so that others don't get upset.'

'You've quite a memory for the recent past.'

'I don't want you to be the analyst, please Doctor, whilst I speak of her. I just want you to listen.'

'Shall we walk another route? Come Tom. Let's take the path through the rose gardens to the river. I shall keep just ahead. I am listening.'

'Other people pick up these rules somewhere,' she tells me, 'which I've missed out on.' 'Like what?' I ask her. 'Like where to walk on the pavement and how fast and what to say if you bump into someone.'

Tom could smell the blooms before they reached the gardens. He stopped talking.

'These roses are arranged in historical order,' Solomon said. 'The first, pale pink with these

loose sprays, are very old- Chinese I'm told, going back to the thirteenth century.'

'This one?' Tom stopped, touched a petal, inhaled.

'Old Blush' I think the General's wife calls it.'

'And this?' Tom pointed to a deeper pink.

'I don't know.'

'Rosa Gallica something.' Tom knelt to read the fading information on its stake. 'Introduced before 1300. Apothecary's Rose'

'Did your mother garden?'

'I want to talk about the girl.' They moved on.

'There's a colour!' Tom pointed towards the wall. 'It looks like a buttercup. Laurel does this little girl thing of holding a buttercup under my chin and...

what does she say?' They both waved at a burly gardener straightening up and touching his cap. 'She tells me that when she was eight at a school somewhere in England she had her mouth washed out with soapy water – for the second time in her life – for calling a clumsy classmate a "bloody nuisance". 'My mother didn't believe in apologising or explaining,' Laurel told me, 'so my teacher drew a blank when she asked me to apologise.'

'What do you say?' the teacher insisted, 'what do you say, child?' and Laurel, confused, replied, 'I say the wrong things.'

'I'll have to speak to your mother, then' said the teacher.

'She says the wrong things too,' Laurel told her and then she laughed. 'I always laughed when others didn't', she told me, 'and older people were always laughing when it wasn't funny, and I never know which fork or knife or spoon to choose. My mother and I lived on pies and sandwiches and gin and ginger beer'.

'Interrupting, which she still does, is something I always do because that's how my mother and I conversed with each other,' she told me,' Just a series of interruptions. And now she's going to interrupt my life again by coming down to Wales!' Tom turned as the two men reached the end where the herb plantation began. He stood still. 'I'd like to show her this rose garden,' he said. 'But I know I can't.' He inhaled and closed his eyes and inhaled her skin and hair and saw her eyes and hands.

'I would like you to meet her.'

'Do you trust her, Tom?' Solomon asked, quite close, quite softly.

'Of course I—'

'Think what I'm asking you. Of course you trust her if you love her.'

'You think I love her?'

'You know what I mean by trust: if she tells her mother or her aunt or a friend, in her excitement or her desire, very natural, to want to share such a secret as she holds, then—' But Tom interrupted him as if he could not bear to hear the rest of the sentence.

'Do you want to spend a penny?' a stranger once asked her as she stood legs crossed, a small girl, on a kerb. 'Yes, please!' she replied and waited for the penny in vain. Moira – that's her mother – used to say, 'Let's take a leak!'

Solomon laughed. Tom joined him.

'I'm going to help myself to some sprigs of thyme and fennel.'

'Well, I'd like to know what you cook in your cabin,'

'I don't even know how to cook an egg!' she tells me, indignant: 'I just don't know how to behave because I wasn't shown.' 'Do you want to?' I ask her. 'Not really, except... well I don't know how to behave with you, Burns,' she often calls me Burns, 'I just have to behove.' 'Behove?' I ask her. 'Yes, behove or behoove. I think it means to just be yourself. But one day when you're free '

'Free?' Solomon frowned.

'You'll want to take me somewhere and I may not know what to do.'

'Yes you will,' I told her. 'It will behove you just to behoove like me.'

Solomon listened, allowing Tom to chatter on, to pick herbs, to share the seeming inconsequentialities of his happiness with innocence. Waiting for the moment to discuss Tom's dream.

***

'Does he wear glasses, your Doctor Solo Man?'

'No,' said Tom quickly. 'Yes. Sometimes.'

'Well, I'm him, and you're supposed to be lying down or whatever you do – go on, do it – and I'm not wearing my glasses today.'

'Yes, Doctor.' Tom happily and obediently lay back on his bed with his feet up on the iron bedstead.

'That's right. Now, Captain...'

'He calls me Tom.'

Laurel's voice was low and steady from her perch on the cabin trunk behind his head.

'We're having a memory test today, Tom. I want you to think slowly and carefully and get it right.'

'Yes.' He closed his eyes, hands behind his head, taking in her serious almost formal tones. 'You sound a bit fierce today, Doctor, and a little too foreign.'

'Don't I sound like him?'

'No. You sound like... General de Gaulle.'

'Ha. Well, I'm Doctor Solomon doing his impression of General de Gaulle. Now concentrate! My first question: are you married?' Tom didn't hesitate. 'Yes. ...No. Yes... good heavens...I can't answer that...'

'Of course you can,' said Laurel's stern voice. 'You must just take your time-don't do things in such a hurry.'

'That's it! That's a memory, what you just said! Those were exactly my mother's words. She sent me a telegram when I wrote to tell her I was about to – do what? Get married? Join the army? 'You always do things in such a hurry. Remember that old car you bought.'

'So you did get married?'

'I can't remember – at all. But I do remember that first car. A Morris. It was always breaking down. So am I married now?' Tom asked, profoundly puzzled. 'I can't be sure. I feel uncomfortable when I search for her name. My wife. No; those words don't make sense.'

'Mmm,' said Laurel thoughtfully. 'You've said 'Sarah' in your sleep.'

'Oh, Sarah was my beloved – my older sister.' He answered with ease then sat up, suddenly agitated. 'Let me write this down – I feel the need to write – just words. I do it for Solomon sometimes…' he fished out his notebook from underneath the pillow, found a pencil beside the bed and started to write rapidly, speaking the words as he wrote them:

241

Sarah.

Sarah Byrne

sister

warm

breasts

woman

soft

gone...

That's it. Sarah ran off with someone. She got married... in ...Limerick? I loved her. But I was too young, six years younger and I couldn't have her. Did I ever see her again? Did she want to see me? What had I done that she couldn't forgive?' He shuddered as if cold though it was a hot and muggy day.

Laurel waited, almost as long as Dr. Solomon would have done, but the next question was asked not in the formal mode but in her own girl/womanly voice:

'Did you... did you like your sister's breasts, Tom?'

'Yes,' Tom almost whispered, 'they were velvety soft to the touch – like yours.'

'I wish I was your sister.'

'You are!'

***

His sawing-horse was nearly finished, the second bookshelf was up, and Tom had half-filled the first one with his dictionary, reference books, Lexicon, the poems of Villon, Byron, Rilke and Pindar, all borrowed from Solomon with a promise of more to come. He needed only a box to keep his tools tidy. He lit the stove to boil a teakettle to warm him after his swim and sat outside in his flannel dressing gown enjoying the late afternoon sun and shadows. Today there had been much activity over at the big house. A marquee being erected on the main lawn. Ladies, he guessed from the trills and cadences that carried across the lake. He'd caught the strains of music. A tea dance? A garden party? He tried to picture the hats, the talking, the giggles, the flirting. Other people's settled lives. Prowling in his imagination around the outside of the tent like an invisible animal he felt distaste at the artificial laughter, mixed with an exile's pang of longing. Families. Children. He, the prodigal son. Now he was beginning to uncover his past, but he could not afford to contemplate his future. As he pushed the thought away, inhaling deeply on his cigarette then going inside to make his tea, a woodpigeon's call could be heard – twice, three times, getting nearer, followed by a laugh and then the creak of pram springs. Laurel!

He poured out the tea into her mug as well as his own.

She wheeled the old pram containing more booty right into the hut: a wooden box full of old leather-bound books.

'Look what I found in the old mansion… for your new bookshelf. A job lot – I haven't looked at them all. But I think they might be a bit… is the word "salacious"?… because there's one on the top of the pile here called 'Confessions'.

For answer he handed her a mug of honey-sweetened tea and a flapjack he'd remembered how to make from watching his mother as a child mixing oats and butter and syrup.

'That's a thank you for bringing me also a box for my tools.'

'You know Tom, I saw a copy of 'True Confessions' magazine in Mrs. Pritchard's shop, behind the Radio Times. A story in there about a man who's trying to become a woman. Did you ever want to be a woman, Tom? Because when I was a little kid and had discovered the difference, I used to practise peeing forwards, standing up. I think I wanted to be a boy….

hey! what are you up to now? You're amazing – how do you do that?' She put down the mug and moved to the bed where Tom now posed, lying back with a smile, one arm above his head and his dressing gown slightly open. Laurel's eyes widened to see that he had turned himself into a woman. With his thighs pressed together and his pubic curls covering what looked like a cleft he'd somehow created in the flesh of his groin. She came closer, awed and silent, and touched the dent gently with her finger.

'A sister! We're sisters! You've tucked it all away!' She joined him on the bed. 'Are we going to be salacious?'

'Are you going to show me that salacious book?' He fastened up his dressing gown and Laurel handed him the book. He dusted the cover with his sleeve, smiling as he did to read the author's name in goldblock lettering on its red leather spine.

'Guess what, Tom. I won something at the fair.' She jumped up to raid her box and flourished a long cream knitted silk scarf which she wrapped round her head like a turban. 'It's a gentleman's scarf, they said. And I went to a fortune teller – she said I shall marry the man of my dreams when I'm twenty-eight.' Laurel looked suddenly serious.

'But I don't like the idea of being married – I never will. And if I ever even remotely did, I would want to get married right now. Here and now.'

'You're too young.'

'I'm eighteen next week. You know that.' Tom nodded. 'But that's not the point. I don't want to get married at all – and anyway I've got you.'

'Am I the man of your dreams?'

'No! Better than that, You're my real man of the woods and streams.'

Tom was now turning the pages of the book Laurel had handed him, half listening.

'But you know, I did dream of a man the other night, Tom – a beautiful naked young man – shall I tell you what he was doing?'

'Was he me?'

'No, of course not.'

'Then I don't want to know. Tell me something else. Stroke my head and my neck like you do and tell me a Truth. I shall ask you a difficult, Laurelish question: tell me the worst or the wickedest thing you've ever done.'

'Oh, that's easy!' Laurel laughed. 'No, it's hard, come to think of it. Because I've done several.'

'The earliest, then.'

'How old?'

'Aged – seven or eight.'

'Ok. At that age… I walked right into a hotel banqueting room just before Christmas and walked out with a basketful of biscuits, cheeses, mince pies, what else? Little red jellies, trifles, the lot. Enough for twelve people.'

'You didn't eat all that!'

'It was for the actors! We were playing panto and staying in a boarding house with no food at all except porridge. My mother was broke, and I was hungry and it was Christmas. The hotel was right next to the theatre, and it had a big sign up: Town Council Christmas Party: Free Buffet. They had a huge amount of food there anyway.' She closed her eyes and smiled. 'I can remember the taste of those trifles right now. It was a feast. 'A veritable feast, darling!' one of the Ugly Sisters said. The stage doorkeeper went out and bought crackers and we all put on the paper hats, even the grumpy old lighting man, and the director opened some Mackesons' stout which we had to pretend was champagne. It was magnificent!'

Tom cut two big slices of the fruitcake Laurel had liberated from Bronwyn's kitchen.

'I was assistant props girl, you see. So, I took Cinderella's basket and went and got some props.'

'You just walked out of a strange hotel with that lot?'

'Well – I made it into the lift, then I seem to remember the hotel porter came over and helped me out with it, the basket was so heavy. And he carried it across the road and into the stage door for me. Very nice man. I'd never set eyes on him before.'

'Did your mother find out?'

'That I'd pinched it? She must have guessed. Where did it come from otherwise? But I'd seen her in Debenham and Freebody's putting two lipsticks into her bag and she never paid for either of them. Mind you, she was very forgetful around that time. Something to do with switching from whisky to vodka.'

Tom wrapped both his arms around her, pressing his face into her neck, his heart bursting for this strong, tender creature who was filling some gap deep inside that he hadn't realised was there. 'What are you thinking, at this moment?' she asked. And so he told her.

Laurel was holding the book. She opened it at random and handed it to him.

'Read to me.'

He settled down to read. 'There was a neighbour's pear tree outside our orchard, loaded with fruit that was attractive neither to look at nor to taste.'

'This isn't like 'True Confessions', Tom.'

'You asked me to read it. So listen – 'Late one night a band of ruffians, myself included, climbed in to shake down the fruit and carry it away, for we had continued our games out of doors until well after dark, as was our habit.'

'This is a boy. Go on, Tom.'

'We took away an enormous quantity of pears. Not to eat them ourselves but simply to throw them to the pigs. Perhaps we ate some of them, but our real pleasure consisted in doing something that was forbidden.'

'Who's that? It's just like me, only worse because we were hungry and we ate every scrap.'

'It's Saint Augustine.'

'Saint! You're always trying to fool me!' She threw the silk scarf at him. 'Up to your old tricks, Tom Tease.'

'Really it is. Written over a thousand years ago.'

'No,'

'Well, sixth century… come here and look.' He pulled her down to sit on the bed beside him, showing her the frontispiece.

'The Confessions of Saint Augustine' she read. 'Goodness. Bad boy.'

'It gets much worse.'

'You mean, Adultery?'

'And the rest.'

'How do you know about him? Oh, I give up asking. You must have been a Catholic… how do you…'

'Let me read you something else. These are very old books you know. Could be valuable.'

'Poo! As long as they're readable and not too mildewed.'

He had selected and opened another book.

'Listen: lie back: this is another Thomas – *'Nothing therefore is sweeter, nothing higher, nothing stronger, nothing larger, nothing more joyful, nothing better in heaven or on earth, than love. For love descends from God…'*

'Tom!' she shook his arm, 'You're not reading that! You've got your eyes closed!'

'Hush, woman!'

He opened his eyes to look into hers wondering if she could see in them what he had just re-discovered.

***

'Are you ever ashamed, Tom?' she asked later, stretching.

'Of what? Ashamed? Of us?'

'No not us, stupid! Of things. Things you've done.'

'Yes, a bit. But I don't think it's strong with me. Guilt sometimes appears and shakes its head at me, but I give it a wide berth.'

Tom was carving a mallet. Laurel was playing with the wood chips and throwing them for Muffin who chased them further than they were thrown so that she could rush into and bark at the water. They were sitting in the sun on the upturned boat. . He suddenly stopped carving and looked at her.

'What did you just ask me? I've blanked.'

'Aha. You should tell the good doctor about that. Feeling guilty, that's what I was talking about.'

'I hate guilt.' Tom had recovered.

'I hate guilt too, but I do feel it a bit because I think that one day Aunt Bron is going to be very upset

251

especially if we just disappeared and can't tell her where we've gone.'

'Does she know you spend so much time with me?'

'In a way. She knows I love walking with Muffin and that I'm waiting for Ollie to come and that I'm a bit snooty or something about most of the local kids and that these woods fascinate me, and she may guess that there's something in the wood that has caught my fancy. I tell her about all the other things. The flowers and birds and creatures. And I ask her – it's naughty really because she'll only say no because of her arthritis which she never admits to or complains about, but it gives her the gyp from time to time and she blames the weather – I ask her if she'd like to come for a walk with me. I know she used to love hiking and riding when she was young. There's a picture of her that Connor likes best where she's on a big bay just trotting off, and her lovely brown red hair before it started going grey is flying back. She looks so young and beautiful. Maybe my age. A bit older, with big bosoms.'

'Are you young and beautiful?' Tom asked, bemused by her chat.

'Of course I am!' she said, reaching for a large wood-chip to throw. 'Can I carve a bit?'

'Sure.' He placed the mallet on the boat with the tool beside it. 'Careful'.

'Where did you get the chisel and the plane?'

'How do you know the names of tools?'

'I'm not just a damn girl you know.'

'I got a whole tool set sent over from the big house and...' he paused and looked serious, 'Go and see what's on the desk.'

'Is it a surprise?'

'Go and see!'

Laurel was off like a gazelle, disappearing into the cabin and squealing with delight. Then silence. Then Muffin noticing she'd gone rushed off too, barking. Tom lay back to feel the sun on his face in peace and await her choice.

'Oh Tom,' Laurel called from inside the hut, 'Can't I have them both?'

'Choose one. The other's for my other girlfriend.'

'You mean Myfanwy.'

'Of course.'

'Here you are, baby,' she said kneeling down to her squirming dog and placing a carved wooden bone between her jaws. Both laughed as Muffin trotted off to bury it, growling. 'And this is for me... you couldn't have carved anything more beautiful.' She was stroking a miniature book carved from oak.

'Yes I could,' he replied, 'I'm just beginning and I need a finer chisel.' And he was visualising what he would carve her next.

'You know what else we need? Music! Con brings all sorts of old records round to my Aunt's and we dance-I'm going to get us some music… Tom, why are you frowning?'

'Who is this Con person? You've mentioned him before.' Tom asked coolly.

'Oh, he's just a crazy man who is sort of courting Aunt Bron.'

'For how long?'

'I don't know. Longer than I've been here.'

'How long has he lived here?'

'I don't know, Tom. Ages.' She peered at his face, but his eyes were closed in the sun. 'Do you feel like a swim?'

'He can't be Welsh with a name like Connor.'

'No, he's Irish just like you.'

'Why just like me?' Tom sat up and watched her picking a shiny stone from the water with her toes.

'He has exactly the same accent as you.'

Muffin brought the bone back muddy and wet through and offered it to Tom who didn't seem to see it.

'Tom!' Laurel rebuked him, pointing at a small dog being ignored. 'Tom, is something wrong?'

'Nope!' He rose and threw the bone into the water for Muffin to retrieve which she did with lightning speed so he had to throw it again. Laurel held her carved book, sniffed it and felt the soft grain.

'And just think I need never open it. And its title is...'she squinted at the tiny letters... 'Laurel Tree'.

CHAPTER 17

The air in the little attic bedroom was so hot and so still that dust motes hung perfectly suspended in the afternoon sunshine long after Bronwyn had shaken out the coverlet on Laurel's bed. That used to be Jamie's bed. She hung the blue brocade dress up in the wardrobe, next to her son's tweed jacket with the leather covered buttons that he'd been so proud to wear at Laurel's age. He'd chosen the air force because of the uniform, he teased her, as much as the romance of flying. Girls liked the pale blue he said, her shy, handsome son. Only two years older than Laurel was now. Girls forever unknown; he must have gone to his death a virgin. She looked at the rows of his books in the corner bookcase; Laurel was reading some of them – was that her excuse not to dismantle the shrine? Here was 'Treasure Island', given to James when he was too young for it. She hadn't been able to protect him from the nightmare of Death coming tapping down the lane to deliver the Black Spot, like Pew the old blind beggar. 'I hear a voice' said he, 'a young voice. Will you give me your hand, my kind young friend, and lead me in?' I held out my hand and the horrible, soft-spoken, eyeless creature gripped it in a moment like a vice.'

Bronwyn was sitting on the bed reading from the blue linen covered book again with tears in her eyes as she recalled those seven-year-old tears. And not just the tears but those dark Arabian eyes in that round Welsh face. She had been mother and father to him but could not prevent him from joining up and crashing down into who knows what sea, what scorching hell of land, Missing in Action.

Now she was as good as mother and father to another young life with the instinct to over-protect as strong as ever. She must resist it. As she looked at the woodcut of the blind man with his stick approaching the inn, there was a loud knock at the front door. Her heart pounding, suddenly recalling the War Office telegram, she ran downstairs. It couldn't be Laurel; the front door was always unlocked in the daytime and Laurel would just walk in. It was Mavis, dear Mavis

Preston, Bronwyn's oldest friend. Black tousled hair and familiar warm brown eyes.

'Look at you, Bron!' Mavis stood in the narrow hallway with both hands affectionately on Bronwyn's shoulders.

'You can't imagine the face on you! Were you expecting a ghost?'

'Maybe.' Bronwyn shrugged ruefully. 'Or I was thinking of them. But you're no ghost, Mavis love. Come on in.'

The two women sat in the same worn easy chairs they'd known since childhood, Mavis automatically choosing the bigger one she'd always had on the right of the fireplace that had been Bronwyn's father's chair, with the ivory crochet antimacassar still hanging over the back. She had sunk right into it in those days. And she recalled Bronwyn's bright-eyed child's face giggling at her as they'd toasted bread or marshmallows on the brass toasting fork in the flames of the open log fire. They had each done support duty for the other, first when Mavis's little son turned out to be retarded, then later, when Rashid had died and Bronwyn returned, pregnant with James, to her father's cottage. She had changed her name to Mrs. Williams on Mavis's advice to stop the gossip. Their boys, so close in age, had played together – James wearing Gareth's hand me downs – and then when Harry had contracted the dreaded cancer, it was Bronwyn who found the books that explained the things the doctor wouldn't.

'Memories are cud,' Mavis's father used to say. He was right, and the two friends chewed over them, reminisced about the men, long gone.

'I've brought this book round for Laurel,' Mavis said when it seemed time to return to the present. 'Met her coming out of the library at lunchtime.' Bron nodded as if she knew, although the truth was that she didn't pester Laurel with questions about how she spent her days, she seemed so busy and contented.

'Been revising, I expect.'

'She said she was looking for the poems of Yeats, but their only copy was lost. I found this amongst Harry's books – won't she be pleased.'

'Yeats?' said Bron. 'Odd – she's done her literature exams.'

'Well. I offered to walk her home, but she said she was going round the long way.'

'Oh, she's a walker, Mavis – out with the dog for hours…'Bronwyn glanced at the grandfather clock with a slight frown. It was six thirty.

'Is she all right, Bron?'

'Oh yes. More than all right, I'd say. There's something about her suddenly; she's blossoming.' Mavis realised that she'd wanted to ask if Bronwyn was all right, she'd noticed something different around her eyes.

'Well, she's almost eighteen,' Mavis said instead. 'She's growing up fast, that niece of yours.'

'And she's happy here. I'm not sure why. I so want her to be happy, Mavis, and to feel free. I want to be a better mother to her than Moira – or a better friend. Is that wrong?' Mavis looked at her closely.

'Why should it be wrong?'

'I don't know… Connor seems to think – but he's an old tyrant really, and he's never watched children growing up. I think she's happy and that's the main thing. Happy and unhappy… is that because she's this age? Suffering from something, because I hear her singing sadly, and sometimes she slips out quite late at night to walk her dog; insomnia or growing pains. I hear her coming back sometimes humming happy songs. A mystery really, the way they change. And Mavis, what a business being a parent, isn't it? Knowing how to get the softness and the hardness right.'

Mavis nodded thoughtfully, still troubled by something but she didn't know what.

'And Connor – is he making you happy, is he good for you? I'm sorry love, but you know how twitchy I get sometimes: must be my psychic Welsh grandmother coming out in me. He's a rum one, your Mr. Walsh. Be careful, Bron.' Bronwyn pushed her hair back and laughed.

'Oh Mavis, whatever would I need to be careful of? Connor is just a big grizzly bear – good for a laugh and a cuddle, but I'm not pinning any hopes of a marriage proposal on that one: anyway, I'd rather share my home with Laurel. I'd rather try and make Laurel happy than Connor Walsh. She's been out on a limb for so long, dragged around by Moira and allowed no life of her own. But she's a good girl just the same, and so affectionate. 'Auntie' she says and almost leaps on me to hug me, and now and again when she's sleepy at breakfast she almost calls me mummy. What do you think, Mavis?'

'I thank God I've got a son, even if he is a bit slow. At least I don't have to worry where he is and what he's doing – though in a way with Gareth I do, too. You know he almost got a job, his first job, as a projectionist at the cinema in town. He lasted one day.

He got so involved in watching the film he forgot to put the next reel on. He just loves the movies…'

'Remember him and James sitting through 'Billy the Kid' three times?'

'And we were worried sick – though with boys it's a different worry…'

'Shh, here she comes.' Bronwyn said. 'I recognise that skipping step. Muffin will announce they're back home.' There was a short bark and a bang as the wooden gate was pushed open and Muffin rushed in. Mavis noticed that Bron was now looking relieved and relaxed, perhaps because of their talk, of the old support system working again. Or maybe it was just that Laurel was safely home.

CHAPTER 18

It was hot. The two men were sitting in the gazebo on the lowest terrace, away from the topiary, both able to look across the water and because the light was perfect they could see the forest clearly and Tom could imagine Laurel being thoroughly feminine, perhaps naked, in his hut, or in the water, or swaying on her branch.

'Do you want to talk about the girl?' Solomon asked.

'Are you leading me, Doctor?' Tom said wryly.

'I want you to talk, Tom. You spoke with a repaired vigour when you spoke of her at our last meeting. As if an appetite had returned, as if you are finding out who you are. And I regret to say there is a bit of pressure coming from above. Certain people want to know when you can be moved on to some assignment, still hidden, but back in the field… they don't understand.

Luckily, I have the final say.' Solomon's eye followed Tom's. He had spotted a chicken hawk hovering.

'If you talk about the girl, Tom, and the effects she has, she might help release the trauma. Warm feelings do release cold feelings.'

'Trauma.?'

'You know the term. Sealed wound.'

'I was interested in the way you pronounced the word.'

'Oh yes, in the German. My mentor, indeed my father, would always say "trauma" like that of course.'

'Disclosure, doctor—'

'Begets disclosure... sometimes.'

There was a long pause. Solomon waited.

'I'm remembering, doctor; hiding with Laurel, hiding from Laurel in the bushes, I suddenly remembered who I'm kept hidden from here. It's the lads I grew up with, my schoolmates. The ones I had to betray. They would kill me if they found me and they'll never give up looking because I'm not one of them, because I couldn't join them, and worse... and it brought a bolt of pain to my gut. I fainted. She found me. She stroked my hair and covered me with leaves out there in the wood – I was shivering. She makes it possible for me to remember.'

'Yes. Talk of the girl if you will.'

'She comes to me every day, almost every day.'
'What does she want?'

'A man like me.'

'Don't pause. Keep talking. Let the words and feelings have free rein.'

'I'm so used to writing. I'll bring you my notes. I write about her. I have no shame about her. She has no shame. Her body is tight. The flesh on the arms and legs and belly. Her belly is concave. want to be mouth to mouth, man to woman, skin to skin, old to young, leg round leg, boy to girl, kiss to kiss non-stop ad infinitum forever. 'Let's not stop!' she says. 'Not yet, not ever!' Then she suddenly jumps up and runs-dances off away down the path as she is or into the lake to wash. Diana – Aphrodite. Then rushing back for bread and wine, and sudden light or deep kisses and I feel completely... real... home... man... happy.'

'What does it remind you of?'

'Happy. Happy and kissing.'

Another pause. Both regarding the arrival of a larger raptor. The chicken hawk taking off.

'Please share the place you've gone to?'

'I'm here, here!'

'Where is here?'

'All right, I'm in Italy. When?' he asked himself, '...50BC. Rome, I suppose.'

'Yes?'

'*Da mi basia mille*... give me a thousand kisses...

Deinde centum... and then a hundred...'

Solomon smiled and started to interrupt and challenge him.

'You wanted the past, Doctor!'

'But you jump into literature and antiquity and prevent our search into your own history and whom she represents therein.'

'She reminds me of no one – she represents only herself.' Tom was angry.

Solomon leaned forward. The buzzard or its prey squealed. Nobody looked.

'*Oh let us live, my Laurel, and let us love;*

And value the talk of pompous old men

At a brass farthing...'

'Go on, Tom...' Solomon urged.

'*Suns can set and return*

For us, when our brief day has gone,

There is the sleep of one unending... Nox...

... Night... Dream... Memory'

'Go on with her. Be present in your past. These literary allusions are... you are angry, aren't you?'

'What about Yeats?' asked Tom his voice calmer now. 'Does that make it present? New poet? Yeats yearning for love...'*and a small cabin build there, of clay and wattles made...*' You want me full of tears, don't you Doctor?'

'I'm pleased with your —'

'Progress.'

'Perhaps. I wanted to say I'm pleased with your return to appetite, with your recovery of lost ground. The detail is a matter of detail now. Lazarus is risen.'

'Does that make you Jesus?'

'No! The girl!...'It's a girl', remember! And it's what this girl can release in you. We'll get there.'

Gulls then appeared calling, and so far from the sea. And there was the General's man moving around the boat on the jetty; the General waving to Byrne then beckoning to Solomon. A handshake, then moves in different directions, both feeling better, clearer, cooler, with rain clouds following the gulls.

CHAPTER 19

The vixen had escaped the hounds. She had got away around the perimeter of the lake, probably across the fields towards the village, then returned to the woods to die. When Tom found her, she was dead. As she was not ripped apart but only infected through the wounds that dogs' teeth leave, he could see that it must have been a slow death. Torture. Strange that she had chosen as that last post, away from other foxes, the tree where Laurel had once worked magic.

It came out of a dare, he recalled as he covered the corpse with leaves and twigs as a temporary grave.

I was lying back on the bed, he remembered, we had just returned from a swim... Tom was surprised at the grief he felt at the sight of this creature curled up at the roots of the tree, not even in its hole... Laurel that day was bustling with water and kettle and tea caddy, having made drop scones for him which she was buttering while telling him about her friend Olivia -

'You'll meet her soon, I'll bring her here.' No! I had wanted to say. But a large mug of tea, three scones and a bar of chocolate had appeared beside him. Laurel had continued, putting down a saucer for her dog, 'Truth or Dare?'

'Both!' I had said… and he smiled as he remembered. He enjoyed reviewing their exchanges.

'Right! Here's the truth question… Tom Burns, if you could get me to do absolutely anything with you or to you, what would it be? She pursed her lips to check a smile, but he knew that she was very satisfied with the question.

'No problem!' he had replied immediately.

'What?' she had asked excitedly.

'You would accompany me.'

'Accompany you?'

'Accompany me on the Schubert fantasy in F minor.'

'Why?' she had sounded surprised.

'Because it is a sublime piece.'

'What is it?'

'A duet. A piano duet. A *pas de deux*.'

'That's a bit dull, isn't it?'

272

'Depends how it's played and I'm assuming we are Schnabel and Margaret Long coming together for the first time.'

'Dare!' she suddenly said,

'Right!'

'Then come into the trees with me!'

Tom was now walking away from the dead vixen, and he found himself making for the area of the forest where the dare had begun. How he loved to recall his experiences with Laurel. 'These I will remember,' he always said to himself, 'when this time has to end.'

'Close your eyes and give me your hand,' she had said as they reached the trees and her hands, soft and young (pianist's hands, he had thought with a sudden fleeting flash of his mother's hands) had taken his. 'And if you don't keep your eyes closed I will blindfold you... I'm taking you to the path... don't talk, just trust me...'

What pleasure to be in her hands, what surrender to time, was the feeling. 'It's dark here,' she had said. 'Green, dark green.' He could feel it and smell it. 'And cool,' he had added.

'Hush! There are orchids here. I came here this morning, just before seven, the sun was already bright. The birds were behaving as if they had just woken, hungry, scrabbling for buds and grubs. I wish I could name more of the flowers, I'm sure you can name them all. But I can recognise an orchid.'

'I've been blindfolded…' Tom had said.

'Hush. You're not blindfolded now.'

'I've been-hooded. A sack placed.' His legs had begun to wobble.

She'd taken his arm again to steady him.

'There's a perfect place to sit here, Burns, it's like a throne… keep your eyes closed while I turn you and sit you down on these roots… there you are. You look just like Tiresias.'

Tom now walked out of the woods looking to see a sign of her on the beach or near the hut, recalling with considerable force the climax of Laurel's little ritual: 'When I take the blindfold off you will find me holding before you an enormous mirror. When your eyes have adjusted to the light I want you to look right into the glass – we were taught to say looking glass but it always makes me think of Alice – look deeply into it and tell me what you see.

'Myself!' I replied, but it was the light that affected my eyes as she pretended to untie and remove the blindfold, her face facing mine… I was dazzled by her beauty. And then as from an epiphany, perhaps my first, in the dark place in the woods bedecked with orchids and light, I saw myself in her mirror. Unimaginable.... Tom would recollect this moment time and again into the future, not in tranquillity but ecstasy.

He swam and fished. He caught his usual perch, gutted and prepared it with potatoes and tomatoes to await her arrival, surprised that she felt late. When she came, she looked strange.

'Come with me!' she instructed. 'Hold my hand. I've been busy.'

'Doing what?'

'Wait and see. Close your eyes if you'd like me to lead.'

'Oh yes!' the sheer pleasure of being taken her way through the trees, through their sounds and scents, crackles, calls, flowers, branches that brushed the face and came with changes of light and shade. The deep cool shade.

'Here's that perfect place for you to sit again, Tom. It's your throne. Keep your eyes closed and prepare a poem or a prayer... please... everything is ready. Only this time you are not Tiresias.'

And this time he peeped.

He watched the tenderness that revealed the hurt she felt at the loss of a small – how small the body of the vixen – wild creature. She laid the little burnished brown body in the neat hole she'd dug.

'Confirmation of death!' she said, her hands on the animal's snout and ribcage, 'Dead!... And I am Persephone the lower depth Goddess who divines that this sacred body has been sacrificed for the sake of the continuation of the wild wood, to the element that contains all the elements, Mother Earth; we commend thy spirit... this is the silent part when the Sky God brings light brighter than the candle I would have brought if I'd known she'd been killed... There, presentation of light!'

The sound of earth on body, earth on earth, he knew it well – he closed his eyes – and expected to hear rifle or bugle salute, but for the first time he heard the real silence of the forest that was deeper than the scent of leaves, the sound of leaves, the breathlessness and fragrance of the girl who stood beside him.

'Your turn, she whispered, and added 'You are Hades the recluse who abducted Persephone but was not all bad. This is Hades out of the darkness on a good day...Go on....'

'*Frater ave atque vale!*' he heard himself say.

'Perfect!... Any more?'

'Trahe me post te! No!'

'Go on!'

'I know a saying from the Portuguese... "a tree that grows bent remains bent". The word is *"pau"* which is almost impossible to translate. Let me see... I do not know much about gods, but I think that the river is a strong brown god...'

'Make up something, Hades... in English.'

'I'll try. Just close your eyes and hold your breath...'

'Yes'

'We will show you the way through this forest death.' She joined in and they alternated:

'Embrace the earth, it will be all right...'

'Though you won't come back you will wake in the light.'

'In the sky there's a tree with a secret door...'

'I've been there myself, but I won't say more.'

Laurel began to clap in spontaneous applause, then turned it into a rhythmic beating which drew a song out of Tom:

'Oh, the sun shines bright on Mrs. Foxy,

She's full of Moxie,

So we'll take her to the Roxy…' which fitted in well with what had now become Laurel's jaunty smiling dance upon the grave.

'This is also a rain dance,' she declared whilst Tom continued to clap.

***

Overnight there had been a storm. An electric storm with branches crashing down in the forest and great claps of thunder. But Tom had slept all through it and right through the dawn chorus as well, waking refreshed in the calm clear morning sunlight. Waking for once without any fear; not the prison fear when he was afraid he was going mad, nor the panic fear from his time on the run when every slight noise was a threat, nor the unbearable physical fear of his torture, nor the everyday dull fear that he would never find contentment or purpose or his real self again.

On this morning, he woke feeling happy then realised he was looking forward to the day. Because of her, he reflected. She had stayed with him the previous night; she'd been able to stay as her Aunt was away. She had held him as he fell asleep and had whispered her secret to him -

'Just before I go to sleep, you know what I do? I give myself a message at the last moment. I say to myself: 'lovely day tomorrow'. Sounds silly, but my Aunt Bron used to say it to me when I was four years old. It worked then and it still works now.'

They were lying like spoons nestling together in his narrow bed, her knees tucked in behind his, her belly warm against his buttocks. Her fingers trailing across his shoulders, up and down the back of his neck, round in circles behind his ears.

'Say it to me,' he urged. 'Not now – I'm awake. Send me to sleep and say it to me at the last moment.'

Of course it had worked for him that night and the next morning. He had his girl there. They'd breakfasted together and he'd felt wonderful.

But on the night of the storm he was alone. He was tired and aching from dragging his firewood in out of the impending rain. He remembered her secret message and tried it himself as he fell asleep. And it had worked. Even though he'd woken with a strained back, sore muscles in his leg and that familiar tremor in his damaged right hand as he tightened it round the lid of a new pot of honey for his toast, he felt happy.

He planned his day: some reading, some walking, finding wood, writing, working on his boat project, cooking a few vegetables and doing the exercises he's been given by the physical instructor. He would sleep well again. If he could plan just one day, perhaps he could start to think about the future without dread.

By mid-afternoon, having written in his journal, eaten his vegetable stew flavoured with wild sorrel and collected wood and had a nap, he was preparing to go out for a long walk when he heard a pigeon call – she was here in the wood blowing their conch shell to attract his attention and he hadn't expected her till tomorrow.

She arrived like a whirlwind at his door, full of plans. No dog today. She grabbed his hand.

'This forest is not the world!' she declaimed. 'Where's your sense of adventure?'

'Where are we going?' he heard himself ask, regretting the words at once, they sounded anxious. The truth was that he trusted himself with her completely.

'Let's just take some apples and cheese and bread and something to drink – and no questions.'

They set out in a direction never explored before, away from the lake and right into the dense centre of the forest. 'How far can you go into a wood, Tom?'

'Half way?'

'Good man. Because then you start coming out. So that's what we'll do.' They tried to follow a straight line regardless of the lack of any paths. Brambles and creeper had to be pushed away or stepped over. Laurel's hands were more scratched than usual. He felt exhilarated, sometimes panting to catch up with her as she slipped like a wood nymph through the trees, sometimes having to step in and help her or lift her over when a branch proved too tough to break off.

The sun was getting low. He was not worried about finding the way back, and gave it no thought. They stopped in a clearing for supper, finishing with a mug of wine from the bottle he'd brought. Then they hurled their apple cores at an oak branch but neither scored an acorn.

They disturbed a rookery, found an owl hole. Laurel claimed she saw an eagle. He accused her of being drunk. Then suddenly, shockingly, the trees ran out. There was a wall. Over it, the brow of a hill. They'd come to the end of the forest and the beginning of something else. Laurel walked along close to the wall feeling it with her fingers. Too high to climb over. He followed.

They walked towards and into the setting sun, going westward. She looked determined to find a way out. He was in her hands. He wanted to tell her how well her secret message had worked last night but decided to respect their silence. The trees beside this wall were very old, mostly oaks. Some elms.

'Look!' called Laurel, 'Our way out!' She had found a fallen tree, a tall old dead-looking oak, top heavy with layers of encrusted ivy. It had toppled over in the storm revealing its roots and had smashed down a smaller tree and a section of wall where it now rested like a sloping ramp, invitingly.

'It's snakes and ladders, Tom. Here's the ladder. Up we go.' And she pulled herself up with handfuls of ivy, almost disappearing in the tangle of branches as she scrambled to the top of the wall. He followed her, using his good left hand to grip.

'Now what? – we jump!' she cried and disappeared down the other side. As he leapt it occurred to him *how will we get back in here again?* but he dismissed the thought, knowing it would be met with impatience by Laurel.

They were on an ancient path, wide and grassy, leading up round the side of the hill. The trees here were sparse. Many had been cut down years before leaving huge root stumps like low tables, rotted away in the weather.

'Where are we?' she asked, awed. 'It's a graveyard for trees.'

'It must have been an old logging track,' he said. 'This was once part of the forest, before the wall, but they cleared it. Perhaps hundreds of years ago.'

Laurel peered down into the hollow interior of a tree root stump, and hooted.

'It's vast, like a grotto. It echoes. An army of rabbits could hide out in here.'

A big sweet-chestnut tree lay uprooted amongst the fallen warriors. One branch was still alive and grew up at right angles to the trunk. It had become a new tree.

'Look at that cheeky chap!' Laurel laughed pointing to a long-dead blackened tree trunk beside it that looked like an old man lying there with one knee bent and one arm sticking up into the air. She was touching a shorter piece of branch also sticking straight up, but farther down the body.

The sun was really setting now. The hill ahead was golden red, its flat top scattered with fallen trees glowing.

'I know this place!' Laurel almost yelled. 'I've been here. My cousin and I used to come, in the holidays. It goes on over there to the moor, *Mynnydd Illtyd*. We came badger watching, years ago. It's Badger City, Tom! Let's watch for badgers!'

He looked around and sure enough, in every group of tree stumps, amongst and underneath the massive old dead roots were the scraped-out holes with their piles of earth, stones, dead leaves outside, the litter heaps. Now he could see that the whole hillside was criss-crossed with red earth tracks between the trees. No farming here, no sheep or cows, no people. Badger paradise.

'Did you ever watch badgers, Tom? You have to sit downwind as still as a rock until way past dusk. Cuddle up to me, here's a tree trunk to sit on. I'll get cold.'

It was almost dusk already. Tom sat beside her, his arm round her shoulders in their thin shirt. He had his jacket at least. He took it off and wrapped her in it. He blinked, suddenly realising: what did he think he was doing? Outside the wall, no way of getting back tonight, his girl going home alone in the dark across a moor, no food. Wine, though. She giggled as he carefully poured out a beakerful, unable to see what he was doing in the shadows. They shared it and then a black and white head popped out just beside them, looked around and popped back in. The first badger. Then they all came tumbling out, the young ones first, larking around like puppies, then an old fat one, puffing, disapproving, lumbered right past Laurel's foot.

He sat tight, holding her, looking at these shy creatures, so relaxed, unable to see them by their tree trunk. The smell of warm girl in his nostrils, her hair against his cheek. Girl hair. -Sarah! Remembering: his sister's name. His older sister, sitting close up to her adored little brother, badger-watching. Telling him to be quiet, shivering, he sharing his jacket, his sweets. Protecting her. Protecting them. She had loved him. But why had he forgotten her name? Was she dead? Had he wronged her in some way? Had she forgiven him?

'Look,' whispered Laurel, 'look at him, Tom!' A small badger was rolling over and over down a slope. Two others followed, giving squeaky little grunts. 'That's badger for 'look at me, mum!' said Laurel. She shook against his shoulder with silent laughter. Alive. The fact of life. He gave a sigh, happy. A badger stopped, raised its head, stared straight at him.

'Sshhh!' she put a finger on his lips. He kissed it. She leant up to his face. He could hardly see hers in the darkness, but he could feel her lips as they met his own.

CHAPTER 20

'Can I write something in your Diary?' Laurel asked. She was about to clear his table, then cook and serve eggs and wild shallots in the way he had taught her. 'I'm supposed to say "may I?" not "can I—"'

'You can. But I don't have a Diary.'

'I won't read it.'

'Solomon reads it. It's just a notebook.'

'Solomon Grundy?'

'The same.'

'I just want to make my mark in it.'

Tom moved to the door, looked out, breathed in the smell of woodland, closed his eyes and marvelled at how he had learnt to love the dark forest. He went out to take a walk along the lake.

Laurel sat at the desk, looked up and considered that this was Tom's view each day as he wrote; their lake, half in shade, half in sunlight, curving like a rounded sickle moon. This is what he sees at night – she closed her eyes – the full moon on the water. 'Ah moon of my delight,' he'd once said to her; no, he had sung. She had laughed. He had stopped.

Now she wrote: 'Once upon a time we went to our glade... The light was lifting the leaves. There is a word for what I saw. 'Sacred' is the word. 'Do you feel it here?' I asked Tom when we were really looking at the moon. I was holding my tummy not knowing how to tell you how happy I was. 'That's where I feel everything,' you told me.'

Laurel put down the pen, but then she added a PS: 'I'm going to put one of my special shells in the lake, near the little pier.'

***

'Well,' said Solomon, after a considered pause, 'we're inside. The rains have come. It feels quite different, being in the house, as if these walls have ears.'

'Have they?'

'Not so you'd get hurt, Tom, believe me. Come and sit down.' Tom moved from the French windows he'd opened a fraction to smell and hear the rain. In rain he had woken and rushed outside hoping to meet Laurel, only to find the boatman, someone new, who waited in silence whilst he dried and dressed and then rowed, with effort, boat and men, across the lake through a heavy downpour.

'And the Marx Brothers…' Tom sat, then lay back on the sofa. 'I meant to tell her I adore, I worship, the Marx Brothers. As much, just as much as beloved Laurel and Hardy, especially *Horse Feathers*… and now…' Tom's hesitation, Solomon could observe, was not resistance but a deep anxiety he was struggling to bring to the surface.

'It might turn out to be too late.'

'Why should it be too late?'

'I'm aware of the pressure to get me operational. I might be lifted soon. I may not have time.'

'I've told you, Tom; not yet, not against my orders.'

'I know; I have to get better, completely better, to know who and what I am, till I can be a man among men again.'

'Though if there were to be any whisper, any report reaching the ears of Security.'

'That my tormentors were on to me, even here…'

'Even here… but I have to say we are well hidden. How are you feeling about all this?'

'I have to say I can see why I might hesitate to recover.'

Solomon looked rueful. 'I can see the danger of falling in love.'

'Yet I must recover, for her sake too. That's my conundrum.'

A long silence followed in which they both listened to the rain beating on window, roof and earth. Both slipping into private thoughts until Solomon asked, looking at his watch, 'Are you ready, Tom?'

'I was running a preview…. 'I've not seen the Marx Brothers!' she might say; then we must do it, I was thinking, even if we have to go to London to catch them. 'When?' she says with impatience and adds… When can you leave…. or, when must you leave… only she doesn't, she doesn't ask … This child, this woman, this slender almond-eyed mature impossibly young creature doesn't pummel me with -'

'With what?'

'Do you know any Irish poetry? I mean, before Yeats?'

'Does this matter?'

'I remember two opening stanzas.'

Tom stood and moved to the bookshelves beside a long teak table used for meetings. 'I feel I've stood here before. Right here, like this.'

'You have!'

'I'll sit: *"I was sent adrift on the waves of the world, Ochon! Ochon! All for the sake of the yellow-curled Slender girl that I wished my own."'*

Tom stood again and although he walked to the windows to stare out, he turned back again to recite to Solomon:

'*I wandered East and I wandered West, Ochon! Ochon!*

And never saw sloe-blossom white as her breast... I can't, doctor.'

'Tom! What are you trying to permit this poetry to say for you?'

Tom sighed deeply, then searched for a direct statement.

'Laurel throws the most wonderful pieces of puzzle for me to unravel... but shall I tell you one?' he sounded uncertain.

'Tell me what you want to say, Tom.' Solomon urged. 'I regret, as per always, we have not enough time. Something to do with Laurel, not so?'

'Yes, Yes!' Tom breathed at last. 'I know what happens when they snatch...'

'Come, come, Tom ~ you mean when it's time for you to go.'

'No. When they snatch. That's what I meant. When it's time to move, I shall just be moved on. But if I'm discovered, by whoever is after me…for they will be after me… then I shall be snatched.'

'Extremely unlikely, Tom. Let us say that eventuality is not part of my calculations.'

'But it's a quick job!'

'You know this?'

'Belgium; another Intelligence snarl-up. It's a thorough job. The Ops Room boys plan it and practise it on paper till its move perfect – a kind of Bridge/ Chess game, only played out, when it comes to performance, by the real thing: Sappers. They don't only whisk me away but every single sign of me. *Tutti*! Total disappearing trick. Not a sausage, not a whisker, not a whisper will remain.'

'Well, Captain Byrne,' said the doctor, 'That would at least mean that no shadow can fall on the girl. That would make her safe.'

***

It rained for three days and it fell with such force that it kept Tom and Laurel apart for a while, although the little dog made a visit to Tom's hut on one occasion, as if to check that he was surviving the storm. Time for analysis…

'I cried last night, doctor. Alone in my hut. It seemed like… for the first time.' Tom paused. 'I remember…' Solomon waited.

'You remember—?'

'My mother. She had an expression… but this was so long ago. Hardly relevant.' He fell silent. Solomon waited again, then said, 'You've never remembered your mother's words before. This is good, Tom. Can you go on?'

'If I fell and hurt myself, she'd say, "big boys don't cry… until the blood turns white". I must have been three or four. I can remember waiting and waiting for the blood to turn white. Very strange. I can hear with a great certitude of… what?… of sense… her voice, low warm mezzo, slightly accented, perfect for *lieder*, and the tone is more important than the words. But the words, like… "You are my little soldier, Thomas" are fairly harsh. She is teaching me piano, and I'm singing a duet with someone about waving corn, summer, and she is saying "This is Handel! This is not Rossini. We want no *portamenti*. Perfect control. No wobbles. Breathe from here!" She is holding her diaphragm; I can see her hands with long fingers and gold ring and emerald. I can't get her face. Did I ever look into it. Did I love her too much? What colour were her eyes? "Never look into the eyes of a cat!" she would say. We had dogs... so I was a singing soldier who wanted a cat.'

'So, then what happens?' Solomon's kindly, gentle probing as they reached a bench with a view right across the lake to a beach, a small clearing and a grey shape which was his hut.

'What did happen at that moment was... Laurel's dog Muffin who was asleep at my feet came and licked my face till I laughed aloud, then climbed happily under the sheets beside me. No girl there, just her dog.'

'We must walk back,' Solomon urged. 'This is good, but General Ashworth wants a word with you quite soon'

'About?'

'He wants to see for himself the progress you've made. And it's about to rain again'

Tom finished his cigarette. 'My mother smoked. The long fingers have a faint stain near the nails sometimes. There is cigar smoke and a cigar box in the house, but I can't see my father. I didn't argue with my father. He cared passionately about things. So... but I cannot see my father yet.'

'Don't look too hard.'

'There's a wind coming up.' They entered their usual room through the big French windows. 'This room,' Tom looked around at the leather chairs, the wood kept polished by someone, the flowers arranged in a tall vase. 'It makes no demands on me. I have no obligation to these things,' Tom fingered a leaf on one of the dahlias that was drooping, 'so I can relax here. And perhaps with the girl it's the same.' Tom frowned, looking surprised at his own insight. 'So I can let her in.' He took out his cigarette case, put it back, hunted in his top pocket for one of the cigars the General had unaccountably started sending over in his weekly supplies. But he'd left them in the hut.

'Don't smoke again,' Solomon said, 'It prevents you releasing some of your -'

'I think... I kept women out, before. Or let them in partially. At a price.'

'At a price?'

But Laurel came charging in rudely without knocking ...or paying. She never asks about the price. Or the future.'

He stopped and stared out of the windows, watching the wind blow the ash trees about, making their leaves sparkle.

'You haven't asked either, Tom, apart from envisaging your removal.' A silence.

'May I lie down, doctor?'

'Of course.'

'She doesn't ask, though she may guess that there will be a price. That there won't be a future. Will the General come along here when he wants to see me?'

'He will ring.' And Solomon indicated the Victorian bell hanging up near the ceiling beside the door frame. Tom lay back on the sofa adjusting the cushions.

'Are you tired today? '

'Yes. A sleepless night, that's all.'

'Dreams?' Solomon asked with interest.

'Talk. All night long. After three days' absence… just chit chat, laughter, games, stories…'

'Tell me one.'

'Let's see…' Tom tucked his hands behind his head and looked at the high vaulted ceiling. 'You know, I love the danger of falling in love,' he said.

'We must consider, Tom, that the greatest danger in all this could be not to you but to her.'

'She told me last night that her progenitor, travelling mother whom she calls Moira, despite consigning her to school and Aunt Bronwyn, would invite her suddenly to join her – when she had a whim or suitable accommodation. And Bronwyn would pack a bag and a picnic and put Laurel on a great puffing train, as she described it, which went from Swansea to Paddington. She told me about the greatest … yes I'd asked her, 'What's one of the greatest treats you've ever had?' – we were asking each other questions all night, her aunt was away so she stayed till morning. She's a lot like you, Walter, only not so patient, much more direct and directive – '

'And working the therapy without any doubt!' Solomon nodded.

'Take a taxi from Paddington to the Theatre Royal, Drury Lane. Ask for Moira Sherborne at the stage door. The Stage Doorkeeper's a dear old man called Arnold. He'll know where I am.' The mother's instructions… and the child found mother and latest boyfriend in the nearest pub. A glass of ginger ale and then an American musical with real Americans dancing and singing just like in the cinema, she said. Then supper in Soho and a drive through snowflakes to Hastings in the new boyfriend's longnosed Humber… we raced, Tom! She said, and next day, Christmas day, we walked on the beach at Hastings and we had a view from the hotel of little black net huts and fishing boats and the gulls didn't mind the bad weather at all. If it hadn't been for Victor le Roux – the boyfriend – it would have been complete perfection, she said.'

'Nothing wrong with your short-term memory, Tom!'

'But she brings such… she's got what the Welsh call *Hwyl*.' 'How do you know that?'

'I read.'

'Of course… you've never lived in this part of Britain before.'

'No.'

'So.' Tom could hear that Solomon was leading him now and he wondered if a preparation for talking to the General would begin, then was surprised by the question, 'And what stories do you tell the girl?'

'Laurel. Please call her Laurel … she asked me what was the worst thing that had ever happened to me…'

After a long pause, Solomon looked at his watch. There were footsteps in the great hall outside the study and from above them.

'What did you say?'

The bell inside the study jangled. 'Go on, Tom,' said Solomon.

'She was holding my wrists at the time, enquiring about the torture, but what came to mind was the feeling of terror, no, of horror, without any form or detail, of a man being crushed, deliberately. Killed.

'Feeling responsible or guilty… then the face, quite clear, of Sarah, an enervating feeling of sadness and of the mystery – which I now recognise – of being loved, plus the pain of this love being connected to the death. Confusion in my head as to sequence. Which comes first, the love or the death, the death or the love?

'"Tell me please," Laurel is pleading, "I want to know." Then seeing something in my eyes as she looks right into them, against my mother's advice, "No, Tom, don't! Tell me instead about the worst encounter you ever had with a member of the female variety." So I made something up, very silly, and we laughed and laughed and then we played a game called True or False in which we had to tell a story so well the other wouldn't know if it was made up or not.'

'Who starts these games?' Solomon asked.

'This time it was me.'

'Do you ever wonder, Tom –'

'– Why I play at lying… yes. It's a useful game to be good at when you are being tortured. And I was good at it. I was tortured twice, you know – I know now, I've been telling Laurel. First for revenge but then for information. I have forgotten the physical details, but doesn't the shock of torture wear off, Doctor? I feel there was something else, worse than torture. So, what am I hiding? Did I give information? Did I give names? Who did I betray? There is a part of me that is not at peace. It seems to be in hiding like a wilful child.'

'In hiding from —?'

There was a long silence.

'In hiding from myself,' said Tom quietly. Another brief jangle of the bell. 'I feel exhausted,' said Tom.

'A good moment to stop,' Solomon said, standing and nodding to indicate that he was now going to allow the General to enter.

CHAPTER 21

How did we make this arrangement? Laurel wondered a few days later as she stood tip toe to push a letter into the damp hollow of the ancient oak that Tom called her tree. Who thought of it as our secret place? Who suggested we have a hidey-hole for our secret messages? Was it Tom? Was it me? 'Was it you, Muffin, you little monkey?' she asked her dog who was scrabbling and whimpering, trying to climb the roots of the tree. One of us started it, and it's maddening and it's lovely not to know which of us it was, or when. Perhaps it was the day of the storm when I couldn't find him. I had a stupid panic; something had happened to him; I didn't dare leave a note in the hut where his army man might find it. We had to have a 'safe drop' we agreed. 'Stop it, Muff! This is a secret place. No one must know.' The dog stopped and stared at her.

And that's how it remained. A secret place. Secrets exchanged secretly, not all of them written.

***

Tom had been splitting logs all morning using the metal wedge and a thirty-pound sledge-hammer until the top of his arms and shoulders ached. They would probably be useless tomorrow.

With his returning energy – which so delighted him – he had developed a series of morning rituals, getting up and out of the hut when the full dawn chorus became irresistible, doing exercises for his weakened ankles and the tendons in his feet, stretches for his spine, some wood chopping for his cooking stove and for the sheer physical joy of swinging his arms, and then having a quiet period just watching the lake and the birds and the sudden splashy eruptions as a fish broke surface here and there in search of breakfast.

Then boil a kettle, cook an egg, cut some bread for himself.

But he rarely got the balance right. He might sit and gaze immobile for two hours or more not realising he was hungry or that his knees were getting stiff.

Or he would start to swing the massive hammer or the felling axe and get into a rhythm, relishing the whole business of muscles and sinews and engrossing physical work that quietened his mind. But then he'd still be chopping and swinging and stacking without a break when it was time for lunch and his muscles were screaming. The next day he could hardly lift the axe.

He'd been splitting oak logs for a couple of hours when he heard the creaking of old pram springs as Laurel carefully pushed The Roxy Dansette Portable Gramophone and its box of records into his clearing.

'What's that?'

'Music Maestro! She called. 'What do you want, Souza, jazz or John McCormack? We have them all.'

'Amazing. Are you an angel?'

He flung aside the axe, rather too hastily, and tried to help her lift the gramophone. She noticed his grimace.

'It's not heavy!' she had the other handle and they staggered to put it down on the flat log in the sun where its polished walnut gleamed. He stroked it with a tired hand.

'It's magnificent. I've been chopping too long. Not fit. Should have stopped earlier.'

'You know you always say that. But you never stop earlier. Never learn. You're so… excessive. Hopeless! Let's lift it onto the bench and get it going.' They took a handle each again.

'You're sounding like my mother.'

'Careful. If I hadn't spent all this time and energy bringing this machine to you, lowering it over the wall, getting stung, I'd just drop it right here and chase you into the lake for that.' Laurel opened the brass catches at the side and raised the lid. It was lined with padded maroon silk. Then she unlatched and swung round the shiny silver horn until it clicked into place.

A Souza march was on the top of the record box so on it went and she unfolded the brass handle with its wooden knob with a ceramic ring on the end and wound the mechanism up. The band struck up at full volume. The trees reverberated. She marched around the clearing, flourishing a stick, laughing. Tom sat on his favourite log and watched her until the tempo started to get slower and the instruments lower and Souza growled along at a snail's pace and finally stopped altogether, mid phrase.

'Rewind, bandmaster!' she called, the stick under her arm like a Field Marshal.

'Not now. Come and sit on the log. Better still, bring my scissors from the hook. I need a haircut. I've been avoiding the Army barber. I want you to do it, I'm sure you can.'

'Oh yes. I'd love to. I'm something of an expert. Used to cut Ollie's at school so I know all about layering.'

'That's it,' said Tom happily, 'whatever it is... I want to be layered by you. And nobody else but you...'

She stood behind him with the scissors and looked at the back of his neck where the hair seemed to curl up from the bottom as well as down from the top.

'Shirt off!' she ordered. The sun was warm on his back. He rubbed a sore muscle in his arm.

Laurel started to touch the back of his neck and across his shoulders between his shoulder blades, lightly with fingertips, up the sides of his neck along the 'guy ropes' of muscle that held up his head and that were aching now. Her smooth fingers skimmed along. They brought their own heat and electric charge. It seemed to be absorbed straight into his marrow, drawing off the pain and ancient tension that he tried to erase by chopping only to succeed in increasing. Her fingers were the solution. As easy as that. How could he prolong this moment? It was bliss. He sighed.

'Don't stop...

She was humming quietly under her breath, and he could feel her swaying slightly from side to side as she stroked.

'Don't you want to know where I got the gramophone?' She was now gently pulling his curls straight, ready to be trimmed.

'Mmmm. That stroking was so good...'

'I know you think I broke in and stole it. Well, I did break in again but there wasn't a gramophone. I managed to resist the pressure cooker I found. In fact, it came from the market, yesterday.'

'You paid for it?'

'Aunt Bron. I made a fuss, so she bought it for me. It wasn't much. They threw the records in free.'

'You give me everything I want. What can I ask for that you can't get me? But what about you, what do you want?' he asked her.

'I want... oh, what do I want? Got everything. I want – to see into the future. No. I don't want that. Definitely not.' She sounded serious and concentrated on snipping off a few more curls. 'I know what I want…' she said suddenly. 'I want you never to ask me about my mother.'

'I never have.'

'So you haven't. You don't ask questions about my past, do you? That's why I feel free here.'

'A free spirit' he said.

'A tree spirit!… Keep still. Now move a bit round, that's it. I have to concentrate. I'm not used to hysterical curls.'

'So who can I ask you about?' he said.

'You're welcome to ask about my father… go on… because I don't know anything at all about him except that he was in the Army and is probably dead.'

'That's what they must think about me.'

'Your parents?'

'My mother, my sister…'

'Where are they?'

'Back in Ireland.'

'That's where Connor comes from. Auntie's boyfriend.'

'Connor…' Tom's voice sounded flat. She moved his head to one side.

'Now keep still. I don't want to cut your ear off.'

'Who's this Connor?'

'I told you – Bron's best beloved. With an awful sister, Zelda. 'A regrettable woman' as Moira would have called her.'

She carefully snipped the close hairs behind his ears, down the skin of his neck. He trembled.

'Are there lots of Connors in Ireland, Tom?'

'Yes. And I knew one of them once. But no Zelda. Good job too; he'd have been trouble.'

'Trouble for you? Why?'

'It has to do with revenge.'

'Would this Irish friend harm you, Tom?'

'Anyone can harm me just by knowing I'm alive and here. What I do know is that I'm supposed to have died in Germany. I think I'm being hidden from people who might want revenge. What I don't yet know is who they are and what I did. So we all just have to keep mum.'

'Oh, I know – 'Careless talk costs lives' – but the War's over now.'

'For some. But apparently not for me.'

'What about Ollie? My friend Olivia, you know. She's coming to stay in the holidays. Next week in fact. I wanted to bring her to meet you. If I swear her to secrecy…?'

'We'll see!' his voice almost sharp.

'Can't the Army keep you safe?' She touched his wrist.

'You'd think so. But they bungled it the first time, during the war. They promised to lift me out. They didn't and I was caught and held… and… well, they don't want to make that mistake again.'

'What did they do to you?' She narrowed her eyes.

'You've seen!'

'Your back! I've seen your back.' She touched it gently. 'And your wrists… at first I thought those marks were your watchstrap.' She took his wrist. 'Two watchstraps. They're too deep, those marks.' She placed the fingers of her other hand on his lips. 'And your ankles. They're like chain marks… they hung you up, didn't they? Chained you and hung you up… tell me?' Her hand still covered his mouth.

'They must have hung you by your hands and by your feet and they must have beaten you. They tried to crucify you, didn't they?' Tom shook his head. She dropped her hand.

'I don't really want you to tell me.' She had stopped cutting his hair. She brushed the curls from his shoulders.

'What were they, Nazis? Was it Germany? Tom? Was it Japan? Was it in France? Was it us, was it the English?'

'Us…' his head dropped. 'I don't ask you questions,' he said.

'But nothing happened to me, just you. And you're always asking me questions.'

A deep sigh.

'It was Ireland.' There was hardly any voice.

'Tom?'

'Yes. It was Ireland. In Dublin itself they held me. A respectable suburb. A small bungalow. The back kitchen; I don't want to know this. It might not even have happened. My memory…' he tapped his head and shook it.

'That's where they tortured you! I don't understand.'

'Nor me.'

'The Irish?

Tom was silent, gazing ahead as if he could see his torturers' faces. In fact, the only face presenting itself to his memory, in reproach, was his beloved father's.

'Did they take pity on you after a while?'

'No such concept. Four days, four solid nights, slow focking death. Yes, crucifixion!' He opened his clenched hand to show his wrists.

'These still don't work as they should.'

'But you rose again!'

'I don't know how.'

'And they work much better, now,' she took his hands and placed them on her breasts.

'I can't recall how I escaped.'

'Oh Tom! She raised his arms. 'Let's dance. We've got the music now. I'm sorry about the questions.'

'No, I've got to know. I think I've got to know.'

'I've brought you jazz. These records. Your favourites with their funny names: Satchmo, Django, Bix what's-his-name Boodlebeck. Don't laugh!' But she was dancing on her own as the gramophone scratched its way into the opening bars of the Royal Garden Blues.

'Besides, you look so kempt and … as they say in the movies, cute. They always dance at the end of a movie.''

Is this the end?' Tom stood up. Laurel immediately took his hands again and stood on his boots. 'Imagine my taffeta dress Tom, close your eyes… we are at the famous Forest Ball by the lake that is so exclusive we are the only couple invited. The only human couple.'

Tom, much bigger than Laurel, was nevertheless once more in her hands, taking her lead, feeling her breath, feeling her rhythm, eyes closed, calm returning. She reached her chin up towards his, knowing that he would sense this closeness and kiss her as was always done at the end of movies, whilst the strains of a cornet bounced bell-like, sharp and clear, from tree to watching tree and across the lake.

***

TO: DR. WALTER SOLOMON, BEAUCHAMPS HOUSE. BY HAND.

Dear Dr. Solomon,

I think the principle upon which you work is that we search for the moments when my mind seized, pry them open and release a great wad of gangrene.

A cleansing catharsis will leave me with a past which will inform my future and enable me to live as I did, only more conscious, and of more use to myself and to others.

And so through a variety of means, which take great ingenuity and patience on your part and not a little curiosity too, you prod my great mud wall hoping it will crack, let out rot and let in light. It's the opposite to the way the priests have worked throughout the history of the Church I think; perhaps its provenance as a method lies in the great argument traditions of the Talmud. Freud like you was a Jew. But the Irish, you know, are the Jews of Europe. And England is Rome.

Analysis works best when you befriend me. When we talk, when you seem to listen, as a friend. It was as if you were not so much listening as looking. I think now of something one of the old Popes said about filling the churches with paintings so that those souls who knew not the letters could nevertheless read the story on the wall. I'm sure you understand. The least important part of me wants to confess that I know which old Pope, to seek reassurance that my mind is working as it did because I say 'Gregory X111'

Or, my father smelt me smoking in the attic when he came back from the Great War on a Thursday in 1918; blind, but wanting to fold, pack and store his Inniskillen uniform. So what?

Friendship at its best is love, and love is the comet. Love is the cure. Love is the miracle. Love is Thomas a Kempis's God. Love is limitation. The essence of every picture is the frame. Her frame is her …I don't know the word. Can I paint it?

Oh, let me be simple. Walter, stop the search. Let me simply stay unconscious in the woods with my wood-nymph. Give me an intermission. Solomon Grundy, release me on a Monday!

In your wisdom you can prevent my being torn apart. On the one hand, that trained part of my brain and conscience that pulls me back to duty. I understand the command completely and it is easy to act upon.

But deeply mysterious is a pull from a primitive part of my brain informed by the whole of my body which compels me to go inconsequentially, irresponsibly AWOL

Like the soldier, pinned fatally to a tree by an assegai. 'Does it hurt?' they asked. 'Only when I laugh' he replied. Only when I love, Dr. Solomon. Do you know what the child, as you call her – ensuring that I remain Telemachus to your Mentor – the girl who, by the way, is really Athene in disguise, did you know? – said to me: 'Jane Eyre is the most beautiful book ever written, even more than the Bible and Jude the Obscure both of which I don't understand, and it's full of good and bad people and moral lessons, but it is about all kinds of love and Jane is so wise. Do you know what she says at the very end, Tom? Do you remember?

'No,' I say.

'You do!' she says.

'Tell me,' I ask. We were busy finding and picking mushrooms. She'd been bending then she stood and made me look at her, her eyes wise beyond her years. Has she suffered – I don't ask – like Jane Eyre, Laurel Williams?

'You are not your wounds, Edward!' That's what Jane says.

I think those are her exact words.' That's what she told me. And I am not, Walter. I am not my wounds. I am not. Therefore, I am not bound to know whence they came.

This woman is my salvation for she reminds me whence love comes.

'*Tell me how love comes...* some poet wrote, I don't know who...

It comes unseen, unsent:
Tell me how love goes...

That was not love that went.

I don't think I knew this before, that love, as Thomas a Kempis told me before I was ready to understand, that all love comes from God. I wish I could remember his words exactly, not that you would be impressed by that. Fluency never impresses you, Sir. You have found more value in my fragments of dreams; more than the dreams fully recalled with no effort in the telling.

I dream now of water all the time. I see lilies in water, great carp in water, my mother's face in water and even myself, moving like a porpoise without purpose but to catch the wave.

I want to marry her by Woodland ceremony. Then I'll be well. I thank you and respect you always.

Tom B.   L6742119 (I remember this).

***

Dearest Ollie,

I've been putting off writing this letter, that's the sorry truth. So you haven't heard from me for weeks.

I've put it off because something has happened so unexpected and secret and gorgeous with my man in the Forest that it seems to have filled up all my time and most of the contents of my head.

Oh help… I can't bring myself to say it or write it down. But you can guess, Ollie! You'll have to guess.

Who would have thought after me writing all that smutty stuff at school that when the real good bright thing comes along, I'd get into such a pickle trying to tell my very best friend!

Now I can just see your head on one side looking at me, as you do, and wondering 'Is Laurie going to be all right here? Will it end in tears?' Well, the thought has occurred to me too – for all of two seconds. It only briefly flitted across the back of my mind. Then it got pushed out because the truth is, dear Ollie, that being in love – which I suppose I am – doesn't leave any room for negative thoughts like that to grow. They just wither away.

So strange: it's like playing, and we do all the time, but it's serious too. He's years older than me and who knows what he went through in the war, yet it's as if he's my younger brother sometimes – or my father – or my son – or, most often, my identical twin. He knows so many things, but I seem to have some answers he hasn't even thought of. We know the same songs and the same nonsense rhymes.

When I go to see him in his hut there in the woods, sometimes we don't say anything at all for two hours – just chop wood or fish in the lake together or light a fire or cuddle. And it's the best conversation I ever had. I can't tell you about the cuddles yet, haven't got the words ready. Maybe words come a long time afterwards, I don't know. But it's all right, Ollie. I'm all right. You mustn't worry about me.

I've been wondering though: all those great love stories, you know, the ones we read in our last year – Anna Karenina, Romeo and Juliet, Madame Bovary, Tristan and Isolde, Antony and Cleo... when you think about it, what happened to all of them? Death, tragedy, destruction. No happy endings for lovers there. Perhaps because they were written by men? But they can all stay on the bookshelves as far as I'm concerned. Happy endings, the Future, they're all unreal.

Only each day seems real, the little shack in the woods, and being with him. There's no more to say about it. I feel full up and empty at the same time.

So, I will love you & leave you for now. Write soon. Tell me all your news. And remember – you're the only human being on earth who knows about this. Apart from Tom – that's his name, and even that is a deadly secret. I can trust you with it.

All love from your best friend,
Laurel.

PS: Myfanwy – alias Muffin – is an honorary human although she crossly denies it, and she knows and loves him just as much as I do.

CHAPTER 22

'I'll tell you a truth or three, Mr. Tom Byrne, without your bidding, and neither or any of them are in any way revealing. They just popped into my head. I think I loved Ollie more than anyone before I met you, and I think she loved me. I love Auntie of course and even Mum too in a funny kind of way when I don't think of her as my mother but just as Moira. Ollie is my sister really. And we both loved a girl at school who was a prefect and the only Indian girl who ever came to our school, named Deepa. Isn't that a name? Deeper than the blue-black sea was the depth of her thick long hair. Who wrote that? And Ollie has a brother called Stephen who does weird things with his Teddy bear, like hang it. He's only seven. Ollie says he was sent away to board too early. What do you think? And I prefer feet to hands. If I did a painting of Christ on the Cross, I'd just do the feet. People would be forced to look up, to want to see the face. Deepa had the softest eyes and softest voice you ever saw or heard in your life. And to think Miss Clarkson made her a prefect. She was useless. It was wonderful. Half the school had a crush on her. What are you doing? You're always tidying this place up. What's to tidy? Are you listening to me? Did you have a Teddy? Have you ever had an Indian girl? Do you believe in Christ?

'What is this?' Tom turned, pretending to be fierce; 'Truth or Dare or something?' Laurel giggled and kicked her legs up from the bed at him.

'Feet,' he said, 'I prefer feet, yes.'

'Then tell me what happened to yours.'

'No more words. Let's play no more words.'

Laurel clamped her lips together, knelt up, moved towards him and, having waited to see if he would break the silence, felt his lips with her forefinger. *These are the softest eyes*, she thought and closed her own.

Her face pressed into his chest.

'Oh Tom, I don't like being blind. I'd hate to have to live in the dark. You lived in the dark, didn't you, like this? Only you were alone…'

Tom opened her eyes gently with his fingertips and whispered, 'No I wasn't. You were there.'

'No, I wasn't.' She hugged him again, putting her arms right round him, squeezing, slowly rocking him. As if they had time.

'You were on your way.'

'Perhaps I *was* there.'

'You were. I summoned you up in the dark.'

'That's what I do Tom, when I get into bed alone in the attic and I hear our owl. I think of you lying here with a hundred owls and I summon you up, like you showed me.'

'And here we are.'

'And where we yesterday?' Tom asked ten minutes later, resting from their caressing.

'Yesterday,' Laurel replied immediately, sitting up as if to leap into the next activity, 'Oh you remember Tom.'

'Remind me.'

'We just drifted about.'

'Did we?'

'Pretending to be fishing. The weather was perfect for fishing.'

'What did we say?'

'You said a lot of nonsense.'

'Did I? What did you say?'

'You'd been talking about Iago and Othello and quoting; no, you were singing underneath your hat, "I believe in a cruel God" you were warbling away – Shhh, I said because you were really loud – "who created us in his own image".'

'I wonder why I was singing that?'

'Oh, it's just opera isn't it? You weren't serious. You looked perfectly happy to me… as you do now.' She quickly tickled his ribs.

'But I think I started you off because I was telling you about my aunt and her boyfriend having an argument while she held a ladder for him to clear some guttering. She knows her Bible and I don't think Connor does.

She was talking about measuring. 'With your measure it will be measured unto you' she quoted, and I asked you what it meant precisely. Then you started singing and I stopped you, not just because of the dreadful noise you were making, but also because I realised that Aunt Bron was talking about God being just. A just God is what she would believe. Then you changed the subject. I think you often do when I mention Connor.

'We must always be able to do this,' Tom now said.

'One day we won't have to. All our days will have run into each other without any interval. You won't need to test your memory, Tom. "Fock yesterday", you'll say, "Everything is one long today".'

Contemplating this sense of dreamtime they almost fell asleep again, till the sound of a sudden shower on the roof and window brought them back to where they were and Tom said,

'Sing to me.'

'I don't know any opera.'

'Sing what you sang to me yesterday.'

'So you remember that?'

'You said it was your favourite song. Sing it again!'

'But I don't sing in tune.'

'It doesn't matter. I like your tune.'

'But I had your hat over my face.'

'Then close your eyes.'

'Slowly, slowly she came up' Laurel whispered, paused, then sang: 'And slowly she came nigh him. And all she said when she came near, 'young man I think you're dying…'

'For love of Barbara Allen.' Tom concluded the song.

CHAPTER 23

'Why does she never ask about the future, Doctor?'

Tom lay back on the leather sofa, hands clasped behind his head, watching a bumble bee at the big French windows whirring its wings repeatedly against the glass. There was a waiting silence from Solomon, a silence also from Tom who knew that these questions of his rarely produced an answer but merely another question.

'Why do you never ask about your future, Tom?'

The bee was now banging itself frantically against the window.

'She wants to be with me – she's fascinated by my past. Yet doesn't ask about what's going to happen tomorrow or the next day. She tells me everything. I don't have to ask. And she's so supple, she's got rubber bones. Bends and bounces all over the place like a Swedish gymnast, except sometimes she might stand on her hands deliberately to let her dress fall back, a spontaneous child, an enticing woman. She told me something so sweet the other day, half confession, half challenge. "Once I thought I was a lesbian," she said, sitting swinging on her tree.

'"Lesbians wear chains on their ankles, don't they?"

'"I didn't know that,'" I told her, putting down my whittling knife in case I cut myself.

'"Oh yes," she said. "Olivia and I found a book on one of her father's shelves which Ollie felt too embarrassed to read on her own… anyway, she and I used to practice kissing in her father's study. We were rehearsing for this."

'"For what?" I asked, and she pointed at herself and me, saying nothing, waiting for me… like you're waiting for me… like I'm waiting for you.'

A silence followed and tensions returned. 'Is she afraid of my answer?'

'What would be your answer?'

'That I don't know. I really don't know, and I don't want to know.'

'Because?

'Because I don't feel good about it… no, don't say it – I'll tell you why. How can I feel good about a future when it's out of my control? When I can't make even the simplest plans. I can't take her to see the desert as she asked, or even to the local cinema. It's all an illusion. I'm a marked man – I might as well be in prison. And I don't even know which bloody side I'm on! Don't look shocked... no, you're not.' His voice, which had been rising, sank back now to his usual quiet inflexion. The bee was now creating a rattling sound as if it had found something else more substantial than its wings with which to beat against the glass.

'How long, Doctor? If you know something you must tell me!' Tom became aware that, although he was no longer shouting, his knuckles hurt. Both fists had been tightly clenched for some time. He must have been angry. Solomon waited for this realisation fully to sink in. Then asked,'Are you angry with me?'

Tom sighed. 'I don't mean you must tell me, of course. Just that I wish you would tell me although it's possible that you don't know. How long do I remain hidden away?'

'You're avoiding my question, Tom.'

'You're avoiding mine, Doctor.'

'Perhaps I have an answer for you, but I'm interested in this emotion of yours first.'

Tom watched the bumble bee, spinning dizzily out of control, plummet to the floor. He started taking slow, deep breaths. Taking control of himself again.

'A decision has been made. It seems the misinformation about your death has reached the desired ears.' Solomon began when he felt Tom was calm and listening. 'In another few weeks, when this has been fully confirmed, you could be deemed to be out of danger. In that case, you would then be able to be free. But I must warn you, Tom,' he added quickly, almost sternly, 'that this is confidential. I should not be telling you. I am breaking every rule, as army officer, as medical psychiatrist. Also, it is entirely provisional. If anything changes... you understand?'

'Yes, Doctor. Thank you. Of course I understand. I am grateful.' Tom exhaled; it seemed he had been holding his breath. 'I'm not about to go delirious with false hope. 'Hope' is not a word in my vocabulary these days.'

'But 'love' is...' said Solomon gently.

'Yes. Perhaps that's why you told me? And maybe a whiff of hope did waft in just then while I wasn't looking.' Tom took out and lit a cigarette, looking over at the doctor to see that he didn't mind.

'By the way, you will keep your journal securely hidden, won't you?' said Solomon.

'From Laurel? Why? I trust that girl completely.'

'No, not from Laurel. "Trust" is also a new word in your vocabulary, isn't it? And it's doing you a lot of good. I meant from any of the Army chaps. Griffiths – anyone in fact who reports back to the General.'

'You report back to the General yourself, don't you Doctor?' Tom was sitting up now, smiling.

'You understand that as one of my jokes...' he went on.

'I do. And thank you for your trust, Tom.'

'I keep my journal well hidden. A different place each time. Sometimes I forget where I hid it myself.'

'Good. Our time is up now. I'll see you next week.'

The two men stood up and shook hands, but Tom, who was suddenly powerfully reminded of his father, realised that he would have liked a hug.

There was a pause, and then he received it in kind.

'Your letter, Tom... your last letter...' Solomon had lost his fluency and Tom listened intrigued. 'The letter you sent to me which had your number written... L 6742119... is that correct? ... it touched me. Yes. It was so instructive to me, as a psychiatrist, of course. It was of such benefit to me... yes, I mean it, Tom...

professional benefit. We too suffer from the great malaise, unconsciousness.

But what it was that touched me was how you were not only able to talk about, indeed to know about, what it is that makes a human being well again, but also to demonstrate it in the very personal way, and therefore, because it is you, the poetical way, of challenging me-by convincing me of the importance of the woman. Yes, I am shying away from the word 'love'. It is a love letter you have written, albeit once removed because you cannot tell her just yet … or perhaps ever… and the dream imagery at the end of the letter is indisputable evidence that you are every bit as well, psychologically, as … for example, I am. Don't be alarmed! …I shall not tell the General.'

There was a long pause. Tom shook both his hands.

CHAPTER 24

They had shared with each other favourite bits from books they were reading, then worked on making a rod for Laurel to fish, then walked in a direction they had not taken before through the forest, finding ancient oaks which Laurel now recognised as Durmast not English oaks; taller, straighter and more 'gracious' she thought (but edited out as it was a favourite word of her mother's). Whilst they walked, hand in hand if space allowed, she observed how he glanced from side to side as if expecting to find someone, except the eyes searched undergrowth and low branches, rather casually. She didn't like to ask him what, or why.

But, after making love, lying on him because the moss felt damp, she immediately entered into the questions and challenges of their Truth game, their way of using time even more intensely, until he fell asleep... and a little later, trying to coordinate her heartbeat with his she rolled off him onto his arm, fast asleep already.

Laurel dreamed that she was lying in a large leaf floating on a lake with some kind of hidden force pushing her along from beneath the water as if she had a motor. 'Where am I going? Where are you taking me?' she asked, half alarmed. 'Back to the forest' came the reply in what sounded like Tom's voice, but from deep beneath the surface. And when she woke up, Tom was snoring in a muffled way that sounded like a motorboat slowly chugging or a voice beneath the water. But she felt quite afraid in case the dream was saying something about avoiding leaves, lakes, men like Tom. She believed that dreams carried meanings, perhaps warnings. The fluttering down of a long-stalked leaf, green and grey, distracted her and she busied herself turning the fissures in the bark above her into a pattern.

Thus, she fell into sleep once again until Tom stopped snoring and his breathing rhythm altered.

She woke feeling lonely and uncertain, with the man so near, why the dream had disturbed her so. I'll ask an impersonal question-she searched then trusted what popped into her head; 'Do you play tennis, Tom?' Then she asked aloud; 'What does deuce mean?

Where does it come from, 'deuce'?' 'Duo… Duos…
Two.' Tom's eyes stayed closed. 'But why at forty-all?
What does it mean to suddenly say "TWO"?'

'There are two clear points to get to win. Or to lose'

'Ah!' she sighed, felt relieved, and opened one
of his eyes with her fingertip. 'Burns, can I ask you
something?' She was suddenly alert again and alive
to where they were, lying under trees in dappled
sunshine, the weight of her head on the top of his
bare arm, the weight of his leg across her naked thigh.
Her voice more serious now.

'If you were hanging upside down, how did you
eat?'

Tom screwed up his eyes, maybe against the light,
maybe the recollection.

'I didn't'

'They never gave you food?'

'It was water I needed most. No, they didn't.'

'So they couldn't have cared less if you died! They
wanted you to die. And they were Irish, too. I don't
understand… what had you done to them?'

Tom gave a deep sigh.

'It was wartime – or rather, not their war: over
there we called it "The Emergency". Some of my
friends were lining up with the fascists. Planning to

help Hitler win. So, I did something very difficult. I had to. It could be called betrayal; it was.'

She stared at him, leaning up on her elbow.

'How did you *wee?*' she asked in a whisper.

'Don't think about it. Don't talk about it now.' He moved his hand across her brow.

'You'll never have to experience such… black… such darkness. God willing. At your age I didn't know about evil, either.'

She flicked open her eyes.

When Ollie comes to see us, I want you to wear something when we bathe.'

'You want me to cover up?'

'Not now. If we swim with Ollie. She might get the fright of her life.'

'…If Ollie sees any of me, Stan; if she knows about me at all…'His old anxiety flashed back, in spite of himself, in spite of her.

Dear Ollie,

I want to describe to you the most exciting day of my whole life.

We decided not to speak, not a word. It started with a dare… he dared me not to speak for half an hour, and he didn't speak… and it went on and on… and we began pointing at things, and ended up pointing at the wall, and over the wall.

We had walked into the forest to the tree where he keeps a great big conch shell and then we took the deer track through the thickest, oldest part of the forest to the far end of the lake where the General's hunt was going to start off after their glasses of whatever they drink… we hid in the trees and my man made the most amazing horn sounds on the conch and when we saw that the dogs and horses were taking off before the humans were ready and in the wrong direction we hoped, we took off too.

We spent the day playing this dare game of pointing at things without saying a word and some of the things we pointed at were precisely the sort of things you're not supposed to point at, never mind speak about, look at, touch, play with, enjoy.

Can you imagine the fun, Ol? Can you imagine playing a really exciting game that feels even more exciting because there are no words to explain it away or to ask or apologise, with someone you feel absolutely devoted to?

And the best was last. Shall I tell you? Okay. Just as it got dark, I went home, spoke to Aunt Bron, said

I was going to the village to see Owen and his sister (and I wasn't lying, not quite.) I phoned Owen from the phone box and asked him to lend me his bicycle which he was only too happy to do. Meanwhile I'd pumped up cousin James' old Hercules bike and took both bicycles to the forest. Then we escaped, my man and I, over and under the wall, and we cycled – him in disguise of course in one of James's caps and a big coat – towards the town. We cycled all the way keeping our heads down for the odd car that hooted and passed us or stopping in the hedgerow. Once we stopped for him to wee in a bush by the roadside. Lovely.

Penorth has got twisty narrow streets and we cycled around, me feeling quite scared because I'm a bit known in the area and people are very nosy and my man is not only persona non grata, as I've mentioned, but he isn't supposed to exist.

But he was full of the joys of being away. We even rode into one of the main streets, Cardigan Street, which is very well lit, and we dismounted because he wanted to look at the architecture of the old museum which used to be the jail or the courthouse. He also said if we didn't find the Castle ruins we would go into St Martin's and kiss in there... there, I've said it. I didn't really like the idea because churches give me the creeps, but he told me that he'd always fancied the idea of shenanigans in a church when he was a boy because it was wicked. So, I reminded him that these weren't Catholic churches so it wouldn't be the same for him.

We were walking, well disguised of course, through a bit of town that is mediaeval, across the old toll bridge, and he was telling me about the famous Welsh regiments and the heroic battles they had won Anyway we were nearly late for our film.

Guess what? It's his very favourite picture because it's really psychological, it explores dreams and deep places of the mind and also it has Ingrid Bergman and Gregory Peck in it. I don't know which of them I like best. Am I a lesbian, do you think? Ingrid Bergman is definitely my favourite actress now, and she's his too, and I'm going to see all her films. Wait till you see 'Notorious' he says. But oh, Ollie, although the film twists and turns and you keep wondering who's good and who's bad, it all ends up at the station with a lovely journey about to begin, with a kiss... and of course we were kissing and touching all the time in the back row of the Coliseum... 'Spellbound'.

Did you guess?

And I made it ALL UP! Did I catch you? Well, I made up the bit about leaving the forest with Tom. I actually persuaded Aunt Bron to take me into town in Jamie's neglected old Morris to see that movie and had fantasies all the way. But one day we'll do it, and it will be just like my fantasy. He'll be free and we'll take a taxi and stay at the lovely Castle Hotel, luxury, and then go to the station, just like in the film, and kiss and set off and travel to the ends of the earth.

I'll tell you more, much more, when I see you. And when you see him.

Love from Laurel.

PS. If you are not really interested in men yet, I might mention that we have wonderful teams that plough in the season, great big muscular Pembrokeshire horses, on our next-door neighbour Mr. Morgan's farm. The boy I went to the dance with, Michael, keeps them in good order, though if you smile at him and show an interest in his horses, he will certainly fall for you: I've discovered that he has a strong interest also in pretty girls.

***

'Jaysus, Zelda!' Connor roared, beating his palm down hard on the steering wheel. 'Will you shut up in the name of all the saints and martyrs.'

'What?' his sister replied, glancing at the stump of his middle finger, feeling a shuddering in her abdomen for shouting always reminded her of the burden of being the older sister, knowing she had gone too far and must stop... but couldn't.

'Don't you dare raise that cantankerous tone of voice to me! Muzzle it right this second!' He stopped the van so abruptly that she had to brake herself on the windscreen.

'You go on about Bronwyn Williams like a banshee record stuck in a groove,' he growled, containing his anger for he saw she was trembling.

'Always giving me the old cod about her. Well, I am too old to marry, woman, and what is more to the point she is too wise. She has no hidden intentions, as you call them, no idea we have the family farm to return to. Farm? Two acres. She has no interest in Ireland whatsoever, will you get that into your thick skull? She's got her own place here. She's never ever asked me why I'm here and not there and not returning and not pining. If I told her why I was lying low, she would shrug and say 'you be careful boyo.' She lets a soul be.

Even this errant Laurel girl that has been landed on her has been spared the third degree and given the benefit of the doubt, the run of the place and the freest rein imaginable. She believes in liberty, woman, to such an extent that she errs in the direction of license where this child of the theatre is concerned. Her religion is irrelevant so will you shut your trap on it. God and marriage are as far from her mind as the Orange king and the union of all the island. What a woman wants is a man who will give her a warm cuddle and a good laugh. And a man needs someone understanding to drink with and talk with, for fock's sake!'

Connor leant across his seething sister, knowing she had received no message whatsoever except his displeasure, wishing her back in County Clare, regretting having invited her to Join him here on his mission when her 'idiot Brendan' had blown himself up, and now wrenching open the battered van door.

'We all choose our comforts, goddammit! Get those nasty canine beasts out of the back, stop them whining, beat them if necessary, take them for the longest walk you can and if you see this Laurel child walking her little mongrel, you report back to me this evening, with any other unfamiliar things going on in the woods.'

'And just how do I see over the wall, then?'

'You keep your ears open, for a change, and your mouth shut.' He glanced across at her, sensing a complaint forming on her deep crimson lips.

'Shut… except to berate those dogs when they foul up this small corner of the great British Empire.'

'You gave me a terrible shock, Connor,' she wanted to say, 'braking the car with such violence.' But instead, she wound her scarf round the back of her neck, kept her dark kohl-rimmed eyes on his and remarked: 'It is going to rain, Con.'

'Good. Get the dogs washed.'

The foot revving up the engine drowned her indignation and Zelda hurried round to the back of the van to release her cairns from their temporary prison. They rushed out barking with the delight that only dogs know while Connor sped away about his business.

CHAPTER 25

The surface of the lake was like brown mirror-glass in the morning sunshine. Tom sat at the desk by his open cabin window and watched Laurel floating motionless, face down, trying to see the bottom through a pair of ex-Navy goggles she'd found in the market. He was writing on his pad his notes for Solomon after a peaceful night, falling asleep with her wrapped in his arms and waking to find himself cocooned inside her.

The evening before he'd grilled trout for their supper with some ugly looking boletus mushrooms with spongy yellow undersides which turned dark blue as Laurel sliced them up for the frying pan.

'I'm not eating these! I've got my whole life ahead of me!'

'So, you won't mind if I eat them and perish, because I'm older?'

'Tom! Don't be silly. They must be poisonous… things that turn blue like that…'

'Just you get on with the slicing, woman, and leave me to decide on the menu. It's my kitchen.'

As they sat together on his bed afterwards with Laurel amazed to be still alive and privately relishing the word 'woman' which he often called her, sharing the last of the wine, he said:

'Doesn't your aunt ask where you go, these nights?' He hardly ever asked her about her life.

'She's out some nights herself. She stays at her boyfriend's place, so she doesn't know about me. By the way, you're a brilliant cook.'

'Don't tell me that intuitive Welshwoman doesn't guess…'

'I suppose she does know about me really. But I want to believe she trusts me to be safe, so even if she did know… Tom, she never even asked me why I was expelled from boarding school.'

Tom smiled.

'I love to think of you being expelled from school. It puts us in the same battalion.'

Now, as the morning sun burned hot outside, he saw her pale naked bottom like the reflection of the moon on the water. It started turning from side to side as she struck out across the lake.

'It was one of your lot,' he wrote in his pad for the doctor, 'some German poet – Rilke? – who gave a definition of love that I respect among all the detritus clustered round that fly-blown word: 'Love salutes, touches and protects the other's solitude.' She does that, Doctor, this girl. She touches, salutes and lets me be. And so I am liberated and able to be alone with her without feeling the walls of my prison cell closing in or the pain in bones and sinews of my torture. I can write it now, Walter. I can talk about it, to myself and to her and to you. I don't tell her much, but I don't need to. And memories keep coming now like faces in a crowd. I just look at them and pass on. They don't seem so important. Though there are still hidden areas connected with certain smells, certain foods, and with some moods of the lake and the weather that bring on the panic still and I don't know why. My dream last night involved a circus. Curious. I will tell you about it on Thursday.'

There was a shout from the water. Splashing. He looked up. Laurel was a long way out. She waved. He leant out of the window and shouted: 'Careful! It's very deep there, very cold. Careful of cramp!' She shouted something he couldn't hear and splashed again. He hurried out of the hut leaving his boots by the door. She was coming in towards him, towards their shore of sandy mud and small pebbles. Face down, snorkel up, kicking with her strong young legs. But his heart was still banging too fast. He waited on the edge of the shore. As she approached the shallows, she stopped kicking and just floated slowly in, her arms hanging limply beside her motionless body. He couldn't bear it. He ran into the water giving strange little groans and seized her under the arms, pulling her roughly up through the shallows until she lay on the beach. He slapped her back, he turned her over, knelt astride her, put both his hands together flat on her chest and pushed down with all his strength. Then he cupped her mouth with his and blew. Pressed her chest again, hard.

His eyes were shut in anguished concentration, so he didn't notice hers were open, looking up at him with a mixture of amusement and surprise. He blew and pressed again. Her ribs were hurting.

'Whoa!' she managed to gasp.

'What's that!' his voice cracked out sharply.

'Whoa!' she repeated weakly, in between his rhythmic pressing.

'I saved a man once during the war,' Tom said, coming to and looking down at her with an odd expression.

'I pulled him out of the sea – he came from a submarine – a big fat man. He was half drowned. You are weightless. You are shivering. *'Wo bin ich?'* he muttered. Quite a shock. *'Wo denken sie?'* I managed to ask him, this German *Oberleutnant* something or other. *'Starnbergersee?'* he asked. His head… his head was bashed on a rock, confused, bloody. We must get you dry…'

'I'm all right… tell me more. Where were you, Tom, what did you say?''

'No, the Irish Sea, I told him. I thought it was a mistake he was there, on our shore. But no, it was planned. Forged papers… Jesus, Mary and Joseph, girl! I thought you were hurt, I thought you were drowning, here, in our lake.' She heard a soft, long groan. 'Don't ever do that again!'

'But how else do I get you to sit on top of me?' She tried to tease but he didn't laugh. He rolled off her and lay still, covering his eyes from the glare, or a memory, with his arms

'What did you do, Tom?' she lay on her side looking at him.

'What did you do in the war?'

'Something...'

'What?'

'I did something wrong, perhaps. I think I... can't... quite... get it yet.' Tom's voice sounded distant, flat, automatic.

'Come on, then,' she was up like a Jack-in-the-box and in the water, diving fishlike, disappearing, reappearing.

'Mermaid,' he thought, despite his nervousness. 'Defiant creature!'

'Come on in, son. If you don't climb on a horse once you've fallen off, you might never ride again, Ollie says.'

'You ride, I'll watch.'

'I won't let you!' she replied, rushing out, her body gleaming in the sun. But she stopped. There was fear on his face.

'God knows what he has to remember,' she thought, and subsided beside him.

'Do you know this one,' he said at last, but not able to look at her.

'Which one?'

'It's coming... just a moment... just getting my breath.'

'I was inspecting the bottom, you know, Tom; floating, not drowning...'

'Shhh... *A mermaid found a swimming lad,*
Picked him for her own,
Pressed her body to his body,
Laughed, and plunging down,
Forgot in cruel happiness
That even lovers drown.

Later as they lay drying out on the grass, she remembered it was Saturday morning, her aunt was returning home and had promised to take her on the train to Cardiff to buy new clothes.

'I must go! Where's Muffin?' Muffin was nowhere to be found.

'Off chasing rabbits,' said Tom.

'She'll be hours!

'I'll keep her safe in the hut till you get back, I'll be here,' he said, marvelling at how good it felt to say 'till you get back' like that. As if she belonged.

'Just don't leave the country!' she called as she raced into the hut for her clothes.

***

Walking quickly along the road with damp hair, she realised that the car coming behind her had an engine sound she recognised. Connor's van. Connor and Aunt Bron, no doubt. It was too late; they must have seen her. She walked along whistling till the van drew alongside. She waved cheerily. There was just Connor inside.

'Morning, Laurel.'

'What a piece of luck, Con! You can give me a lift: please! Legs tired. Where's Bron?'

'I don't know. She went temperamental on me.'

'You haven't been a beast to her, have you Connnor?'

'You've got the wrong man. Hop in, girl.'

'It's a great day for a walk,' she said once she had climbed up to sit beside him.

'Looks as if you'd been for a swim.'

'Yes, I did decide to just have a dip in the river. So hot.'

'Well, you're walking a long way round from the river. Where's the dog?'

'Oh Muffin – probably asleep – didn't come… hey, Connor, have you seen *Wuthering Heights*?'

'It's a turgid book.'

'It's a great film though. I just love Merle Oberon. She might not be a good actress but she's so beautiful as Catherine.'

'She betrays her class. That story is all about betrayal.'

'Betrayal again?'

'Think about it.'

'It's not about betrayal, that story's about love – passionate love,' said Laurel firmly.

'And what do you know about passionate love, madam?'

'Well… I suppose… well, I have read Antony and Cleopatra…' Laurel's voice faltered but soon rallied. 'So what do you know about betrayal, Connor?'

'*Sancta simplicitas*!' he said fervently, 'What don't I know! I've lived it, my girl, not just watched the movie.'

'Are you political, Connor? Oh, of course, you're Irish. I forgot.'

'The Irish never forget, Laurel. You'd better remember that. We're like elephants. That could be our problem.'

The van braked and pulled into the grass verge.

'Here we are. I'm dropping you off at the end of your lane. Oh, and by the way, Laurel…' his voice had become hard; 'before your Aunt gets home maybe you should change into your own shirt. Goodbye.'

Laurel looked down, startled. She was wearing Tom's khaki army shirt with the three pips of his rank on the shoulder. She looked up, but Connor had already driven off.

CHAPTER 26

Drawing maps had always been one of Laurel's favourite pastimes on a rainy day. She'd drawn highly imaginary maps of towns when on tour with Moira, putting in the theatre, the pub, the pier, the pie-shop, and any place that had taken her fancy, plus neat little representations of tunnels, caves, bunkers, ammunition dumps, pirates' lairs, and always an X 'to mark the spot where people will least expect to find the treasure.

She drew a map now for Ollie in anticipation of the longed-for visit and filled the page with places she was fond of in the village plus items represented by symbols (and a key) which she knew would make her friend giggle. Beside the post office was a nightclub. In the crypt of the church was a brothel. Cinemas were dotted all over the terrain which included an oasis, an airfield, a tropical island and an arrow pointing to 'wooded area off the page where X marks the spot where Gregory Tom Peck resides. A dead secret between you and me and Muffin who you also have to meet.'

Bronwyn, catching a glimpse of the map being folded into an envelope, embarked on the dreaded conversation as to where or whether Laurel would continue her studies once the summer was over.

'You must make up your mind, girl!'

'I have!'

A brief argument, a chase-the-ball game across the garden with Muffin, a hasty re-hanging of sheets and towels on the washing line, then a walk to the post office as the sun came out as if there had been no rain at all.

Waiting for her aunt after posting her letter, Laurel looked at the boys hovering on their bikes outside the shop where she knew Bronwyn would have trouble breaking away from Mrs. Edwards' latest piece of news. She waved hastily at Mike whom she'd been rather ignoring since the dance. He was driving past in a tractor full of feed bags. Owen she spotted too, wearing his Scout uniform and looking a bit embarrassed that she'd seen him in it.

She was in fact impatient to get to Tom, imagining him fishing or carving or keeping his notes, imagining the curls at the back of his neck as she crept up on him sitting at his table. She walked past Connor's little shop without looking in but she heard his gruff voice:

'Where are you going to, my pretty maid?'

'Aha!' said Laurel, 'Come here, Muffin!'

'Where are you off to then?' He stood in the doorway fiddling with a small wireless that he had taken to pieces.

'I saw you three girls sneaking into the village, trying to avoid your friends.'

'We're going to see a film later on, me and Bron.'

'Just the two of you? No room for me?'

'You wouldn't like it Connor. It's about Romance.'

'Oh yes,' he laughed, 'Like your *Wuthering Heights*. Is Merle Oberon in this film as well?'

'I'm not saying. It's a secret.'

'A secret! Have you lots of secrets then?'

'We're going into town if you must know, Mr. Inquisitor, and the leading actress is not my favourite but everyone else's favourite.'

'Never heard of her!' Connor kept glancing up the street lest Bronwyn avoid him again. 'Where's your Aunt then, girl?'

'Guess… she acts with her eyes closed, sticks her chin in the air and warbles her voice like this: "I vunt to be alorn". Swedish accent that.'

'Wallace Beery!'

'You're getting warm.'

'Charlie Laughton.'

'Not so pretty. Anyway, it's a wonderful film and the leading actor is my favourite and it's a love story set in —'

'I give up.'

'Greta Garbo in Anna Karenina.' She pronounced the name carefully.

'Now that's about betrayal if ever there was,' he snorted.

'Oh Mister Walsh what's the matter with you? Come here Muffin! It's one of the best love stories ever. And Fredric March is wonderful!

'He is betrayed, the husband! The child is betrayed!'

'It's Anna who is betrayed. Her husband neglects her and the little boy. And worst of all she is treated wickedly by her lover!'

'Lover. Does your aunt know you use words like lover?'

'And I suppose you wouldn't be able to understand Jennifer Jones as Madame Bovary. You'd say, Oh that's just a story about betrayal.'

'Isn't it?'

'It's about love, Connor, and-what else?... Courage.' Connor's dark eyes seemed to get quite black, the colour of his eyebrows, as he almost glared at the girl in his doorway.

'That's what betrayal is all about, the betrayal of love...' he told her sombrely, 'love of someone or love of country.'

'So what is a film about love of country, then?' she asked, teasing, provoking, not entirely serious; 'Ninotchka?'

Connor cleared his throat, turned away, thought to spit, searched his pockets, pulled out his Woodbines and matches, put down the wireless, lit a cigarette, inhaled, then replied, 'Ninotchka? With your least favourite actress?'

'Yes, I know, and with—'

'It is about a woman choosing frivolous love and there is betrayal in the writing and the directing as well; these so-called artists turn a serious revolution into a romantic Hollywood comedy!'

'But Russia... Oh Connor, you've gone all – what's the word? – look how Muffin is staring at you. You've lost your sense of humour!'

'I have not!' this was almost barked, and Muffin growled at him from between Laurel's legs.

'Look at your hands. You're crushing your cigarette!'

'Where is your aunt?'

'Why do you smoke?'

'Never you mind! Don't change the subject.'

'Anyway, aren't you married? Weren't you married once? Aren't you a Catholic? And why aren't you living in your own country if you're always going on, as Aunt Bron says, about the importance of Welsh Nationalism and what we should do here?

Muffin pulled on the leash.

'Also, what's happened to your nice friend Milo who used to come to visit you?'

'Why do you ask?' This time he sounded really angry though his voice was low. Muffin cowered and whimpered.

'What's the matter with this little runt?' He poked at Muffin with his boot.

'Don't do that!' she checked herself, looking up the street, hoping Bronwyn would appear. 'He was nice, Milo. I called him Horlicks. He was friendly and funny and he just disappeared.'

'That's what people do.'

'Did he go back to Ireland?'

'Of course he did!' the voice was sharp still.

'He told me that on a clear day you can see the mountains of Wicklow from Wales.'

'I didn't know you talked with him. Do you know any other Irishmen?'

'Why are you so cross? Insulting an innocent dog and —'

'I'm not! It's hot. Where's the rain gone, girl? It's supposed to bring relief. The beer is terrible in this country, has anyone ever told you that?'

'With so many things making you fed up, Connor, I don't know why you stay.'

'Nor myself.' He plucked at his eyebrows.

'And you're not even very nice to Aunt Bron these days.'

'Ah no,' he softened, stamped out his cigarette stub and picked up his wireless. 'No, no! That's not like you, Laurel, to be so… wide of the mark. I would never do anything that I thought would cause any distress to that woman. Not at all. I am not cross.'

'What is it then?' she asked sincerely. 'What are you Connor?'

'I'm a bit fretful, that's all; everything has been rationed too long.'

'Yes, that's it. It's the rationing of the Bushmills.'

'What do you know about Bushmills?'

'Milo used to drink it from a funny long oblong bottle. He kept it in his pocket. He gave me a swig.'

'Swig indeed. You're a scallywag, you are...'

'Scallywag?'

'Rapscallion then.'

'What about varlet?'

'Have you taken any more swims in the river of a morning very early, young lady?'

'I'm off; I'm going to trundle off now!' Laurel made a move from the doorway then turned to say 'You should go to see Fredric March in *Dr. Jekyll and Mr. Hyde*. That really is about betrayal, Mr. Walsh.'

'Mind how you go, girl!' Connor laughed as if to reassure her but also because he had caught sight of Bronwyn coming towards them at last. 'And try to keep away from—'

He didn't finish, and she wouldn't have heard for she ran now, hair flowing; it had grown in the weeks of knowing Tom, smooth and fleet as Artemis, he said, the goddess of the chase and the forest.

***

Solomon allowed a silence that reverberated for almost half an hour in which the faint creaks of the old house, the fluttering of birds amongst the vast mauve wisteria on the walls outside, distant footsteps on the gravel somewhere, a gardener's cough, horses hooves, were all heard by him as his concentration on his patient wavered and his thoughts flitted back momentarily to Eastern Europe

'Are you on your own, Walter?' Tom's question came loud and clear. Solomon looked away towards the French windows. 'Why do you ask that?'

'Well now, I am quite sure you can work out what theory is behind the return of a question.'

'You mean it is not just a Socratic device?' 'I am not a teacher, Tom.'

'Is your return of the same question a way of indicating what you, I believe, call a projection of my own state of mind?'

'Are you on your own, Tom?'

'By the way, you are a teacher, Walter; and I believe I was a teacher too, in a very different field, once upon a time.'

'And so what is a teacher?' Solomon asked.

'A person – I think – who elicits questions... No, I do not feel I am on my own, at the moment.' Tom rose from the sofa, moved to the windows then returned to lie back, as if fully to enter into analysis this morning.

'In the future...' he went on, '...My God it's going to be hard without her... yes.'

'Because...?'

'Well, I'll have to give her up, won't I? I know there is a whole new young woman's journey ahead of her, children, a family, a conventional life perhaps. I am no longer impotent, but I am probably infertile. And a fugitive, always perhaps a fugitive... Yes, I will be on my own. Your turn, Walter...' Tom turned round to look at his analyst who was sitting at his desk, arms folded at the elbows so that his fingertips were just touching his lips. Then he rose; his turn to move towards the windows.

'I am trained, Tom, to turn all personal questions around, and even on their heads sometimes, but never... in fact to disclose nothing.'

'Not even if disclosure begets disclosure?'

'Why do you say that?'

'You said it to me once, and Laurel has taught me that it's true.

'My wife disappeared. She delayed leaving Budapest. She managed to reach Cologne, I was told, of all places. She was determined to finish… imagine… her research into children's language.'

He returned to the desk, rang for coffee, and Tom knew that this was as much as he would divulge.

'Thank you. Laurel calls you Solo Man. Walter, you know all about it. We have got to help Laurel if she needs it. Please.'

'You feel responsible for her.'

'Yes, Yes.' Tom sat up. 'And you are, too. We are, both of us. Who said – I can't remember —'

'To love is to tame, and we are responsible for what we tame.'

'You have my promise, Tom.'

'You're breaking all the rules today. Not that she appears tame. But the heart… the heart… oh why have you disinterred my heart?

'So, it's you we're really worried about!' they both laughed. 'No… something must be done for her.'

Another long silence while they waited for the coffee.

'You have made a promise Walter.' A bell rang. There was a loud knock and General Ashworth entered.

CHAPTER 27

'What are those bright pink flowers right over there?'
Laurel was sitting up, Tom half lying on rugs and
cushions after their lunch. The General's man had
brought fresh local salmon and asparagus grown in
the kitchen gardens at the big house.

'Rhododendrons.'

'You're just saying that without looking.'

'There are some things that I know... in fact
I've been there and seen them. Massive bunches
of blossoms on big old tangly bushes planted last
century. They spread like mad.''

'I feel like going over there...'

'I tried to swim there once.'

'Let's go!'

'No, we can't. You'll be seen.'

'Ah. Your Army guardians in the big house. Your
girlfriend on the brown horse.'

'Chestnut. I've seen her in the distance. A haughty lady. Never speaks to me.'

'Of course, you've not been introduced to her! Neither was I to you.'

'So, you see I do get about.'

'So, you see I do know how to behave. But Tom, you don't go anywhere… except in my fantasies.'

'I don't want to go anywhere.'

'Aren't you wondering about where you are? And what's going on? Why don't we take a walk to the wall where I climb in? The outside world starts there. You could peep.'

Tom lay back sighing, heavy reluctance weighing down his limbs. Soon enough, he thought, I shall be over that wall: I shall lose you soon enough. Too soon. Her smooth arm with its down of fair hairs leant on its slender wrist near his face. He could move his head and breathe in her skin. He closed his eyes. Storing up moments like this. Maybe he could just fall asleep and she'd still be here when he woke. What would that prove?

Laurel leant down and whispered in his ear:

'Let's go for a walk. Come on. I'll take you to see my secret hole'.

He gave her a sleepy grin and ran his fingers upwards along her thigh. 'Seen it already.'

She lifted his hand away and sat up again, too keen to take him exploring to succumb to caresses.

'But this one you can climb through.'

'Don't need to.'

'Don't you want to a bit? Aren't you curious?'

'What would I see?'

'A road. Cars perhaps. Different trees. Roofs. The beginning of the village... oh, I'm not going to tell you.'

'Sounds like too much excitement all at once.'

'Come on,' she was now pulling him up, 'you're a namby pamby, it's completely safe. The road's usually deserted. At, least you can see the way I get in.'

'All right. I'm coming. I'll do it for you.'

'Good man!'

'I need a walk. Getting fat and lazy with all this food. And your auntie's cake you brought; didn't she miss it?'

'Told her I was going on a picnic after school -'

'She thinks you're at school?'

'Maybe. Or maybe not. She doesn't comment, she just lets me be'

'You know, she's a saint of an aunt.'

'My sainted aunt.' They walked arm linked in arm comfortably, taking the same sized steps, joined somehow at the hips like Siamese twins.

'It's the last week. I've finished the exams, so I just go in for the register, and my friend Bethan has influence with the class teacher. She's apparently walking out with Bethan's uncle. And by the way I think young Michael who took me to the dance has finally got the message: I've seen him looking moony at Bethan.

She's not going into school either, she hangs around with him and helps her mum at home.'

The world sounded so free and easy. His heart ached. If only his life could be as simple. So he could go or stay as he pleased, play truant with this girl. Run away together on an endless picnic and never turn up for the register.

They were pushing through tall pine trees now which grew close together, making deep shadowy paths crackly with dry pine needles. They went single file, she leading him by the hand.

'Bethan has older brothers, so she knows about men. She told me you can tell everything about a man from looking at his fingers, including what sort of lover he'd make and the shape of his penis, so she says.' She stopped, took both his hands and began examining them minutely; the small scar at the top of his thumb, the ridges on his little finger nails, the lines across his knuckles. She gently turned them over and noted the calluses at the base of his fingers from the felling axe, the deeply etched lines across his palm, the burns on his wrists. She seemed moved.

'Will you make me something for my birthday?'

'Yes. I'll make you…'

'Don't tell me. Will you make me some kind of creature?'

They walked on in silence out of the pine trees now into sunlight and a clearing of old oak trees. They were near the wall. After a while she glanced at him and said, 'You can have a pee now if you want to so I can cross-check my facts.' Go on.'

Tom, unbuttoning, started to laugh but then they both froze. Horses' hooves in the distance. Someone approaching, this side of the wall.

Laurel hardly hesitated: seizing the lowest branch of an oak, she swung herself up and climbed higher to hide herself in a fork amongst the leaves above his head.

'Fly,' she hissed down at him. For a moment the instruction confused him. Then he remembered and buttoned up hastily and just in time, for the rider was now close and approaching their clearing from the other side at a canter. An elegant, straight-backed woman with beautifully tailored jacket and shiny brown leather riding boots on a magnificent chestnut hunter.

'Good afternoon, Captain. I know who you are – you must be our man in the woods. I'm Alice Ashworth. I know we haven't been introduced...' She swung down from her horse easily in her tight moleskin jodhpurs and stood very close to him, taking off her riding hat to let her hair fall to her shoulders. It was chestnut, matching the horse. Her nose was very thin and her eyes a greyish blue. Tom didn't speak.

'I'm glad you're not a poacher. I sometimes wonder when I hear things; but of course, I can see you're not.' She held out her thin hand. 'So hello!' He took the offered hand for a moment.

'Glad to meet you... Mrs. Ashworth.'

'Call me Alice. You must be very isolated here. I'll ask Gerald to invite you over one evening. Do you play bridge?'

'Afraid not. Chess.'

Surely she wouldn't have him to a bridge party?

'Oh! Too clever for me, I'm afraid. Never mind. Come to supper sometime soon... Saturday.' Her voice, which he had heard in the distance giving loud orders to gardeners, was now quiet and husky, so quiet that Laurel up in her tree would probably not catch the words.

'Anyway, you'll be back in the wide world quite quickly now, I'm sure. Bit more fun than this, hmm? Expect you can't wait to be up and about again, no? Yes, of course. You're a young man, younger than I'd imagined. And quite a looker' She was now running her long hand slowly down the curls at the back of his head and round to caress his beard. 'Gerald should lend you his barber. Then you'll be ready for anything' She gazed into his face. Her eyes were not blue, he could now see, or they had changed to the indeterminate colour of a pool of water in the shade.

Abruptly she turned and swung back up onto her horse and called over her shoulder: 'That was a good ride round the lake, I must do it again. Goodbye for now, Captain!' and cantered off.

Tom stood still. She was soon out of sight and earshot. He felt unsettled, annoyed at himself. 'I'm not ready,' he muttered. Laurel had slithered out of her oak tree. She was standing facing him, yet he didn't look at her but into the middle distance, trembling slightly. Her arms went round his waist pressing her body gently into his as they stood there, fitted together like a successful jigsaw puzzle. Now she could feel what she had noticed as she climbed down from the tree: he was semi-erect. She pulled his buttocks towards her. 'You seem ready to me, anyway!' Her gentle, teasing voice. He stood up against her, as close as it was possible to get without being inside or without dissolving completely.

'Not ready for out there,' he said. For betrayals and consequences and compromise, he meant. 'For tough women, 'he said.

'And weak men,' she added. Slimy old Toff! She had wanted to yell after the rider for she'd felt a sharp spasm of jealousy.

'How do you know about men?' he asked, incredulous. 'You're practically a…' he was going to say 'child' but the word seemed absurd as he held onto her with his arms and his torso and his guts, the eternal feminine, for dear life.

***

'Byrne, I'm getting good reports. As you were, do sit down!' General Ashworth made a sweeping movement with his hand to indicate that Tom should relax, expand, possibly even feel encouraged; although his permanent military bearing and his Sandhurst voice seemed to work in the opposite direction.

However, there was something about the eyes, thought Tom, that told you he was intelligent strategically and socially.

'Isn't that so, Solomon? Excellent reports.'

'Yes Sir. There has been a quite rapid progress.'

'You had a rough time, Byrne. We were surprised you pulled through. Your amnesia, I am told, is a natural concomitant of such events. Certainly came across it personally many times. My father after extended action in 1915 was semi-amnesiac for several months. We had no Doctor Solomon around then and the word psychiatry itself was hardly in usage. But you are a rare find for us with your non-English Englishness and Irishness of course, and your command of languages. How is that side of things?'

'The rude words are coming back first, Sir!'

'Excellent!' the General half laughed. 'How well do you recall your last piece of action and its aftermath?'

'Not the events themselves, Sir,' Tom replied, 'but before and after is falling back into a recognizable shape, more and more every day.'

'Hmm, good. Is there anything else we can do for you? Anything you think could aid and speed your retrieval?'

'No Sir. Thank you. I am very well provided for.'

'Glad to hear it.' The General half looked round at Solomon, both nodded, both rose and the General strode towards the door.

'Oh by the way – nearly got demoted there – the good wife wants me to ask you to supper. I'd say, when you feel ready. So consider yourself invited. Mufti. You should get some clothes sorted out with Griffiths. Doctor, keep me posted.'

'I will, Sir.' And he was gone.

***

Solomon had been watching Tom's reactions to the General and his invitation to supper. Already he could observe a perhaps unconscious hint of a military bearing beginning to return to this academic Irish soldier in the British Army who perhaps came from generations of fighting men. It was Solomon who spoke first.

'What about the… male side… before we end?'

'What do you mean?'

'You talk about the female. What about the male?'

'You mean psychologically? Or do you mean generals, patriarchs… let me see … what does my reading tell me…'

'No, Tom.'

'Well. I think I have always wanted to find a strong male figure. Strength from him. The army? Academia, in a way? My father.'

'Was he strong?'

'I don't know… I never knew… He was kind. My mother was strong. I think I have only ever come into contact with weak men… or found them so. All good sinners, army friends, drinking, whoring, running like hell. I feel you as strong.'

'Perhaps the question is, are you?

'Am I strong? … I don't know…' Tom was facing Solomon.

'I think I am good at pretending I am strong.'

'Perhaps that is what male strength is.'

'Male strength is pretending to be strong...? Is that it?'

'No. There is more...' Solomon didn't wait long for an answer, he knew time was short. 'Pretending and acknowledging that one is doing so. It's the same with courage.'

'Is it the same thing? Strength, courage, being a man?'

'Maybe.'

'Laurel is strong.'

'Yes.'

'And is this your canny way of getting me to talk about the female? And don't say maybe.' Tom sat.

'Yes...' Solomon was tempted to say more, to explain. But he resisted. He was aware at this moment of his feelings of fondness for this man who was now, with time almost up, lying back to relax at last.

'I've got a dream,' he said. 'You like dreams. Once upon a time there was a male and a female and a Prospero... or to put it on a more surface level, an Irishman, an Anglo-Welsh woman, and a Jew.'

'Ah, a daydream...' Solomon enjoyed the smiling silence that followed for a full five minutes.

CHAPTER 28

Laurel liked drying whilst Aunt Bron chatted and washed. There had been a time, not so long ago, when she was not permitted to reach up and put away her aunt's good china…now, she felt like an equal as she worked alongside her second favourite person in the world. She considered how she also felt grown up in the company of Tom. She couldn't guess how old he was.

'I think of him as Tom but speak to him as 'Burns' she thought. 'I wonder how he thinks of me… as Laurel? Something else? And does he forget me until I turn up?'

'I like drying up with you, Auntie,' she said.

'Do you, Cariad?'

'And I like hanging out the big wash.'

'I like you helping me, my precious.'

'Is Connor coming round?'

'Wednesday: you know he is. Concentrate, now, we don't want you letting a bowl slip!'

'Oh, Auntie darling, I think I'm attached... I'm attached to someone...'

'Oh really... well...'

'I wish I knew why'

'*Where the apple reddens...*' her aunt said softly, looking at the hills through the window as she rinsed the plates.

'What does that mean?'

'It means, don't ask. A very old song. Your grandmother would sing it.'

'How does it go?'

'Where the apple reddens, never pry;
Lest we lose our Eden, Eve and I.'

Laurel stood motionless, and the large, wet casserole dish she was holding dripped steadily onto the floor. 'That's it!... our Eden... Oh yes.'

They worked on in silence with the Home Service offering conversation from the shelf above the cooker. 'But it's something... of a secret, it has to be.'

'You keep it secret for as long as you want to, my dear one.'

'You do that sometimes, don't you?'

'Oh always, always; I tell as little as I want to.'

'But I could tell *you*. If, when, I thought felt … like it.'

'And not a moment sooner, if at all.'

'I love you, Auntie!'

Laurel embraced her aunt round her flowery apron, with dishcloth and damp hands, and then a kiss on her cheek; holding on, staying there. The wireless turning to music.

'John, dear John MacCormack… listen!… Mother McCree… That's me!' sang out Bronwyn.

'That's you, my dearest Auntie Mother McCree!' and Laurel danced out of the kitchen and into the garden and towards the gate.

'I thought you were waiting for Connor, Laurie?'

'Not really. Not now.' And she was off down the little drive towards the wall and the woods. The little dog chasing and barking and leaping at her feet.

But he was not there. Muffin discovered it. She'd gone on ahead as they neared the shack, not barking, doing a sort of swift, padding run, tail held high and swaying from side to side like a banner in a cavalry charge. One bark inside the hut then she ran back to Laurel, tail down, eyes tragic, and sat at her feet.

'Oh dog! He's not there! Where is he, Muffin?'

Muffin wagged helpfully but she didn't know either and could only follow his scent to the jetty at the edge of the water. They both looked across the lake to the tiny distant chimneys of the big house. Too far to see any sign of life. She wasn't sure what else he did over there apart from see his doctor. He never talked about his visits.

'Secrets, Muff. The Isle is full of secrets. And so are we, aren't we?' She pushed open the door of the hut and found the old Earl Grey tea caddy. Two shortbread biscuits, one for Muffin and one for herself. And then back home for supper with noisy old Connor whose boisterous teasing and rough housing she had once enjoyed but was not so sure about now. Strangely, Muffin wasn't sure she liked him much, either.

They had another guest. She saw the blue car parked down the lane. The only blue car in a village of black ones. Connor's sister, Zelda. Her heart sank. Muffin stepped cautiously across to the furthest side to pass it, practically walking inside the hedge. Zelda had a yappy mongrel called Minnie. She didn't bring it into Bronwyn's house anymore, it drove Muffin demented. Sometimes it was left in her car outside.

Supper was lamb chops and green beans from the garden and homegrown rhubarb crumble. Her aunt and Connor were discussing the growing volume of Army traffic to and from their local headquarters at the Big House. 'Bloody Kings of the Road they think they are, five miles an hour through the middle of the village with all their lights on...' said Connor. It seemed that General Ashworth had put in a request to the Council for the sixteenth century stone bridge to be widened. Connor was damned if he could believe the man's cheek. Then a letter came from Whitehall. 'Bloody hell!... Over my dead body!' said Connor. Laurel was forced to make polite conversation of sorts with Zelda as she waited hopefully for a second helping of crumble and custard. But Zelda did not care to hear her observations about mating buzzards, she was more interested in the goings-on at the Big House.

'I've met that General Ashworth. He's no gentleman, like lovely Colonel Preece-Williams, a dear, dear man. He shouted at me from his car yesterday.'

'The Colonel's dead, Zelda.'

'I know, Connor. Thank you. I was at his funeral. I meant that General Ashworth shouted.' Connor shovelled pudding into his mouth as if to stop up his exasperation.

'He frightened poor Minnie. We were only walking down the road past his gate, wouldn't have dreamt of going in.'

'What was the matter with him, Zelda?' asked Bronwyn, pouring out coffee.

'Can't have dogs anywhere here! Not allowed! Hadn't I seen the notices? War Office policy-no dogs whatever!' Her voice was strident. 'Well, I had my reply ready, of course…'

'Of course,' mumbled Connor. Bronwyn shot him a look.

'But no sooner had I opened my mouth to speak when Zoom! the windows go down and he roars off up the drive.'

'Rude man!' said Bronwyn sympathetically.

'I was furious. You can imagine. Apart from poor Minnie – well, it's her usual route down that road, and of course she understands the word 'dogs'. Apart from that… the point is, he's a liar! They do have dogs in there. I've heard them. Several times.'

'I've never seen any dogs…' said Connor.

'Not seen them; heard them barking. A young dog, probably, like yours, Laurel. Like that barking your puppy does when she gets excited.'

Laurel carefully scraped the very last remnants of custard from the inside of her bowl. She noticed Aunt Bron glance at her briefly over her coffee cup.

'Zelda, more coffee?'

'Thank you, Bronwyn.'

'Well, I think Minnie's looking marvellous since her visit to the vet.'

'Oh Bron, do you think so? It was the back teeth you know. An abscess. Had to have them all out. It's made all the difference. Of course, I have to puree all her food.'

At this Connor noisily poured himself a large whisky and Laurel quietly excused herself and went up to her room.

***

'They were asking me questions last night at supper, but I fobbed them. Right off.'

Tom was buttering fat slices of bread to spread with the fragrant Welsh honey Laurel loved, for their tea.

'Who were 'they'?'

Laurel didn't seem to notice the edginess in his voice, he hoped.

'Oh – Auntie's boyfriend and his dippy sister. Not my aunt, she's not the questioning kind. And she's on my side. You'd like her.'

Tom wanted to ask, 'questions about me?' but edited the words in time.

'Questions about?'

'About, oh, big issues, like what was I going to do; what about my exams – my Highers…going to University…'

Tom busied himself with kettle filling to hide his relief.

'It's all a bit of a mess. They've got a different syllabus down here… you don't want to know… and I can't bring myself to care that much.'

Laurel wrapped her bare legs round the stool that she habitually perched on and selected a banana from the box of fruit sent over by the General's chef every week.

'Connor wanted to know "what I wanted to do with my life, young lady". Well, I told him, in the light of all possible alternatives, I wanted to *live* it.' She was now holding a small sharp knife close to the bottom tip of the banana.

'I shall ask this banana a more interesting question… look, you cut off the end here for the answer... their questions are so predictable and boring. What I want to know, oh banana, is....' she paused and puckered her brow.

'He loves me, he loves me not?' Tom suggested.

'No – you have to ask a Yes or No question.

'So – does she love me?'

'A bit predictable still and all.' She sliced off the tip of the banana and revealed, in the centre of its flesh, a deep browny black and definite Y.

'There you are, yes. No surprises.'

'Does a banana ever say No?' Tom asked.

'Of course. It depends on what you ask.'

'And what are your own big questions, madam?'

'Is this Truth and Dare?'

'I dare you to answer.'

'Oh well, that's easy: Why are we here? How should we live? What's the point? – But aren't those everyone's? – and one more of my own: If you were to die or go away, would I quickly get over it? Those are all my questions.'

Tom was shaken by the last one. He poured out two mugs of tea standing by his stove, feeling both helpless and protective at the same time, which served to confuse him into silence.

Laurel unfolded the checked cloth she had brought from her aunt's which added an incongruous daintiness to the rough splintery table.

'As for 'how should we live', she was now shaking the tablecloth vigorously open, 'trouble is, everyone knows that, but it's not convenient or it doesn't make sense, so we all forget about it.'

'Do we?' Tom smiled. She looked so solemn. 'Do we really know it?'

'Oh Yes.' She started slicing up the banana deftly with his sharpest fish-gutting knife. 'But everyone's busy following their noses. Looking after their own little needs. Ignoring their souls, you know?'

'So that's the point, is it? To look after our souls – who told you that?'

'Nobody told me. It's common sense.' Laurel was eating her way enthusiastically through her second slice of honeyed bread smothered with sliced banana. He watched the pointed tip of her tongue lick up a drop of honey from her finger. He wanted to put another drop there so he could watch her do it again.

'Anyway, it's in all the decent poetry. You know poetry. And the hymns. You just pick it up by osmosis. Mind you, most hymns are dreadful rubbish. Can I ask you one now, Tom?'

'If I can have a kiss first.'

'Kisses come after the honey. You know that. Here's my question: have you ever seen anyone die?'

A sudden flush. The unexpected heart-thump of rising panic. The face of a different questioner, close to his: have you ever…? His clenched fingernails digging into his palms to stop himself screaming. It was over in a moment. Now Laurel's face, calm, waiting.

'Hmm. Why all these thoughts about dying?'

'Ha! Evasion! Penalty, as agreed….'

She reached over to grab him to take off one item of clothing, which nearly always turned out to be his trousers. He grinned and quickly undid his belt and buttons and slipped them off and sat down again, with his mug of tea, in his underpants.

'Well, I've just been to a funeral, in fact. So that's why. Or at least, I walked along behind the procession until Muffin saw a cat. On our way here.'

'Who was it?'

'Oh, it was sad, Tom. My friend, Mr. Rees. The old man who drives the taxi. Who drove the taxi – I've known him all my life, so I can't get used to it.'

'You liked him.'

'Yes, I must have. Quite a lot. Because I do feel sad. He liked me too. It's hard to lose any of the people

389

who like you in this world.' She fell silent. Muffin came rushing in from outside, found her usual saucer of water, slurped noisily and then stretched out with her head on her paws facing them, watching them, content.

'Tom, there's something I've got to tell you.' Laurel sighed. 'They were sniffing around our secret last night, getting a bit warm. At least, Zelda was.'

'Zelda?'

'Connor's sister, you've such a bad memory for names. She'd heard a dog like Muffin barking in the wood, apparently. But my good old aunt changed the subject.'

The memories and the flicker of anxiety produced in Tom like a reflex at the Irish name 'Connor' were almost completely routed by the unknown, never-known 'Zelda.'

Laurel stopped jigging around. 'Hey, don't look so worried. I know you have to be secret here. I'm as safe as Fort Knox. They can't crack me – they'd have to pull all my toenails out first, one by one.' Tom unrolled his thick eiderdown and laid it on the floor by the fireplace near to the dog. He took a blanket from his bed. Then he came up behind Laurel on her stool and wrapping both arms around her, he lifted her up, turning her round to face him, sliding her down with him onto the eiderdown in front of the fire so they both lay there close together in silence watching flames jumping around on the logs, her face on his shoulder, peaceful.

She sighed and closed her eyes. Snuggled up. He moved his leg to cover hers, gently. She felt its naked strength. She felt his warmth. They wouldn't need a blanket.

Her breathing slowed down, grew deeper, her head heavy now on his shoulder, her trusting wide open hand inside his open shirt on his bare chest. She'd be asleep in a minute. He was perfectly happy.

***

It was now getting dark. Tom concentrated on lighting two candles on the mantelpiece and Laurel leaned up onto her elbow to watch him. With his curling beard in the candlelight and his slightly pointed ears he looked like Puck. Or Pan perhaps... what was he doing the great god Pan? Staring into the candle flames, solemn. She reckoned he *had* seen someone die.

'I've just had a dream,' she said.

He flinched – he obviously hadn't realised she was awake. 'You were in it.'

'Tell me.'

'I dreamt you had made me a present.'

'I have.'

'Can I see it now?'

'What was it in the dream?'

'It was made of wood.'

'So it is.'

'That's all I know.'

'Close your eyes.'

'But Tom, I have to go!' Laurel had closed her eyes, opened them again and was looking around for her clothes, suddenly aware that something significant was about to happen. Then she saw it: on the mantelpiece sitting between two candles, light flickering in such a way that its wings appeared to be lifting, stood a bird, very still. Tom was watching her.

'Oh no,' she said. But he knew this was an affirmation for she covered her face with both hands.

'It's my creature! It's my present! You carved it.'

She stepped up to touch it, amazed at the deep dark browns that marked the bold form of a bird with its head raised, and the silky grain suggesting delicacy of feather and down to such an extent that she did not dare to touch it lest it fly away.

'You know why it's a gull?' he asked.

'Yes… away from the sea.

She reached up and planted a kiss on his forehead to forestall a frown, then lightly brushed his lips with her own.

'Now I must go. It's hard to go, it doesn't get any easier with practice.' A small sigh from Tom, then 'Come on, Muffin!' and girl and dog disappeared into the dusk.

Tom was left alone with a foretaste of what he most dreaded.

***

First Muffin and then Laurel popped out of the secret hole in the wall to pause in the thickets and check their concealment.

Then out onto the grass verge beside the road that curved round through farms and cottages to the village.

Once out of the forest Laurel felt herself back in a world that seemed unknown for as long as it took to reach the path that led to her home and Aunt Bron.

Today it felt unreal, it was even a different climate out here.

It had been warm and still by the lakeside trees where she'd left Tom in his hut, but here outside the sky was darkening and changing rapidly and as they stepped off the verge the suddenness of a wind gusting up brought noise and leaves and excitement which prompted Muffin to bark and chase. She turned to face the darkness of great rolling clouds storming in, feeling the wet on her face and her dress, and observing that the looming waves of vapour were shaping into a large squat figure. 'It's the vapour God!' she yelled, the droplets letting up for a while. 'No, it's...' she searched for the name. 'Nandi... it's Shiva's Bull... it's made of solid Basalt!' She could hear Tom's voice in her head and wanted to shout across the wind, across the forest, 'Look at the sky, Tom! Look to the East! Your enormous sphinx has come to Wales all the way from India.'

'Will you take me to Ireland?' she had asked.

'I thought you'd want me to take you to India.'

'I do! But I want to see Ireland first.'

'You might have to wait for that.'

'Why?' she had wanted to ask, and now as she turned back towards the village, resisting returning to the forest to smell the rain on the trees and be with Tom, she ran after Muffin encouraging her to bark, enjoying getting soaked and wondering why and why and when.

She wasn't worried, just a mixture of curious-impatient-excited, while the heavy downpour now increased and a tractor came towards them with a farmer waving, and then a Hillman hooted, driven by Mr. Humphries, and she asked herself what will be the third vehicle, shouting 'Move, Muffin, move!' as she shooed her onto the grass verge from her tailwagging walk in the centre of the road, and then she realised with an inner thud that she had left her seagull behind in the hut. 'What will Tom think? …What will Auntie say if I'm late again, especially as I've promised to peel and prepare? Too bad.'

She was already rushing back through the rain to the hole in the wall and the forest. The third vehicle that went past, unnoticed, belonged to Connor, looking forward to Bron's meal, straining to see and just able to identify girl and dog climbing into thickets alongside the wall.

***

On the washing line Laurel's thin blue dress flapped and dried in the wind. How young it looks, how small it looks; does Tom wish I wore different clothes, womanly clothes, she wondered, musing on how she might look, remembering the stir she had caused at the ball, but not for long. Tom was always looking at her limbs or into her eyes or stroking her skin or her hair. He doesn't care about clothes. 'What are you?' she had asked, 'a Buddhist?'

'No…'

'A Shiva follower?'

'No, not a Hindu.'

'What are you, then?'

'I'm a…' Tom had paused, looking above her head. 'The word won't come

'Give us a clue.'

'It's not a religion, Jack.' He had stopped calling her Jack now for a long time.

'Where are you? Where are you, girl?' Aunt Bron was standing beside her looking out of the window in the kitchen. 'Lovely wind… penny for your thoughts, girl…'

'Oh Auntie, I'm sorry I was late for lunch.'

'Well Connor was too.'

'And Sunday too and my turn to do vegetables'.

'Nothing's broken.'

'Except a promise.'

'Never mind. Look what's arrived, birthday cards for tomorrow.'

'On Sunday?'

'Connor brought them – you know he's been rewiring the Post Office; he often brings me the mail. Do you want to open one?'

'This one's from Ollie... it's opened. It's been resealed. Bron! You were peeping!' Laurel took out a fine hand-painted card showing an owl sleepy amongst a pile of wrapping paper, with a birthday balloon in its beak.

'Ollie always sends me an owl somehow for my birthday.'

Bron looked at it in surprise; she had certainly not opened the envelope. She shrugged. 'Where were you Cariad? Stuck in all that rain?'

'I'd gone to get my present from my friend. I'd had to run back...' she shuddered.

'Are you cold? Get dressed girl. You're much too thin.' Aunt Bron smacked her bottom. Laurel giggled and ran upstairs, Bron following.

'I'm not cold but something walked over my grave, as Moira says. When I'd run through the forest the hut was bare. I mean he wasn't there. He'd gone to see Mr. Solo Man, I suppose.'

'Who?' Aunt Bron was choosing a jumper for Laurel

'But I didn't want to take the lovely carving he's done for me without him being there, so I left him a note to tell him how much I loved the seagull he made. Oh, the forest is magical in the rain…' She was slipping into trousers and one of her cousin's shirts.

'Is there something you want to tell me?'

'Yes… no, not yet.' Laurel looked sad. She turned to face her aunt and they sat together on Laurel's little bed. She sighed silently, like her dog did when desolate, her eyes growing rounder. 'I'm eighteen now,' she thought. 'I'm a woman. Here I am – Laurel Williams, no school, no job, no fixed abode, no particular talents, no remarkable features, Friday's child, no prospects. What have I got? One scruffy dog and a secret lover.'

'Do you really want to wait till tonight for your present?' Bron asked.

'Oh Auntie…' Laurel gasped, her eyes large and about to flood. 'I've got you,' she thought, 'no one is better than you, more loving than you. I'm so ungrateful,' she wanted to say, the flicker of guilt assuaging the tears.

'Oh Auntie, what…?' Bron enquired gently, her hand on Laurel's knee, searching by look and touch for disclosure of the great burden of the unknown future that her niece had suddenly felt.

'I wonder if you'll like my seagull, Auntie?'

'Of course I will. The man's an artist, I'm sure. Do you like him?' she paused for Laurel's look of indignation, the frown, was an instantaneous rebuke. 'Of course you do,' Bron continued, 'you probably wish you could invite him tonight to your party-supper. Can you?'

'I think it's just my period… or the time of year. It's almost autumn isn't it. Or the year itself. Perhaps 1951 is at odds with all the other forces in the cosmos.'

'What are you trying to say?'

'You want me to choose a school, don't you?' Laurel rose and walked to the little window to look across a slight haze in the direction of the distant forest.

'You want me to go into the sixth form and be a prefect or something. You want me to go to university or become a schoolteacher and wear my hair like Miss Montrose.'

'Who's Miss Montrose?'

'Don't even ask me to try to describe Miss Montrose, Aunt Bron, she belongs to one of Moira's plays… it's raining again.'

'Good! The garden's smiling.' The two women stood looking out at the rain, Laurel leaning forward a little to inhale the rich odours of wet earth and shrubbery. 'Perhaps I shouldn't bring my seagull here, away from the lake…'

'I do want you to go back to studying, when you're ready. Soon, I hope. Next month.' They spoke at the same time.

'Why did I have to do needlework at school?' Laurel asked with a tearful intensity, 'and all that Domestic Science they dare to call it. And deportment and elocution and being a Miss Montrose. Why is it girls aren't supposed to be good at some things?'

'Laurel, what's happened?' Bronwyn pleaded, her arms around her niece, aware that potatoes needed peeling, the oven needed heating, but she checked her voice to say gently, 'Tell your old Auntie, Cariad.'

Laurel sniffed. 'You know, when men say "women don't like working with wood", they really mean, they can't. Well, it's true.'

Bronwyn couldn't help smiling. 'You can do so many things…' she reassured Laurel, aware that it was with immense relief that she'd heard her mention her period for she knew, she felt in her bones, that Laurel was now sexual, no longer a virgin. She looked different, moved, walked, talked no longer like a child. 'You can change a fuse,' she continued.

'Only because you showed me.'

'So; who do you think showed me?'

'But I never learnt to use a saw properly.'

'You can make whitewash, and you rigged up a pulley on my washing line, remember.'

'Oh yes, and I can fasten a line to a pole with a timber hitch.'

'And you can estimate the height of a tree…'

'And I can shorten a rope with a sheepshank. What else?'

'You can make a kite.'

'It never flew.'

'But darling why do you look so sad?' Muffin barked from under the bed.

'Oh, shut up Muffin!'

'Who has been saying you can't do things? Why are you so upset?'

'I was running and running and running through the forest and the rain with Muffin going mad, barking her head off, I didn't want to be late back, and then Tom wasn't even there… and I felt all… I don't like feeling all alone. Usually, I don't even when I am… but I did… it was like he had really gone, forever.' Laurel burst into tears and Bron held her, arms right round her, making soothing noises while Muffin looked on and whimpered. Then Laurel chuckled; 'Listen to us!'

'And you're very good at peeling potatoes!' They both laughed. 'Come on,' Bron continued, 'there's nothing like a good cry … have you finished?'

'Yes. Come on Muff, let's feed you.'

'She must be hungry and so must you.'

'I've forgotten what we're having for supper.'

'Come and see.' Bron led the way down, Muffin bounding past her and skidding at the bottom of the stairs, then into the kitchen.

'Oh the wood, Auntie; the softness of the wood!' Laurel said as they put on their aprons, 'it feels like feathers. I'll want to take my seagull to bed, poor thing. I wish I'd brought it home, but I couldn't. He'd have wondered what had happened.'

'Where was he?'

'Probably gone to see his Doctor.' Bron raised her eyebrows as she put a tray of vegetables in the oven to roast. 'He's been badly wounded, Auntie.'

'But the war's long finished, girl.'

'Well, he had to stay and mop things up or something… something undercover. Oh, parsnips… my favourite! How many are coming to supper? Is Connor coming?'

'Surprise. Wait and see.'

'Well, in case he is I'll put out his special tankard.' Bronwyn, watching Laurel lay the table, could not remove from her mind the thought that her beloved niece had suffered more than she'd realised from not having had a father in her life.

CHAPTER 29

It had been a fast trip across the lake and then Byrne had to wait, paging through a 1930's *Punch*, whilst the General kept Dr. Solomon busy. The psychiatrist apologised then, uncharacteristically, commenced the session himself.

'Are you not curious about the girl?' Solomon asked, and Byrne was surprised at the question, didn't really understand it, was silent. It wasn't the sort of thing Solomon did, ask a question like that about the present with an inflection almost suggesting reproach.

'Are you not curious about where she comes from, her family, their rules, her age?'

'Of course I am.'

'Well…'

'I don't ask her questions because I don't want to slip into this with her.'

'This?'

'That you and I do; analysis.'

Silence. Then the waiting that Solomon did.

'Besides,' Tom smiled, 'she plays this game with answers to satisfy my curiosity.'

'Truth and Dare'

'Did I tell you?'

Solomon nodded a reply.

'I'm curious about everything, damn it! Even you. Can I smoke?

'Are you angry?' Solomon asked.

'Almost. I want to know where you come from, your family, your rules, your age, your accent, your persecution. Why England? Besides she shows me everything even when she doesn't tell.'

Solomon waited. Tom lit up, watched the smoke.

'Sometimes she doesn't want to make love. She doesn't say so but she looks different and on those days she talks about making love and has large deep eyes and she just wants to talk and … nuzzle.' He exhaled slowly.

'Sometimes she… do you know, she doesn't like smoking, my smoking, but she doesn't say a word.' He blew a smoke ring.

Solomon did not often look away, but he did now by reflex as one of the General's dogs came wagging at the French windows at the same time as the wind, which had blown the boat across and kept them inside with its force and promise of more rain, now blew the first large drops onto the panes. The great red setter rushed off to get wet, his tail beating on the glass before he charged.

'Sometimes she...?' prompted Solomon.

'Why are you so interested in her?'

'I'm interested in your relationships with all women, Tom.'

'Well, I'm interested in how you got caught up in the military, Doctor.'

'It's only part time, with the Army. It was a condition of my staying here. My last home was Cologne. Your home was Skibbereen, or near about, beside a small loch, before the family moved to Galway and then Sligo; your father even when blind practising medicine where he could and moving gradually back to his root of roots, Enniskillen.'

'And my mother?'

'She was a musician, as you know, playing Irish instruments I cannot name or pronounce, and she taught the violin and piano when your father was in struggle.'

'And my sister?'

'You remember your sister?'

'Yes. But describe her, if you know.'

'A beauty like your mother. Red gold hair and green eyes. I read the notes whose details are naturally prosaic, birthmarks etcetera'.

'Why are you answering these questions?'

'The General insists I hasten the business of "getting his marbles back" as he puts it.' Tom noticed a wry smile briefly visit the doctor's face.

'Have you told him about Laurel?'

'Oh no!… And I shall not.'

The rain had stopped, the wind dropped and now three dogs appeared, one at the door, the others leaping up at the General's wife as she passed, well wrapped, striding past then waving and looking in at Tom.

'Women are curious, are they not, Doctor?' They heard noises, footsteps, in the room above them.

'Are there people here?'

'A meeting. Some action soon.'

'So, you're hastening the business… is that why you asked me about my girl?'

'No. I'm trained to use my intuition, believe it or not Tom. I trust the girl. I ask you about her and push the discussion towards things emotional and even sexual with her in order to understand you... and to prepare you fully as a man again. You know that you had given up on that'

'She asks me why I sleep outside when she is not with me.'

'So, she sleeps the night with you, Tom.'

'She asks me, "What's the most exciting place you've ever visited in the whole world?"

'"You!" I say. "Here!"' I say.

Both men wait for the other to smile... 'Africa!' I tell her truthfully.' 'Why?' she asks. 'I'll show you something', I say. 'If you shake hands with an African, with a Shangaan or a Zulu, he will take your hand like this:'

Byrne rose to demonstrate to Solomon who stood to be shown. As they shook hands, Tom's left hand lightly supported his own right wrist, and his head bowed. Solomon followed suit. Their silence made audible the soft rain falling on the long windows.

He dropped the doctor's hand, half smiling and clearing his throat. Solomon said, 'Go on'.

'You're impatient today, Doctor. Not yourself.'

'That's a first for me!' Laughter. 'A patient informing me I'm not myself.' Tom was standing at the window peering at thin mist hanging over the lake, aware that Solomon was not quite playing his customary taciturn part, and that he too felt very different in a way that he wanted to be able to convey.

'*Amo et amo*,' he said. 'Walter, there's a good story that keeps coming to mind...' then Tom interrupted himself, 'I was not loved before...' He did not know which way to proceed so he slipped into silent reflection.

'Tom? Tell me the story,' Solomon urged.

'I can talk about Laurel, or I can tell you part of the story. Which?'

'Is it possible that they are connected?'

'The images of Beauty and the Beast keep popping up in very vivid pictures.' Both of Tom's hands opened and closed to signal small explosions, then he held them as fists, 'But I can't for the life of me remember the ending.' He turned to Solomon. 'I'm just stuck with illustrations and little fireworks of thoughts.' His fists flicked open into spread fingers and back, several times.

'Tom,' Solomon gestured too late to stop his patient turning away to blow warm breath upon a windowpane then with forefinger start drawing a shape where the glass had clouded. Hoping to hold

410

a focus Solomon added, 'We can make time today, Tom, if it is required. You're not writing your notes anymore, you've finished with that. You've stopped listing. That primitive syntax has resolved itself now into the convolutions of normal thought. All minds race, Tom, and there is no thinking-cap that can prevent ideas running in different directions both at the same time.'

'That's not mad?'

'No. Absolutely no. That has never been your problem. Come and sit down.'

'I still get flashes and blanks. Blanks and flashes. I know the memory is working but it floods and stalls.

'If you can describe your condition, you are okay. You are okay, Tom.'

'I have shaped a heart in this steam on the pane. What a silly boy. I can remember carving a heart into a birch near some water back home. Then I blank. I can put a face but not a name to my first sweetheart. But when I go home in my mind, or nearabouts, there is another face, it is horrid, it is livid. Oh, most pernicious villain, I want to say but not to it, not to him; to myself. A Frankenstein beast is what I see through the mist of my memory. Too many pictures, too little story.' Tom leaned against the windows.

'I wonder,' Solomon asked, 'Did you ever see when you were in France a piece of cinema made by Jean Cocteau, *'La Belle et la Bête'*?

'I don't think so. When was it made?'

'Just after the war. 1945 or 46.'

'Love,' coming back to the sofa Tom lowered his voice…'Love is the catalytic agent, yes? Or the fairy magic in the story, not so?'

'Go on.'

'I'm tired.' He stretched out, reached in his pocket for his cigarette tin but stopped himself. 'I wouldn't mind a coffee.'

'You will very likely know the name Carl Jung.' Solomon moved from his armchair to sit against his desk, nearer Tom. 'The psychologist whom others liked sarcastically to call 'le Mystique'… well, he speaks of an alchemical transformation which … Tom, do you know the myth of Cupid and Psyche?'

'Another fairy story… tell it to me, Doctor.' Tom's eyes were closed.

'On one condition, Captain.'

'What?' Tom's eyes opened, surprised.

'That you give me the original meaning of the word psyche.'

'Soul,' Tom answered, sinking back. 'Are you going to give me an allegory of the soul's journey through the vale of woe?'

'Once upon a time, Tom,' Solomon cut across the irony and spoke with resonance, 'a king and queen had three lovely daughters, the youngest of whom, Psyche, was so breathtakingly beautiful that the people of the kingdom began to turn away from Aphrodite in order to worship the radiance and innocence of this young woman. Well, as you can imagine, the Goddess was not best pleased and she instructed her son Cupid to pay Psyche a visit and excite her into falling in love with some quite unworthy, wretched man. Naturally, Cupid fell profoundly in love with Psyche himself.' Solomon, amused, laughed.

'What happened then?' Tom asked, lighting a cigarette.

'Well, to cut short a long and arduous tale, which love always is, of high mountains, evil spirits, jealous sisters, a fearful monster, yes, and a journey into the underworld to consult with the blessed Persephone, why even a period of love-filled nights in a palace in a forest, no less, followed by a wicked, spell-induced endless sleep until… her helplessness comes to an end with Cupid finding her and waking her by loving

413

her. He then persuades Zeus to honour Psyche with divine status so that his mother Aphrodite will find her acceptable. Also, to crown it all, a baby girl is born to this enchanting couple whom they name Pleasure… Voluptas.'

'Yes,' Tom sighed, 'a palace in a forest, or a hut in a wood…Walter… what I was finding words to say when I was standing at the window earlier… is …I was not loved before, because I could not…receive it.'

'Man's great affliction.' Solomon confirmed. 'It is what I call the condition of the closed heart, very sad. In the end, blood being not sufficient in itself to keep the heart pliant, the heart hardens, cracks and breaks. Now what can be more tragic, Thomas, and impossible to treat, than the love-rejecting heart?'

'And what is woman's great affliction?' Tom asked, wide awake.

'Waiting. This is what we find in one form or other in all the stories, existential and mythic. Women are condemned to wait. No matter how productive or delightful, they wait.'

'Not Laurel!'

'She does not know it.'

'She's waiting?'

'She's waiting to lose you.'

Tom looked shocked.

'And then?' His voice was very low.

'I think she will be waiting to find you again.'

'And what about your wife, Walter, was she -'

'Waiting!' Solomon intervened then heard himself add, in his mother tongue, *'Allein.'*

The general's wife walked past the windows carrying secateurs and with the dog bounding after her. She glanced in, ready to wave, but both men were absorbed, caught in the web of what Walter Solomon had called, in one of his publications, 'The mutual unconscious'.

'I think it's time,' Tom said eventually. 'The lake looks clear. I want to row myself. Will it be my last trip? Am I recovered?' His voice shook a little. He sat up.

'Let's take that coffee first.' Solomon rose to ring the bell beside the mantelpiece. His good leather shoes sounded on wood and carpet in the silence of the big house.

'I think my sister Sarah was... I once heard my mother say to my sister Sarah "You don't have to play the piano if you don't want to, you certainly don't have to play it like that. Nobody plays the martyr in this house". I would sit at my desk with a view and hear my mother's music. It was angel's music. She taught me everything – this silly boy with big ears – words as well as music. How to sing. How to dance. How to work. How to laugh. The love of Italian. Vero. The love of truth. She taught me how to wash and how to clean my soul. Jaysus, she even directed some of my love for her onto my father and she had a way of cutting through his blarney, not unkindly, and then when he was blind, treating him as if he had extra sight. Wasn't it a splendid thing to say to a Catholic girl, "Nobody plays the martyr here". Perhaps mother was a Protestant. Do you know I can see her right now sitting at the piano playing and singing 'Drink to me only with thine eyes.' Do you think my mother was English? Mary mother of God, what a possibility! No wonder, if it's true, I feel such ambivalence. Oh, but she was a grand woman, whatever she was! German, Walter, more than anything else, she sang in German, *leider*, Mendelssohn, "all melody" she said, and Schubert of course, *"leibe Franz"* she called him as if she knew him. She did.'

And there was another language... what was it? Haunting, almost oriental songs she sang in this tongue. "Songs my mother sang me," she said. What was it? Walter? Do you know?'

Solomon's eyes, dark and large, were fixed on Tom who sighed, exhausted.

'I think it's time to go.' Both nodded, but they waited for the coffee.

CHAPTER 30

Connor was surrounded by women, none of them under sixty. He sat with his pint of bitter and a chaser at a table near the door and reflected that around here real men were a vanishing breed. The young ones had left the village to look for work or to fight Hitler, never to return, others were wasting themselves teaching in England he thought bitterly, and the over fifties were mostly listed alphabetically around the base of the stone statue of a First War infantryman in the Market Square. Two survivors, retired farmers, were sitting at the next table amongst the old women, gossiping. Old women themselves, thought Connor. Shrunken down in their seats. He wouldn't get like that.

'Never saw the like of it – went right through his foot; sock, boot and all.'

'Get away!' said the other old man.

'Right through, it was. He was lifting a heavy bale, you see, stumbled with it. Fell onto the elevator – those new petrol motor ones – and the spikes stick out further nowadays.'

The old women talked across them in counterpoint.

'Saw Joan Preece yesterday. She was in the hospital with her feet again.'

'No! that's the sixth time at least!' said the other old woman.

'You must get the bales on faster than the old ones we had in our day. So the spikes have got to be longer, see.'

'It's all much faster nowadays,' said the other old man, 'or it's my brain that's slower!'

'It's not good news, Mrs. Preece, they said…'

'He didn't take his boot off, you see, that was his problem. Didn't get it washed. Not for the rest of the day. Just kept on stacking the bales, blood coming out all over the place….'

'No, said the doctor, I can't offer you any hope, Mrs. Preece now…'

'Well, he couldn't get his boot off later, see. Foot was all swollen up…' It was like watching a tennis match, Connor thought. Bron's friend Mavis came in just then, looking around.'

'Mavis! come and join me. Lighten my darkness.'
She smiled in his direction and went to fetch a drink.

'They had to cut through his boot with a scalpel to get it off. Terrible smell…'

'So, all the doctor could say to her was "your feet won't be much good to you any more, Mrs. Preece. Not *as feet*".'

'That's gangrene, said the nurse, that smell. Had to have it off.'

'Get away!' said the other old man. Then they all lapsed into a satisfied silence.

Mavis brought her half pint over and sat next to Connor. 'Good news, Con. Gary's got a job.'

'Let me guess: working for the Army.'

'Connor! You weren't behind this, were you? You old fraud! I thought you and the military were daggers drawn.'

'I am, my dear. Can't abide the buggers, excuse my French. Wasn't me. But they're the only employers left around here, aren't they? And not too bad to work for, I'm told.'

'Well Gareth said he met some chap called Griffiths who was looking for an assistant gardener and tree-cutter at the big house. Gary's marvellous at that sort of thing, about all he is. Even topiary. So it seems he talked himself into the job.'

'I'm glad. He'll do well. As long as they don't scoop him up and put him in uniform.'

'Gareth would love that. Not everyone shares your prejudices, you know Connnor!'

'You're a Celt, Maeve! This is a foreign army! Where's your sense of history?… only joking. But good about your boy, and they don't pay too badly.'

'And what about you then? I don't know how you make ends meet, Connor. Your little shop. People don't call on electrics that much, do they?'

'They do when they need to.'

'In a tiny place like this, I mean.'

'I keep things ticking over.'

'You do, don't you. And you don't say much about yourself, do you? Not even to Bronwyn. She has nothing to say about you.'

'I'm glad to hear it.'

'No nice little titbits to keep us going.'

'What keeps me going, Mavis, is a small pension.'

'Were you in the war? Surely not?'

'Not exactly. And where I come from, they called it "the Emergency". It's what they call a modest stipend.'

'Like a clergyman.'

'I wouldn't put it like that.'

'You're a Catholic, isn't it Connor?'

'I wouldn't put it like that, either.'

'Am I being too...'

'Inquisitive? Possibly. But you're not in their league yet.' He indicated the old gossips at the next table. 'You can ask me about Zelda...'

'Ah yes, how's Zelda? How are the dogs?'

'Yapping, yapping.'

'Is she the Catholic one, going to Mass and such would you say?'

'Yes, you might say. Have a Woodbine.'

'Ta. Bronwyn tells me nothing.'

'Pleased to hear it.'

'Except that she's your sister.'

'One of five. Will that do?'

'No brothers?'

'Have a light?' Connor looked at her broad face and wide eyes and full lips smiling, inhaling, and he wondered... but stopped. Mavis wasn't really flirting, just teasing and intrigued, he thought.

'There were four. Two are dead.'

'Ah.'

'I was slap bang in the middle of this average Irish sandwich and squeezed out. I got an education. And

Zelda too is a reader, an educated woman, nice voice when she greets you, but she's always with her dogs. She had no children.'

'Ah… is it better to have none or lose one, I wonder. Poor Bron. At least I've got my boy. Simple but nice. Look at him now!' Mavis indicated Gareth at the bar. 'Walking tall, buying his own beer. Here he comes. He's not a bad-looking boy, don't you think Connor? Not bad.'

'Just like his Mam, not bad at all.' He blew a smoke-ring.

'He's blossoming now. The first paypacket, you know.'

'Hello Mum! See!' The boy held up his beer, triumphant.

'Hello Mr. Connor – Mr. Walsh – can I get you a pint?' Mavis nodded happily.

'Yes, but I'll have just a half, love, thank you.'

'So will I, Mister Wage-earner. Half a pint of stout.'

The old men and women had lowered their voices so that Mavis knew they were discussing her son, 'the backward boy' who had always been a focus for pity. News of his first job – especially employment at the big house – would have spread fast.

'The whole of Wales will be employed one day, you'll see,' said one of the retired farmworkers and she couldn't determine whether he was pleased or not. Mavis and Connor smoked their Woodbines in silence and watched Gareth strutting back from the bar with the two halves of stout. He sat down carefully opposite them and only then did he put the beers down on the table.

'Hey Gary, how's it going then?'

'Fine thanks, Connor. I'm doing well. The Corporal says I've got a good two seasons' work ahead. And he says I've made a big impact on the rhododendrons.'

'That's good eh!' said Connor. 'Who's the Corporal?'

'Griffiths. He's my boss.'

'What does he do, an NCO- Just the trees and gardens?'

'And the lake. And he rows the provisions across the lake.'

'Provisions?' Connor's eyebrows began to bristle.

'To the hut.'

'There's a hut? Oh yes… I know about the hut.'

'Not this hut you don't Connor,' said Gary quickly. 'Nobody knows about the hut. Corporal Griffiths says.

'Well, maybe I don't know much.'

'Nobody does. It's Top Secret.'

'Sure. Top Secret. That's right.' Connor had lowered his voice. 'But is there someone called Tom there in that hut, Gary? Have you heard?'

'Tom? No. I don't know. But I can ask Corporal Griffiths if you like, Connor.'

'Oh no, don't do that – don't bother about it, Gary. Not important.'

'Who's this 'Tom'?' Gary asked, looking interested. 'I will, I'll ask Griffiths for you.'

'No, just looking for an old mate of mine, but I'm sure I'm wrong. Don't bother. How did your team do on Saturday, Gary? Win a match yet?'

'Sensational, Mr. Walsh. We only lost by two goals!'

'Tell me about the match,' Connor invited and as Gary started the longest speech he'd ever been able to make without interruption on his favourite subject; his mother listened impressed at the older man's interest in her son. Connor relaxed with his beer as the boy maundered on, thinking his private thoughts behind a faraway expression and reflecting on the bizarreness of coincidence.

He leant across to Mavis with his face so close she expected, half alarmed, a sudden kiss on her cheek.

Connor winked, his right eyebrow shooting up, and whispered as if in confession but for somebody else: 'The name her blessed mother gave her was Nora... never Zelda – pure invention ...Nora Frances Bernadette.'

'Aha!' replied Mavis, delighted with this news and wondering if her best friend Bron was so privileged.

***

Mr. Rees's old taxi roared up the hill with its new young driver and pulled up outside Bronwyn's cottage. She was at the top of the stairs standing on a chair balanced on two planks across the stairwell, painting the ceiling. On her head was an old canvas fishing hat to catch the drips. She heard a distinctive female voice outside: 'Oh thank you! You're really kind!' It gave her an almost physical jolt like an electric shock, and she nearly toppled off the chair. That voice. That strangely rolled 'r' which some people thought sounded French. Her sister, Moira. Bron had watched her as a child, fascinated, as Moira practiced saying this 'r'. She'd seen how Moira's teeth touched her bottom lip for a moment, which Bronwyn found could only produce a 'v'. She, the younger sister by three years, could not help giggling at the sight. She'd had her arm twisted so fiercely behind her back that she could still now remember the pain.

'Oh Bronwyn! Laurel! Coo-eee!'

How odd, thought Bronwyn sliding carefully down from her platform, that all the family names her sister was required to pronounce contained an 'r'. She even claimed that Laurel's father had been called Jeremy. But Bronwyn suspected he'd in fact been a Canadian serviceman called Steve. She ran downstairs to open the door.

'Who painted Granny's front door this dreadful green?' Moira was certainly back. Bronwyn gave her sister a quick hug and picked up her suitcase.

'Oh Bron! That *hair*, dear!'

'What… have I got paint in it?'

'No; but darling, I hope you're going to dye it.'

'Certainly not. I like the bits of grey. Anyway, how are you?' Bronwyn noticed that her sister had put on weight, her cheeks were quite puffy.

'*Exhausted*: hospital is exhausting, even when you have a private room. I need a rest. Lovely to see you dear… you got my card?'

'You're better?' Bronwyn in fact hadn't got her card. 'My kidneys are functioning properly again. I can eat.'

'But not drink?'

'Moderation. Where's Laurel? Oh look, that old picture of the bluebell wood. I always thought that was heaven as a child.' And Moira gave a series of husky coughs.

'Won't you settle my taxi, dear? Whatever happened to old Mr. Whatsit?' Bronwyn shook her head.

'Later. Come and sit down, I'll do the taxi. Then we'll have a fire. Laurel's gone to Manchester to look at a college she says she doesn't want to go to. Maybe you can sleep in her room till she's back.' Bronwyn found herself very relieved that Laurel wasn't there. She watched Moira settle her long legs clad in a pair of well- cut caramel-coloured slacks made from what looked like raw silk. And that jacket was surely suede. Moira took out a cigarette case and offered it to her sister.

'No thanks – here's the matches.' She probably has an expensive lighter too, thought Bron, but she's taking a light from me as her first act of contrition.

From her sister Bronwyn had learnt, early on, what she found to be two of the main lessons of life: that the meek may well inherit the earth, but not so you'd notice; but also that those who live by the sword usually get the best Christmas presents.

It should be easy enough to forget, now Bron sat on the comfortable old chair that had been her Grandmother's, that the elegant blonde middle-aged woman who was drinking her dry sherry on the sofa opposite, had once taken her, terrified, into the woods at dusk because she 'merited sixteen punches' for some childish misdemeanour. Or had transfixed her with fear of the evil witches who lived behind their bedroom door or had threatened to 'invoke the holy ghost' to punish her if she went ahead and recited *'Twas the night before Christmas'* at the family celebrations, aged six.

Those eyes, drooping now and fringed with eyeliner and mascara, had stared at her so hard – no doubt 'invoking' away – when the recitation was duly announced, that the child Bron had been unable to get past 'Not even a mouse!' and had had to feign a coughing fit and rush from the room. She'd had real problems at her convent school with the creed and the catechism after that.

Now she watched wryly as her sister tapped the cork tipped cigarette on the silver case then fitted it into an ivory holder, flicked her match into the fire, inhaled deeply, sighed and exhaled with her head tilted to the ceiling in profile.

No; she clearly hadn't forgotten – but now, watching her sister's thin fingers nervously fiddling with glass, cigarette holder and ashtray, noticing the lines of disappointment curving down between nose and mouth – she thought that she had at least forgiven.

Moira yawned, looking at her watch.

'Well little sister, our news will have to wait till the morning.' She got up, staggering slightly, and stubbed out her half-finished cigarette.

'You may think of me as Racketty Moira – but these days ten p.m. is as late as I get, if I'm not in London. So I'll turn in, if I may.'

Bronwyn was touched to see an expression of weakness, of vulnerability flicker across her sister's face.

'She looks her age for the first time,' thought Bron as she hurried to help Moira and suitcase upstairs to the attic room.

'You won't mind Laurel's sheets, Moira, will you? Only two days old.'

'Of course not, dear. I'll just put my head down on anything.' And she gave Bronwyn a surprisingly warm hug. 'It's good to come home.'

'Home!' thought Bronwyn, unsettled, and went downstairs to a double measure of Connor's special Irish whiskey.

CHAPTER 31

Laurel was swinging the scythe fiercely through the long foliage by the side of the hut, slicing down nettles and tall stalks of wild hemlock and cow parsley.

'I go away for a few days and the place gets completely overgrown!' she called over her shoulder. He looked across at her from his woodpile. The curving wooden scythe handle was as tall as she was, the blade was long and heavy. The word 'careful!' sprang to his lips but he said nothing.

'It's gone blunt!'

Tom was hammering sharpened stakes of larchwood into the ground in a rectangle to make an enclosure for his expanding compost heap. He'd planted rhubarb. He had plans for the autumn. He would get some bulbs… he must tell Solomon he was putting down roots.

'Oh, stuff it!' Laurel interrupted his thoughts, 'My arm aches. I'll get sinusitis. That's what Auntie Bron says. It's either one of her jokes or she means something else. You can't tell sometimes.' She rested her scythe up against the wall of the hut and sat down on her newly cut pile, selecting a long piece of broad juicy grass and stripping it rapidly in half down the centre.

'Where have you been for three days?'

'Shut up. You are about to hear the demented owl shriek with which I welcomed my mother home when I found she'd already arrived…' She stretched a strip of grass along the outside of one thumb and trapped it in place with the other thumb beside it.

'This can be deafening.'

'Your mother? Moira? Is she here?'

'Not exactly here, thank heavens. At the cottage. Listen.'

She cupped her hands and put her lips against the knuckles of her thumbs and blew. A furious magpie shriek cut through the peace. Tom stopped hammering.

'Don't you have this grass in Ireland?' She gave a few more bird calls going up and down the scale, varying the rhythm though not apparently able – or willing – to lower the volume.

She stopped abruptly and the echo faded away across the lake.

'Oh Tom! It's desolation time. Moira just arrived out of the blue. Bron pretends it doesn't affect her, but it does, and it affects me too, and I can't bear it.'

She threw a stick for Muffin.

'It doesn't take long. About half an hour, that's as long as we remain civil. Maybe it's the effect I have on her.' Laurel had an expression in her eyes that he'd not seen before and appeared to be tearing off enough grass for a whole series of banshee howls.

'Talk to me, Laurel. We've done the owl. Tell me about her.' Muffin returned from the lake and covered them with spray. 'Moira's an Irish name, you know,' he prompted. 'Her father was. Apparently, mine was a bit Irish too – but it varies. I wish she didn't smoke.'

'Your father varies?'

'You could say that. The story varies. You know, she's been smoking her Sobranies in my bedroom.' Tom was sitting on his newly constructed bench made from logs and a plank covered with a plaid rug. He pulled her hand down, so she sat beside him.

'Did you know that "Moira" is Gaelic for "Fate"? And you don't have to tell me about your father.'

Laurel seemed fidgety. He noticed she was wearing shoes.

'She once said he was tall and thin, my dad, with fair hair – and he played the fiddle in an orchestra. Which is how she met him, in some musical comedy she was in.' She stopped and gazed across the lake. Was that a boat over there? That tiny speck, coming this way? Maybe not.

'Anyway, I clearly remember years ago, one Armistice Day, she got quite weepy during the two minutes silence. She said it was about my father. He'd been a short dark-haired Celt with the West Sussex Regiment or something who was lost at sea when his troop-ship was torpedoed off the coast of Madagascar. She must have forgotten she'd told me he was a tall musician.'

'So she doesn't play the truth.'

'It's about the only thing she doesn't play. I don't think she can remember who my dad actually was. Wonder what's on my birth certificate? But I expect she's lost it.'

'Do you mind?' Tom asked.

'About the birth certificate? Couldn't care tuppence.'

'About your father.'

Laurel thought about this. She perched on Tom's saw-horse. She'd been asked this before, by Ollie, even by Bethan, both having fathers. The answers she'd given were the easy ones: 'Oh, just one less obstacle to climb over,' and, 'What you never had you can't miss.'

'Laurel?'

'Do you call me Laurel when I'm not here? I want to stop and talk but she wants us to take a run to St. David's for no reason that Bron and I can work out. And she wants Bron to drive and it's quite a long journey and I have to hurry home, but it's not a home now.'

'Are you afraid of her?'

'I'd like to choose a father, that's what I'd like to do,' Laurel said with a burst of energy, almost of anger. 'I'd like to run auditions or something.'

'You could advertise in The Times, in the Personal Column.' 'Or the Situations Vacant. Dad required.' Laurel laughed. 'Would you reply, Burns?'

'Too young – far too young.'

She was off the sawhorse, standing up.

'I'm late!' She wanted to do her White Rabbit act to make him laugh but she couldn't, and the answer came to his last question: 'I'm afraid of something I don't want to think about... Everything is a mystery and just as the mystery begins to clear and Tom Byrne begins to clear like you are right now.

He nodded.

'And when Bron becomes my very best friend… Moira arrives in her high heels and treads on everything and everyone without even bloody knowing what she's doing. And she doesn't like dogs. Oh Mother – what timing; why did you have to arrive just as I am changing. Tom?'

'Yes,' he replied, full of her mystery, feeling her confusion, never closer.

'Say that Irish word you say when you really get angry and want to hit out.'

'Fock!' he said in full resonance.

'Again!' she urged.

'Fock! Fock it all! Fock the whole shooting match!'

'Yes… That feels better… I can face it now… Thank you.'

Though she was hesitant she was ready to go. He called as she sped off, 'What about Muffin?'

'Look after her for me. She's probably hiding in the hut.' Laurel stopped. 'Oh Tom. Most important of all which is really why I came.' She moved back to him. He saw that the dress she wore was unfamiliar and her eyes were emerald green.

'Tom, my sweetheart … the gull…' *There is nothing more painful than love,* he thought. 'My gull you made me. You might wonder why I've never taken it away and just left it standing on your desk looking at the lake. This is where she wants to stay. Her feathers come from this forest, from these hands.' She wanted to bury herself in his hands but merely looked at them lest she stay. 'This is her home. This is my home. Ask her. She'll agree. Now let me flee.'

He stood to watch her as she started to run through the trees, then stopped.

'Tomorrow, Tom!' she called softly. 'Tomorrow night. They're going out. Meet me by the wall, by the new exit.'

'When? What time?'

'Nine. Just after nine.'

'I'll be there. Secret?'

'Shhh…' And she was gone.

CHAPTER 32

They were walking down the road towards the moon, completely swamped by the magic of the night and night noises, the smell of damp earth cooling, the mystery of the road with no one but themselves walking barefoot uphill towards England, the excitement of the risk they were taking. An after-midnight car might come. Mr. Bright the policeman was occasionally called out because of sheep rustling.

Over the wall via the fallen tree they had clambered, Tom leaving his boots in a hollow at Laurel's request. 'Then we will be really quiet, Burns, and you won't get shot!' She turned round. 'This time let's remember how to climb back…if we decide to come back.'

They walked for half-a-mile in silence, side by side and slowly in the middle of the road as if they were leading a solemn procession. Laurel stopped and took Tom's arm.

'What's that noise?'

'Guess!' Tom kept walking.

'Is it a bird? Is it a seabird? Is it an omen? Stop Tom! Listen!'

'It's a creature on heat.' He stood still, looking into the darkness, listening.

'That's an omen!'

'An omen is a portent.' He padded off again. 'A fore-shadow, a fore-echo of a future event.'

'You sound like a teacher!' She caught him up and pushed him.

'I am a teacher. I was a teacher, once upon a time. I remember that now.'

'Oh poo! Don't you wish we had a car. What would you like to be driving if we could have anything right this moment?'

'A motorbike. A Velocette 500 would do.'

'Oh yes! Yes: we'd just keep going, wouldn't we, and I'd hold you like this!' She leapt behind him to hold him tight and walk in step. 'To London we'd go!' she shouted over his shoulder as he turned a purr on his tongue to a growl in his throat and they felt their engine roaring off.

'To Paris, Tom! To Berlin – poor Berlin! To Dublin and Timbuktoo just me and you. Zigzagging like this!'

'Who's steering?'

'Stop! I'm getting off the bike.' She unwrapped herself and moved round to face him.

'Good news Tom: Moira has gone. I've got my room back. She may return – who knows. Ow!' He bent to pull a thorn from the pad of his foot.

'That's where they hurt you, isn't it, under your feet?' She knew he would not reply.

'What was the poem you were thinking of, Burns? Is it your favourite? Is it a love poem?

'So who is your favourite Woman Poet then?? Goodness gracious, what big feet you have, Mr. Wolf. I've never seen them looking so big before!'

'My favourite woman poet's first name begins with an E.'

'Do you remember her words?'

Tom stopped, looked at his feet, then said:

I never saw a moor
I never saw the sea;
Yet know I how the heather looks,
And what a wave must be.'

'Is that her, Tom?'

'I never spoke with God,
Nor visited in heaven;
Yet certain am I of the spot

443

As if the chart were given.'

Tom cleared his throat. Laurel waited, expecting more. 'Is that it?'

'That's it.'

'Can I stand on your feet, Tom? Look how small mine look next to yours.'

What a tableau they made in the middle of the road, in the middle of Wales, in the middle of the night, frozen together, about to walk off with comical strides then dance a kind of Tango, formal and sensual, but holding on foot to foot, head to chest, arms wrapped right around each other, very still, very close, closer than they had ever been in their lives. They would never forget to remember this moment.

It was Laurel who broke the spell.

'Shall we go back?' Then she said 'Tom, have you ever killed a man?' she asked and quickly added, 'Don't tell me! Oh Tom, I feel it here!'

'What?'

'It! Here!' she placed her hand on her stomach then moved it up to her breast. She was swaying in the road as if to dance, but not able to find the steps nor find the words. She turned around.

'Why are we going back, girl?'

'Because there's a Festival of Britain and the whole of London and the river and then the sea, and soon there'll be no more ration books and no more bad effects from the war and no more wars ever again and because we could go on and on and on, but the moon has to rest and the sun has to come up.'

'And we forgot our boots and shoes.'

'And one day when you least expect it, they're going to say "You're free to go now, Captain Byrne, Sir!" and you won't be hunted, and we won't be on the run.'

'Listen!' Tom was impressed.

'Is it a corncrake?'

'You know it's not a corncrake.'

'It's an owl. A good omen. Good bird. We're safe now.'

***

They had parted at the wall without knowing why. Laurel could quite easily have followed Tom back over the wall to walk the winding path to the hut. To sleep together to continue their enchantment. Stay on this moonlit road had been Laurel's vague thought, and now as she woke in her own narrow bed to the sound of digging in the garden, a misty memory of Tom having said words like 'You'd better get home to your aunt tonight' popped into her head to wake her completely.

Buttering toast, with crusts for Muffin, she found herself wanting to increase the excitement of the previous night by trying to make a plan. 'Eureka!' She gulped down her tea and almost tripped over the dog as they ran into the garden.

'*Bore da*, Aunt Bron, will you teach me to drive?' Laurel knelt beside her aunt before a fine trellis laden with scented sweet peas.

'*Nos da*, I should think! Have you been to sleep at all?'

'You know I have Auntie, I heard you look in my room.'

'Pretending to be asleep, was it?'

'Half asleep.'

'Well, speaking Welsh won't let you off the hook.'

'Oh, Auntie…'

'Here, hold this!' She handed Laurel a ball of string. 'You've never been *on* it as far as I'm concerned. Give us a kiss. As long as you're not keeping other people awake too late.'

'As long as I don't wake you up, Auntie.'

'I sleep the sleep of the innocent, more's the regret. Nothing wakes me, girl.' She finished tying and lowered herself to sit and look at her niece. 'What is it child? Have you had your breakfast? But you're not a child, are you? Just look at our Muffin. Are you wearing a bra?'

'Please, please, if I'm not a child anymore will you teach me how to drive?'

'The car. Oh shame, standing all neglected like that. But it's not a very reliable little car, you know. Jamie only bought it second or third hand from Mrs. Rayer when her husband passed away with lots and lots of mileage on the clock. Mr. Rayer had to visit his mother regularly every weekend at least in Llandrindod Wells – quite a drive – and it often broke down, which she denied to James when she sold it. Mind you, she gave it him for a song. Everybody liked James, I don't know why. Of course I do. Don't dig there, Muffin!'

'Oh please, Auntie. Stop it, Muffin.'

'Well,' Bronwyn knelt up again, 'I sometimes can't get it to start. Jamie had the knack. Kickstart, he called it.'

'I could learn that too.'

'There's one of the springs under the passenger seat almost gone. Connor calls it the suspension.'

'Well, we could go very slowly, just along the quiet roads… Round Forest Fawr for example.'

'Where *is* that string?'

Laurel knew that her aunt was now giving the plan some thought so she changed the subject very briefly. 'Shall I fill the watering can?'

'Oh yes, we'll need that, but we'll do it this evening. I like to water when the sun goes

down. You should wear a hat, Laurel. It's very hot already. Poor garden. Poor farmers!'

'Can we do it on a Wednesday?' Laurel was canny. 'Could you

take me for my first few yards on Wednesday?'

'On a Wednesday? Why a Wednesday?'

'Well, tomorrow is Wednesday.'

'We'll do it maybe when it gets cooler. That car becomes an oven. Preferably when Connor's on one of his trips out of the village. You know how he fusses. Your dog's got the string. Quickly, rescue it, cariad!'

Laughter and barking as Laurel coaxed then wrestled a damp, mauled ball of string from a bored dog waiting for a long walk.

'We had a nice little row you would have enjoyed last night.'

'Who did?'

'Me and Mr. Walsh.'

'Did you? Why? '

Laurel was alarmed that it might have been about her absence; that Connor might take it upon himself to find out where she went and become bossy.

'What happened, Auntie?'

'This string is all wet, you naughty doggy.' Bron chuckled. 'He annoyed me with something to do with that sister of his, Zelda, wanting to borrow 'a packet of candles' he asks for as he steps in the door. 'What does he want candles for?' I ask, picturing them arranging some private mass in that little flat above the shop. Black Mass probably. Not seriously of course. She looks like a witch, mind you, Mavis always says, with all that mascara round her eyes, long black hair, black stockings, high heeled shoes. Or she wants to borrow a packet of tea or some soap when it was difficult to get. Because she's too proud to go to the shop and it's just up the road. It's not about money because neither of them is mean. Connor always brings something if he comes to tea and is very helpful if something breaks down. Likes to help. Slow, mind you. And on the occasions I've been asked round there – twice, well, Zelda's practically a hermit – she has always provided a good tea, a fine ginger cake and fresh bread.'

'You don't really like her, do you Auntie? – Muffin's peeing on the roses!'

'Good for them. Pee is good for roses. Our Mam, God bless her, used to be out with the chamber pot every Spring and Summer morning – it upset Moira no end, I can tell you, but it did the blooms a power of good. It's my Guinness does the trick, our Dad liked to say. And she won a few prizes with her roses in the local show. Where was I?'

'Zelda. You don't like her, do you?'

'I do not. She's got her good points I suppose, and a widow too … where have all the

husbands gone, that's what I'd like to know… but there's something creepy about her. Always dabbing her eyes at the oddest of times. Connor always says she's not happy. "*Dagrau gwyneud*", I said to him last night when he said she'd burst into tears just because he remarked she snored too much; he's a fine one to talk.'

'What's it mean, Auntie?'

'Crocodile tears.'

'Crocodile tears. I know someone who knows about crocodiles, real crocodiles, been to Africa.'

'It's just an expression.'

'I know that. Ollie does it sometimes, she turns on the tears.'

'Does she? Ooof, it's hard work, sweet peas. A lot of girls do it. I don't like it, I must say.'

'Me too.'

'Just turn the tap on for effect. Anyway, that's what I said to Mister Walsh. "Speak to me in English, dammit woman," he says. "Speak to me in Irish, dammit man," I reply, "What sort of a Nationalist are you?"'

'Oh wonderful, Aunt Bron! What did he say?'

'Well, it lit the fuse, he took off like a rocket. Turned quite nasty, got quite personal.

Accused me of dereliction of duty, he called it, indulging you something rotten by letting you pick and choose your education – in his day you went where you were put – and giving you too much rope.'

'What's it to do with him?'

'That's what I say.'

'He's not family.'

'Spoil the dog,' he says, and... oh what's the expression he always uses... something about sheep and the shepherd and losing the way. Something very Irish.'

'Cheek! I'm not a dog,' Laurel growled, 'I'm not a dog, am I Myfanwy?' She threw a stick,

Muffin chased it. 'Did you get upset, Auntie?'

'No, no, it soon blows over with him then he's nice as pie… ohhh!' Bronwyn stood up stiffly, stretched her leg, rubbed her knee, looked up at the sky for clouds and wiped her brow with the back of her wrist. Laurel rose too and without knowing took up the same stance as Bronwyn, hands on hips, looking beyond the garden and the hedges towards the forest. There was silence, except for a robin, until Laurel asked as her aunt returned to her tending:

'Where were we, Auntie? Where were we exactly?' She threw the stick again for Muffin to fetch.

'Oh, you have to tie these damn things not too tight and not too loose. More bother than they're worth, I sometimes think, sweet peas.'

'Popeye's baby's called Sweetpea.'

'Nicer than the Latin name which I used to know. Our Mam, your grandmother, knew all the Latin names for the flowers, you know; and the Welsh ones too, or she made them up in Welsh, I wouldn't have put it past her. She could have been a scholar if she'd been of your generation. Bright like you, she was, full of wisdom. And fortunately, the Welsh believed in education, even for girls, even if you came from a humble home like she did. She loved flowers, she did all the arrangements in chapel with Mrs. Bynon. She even helped at the church where our dad sometimes attended because he liked the name 'St Peter the Fisherman', not that he was religious, much too free-spirited. Where were we when, Cariad?' asked Bronwyn, feeling the closeness of her niece kneeling beside her and watching every movement. Laurel smiled and wanted to kiss her aunt. She loved to hear her voice, fully aware that she was spending time with Bron to work her plan but feeling almost virtuous in any event because of the strong sense of love that stirred as she observed the nimble fingers that did so much good, felt the joy of living in this other person who had lost her parents, her lover and her son. She doesn't believe she was put on this earth to boss and bully. 'You're not like any adult in the world,' she wanted to say, 'and I want to become like you with a full mane of hair which I tie up in a net to do the garden. I want to live in a cottage like this with a man as good as your Egyptian, like Tom... once we've travelled the world.'

'Where were we when you drove me to our first picnic, with Muffin. Do you remember?' Is what Laurel said.

'Oh then. Near your school, wasn't it? Somewhere between the woods of the Wye and the farms of the Usk, as your grandfather used to say… or is that not what you were asking?' Bron put down her scissors and tucked away hair that had escaped.

'I mean, Auntie, where were we then and where are we now? What's happened to time? It feels as if I'm in another life now and it's got nothing to do with… I don't know what.'

'Growing up can happen so suddenly,' said Bron, speaking as if talking about herself, 'There it is one day. Here I am. Who's this in the mirror?'

'That's it!'

'And it's got nothing to do with events outside yourself, not really. There might be other places and people that are new and important but there's some kind of fermentation that occurs right here inside you like a good cider suddenly coming right before its time because of something that went into its preparation without anybody knowing, quite by accident really. Who knows what went into your life that makes you this young woman in this garden in this conversation right this moment.'

'I don't.'

'Definitely not Moira... never mind that... or she's had something to do with your gift for survival. Your grandmother once said to me when I was at about your turning point, drawing me into conversation as we set up for Sunday dinner: "A girl is always ready," she said to me, "a girl is always ready, in her heart she's always ready". Now she wasn't just talking about love, Laurel ... something more... there's a word in Welsh... responsibility is near enough, only it's not as duty-bound as responsibility, this readiness. It's something to do with a girl's natural responses.'

'Fertility... are you talking about being fertile?' Laurel offered, almost gasping.

'No, no. She wasn't trying to lecture me on what to do. All was virginity then, I can assure you. She was being philosophical about how women are different, older and wiser than men in most things. She would have added that God made them so, but at least she knew it for herself from her own knowledge of herself and our gender, not from any scripture.

The trouble with Wednesday,' Bronwyn went on, with a chain of thought that was not discontinuous, not to her and not to Laurel, 'is that me and Mavis Preston go up Hylfford on a Wednesday.'

'Every Wednesday?' Laurel asked, throwing another stick to hide signs of the anticipation she felt beginning to bubble. 'Stay patient' she reminded herself internally.

'You know that. You know that by now. It is our sacred duty to take our day out, on the bus, to shop on the riverside, lunch off Castle Square, take in a matinee or a concert at Mill House College. Look, Muffin's burying her stick like a bone. Turn the earth, girl, turn the earth!'

'How about Thursday, then, Auntie, instead of Wednesday?'

'Thursday? Warm up the engine a bit, charge the battery? Why not. Jamie would have liked that, I think. Wouldn't it be wonderful if Jamie could be teaching you to drive? He'd know what he was doing.'

A cloud came across the sunlight briefly, followed by a series of fuller clouds. Both looked up.

'Rain clouds, Auntie!'

'Yes. And it would give us an excuse to give that little Morris a good clean and polish – what are you smiling at, you cheeky monkey?'

'Auntie, that car couldn't shine brighter if it were new.'

'Yes indeed. We'll take the quiet road that goes around the forest. Fewer tractors for you to pass. You don't know how lucky we are, Laurel dear, living where we do to have such an ancient wood when Pembrokeshire is the least forested county.'

'I do know how lucky I am. I do, Aunt Bron, I really do.'

***

On Wednesday one week later, when she knew that Bronwyn was safely away, town, Laurel's plan was brought to fruition. And in the days of learning, practising and waiting with agitation for this very day, the following had ensued:

'Truth or dare or promise. Say promise, Tom.'

'Promise.'

'Fine. Now, choose first from Black Mountain or blue sea.'

'Easy. Blue sea.'

'Wednesday or Wednesday.'

'Wednesday.'

'That's a promise, then. From me, too. Wednesday, blue sea. All you have to do is disguise yourself with a hat and coat – and drive.'

'Drive?'

'Hish! Stop it!' Tom was tickling her ribs so that her serious face would grin as he was grinning, for he thought this was one of her jokes.

But on Wednesday there it was. A gleaming dark maroon Morris Eight with Laurel at the wheel in one of Bron's cloche hats, relieved to see him at their newfound exit spot over the wall.

'Do you remember how to drive? Of course you do. It's not easy, mind, these gears are

terribly stiff but at least I managed to stay on the left and I didn't meet one car, only Davies the postie on his bike and he waved politely so he can't have known who it was and anyway he's not a gossip like his wife. What are you looking at?' She knew the look, a loving look of amazement which always made her blush and then try to hide the blush.

'Get in and drive, Tom… that direction. I haven't got a map but here's Jamie's compass

and I know the coast is west.'

Tom laughed a roar of delight, and he pushed her with his hip across the car into the passenger seat.

'The day is here
The coast is clear
The way is west

Who knows the rest!' she sang and stopped to give the order, 'Put your hat on Tom,' adding, 'Not like that!' as he pulled it down over his ears.

The sea drew them on. In silence, in wonder, with hardly a touch they drove down country roads, over bridges, past farms, through hamlets, Tom happier, she thought, than she'd seen him before. Fewer and fewer trees she noticed, no woods. Hedgerows, a pub, a ruined building, black cattle, sheep, a horse, then gulls. A field with hundreds of gulls feeding, a few flying round. Till they smelt the salt in the air and stopped, parked near a gate on a single-track lane.

They took the first footpath just after a small chapel, a gravestone so weather-beaten Laurel could only decipher the last word, 'Reunited'. Crows, bare trees bent by the wind, flat trees spaced far apart, colourless gorse. The wind now in their faces, air like ether, gulls screeching. Suddenly over a rise, brilliant colour, light and dark, grey and green. The sea. They stopped.

Near the edge of the low, red-brown cliffs with the ocean stretching out and washing in at various rates all around them they stood silent for a very long time. Then they sat against a rock and looked. The colour of heaven and ocean. The light.

'What's going on in this man's deep mind?' she wondered as his profile came into the arc as she scanned all around and above her. 'The same as in mine. A thought without word. A thought that is feeling. A knowing that though one could never tell a soul – no need – there's no doubt that God sits here beside the ocean and stares out to sea just like Tom.'

'What's over there?' was the sound that broke the spell and the voice was so breathless that either could have asked it.

'You tell me,' Tom said as he caught the question and knew it came from her. She was kneeling.

'Another island,' she answered, 'another sea.'

'Yes,' he agreed.

'Home?'

'What?'

'It's home. It's your home. Over the water.' She pointed, and the repetition of the word and the slender finger pointing so assuredly at that place in what looked like infinity, suddenly, with great force, impacted. He gasped. She took his hand. She kissed his hand. He sat up straight, bolt upright.

'Let me tell you…' the gasping was as if he had lost his breath as well as his memory and now, in this whirling of wind and gulls with the softness of her hand, both were coming back. He breathed in deeply then released, on the outbreath, concentrates of recall.

'Another sea … yes indeed… the Atlantic. Our own beach windswept and rainswept for much of the year. Cliffs too, higher and paler than this, therefore a climb down to our boat in the shelter of the cove. The climb back to the terraces, the broad verandah. The well-lit living room with a grand piano. My parents' bedroom, and my sister's, looking onto the sea. Sarah, Ruth and John. Sometimes Sean, Doctor Byrne to his patients. Doctor Sean to the locals, sweetheart to my mother. Blinded by gas in 1917, moved deeply by my mother's music especially the Spring Sonata, 'at any time of year,' he'd say, and my sister Sarah playing the fiddle … later myself on the piano, Marche Militaire, Schubert.

Tom closed his eyes in recollection.

'I never married… the Jesuit College, languages I read, my mother's native language, German… my father's politics… republican devoted, almost anticlerical, a good man… helped with my decision to serve. 'It's an Irish Regiment, not English. Your mother's Jewish.' So, I served. But I couldn't tell him about my transfer to Intelligence, my 'change of side.' 'You have no choice in wartime.' That's the only piece of cant that my honoured Doctor Solomon fed me these last months. You do. You always have a choice. The Nazis found a bolthole on the west coast of Ireland. Money and guns to bring in to support a cause somewhat loftier than their Third Reich taking over the world: the unification and liberation of Ireland. And all they required in this devil's bargain was the backdoor into Britain from the West. "England's embarrassment is Ireland's opportunity", that's how those nationalist friends of mine saw the War.'

And I sneaked off to Intelligence, muffled meetings in back rooms. Just the ticket, choose it, lad; with your fluent German… with all your Republican friends… we can use you… what a challenge … what a farce. British Intelligence: Irish hubris. We'll protect you, said my new English masters. So many of them shipped over to Ireland then to try and stop the IRA.

What a performance in County Clare, welcoming Nazis ashore at night, out of the sea, welcoming them with false papers to safe houses, with their money for Republican guns. And then back to have them rounded up, interrogated, jailed or shot, and not just Germans but my fellow Irishmen too, whose comrades sniffed out the betrayer that I'd chosen to be, stony-faced Iago. Then what a chase, right across the war years and beyond as if I were King Billy himself. But before that, what I've been forgetting, the capture. My protection bungled. Trapped, captured, incarcerated, execrated, tortured. Day after day though for only four days with one day to go before being shot, with only one chance of salvation the determination not to give names … whose? To whom? And who is the enemy? I must choose. I had already chosen to betray my father – his cause – breaking his heart. Now, I must kill. I wasn't trained to kill, only to dissemble, and I have to kill an Irishman to live. I have to crush his skull against the wall with the door. Take his knife, cut my ropes, take his gun. Kill his mate who is sitting on guard with the radio playing a jig. I knew his name. His mate was my schoolfriend's little brother. Phil and Gerald, who also had to choose between two foes. *"Those whom we fight we do not hate, those whom we guard we do not love"*. My father was a doctor, a healer, a model of what a man should be to men, and I – a mad dog with rope burns and matted blood, running and hiding and even afraid by now of my minders, my handlers, with their cut-glass instructions, jolly good … and hiding therefore in amnesia, according to Walter… good man… good woman… the forest and the lake. My mind recovering in your hands… my heart no longer stone… meaning… your forgiveness though you know not what I've done… you… now… over. You made all this…' He gestured with hands and arms opening wider to include Laurel and himself, the sea, the sky and the fields behind them, lying on his back to do so. 'What sky! And you're its Goddess.'

The silence returned for there was nothing to say. She felt she knew him, even before his recent recall.

It was as if there was nothing to tell. There certainly was nothing to tell him. He knows me. It's not sacrilege to be his Goddess. 'What is the sound of his voice,' she asked herself, feeling very mortal. Will I always remember it? Even when he's gone because he has to go, as he thinks he does, or because he dies one day naturally long into the future in our bed…?' she looked at him and closed her eyes and lay back beside him.

'What is the sound of the sea?' she asked softly, listening and prompting him to listen to its movement, her voice saying: 'Not whispering, nor sighing, nor shushing or whining or licking or lapping or lulling or sucking or crying or tearing or roaring or… singing… it's all of these sounds at the same time, especially as it tumbles up the shore across the shells. Oh sea, oh sea!'

'Yes,' he replied, 'one day I'll take you this way –
west – sure, and west and west till we're east and what
is called 'down under' – *Kurrumparree*.' She wanted to
utter the name he had just given her, but it sounded
too magical to repeat, too mysterious to get into so she
tried to change the subject.

'We'll play questions,' she said. 'You start.' The
feeling of mortality was beginning to disorientate her.

'What is this place?' Tom asked, also trying to
return to focus.

'I don't know. Pembrokeshire somewhere. Don't
you like to breathe this wind? It's not cold.'

'What's that sign say?' he pointed through the
clear light to

a notice along the cliff some fifty yards to their
right.

'I don't know.' She looked, frowned, could just
make out *'Pergyl'*.

'Peril?'

'It's Welsh.'

'It's universal.

'It means Danger. There used to be guns here not
so long ago, perhaps, or it's because

these cliffs are slowly falling into the sea. My turn,'
said Laurel.

'What is this grass we're lying on?'

'I don't know.'

'Spongy grass.' She rolled her bottom on it.

'We are as grass,' he rolled his legs.

'Deep dark green thick, soft cliff grass laid here to make love all over until you roll

into the sea or the cliffs just collapse because they're old and trembly. You're the expert on geology, what are these cliffs, Tom?'

'It's my turn. Why do I love you so purely?'

'Purely?'

'Yes. Tell me.'

'Because I love you so impurely. What is Kurrum… parree?'

'It's a sacred place. I've never been. It's an Aboriginal word for where the sun goes down and burrows its way under the desert to come up.'

'Imagine the desert. Imagine us there already.'

'I'm happy here.'

'Close your eyes. Cover your ears so you don't hear water. My nose is running.'

'Catch it!'

'No, lick it!' She leapt onto him, bouncing off the grass without warning to push her face into his. They laughed and kissed at the same time. They became silent and slipped into each other. They disappeared. They had gone both into the desert and the sea, into the oceanic sky where body becomes spirit.

When they came to, before becoming conscious of time and the task of getting the car back to its tarpaulin garage, Tom said:

'Turn away from this view, Laurel.' She rolled onto her stomach and turned to look up the slope to the fields. 'Just over this wall, just there out of view there are lambs right up against it sheltering from the wind.'

'And hiding from humans who do funny things.'

'And if there are no walls and the wind is cold, they know which side of their mother to lie for shelter.'

'I like that… knowing which side of your mother to lie for shelter.' She buttoned her thin blue dress. 'How do you know?'

'I know about sheep. I know about everything that I once saw from my window in my bedroom at home as I looked inland at the fields and hills.'

'Tell me more. I'm not cold.'

'Sometimes the ewe has twins, quite often, and they become friends of course and bounce about and butt their mother for milk, and occasionally you get twins where one's black and one is white. But you

467

never get a black sheep with a white face, though you certainly see white sheep with black faces.'

'Tom, do you know about hippopotamuses?'

CHAPTER 33

There was upheaval at Bronwyn's cottage. Moira was returning the next day. Ollie was about to arrive. Connor, a day later than promised, had been helping Bron to move the old cabin trunk and the suitcases out of the tiny boxroom in order to fit it out as a room for Moira with a folding bed he found in the back of his garage. The two girls were to share the attic room, which had been Laurel's until Moira's arrival. James's army camp bed had been assembled there for Ollie, and Laurel was busy reclaiming and rearranging her piled-up possessions.

She opened the small, half-circular window that looked like the top part of a porthole and wafted the open door backwards and forwards to get rid of the lingering smell of Moira's cigarettes and scent. Probably impregnating the blankets and the curtain, she thought. Even Connor had been smoking his pipe up here while he moved the furniture, she could tell. She checked carefully underneath the bed for any half-full ashtrays or discarded lipstick tissues. Her mother was always inclined towards chaos.

'Life should be spontaneous, dear,' she would say to the young Laurel, 'One should be flexible.'

There was indeed an ashtray and an empty tumbler and a hankie under her bed, and lying next to them Laurel also found her diary.

She'd kept it under the mattress so perhaps it could have just fallen. But the plaited elastic braid that secured it was gone. And her bookmark, a cheeky seaside postcard from Ollie, where was that? It was certainly not in its place. There it was, between blank pages right at the back: how had it got there?

'I can't help being curious about human nature, dear; being an actress,' was another of her mother's expressions. Laurel remembered it with a shudder from late nights in the dimly lit residents' lounges of small provincial hotels, Moira unable to tear herself away from fellow actors and camp followers who smoked and drank too much and laughed at the failings of others, in order to take her sleepy young daughter up to their shared room.

'Here's the key, dear. You just go to bed.'

'But it's dark…'

'I'm busy.'

'That's not busy – it's just gossip.'

'Nothing wrong with gossip … good God, have I given birth to a prude? Love and gossip are the two main pleasures in life Laurel'

'And whisky!'

'That's right, dear!'

'But it's midnight, and you'll wake me up when you come in.'

'It's high time you stopped being afraid of the dark. How old are you? Eight?'

'I'm seven.'

'Well, seven then. Old enough.'

Laurel wasn't really afraid of the dark. The dark was comforting and fed her imagination. It was her mother coming in noisy, drunk and unpredictable that she didn't like. Or tiptoeing in with a man.

Now, with her diary open in her hands, she felt the same mixture of dismay, guilt and nostalgia for an impossible 'motherly' mother that she had felt all those years ago. 'Today I managed to persuade Aunty to give me a big chunk of her delicious Welsh fruit cake for my 'midnight feasts' as she calls them. Burns loves it, so I'm off to the forest to surprise him.

It goes well with his homemade wine, after cuddles…'
No, she surely wouldn't have read it. Mothers don't
read your diary. Do they? But as a mother, Moira had
her own rules and the first rule was that she should
not be called 'mother'. It was the only consistent one.
She changed her opinions and her behaviour like she
changed her nail varnish and her hair colour.

Moira claimed to value personal privacy. Laurel
had often heard her telling lovers or would-be lovers
'I'm a very private person' in order to keep them at
a suitable distance for when she wanted to make her
escape. But she could easily have read her daughter's
private diary. There was no telling. And now there
was no remedy. Perhaps Tom was already betrayed.
Laurel felt cold.

She wrapped the diary up inside one of her
cousin's Fair Isle sweaters and stuffed it at the back of
a drawer. She felt jittery and on edge and had to shake
out the pillows and make up her bed and Ollie's camp
bed with clean sheets and nicely tucked in 'hospital
corners' as they'd been taught at her boarding school,
to calm herself down. She'd picked some wildflowers
to put in a vase for Ollie.

As soon as she thought about meeting her friend
at the station next day, showing her the cottage,

introducing her to Muffin, hearing her news, taking her to discover Tom and his hut in the woods, she felt a warm flush of anticipation which flooded out all her anxious thoughts.

By the time she'd finished the beds she was calm and cheerful and was singing *'What's the use of wonderin'?'* from Carousel as she ran down the stairs. She found she'd chosen the verse:

'So what's the use of wonderin'
If the ending will be sad,
He's your feller and you love him -
There's nothing more to add.'

And she almost walked right into an almighty row that was drowning out her song.

'I'm *not* demanding…' came Connor's voice, 'but why won't you come to my place?'

'You know I can't.'

'Now it's bloody Moira gets in the way… any excuse…'

'You've said enough, Connor.'

'I won't be censored '

'Enough.'

'You may have heard enough, Bron, but I haven't finished…'

'You misunderstand me…'

'I understand you too well. You used to come round. You used to love it.'

'Oh Connor, cut it out. I must spend time with Moira, she's not been well, she's depressed.'

'Bollocks! Where is she tonight? All day, while we've been working as removal men, off with her cronies drinking. Down the pub. That's where the blessed Moira has taken her illness and depression.'

'Old grievances, Con. I can spot them a mile off.'

'No, Bron. Not me. I was never in the queue for your sister. Never ever. I just don't want to see you used. I want you back.'

When Bronwyn spoke again, she sounded calmer.

'Moira's been off in Cardiff, auditioning—'

'So she tells you.'

'It's true. An old friend from the Cafe Royal days has a theatrical project of some sort down there. I think it's a revue. He came over in his car and collected her. He was all over her, she's still attractive you know. Anyway, Connor Walsh, you've got a sister – you spend time with her occasionally – quite often in fact!'

'This is not about my sister…'

'I don't think it's about mine either. It's about you needing more attention.'

'Bloody rubbish!' Connor's voice was raised, and Bronwyn was standing up, flushed and dishevelled as Laurel announced her presence by unlatching the door at the bottom of the staircase and walking into the middle of the room to hear the word *'Bandjaxed*!'

'I'm going out' she said, collecting Muffin's lead from its hook by the front door. The adults remained silent as girl and dog went out into the twilight.

The front door closed. Bronwyn was still standing in the sitting room looking at Connor's frozen face. He waited for the front gate to creak shut before moving closer to her to say:

'You don't look after that girl, either. She's always off somewhere.'

'I trust her good sense, Connor. More than you trust mine.'

'How do you know where she goes? Or who she's seeing?'

'And what exactly does that mean?' Bronwyn asked, moving away slowly.

'You're so bloody relaxed. You just don't know, do you?'

'What don't I know?' Bronwyn's voice had a steely edge.

'Well – like mother, like daughter. Are you prepared to find yourself bringing up a little bastard one of these days?'

In all her fifty years Bronwyn had never struck a man in anger. But now she did, and although straight afterwards she knew she'd never want to do it again, she also knew that it felt good at the time.

***

Muffin had a way of walking that fitted in exactly with the way Laurel was feeling now. The little dog padded along quietly and lightly, her haunches and her tail down, ears stuck out to the sides instead of pointing straight up, giving sidelong glances at her mistress from lowered eyes. She looked like a disconsolate young owl.

They walked together in silence through the outskirts of the village until they reached the junction where she usually turned right to go towards the woods. Undecided, unhappy about her diary and the row between Connor and Aunt Bron, Laurel stopped. So did Muffin, although stopping at kerbs was never her strong point. The dog sat down and gazed sadly at Laurel from eyes that seemed to be brimming with tears. Laurel knew she was expecting to be taken to the woods. The dog must sense they were not going. She felt guilty about the diary. She could not burden Tom with her fears. He would see through her. He could sense her moods, just like Muffin. She bent down and gave the dog a hug.

'Myfanwy; we just have to cross our fingers. I don't know what I'm worried about – be scared of my own shadow next! Cheer me up, please cheer me up!' And Muffin perked up her ears, wagged her tail and gave Laurel a generous lick right across her forehead and down her cheek. 'Thanks, dog! Let's go and get some ice cream.' And they turned and made for the village shop, Laurel looking at the bonnet and dashboard of an unfamiliar car parked near the post office.

'Let's hope nobody's there,' she said to Muffin who knew now where they were going, 'except Mrs. Edwards' fat cat. Don't growl at her, she'll give you a scratch like last time. Just let her be, dog – are you listening?' Muffin put her head on one side and they both turned the corner where just ahead of them large bottles of sweets glittered in the window and four noisy lads bustled out of the shop.

'Oh no, look Muff!' she exclaimed, 'Youths! Oafs!' It was Owen and his friend and two older boys with their shorts below their knees.

'I saw their guns…' said one of the bigger boys, bursting with discovery.

'Any machine guns?' asked Owen, breathless. 'Oh, hello Laurel.'

'Don't be daft, soldiers on motorbikes carry pistols.'

'And the ones in the jeeps?' They were all asking questions and chewing.

'They had revolvers. I saw the holsters anyway. At least five jeeps, six men in each. Then there were the two sentries at the gate. They had rifles.'

Laurel asked, 'Where's this?' although she had already guessed.

'The big house, that Army place,' said Owen, 'you know, the place where you…' he blushed.

'Where I sometimes take Muffin for walks' said Laurel quickly, in confusion.

The older boy was still riding high with his story and scratching the back of his neck.

'So I hid behind a tree and waited, for ages. The sentries just stood there. Later, there was a big, closed van coming out quickly with a couple of motorcycle outriders. Blacked out windows. Looked like an ambulance or something.'

'A shooting accident!' said Owen, nodding.

The boys fell silent to consider this and to chew their toffees. Laurel stood stock still and had to remind herself to breathe normally. The younger boy called Barry broke the spell.

'Poo! That was General Ashworth, I bet. My mam works at the surgery. She says he's got a terrible gout from drinking too much port. Probably dashing him to hospital with a proboscis.'

'How d'you mean, proboscis?' asked the oldest boy suspiciously but excitedly, trying not to look at Laurel.

'That's when your blood goes all thick inside your leg and it swells up, like a clot.'

'Like you!' Punches to the top of the arm were exchanged.

'That's *phlebitis*,' said the older boy, 'our sister calls it *phlebitis*.'.

'Same thing,' said Barry. 'Let's get some gobstoppers. I've got sixpence.'

'You haven't!' pushing instead of punches now.

Laurel had half closed her eyes and was doing now what she had learned from Tom, she was summoning up lists of pleasant things to think about until Olivia arrived to distract her. Only she was listing in order not to think.

'Tom Burns is okay! Ollie will see him soon! He'll kiss her on the cheek. He'll have to bend to do it. He'll kiss me on the mouth. Kisses, hugs, trees, flowers, rods, flies, woodfires, picnics, songs, dances, canopies, moonlight, jazz, journeys, cars. He loves cars.'

'My Mam says that General Ashworth has got a girl of a wife who is very arty!' one of the lads was saying and the others, except Owen, laughed and made suggestive gestures. Laurel stood and watched them in disbelief, allowing her scorn to disperse her apprehension. 'And these boys are just about my age,' she thought with a shudder.

'How do you mean, "arty"?' Owen now asked, half hoping Laurel would hear his contribution. 'Do you mean loose morals?'

'It means she's an artist's model, most likely,' said the largest boy, somehow managing to scratch both his throat and the back of his neck while he spoke.

'Yes, but who is the artist then?' asked Owen. Laurel observed that the four boys fidgeted from one foot to the next as if about to dash off and kick a ball at any second.

And they did shoot off but turned again, pushing the boy with the sixpence back into the shop to buy something that would make a change from toffees, all pretending that Laurel did not exist, even Owen.

'What regiment then? What regiment were they? Borderers?'

'I don't really want ice-cream, do you?' Laurel whispered. 'Mrs. Edwards' little shop is going to smell of boys!' Muffin, sniffing at other dogs' markers on the wall and adding her own, was already tugging to walk on. 'Yes, all right, we'll take the long way down to the station and make a plan. And Bugger that Connor! And Bugger Moira! And Bugger the soldiers! We won't give them another thought.'

This was relatively easy to do because there was so much birdsong in the lane, all unidentifiable and challenging to her, except the robin, and Muffin was doing her zig-zag walk which said 'the cars have stopped, release me' – which she did and watched her tear off to imagine the autumn squirrels were back, leaping at a sycamore, scratching, barking; then ferreting into the hedgerow which smelt of shrews and fuchsia, growling and shaking bushes till petals fell and Laurel laughed at last and then had to call and whistle and slap her thigh until Muffin came to heel.

There were sheep in the field and a farmer staring with hands on hips. Then they played at chasing a chunk of wood which always ended with Muffin dropping it in the stream and Laurel watching it float off under the little bridge when she suddenly realised she might be late for Ollie and began to run towards the station, Muffin delighted beside her, trying hard to keep dark thoughts from her mind.

'One day I'll have a little car and I'll drive us, you and me and Tom into the country proper, up north to Anglesey or the Hebrides in my Italian Fiat. Tom had a Fiat, and he had a Dyna Panhard. He's going to teach me how to drive.' She was listening for the train as they ran.

'I thought he said Dinah Panhard and that it was one of his girlfriends. He laughed. He can't remember other women in his life. He only remembers me.

But I think he had as many women as cars, probably.'

Muffin barked at a bicycle approaching with the postman. Laurel waved and had to leash her little dog. They were there. The platform was a blur until... the grin she adored.

The train had arrived.

'Ollie!'

'Stan! I'm here at last!'

'You look like a star! Look at your hair – it's so long...'

'But your legs, Laurel! they've grown at least three inches... you look like a dancer.'

'Yes, I can almost Tango.

'I went to see 'South Pacific' with mummy – brought the record – wait till you hear *'Some Enchanted Evening'*

'Aunt Bron's got us a bottle of white wine...'

'Guess who Josie Havergill's engaged to...'

'No! She's the same age as me, a couple of months older...'

'Are you learning Welsh?'

'Yes. No. I adore your yellow dress... oh Ollie! I'm so glad you've come at last. I've been counting the days.'

'So have I. Oh Muffin, aren't you sweet.'

'Wait till you see the cottage... wait till you see Muffin off the leash... till you see my forest and –'

'Wait till you see my photos of Alistair, he's delicious... he's lost those spots... is your mother really here in Wales?'

'Here or hereabouts.'

'Oh, is that our taxi, Stan?'

'The only one there is. I know how it looks, Ollie, but it does go up the hills. Come on!'

Both girls ran, arms linked, behind the porter who had already loaded Olivia's suitcase into the boot of the taxi and was holding open the door for them. Laurel gave him a threepenny bit, and after a certain amount of 'After you, Stan!' 'No, after you, Ollie!' they were off. They were about to grow up rapidly.

CHAPTER 34

They hadn't wasted any time. 'Come on! Follow me!' were Muffin's constant signals as she led the way with Laurel walking fast or breaking into a trot, with Olivia, breathless and excited, trying to keep up.

'Oh Ollie, what can I say? I want to try and tell you... They had reached the big trees, the corner of the high stone wall that formed the boundaries of the great wood that held her amazing secret.

'Laurie... why is Muffin behaving like that?' Muffin had started barking wildly and rushing around in small circles in and out of the scrubby bushes beside the boundary wall. Laurel raised her eyebrows mysteriously in answer, putting her finger to her lips. She looked cautiously up and down the empty road and then drew Olivia by the arm close to the wall at a spot where thick foliage hid its base.

'You mean to say there's no gate?'

'All is secret. There's no way in but Muffin's way.'

'Then we're not supposed to go inside.' Ollie pulled back a little, looking up at the wall nervously. 'Won't we be trespassing?'

'Yes. Muffin and I have been doing that every day.'

The dog had now disappeared and could be heard softly yapping at them from the other side of the wall.

'Who does it belong to, this forest?'

'Never mind. I'm not sure. Come on, Ollie. It's hands and knees here but I've cleared away the nettles, mostly.'

Laurel rolled away a large stone and had soon squeezed through a smooth hole at the base of the wall. Olivia followed with Muffin licking her face in encouragement as she emerged into the deep green of the silent wood.

'But Stan – your secret, your Man in the Forest, how does he…'

'Shhh!'

But Olivia persevered, whispering now.

'If you come to see him every day, this man, it must be okay to climb in? Doesn't he invite you?' Ollie stood still, biting a lock of her long blonde hair as she always did when worried.

'He doesn't own the forest!' Laurel laughed. 'It's all right Ollie, trust me. Look at this…' She pulled her friend further in away from the wall.

'Quiet now, we'll talk quietly. It's a bit like going into a Cathedral.' Ollie looked up at the tall trees meeting above them, felt the silence. Muffin once again led the way, taking them along her path but silently as if she knew the rules.

'You know I went to see 'the Song of Bernadette' again, with Mummy' Olivia whispered.

'I'm not surprised,' Laurel teased, 'you want to be a nun, don't you?'

'I do not! Not anymore.'

'A girl who does everything with her mother is bound to end up a nun.' Laurel lifted up a tangle of brambles to let her friend pass.

'She wouldn't let me go to see Ruby Gentry.'

'Typical. She wouldn't let you see 'Duel in the Sun' either, would she?'

'What's this?'

'What's it look like?'

'A log. Are we going to sit here? We can pretend it's our bench behind the hockey pitch where we did all our talking.'

'No, we can't.'

'We told each other everything there, didn't we?'

'We kissed there once, didn't we?'

'Right out in the open, didn't we?' Olivia blushed; Laurel kissed her cheek.

'And nobody saw us.'

Then Ollie suddenly said: 'I'm scared.'

Laurel looked at her. 'You know, I've got a funny feeling too.'

'Is that why we're waiting?'

'There's something important I want to try to tell you before you meet him.'

'This forest is so deep,' said Ollie gazing upward, 'I can't see the top anymore.'

'That's called the canopy. Listen!' Laurel cupped her hands, pursed her lips and blew hard between her thumbs. Out came the call of a woodpigeon. Then silence. She frowned.

'They're supposed to reply. Perhaps they've gone. Come on...'

They charged off but had to stop because they couldn't run together without bumping and laughing – 'Shhh!'– until the very faint path seemed to end. The Cathedral closed in on them.

'Look over there,' whispered Laurel pointing into a clearing of young oaks. 'That's where a very special creature is buried.'

Muffin had bounded on ahead. They pushed carefully through low hanging branches. Olivia wondered how her friend could find the way.

'Do you know, this man can name every tree in the forest. And he knows about the age of ferns: they go back millions of years. One day he says they'll take over the earth again and serve us right. That's what he says. Well, he lived through the war.'

'It's a terrible world, when you think of the war,' said Olivia. 'You know, my father won't tell me about the war, Stan…why are you biting your nails? You don't do that.'

'The war's one of his secrets too. He can't bear to even mention it. All that happened to him. I'm just chewing the skin…' Laurel's voice died away, she was abstracted. She was wondering why Tom had not responded to her pigeon call just now.

'What's that?' Ollie asked abruptly, pointing to something hanging from a tree just beside their track.

'Don't worry, it's not a giant snail. It's a conch. My man blows it sometimes to distract the hunt. The sound carries right across the lake. It drives the dogs crazy, but Muffin loves it.' Olivia reached for it gingerly.

'We won't blow it now, Ollie; it may give him a shock.'

'Are we going to wait here for your man?' Ollie asked after another silence.

Muffin now caught their attention by dancing round and round another tree on her hind legs, tail wagging, head thrown back, yearning upwards and looking into the top branches intently.

'There must be a squirrel up there,' said Laurel. 'Look, she's given up the idea of climbing it – she's trying to fly! Oh Ollie, he cares about so many things – about squirrels and foxes and cricket and poetry and birdsong and orchids and Ireland and me! He taught me to summon him up when I can't be with him. He summons me up. I can even summon up his smell.'

'His smell?'

'I love his smell. You know what he says? Long before I arrived in his life, he says he knew I was on my way. He says I fill a gap inside him he didn't even know was there.'

Ollie leant her back against a huge oak, her hand across her heart, eyes shining, gazing at her friend.

'Oh marvellous, Laurie. Whatever do you feel when he says those things?'

'It's hard to describe. The feelings change so fast. Oh, and touching him, Ollie!…' She fell silent, smiling vaguely and holding onto the lowest branch of the squirrel tree with both hands as if to swing.

'Tell me, Laurel! You can't not tell me about the touching and the… well you know, whatever you do, when you do it, which of course you don't, do you?' Ollie's voice was a practically inaudible whisper now. 'What's it like? If you do?'

Laurel sighed, smiled, and as she started to answer, Ollie noticed that she was slowly stroking the tree branch with the palms of her hands, almost absent-mindedly.

'Oh Ollie, let me tell you everything. I've got to tell someone everything, things I can't

even tell him because sometimes I can't talk at all when I'm with him. It's been so hard not to be able to tell you, face to face, like in the old days. They stared at each other. Ollie flushed.

'What?' she gasped. 'What is it Stanley? Is there even more?'

'More? I haven't begun …' Laurel's hands left the branch and went up in the air and round in two arcs.

'I never knew, no-one told me, books don't tell you what it's like.'

'Stanley, what?'

Laurel stood. 'Can you see that it's me? Do I look as if I've changed? Am I different, Oliver Hardy?'

'Well, you don't look like... Stanley. Your...' she nodded towards Laurel's breasts '...seem to be growing, fast!'

'It's the making love. Everything grows. Oh, it's not a parsnip, it's not a vegetable at all! It's a... like a little idol only it gets so big, it's like marble, shiny, hard, but not cold, it's warm and sometimes it's as soft as soft. Don't look away!' Laurel took both of Ollie's hands in hers and said, 'I won't talk about that. It's frightening I suppose, if you haven't... if you don't know. And the best bit of all is not *that* anyway...'

'What is it?' Ollie's eyes were enormous.

'Just the feeling of feeling good... not worrying about anything else or anyone else and knowing he feels just the same as you do and that feeling is there even when you don't speak to him all day or see him or you're far away and can't get to him and you're missing him and it hurts and even while it hurts you know he's thinking of you just as you're thinking of him, and it doesn't harm your life, this feeling, or interfere with your life, just the opposite. It's… better than just life, this feeling. It's like it's not even a part of this life, this feeling.

Ollie looked hushed and confounded.

'It belongs to the forest, to the Hundred Acre Wood. It's as if love comes from the time of being a child and it jumps from time-then to time-now and just flows out when you're ready… if you wait. Except that it also feels as if it comes from the opposite of being a child.'

'From what? From what, Laurel?'

'From God.'

'Are you serious?' Both were shocked. Laurel never spoke like that.

Oh Ollie, shut me up! I'll show you… Race you!'

They charged off immediately, holding hands, but had to stop because they couldn't run together, keeping step, without bumping and laughing once again. A woodpigeon replied to their laughter. That's not an omen, Laurel thought to herself, but she stopped.

'Is something wrong?' Ollie was breathless.

'I have a small problem, yes. So, you wait here and catch your breath while I clear the ground. I've not quite got his permission to bring you here today, exactly. Though of course he knows about you.' Olivia stopped in her tracks.

'Don't say he's a trespasser too!'

'Oh no, he's official. He's hiding out, he's an official fugitive.'

'Is he a criminal? Are you in love with a criminal?'

'No. The opposite, he's a hero. But not to everyone's way of thinking. So he has to be hidden and guarded in case the wrong people find him.'

'I'm even more scared now…won't he shout at me or send me away?'

'You just have to wait here while I go to his hut and negotiate. You can't see it through the bushes but it's over there by the lake.'

'There really *is a* hut?'

'Ollie! Of course…what did you think?'

'Might have been a tease…'

'But I wrote to you…'

'Not about a hut…'

'Yes I did! I told you his name and everything in that particular letter and how secret it was.'

'You never told me his name…'

'I remember I did!'

'Oh. Maybe you forgot to post it.' Ollie was scratching her knees with nervousness.

'I did post it. I sealed it carefully. You must have got it. I definitely sent it.' Laurel's voice was

raised, nervous.

'Maybe I'm forgetting… I got a lot of letters from you… I'm such a noodle, maybe you did tell me about the hut…'

'And his name; Tom…'

'Well, maybe you did. But surely I'd have remembered reading his name: I've been dying to know his name.'

'Oh Ollie! No wonder you can always be trusted with secrets – you always forget them. Never mind. We're nearly here and you're about to meet him. You'd better hide amongst these trees while I go and talk to him.'

'What if he says no?'

'You can't see me taking no for an answer. Now hush completely. I'll be back in three minutes. Stay, Muffin.'

Olivia crouched in the foliage with Muffin, stroking the little dog, trying to be calm. A few moments passed; Muffin seemed tense. Then they heard a scream. Muffin leapt up, barking wildly and Ollie ran panic stricken after the dog. As she emerged from the trees by the lake, she saw Laurel with her hands covering her face as if she couldn't bear to look.

Muffin was racing round, zigzagging, sniffing, reacting doglike to something that didn't seem to be there.

'What is it? -what is it? Stan – Laurel – tell me: what have you seen?' And Ollie ran up to hug her speechless, white-faced friend whom she had never seen frightened before.

'Please tell me what's happened,' she begged.

'He's gone. It's all *gone*. The woodpile. The fishing rods. The slippers he made me. It's just gone, all gone, completely vanished. He's gone, and he's taken his hut with him.'

Tears were streaming down Laurel's face. Ollie looked around. Nothing there. No sign of a hut. Just a flattened oblong of ground. She looked across the lake.

'Maybe he's over there, in that big house,' she ventured.

'No, that's the Army's place. They were supposed to be guarding him. Perhaps it was me. Somehow, I gave him away.'

'What could have happened to him, Laurie?' Olivia was rocking her friend in her arms. Laurel muttered into her shoulder,

'He's gone. Not even a note. Someone found him. That letter. It's my fault. Connor. The bloody, bloody Army! He always said he should never have come – and now he's dead! Oh why didn't they guard him from *me*?'

'Are you teasing me, Laurel, please tell me,' Olivia asked in complete confusion and alarm at her best friend's wretchedness.

'Is it all a big tease?' she asked again, Laurel now mute, hoping it was but knowing that it wasn't.

'The little shell,' Laurel spoke at last. 'I put it under the pier, his pier...' she moved from her friend to the water's edge.

'What pier, Laurie?' 'It's gone!... everything's gone... my wooden seagull. Gone.'

CHAPTER 35

Beauchamps House was embossed on the letterhead as if it were an invitation to dinner, but the message was military in form and content:

TAKE THIS AS A FORM 216. PATIENT B TO VACATE 23 HRS. 4TH INSTANT. CODE GREEN. GENERAL A. 2:9:51

The impact of the message was brutal, for Solomon had just returned to Wales after a week working in London and Cambridge. He had not been contacted, he felt he had not been sufficiently warned, and Patient B., Tom Byrne, had been extracted. Too late.

'Where on earth will they put you, man?' Solomon asked of the absent Tom as he stared through the windows towards the lake, nothing visible through the rain. 'And what on earth will now happen to the girl?'

CHAPTER 36

'Aunt Bron, he's gone!'

It came out as a hoarse yell, completely out of keeping with the sleepy afternoon cottage kitchen.

'You mean your friend…?'

'Like he was never there! Never in the woods! Gone!'

Aunt Bron was ironing in the sunshine, the Home Service playing dance music in the background. Olivia stood at the kitchen door, Laurel was holding on to Muffin as if she too might run off.

'Connor has also disappeared. Nowhere to be seen.' She put the iron down. The wireless was switched off.

'But Tom was talking to me yesterday!'

'What did he say to you? Sit, sit down darling!' Laurel collapsed into a chair.

'He said… "Hippos walk on the bottom of the river, Laurel", that's what he said to me; he said… "Hippos swim on the surface and walk on the riverbed". When Ollie started to laugh because she couldn't help it, Laurel burst into tears and Muffin leapt from her arms and her aunt arrived to console her.

'Come now, Cariad.'

'It might be a code,' said Ollie.

'How do you know, have you seen them, hippos? I asked him. 'They are very dangerous animals,' he said. It's his favourite country after Ireland, he told me… Africa. But he didn't tell me that yesterday. He told me… what else? About vapping.'

'Vapping?'

'I think he said vapping. It's what fishermen do. It's sort of disturbing the surface of the water, making ripples when you're fishing with flies. He's a fisherman. He says he's fished every river in Ireland.'

'So, he's Irish!' said Bron, the penny dropping.

'Sort of Irish.'

'So is Connor. Oh dear me…'

'What's going on?' Ollie now asked, near to tears, observing Bron turn pale. Laurel hardly ever cried and now she couldn't stop. 'But Connor is real Irish, Auntie.'

'He's that indeed.'

'Not Tom. Tom's posh Irish.'

'Irish is Irish where certain things are concerned.'

'And now he's gone!'

'They're both gone,' said her aunt.

'But where? Where?'

'In different directions I would sincerely hope. Oh, dear me!'

'And now Muffin's run away. What can we do?'

'I'll find her!' cried Ollie, escaping into the garden to search the shrubbery.

'And I'll find Tom. I will! I promised him.'

'Oh sweetheart!' Aunt Bron was holding her heart. 'Come here, come now!' As they embraced, both sobbing, Laurel managed to suggest 'Perhaps he left a clue? I didn't find one, no note, nothing. Perhaps I'll have to search our little places in the forest. There's nothing in our hollow tree.'

'What did he say, what did he tell you he was doing there in the first place? Try and remember what he said!'

'He said – when he condescended to speak to me at last, he thought at first I was a boy or a child.'

'You are a child.'

'I love Nature's arrangement!' he said…I remember that… but he didn't use the word 'love'.

He said he 'admired Nature's arrangements.' How root and fern and rock and moss were

placed wherever you look in the woods. One day we saw an oak leaf fall like a little parachute, long stem first, slowly down onto other leaves which were shaped in a wonderful pattern. There were patterns of leaves wherever we looked so that we didn't want to walk in case we destroyed them. We stood there talking about how it would be in autumn, these patterns. There were thousands of things he was going to show me. The fox… stoats. He was interested in all the creatures of the woods and what he called the margins. He'd seen a stoat take a hare and all sorts of gamebirds. They hunt them on the margins, he says, and chase them across fields and even roads. They usually catch the cocks who are so busy stalking around their territory, and stoats are bigger than weasels, he says, and quick and clever and deadly.'

Muffin trotted calmly back into the kitchen and dropped a small twig on the linoleum.

Bronwyn wondered how near Laurel was to hysteria, how long either of them could hold on.

'You can tell a stoat from a weasel by the black tip on its tail, but I can't tell which is which and you tell a coot from a moorhen in a more interesting way than whether they have a red or white beak: they have different tracks. The moorhen has three thin toes, and the coot has three quite fat toes. Tom showed me and he called them messages in the mud. There are always clues he said. Otter and badger have quite similar spoors. He drew them for me and then he showed me. And one day I showed him a fox's spoor, but I don't want to talk about the fox. We blackened our faces with gypsy wort and pretended we were gypsies one day when he'd cooked some mutton he'd poached when we were tired of the usual fish.'

'No wonder you weren't eating, girl!'

'He cooked it on a wood fire with reedmint, I think, the reeds were full of everything. And we saw grey and purple herons often, just standing. 'Well spotted!' he said to me nearly every day and he said it to himself 'well spotted' he said when he found a mole on my...' Laurel stopped, then giggled, 'on my shoulder blade.' Ollie giggled too. Bron folded the ironing board.

'He taught me the word "raptor"... and we spotted, both of us, what sounded like a buzzard but turned out to be a red kite. Rare, he said, for this part of the country. Oh, that brought him a smile. 'One day I'll show you the difference between a cormorant and a shag,' he promised. 'And if, one day, I return to Ireland I'll show you... '

'What, Stan?'

'He even taught me about rocks, never mind birds and beasts, it was a way of teaching me about trees.'

'Rocks?' Olivia asked.

'Listen, Olivia, she'll tell us all about it,' Bron urged gently.

'Oh, Auntie Bron, why are some things so important? Why are trees so important?'

'Trees?' her aunt responded. 'Perhaps because you climbed them when you were little. When your mother and I were little our father made us a swing from the tree in the garden.'

'Oh, Grandfather Lloyd, I remember. 'Pretend I'm a tree' he used to say.'

'I am the tree, and you are the vine, Jesus says in St John,' said Bron who was now standing behind her niece's chair and gently massaging her shoulders.

'I think it's the leaves,' Laurel had her eyes closed now, as if she could see them. 'That day we saw an oak leaf descend, like a little parachute... "It's carrying a message," Byrne said, 'Messages are clues.' Are all the answers really in the Bible Auntie?'

'Some of them, girl. Would you like some tea now?

'"Once upon a time," he told us as we sat on a mound looking at the gnarls and knobbles on a great tree, "about three-hundred million years ago to be exact, Lorelei, in a time known to geologists as the Carboniferous period," I think he said – I wrote it in my diary – "when the sea was teeming with fish and shellfish and all sorts of sea creatures and as they died their scales and shells and skeletons fell down to the seabed where they accumulated over many, many years and compacted to form great beds of grey rock. But there were a series of violent earth movements and parts of the ocean bed were raised to form mountains and great chunks of continents disappeared beneath the sea.

All sorts of things happened but the final shaping of the landscape – I don't know if it's final really – began about fifteen-thousand-years ago when the last Ice Age arrived," he said. "And most of Britain lay under ice which moved like great rivers carving up the countryside until it stopped, and temperatures increased, and plants began to cover the bare ground, and then mosses and lichens and then grasses and herbs and reeds, and then finally shrubs and trees, to create a dense cover of woodland." Oh, he loves trees.' Laurel paused.

'It's time for tea,' insisted Bron, feeling discomfort and wondering how long to let this outpouring continue.

'You see how much I've remembered? What is your favourite tree, Aunt Bron?

'I like our bay tree. Would you like a piece of Bara Brith?' she added worried that after the outburst there would be a collapse. 'It's our fruit cake, Olivia, Laurel's favourite.'

'He taught me everything,' Laurel continued.

'And I wonder what you did for him? Not exactly nothing, would be a fair guess!' and she added to herself, 'bite your tongue, Bronwyn.'

There was a silence. At last Laurel said, 'He told me I taught him about love.'

'Love?' said Ollie, impressed.

'Yes,' said Bron, quietly. She found she had been holding her breath.

'But who taught me?' Laurel beseeched. 'Not my mother. She was hopeless at it. Love always made her cry and drink. I never saw her smile because of love. I don't think she liked it.'

'Well,' said Aunt Bron, 'I think your Tom was talking about something else, something more.'

'What?' asked Ollie.

'Tell her,' Aunt Bron prompted.

'Well,' said Laurel as if the greater clue was about to be revealed, 'One day…' she paused.

'What?' asked Ollie.

'Just as the sun was setting, both of us dressing for supper, a propos nothing, Tom said to me, 'Laurel, if I worked on the roads and I drove a great steam-roller and if I invited you out and I turned up in my steam-roller because I didn't have a car… would you go out with me?'

'What did you say?' Ollie asked urgently.

'I didn't have to say a thing. Tom was already saying: Because if you did go out with me it means you love me.'

Ollie looked stricken. Bronwyn had her head lowered over the teapot as she poured, perhaps to conceal how much she was moved.

'And he did leave a clue! Of course, he left me a clue, I'm such a sap.' Laurel drank up as if thirsty now.

'I thought I'd have to search through the woods for something hidden in a bottle or buried in his bait-tin at one of our special spots. But he told me, all along he told me. Walter Solomon, that's it!' Laurel's voice rose. She rose too. 'Doctor Solomon holds the answers. He's our best clue.'

CHAPTER 37

Aunt Bronwyn was doing the washing with a small prayer for the cloudless sky to remain so and a deep prayer for her niece Laurel to recover from what Doctor Prosser had diagnosed as 'a combination of girls' growing pains and sudden shock.'

'So what do we do with her, doctor?' An apprehensive plea. 'She can't eat. She can't step out of the house. She can't -'

'She can and she will, when the time is right, Time is the greatest healer, Mrs. Williams, and Time as you know, is one of the Lord's prerogatives. Look now how you yourself recovered from your impositions.'

'She is just a girl of eighteen!' Bron's reply had been. 'She is going to waste away!'

Inspiration, however, came to the Aunt as she remarked with consternation and some volume: 'What about your little canine friend then, Laurel; is she to starve to death too? Look at her!'

'They blocked up her hole. She can't get into the forest anymore.'

'She won't eat unless you eat! She's taking her cue from you, girl!'

'That's her favourite walk.'

'She won't walk until you walk!'

'I'll never go out again. I've nowhere to go…' But Laurel looked, reached forward a little, almost to stroke her dog who looked back with haunted eyes, heartbroken too.

'If you come out with me to see old Mrs. Rees up the hill after we've hung up the washing, then Muffin will come. She needs the exercise. A dog that doesn't run just departs; you know girl. Dogs pine away…' Bronwyn began stretching towels, pulling on the damp material with a vexation still fully to be expressed.

Beside Laurel on the kitchen table lay a pile of magazines that her aunt placed before her every time she sat listlessly. Laurel ignored them. It had been a long fortnight since Tom had vanished and the whole wood had been put under guard.

'After the horse has bolted' was the phrase that kept running through Laurel's confusion. 'Why didn't they patrol the forest before?' she would ask herself. 'Because then you would never have met him!' came the answer. 'And would that have been such a bad thing?' came the voice from the hopelessness which would then take over. No answer.

Her fingers brushed the copy of Punch which lay on the top of the pile. She touched Mr. Punch's nose, then his quill-pen. She looked at the elaborate frieze around the cover; at the date – November 1, 1950; and the price 6d; then she saw Mr. Punch's little dog sitting on a pile of books, in a red ruff and a feathered hat and with an expression she could not decipher. Bronwyn and Muffin noticed her concentration, felt a flicker of a shift in her demeanour. 'Hello Muffin,' she said turning to the first page. The dog was on her lap in an instant. 'See, that's a cuckoo-clock and that's a Pyrex-dish and look, that's what Aunt Bron uses… 'hand-finished Imperial Leather'… and that is what Tom Byrne might have smoked… 'State Express, the best cigarettes in the world', and there might be something for dogs in this magazine… Yes, 'a nice rasher of York ham, please'.

Slowly pushing back her chair Laurel placed Muffin on the floor and moved to the refrigerator. She was observed selecting a dish of cold roast, picking at it, sniffing, tasting then biting and offering half to the dog. Reluctantly then quite eagerly they shared cold mutton whilst their Aunt, with great strength of mind, resisted adding tomatoes, lettuce and cheese to the ending of the long fast.

Then as they all walked up the hill, Bronwyn resisted once again the temptation to intervene, to lead the conversation in the direction she desired. Old Mrs. Rees remained the subject... her lumbago, her delphiniums, her cat... until Laurel said suddenly, much to the Aunt's amazement,

'Tell me about Connor gone.' Connor gone. Jamie and Rashid, too, she thought. For Bronwyn, the loss of all the men.

Bron had to stop to pretend the basket she carried was too heavy, change hands, indicate the postman freewheeling down towards them, wave, then continue the journey aware of her own heavy heart, the sadness and its source having been suspended, lest the memory of her lost son and lost love all come back in a flood; and because she had the charge of a niece in anguish. 'I know this vale of woe; I'll help her get through,' she reflected.

'Let's talk about Connor later,' she said. Laurel took her arm and gave it a squeeze. The hill became steeper here and it seemed that the young girl, with her days of inactivity, was more breathless, more in need of support on this climb than her aunt.

'I've changed Mrs. Rees's library books for her,' Bron said. 'The old lady likes a bit of a romance with a bit of a mystery so I've got her two Georgette Heyers.

'Oh look!' Laurel had spotted swallows dipping low over a roof in the village just down below them. It was Mavis's house and Bronwyn gave a deep silent sigh. 'Thank you, God, for getting Laurel out today, and for Mavis Preston and her little house and her big tree and her big heart so near to me that I can take her for granted.' She saw the swing in the garden, Gareth's swing hanging very still from the full-crowned walnut. A twinge. She saw her son James swinging his companion, Gareth, allowing himself to be taunted as 'the dumb-boy's friend', walking up this hill and down into the valley to fish or finding a hole in the wall to search for nests in the forest. The forest. Was it spellbound?

'Come Muffin!' They had paused and caught their breath whilst the dog, as decorously as a cat, having sniffed carefully first, squatted low, shook herself, trotted off, scratched.

'As for Mister Connor Walsh,' Bronwyn began, jaw set, 'well according to General Ashworth's young *aide-de-camp*… are you sure you want me to tell you, Cariad? Because all of it is connected – an Irish connection of course – with your Tom… a nasty business.'

'Auntie, do your ever think about the war coming back, or the world ending?'

'If you leave it in the hands of these men, when you can't trust them, not even the nice ones, then yes; it will all be over by the end of the century.'

'I shall be about sixty something then and Tom will be … What did Connor do to Tom?

'Betray him!' the reply came like a dart. Muffin flinched.

'Betray!' she boomed, as sheep in the fields turned collectively to check the unfamiliar call.

'That's the word! That was his favourite word of condemnation, and in the end, he practised it. He betrayed Tom! He betrayed you! He betrayed me! And those trips he took to Cardiff and Bristol saying they had something to do with his business – a fiddly little village shop with its wirelesses and clocks. I mean he's Irish! I'm Irish, half Irish. He drinks tea and beer and eats porridge and fries. I'm completely at home with the Irish, he's one of us. We're fellow Celts. And dammit…to think of the promises and offers I fell for. He had just about as much reliability as washday sunshine – I knew that – but I didn't think! What in God's name is a good-looking blarney-sodden Paddy doing in a dull little spot like this? With a sister like that? Making bombs in that nasty little shop, I dare say. And what guarantee that she really was his sister. I shudder to think… Zelda, what a name! Then the two of them slipping away like eels in the tide. What a coward him! What an idiot, me!

'But I—'

'No!' Bronwyn gripped Laurel's arm hard, 'I heard you in your delirium telling Doctor Prosser that you were the one to blame! Not so! It was Connor, not you! It was him responsible for all the upset and rumpus! Men call it politics. Have you anything to do with politics? Have you?

'No!'

'Just you remember that! This is about two ancient enemies, two armies, the Irish and the English and nothing to do with us except we got caught in between.'

'Tom got caught in between.'

'That may well be. But he is not as innocent as you and what you brought to him is the opposite of war and politics, I've no doubt of that. It is no cause whatsoever for blame of any kind. You remember that!'

'And in any case,' she said to herself 'I'm the one to blame, I let you out on the longest leash ever given to a girl, just like your mother – whilst I, as if I were a girl myself, dallied once again with a man; just like your mother. No, darling – I'm not sure what it was that Connor did, but if he was innocent, would he have vanished like that?'

Bronwyn's passion had carried her, with Laurel and Muffin in tow, right past Mrs. Rees's cottage, a cat watching inscrutably at the window, to the top of the hill where she laughed suddenly to see where they were, and Laurel had to smile. Below them lay one of the roads winding all the way towards the sea; before them, rolling, green and endless, patterned and dotted with fields and sheep, lay Wales stretching westwards, thrilling to view for it seemed to beckon: 'Come on! Keep going!

They paused up there, catching their breath again, then retraced their steps, listened to the old lady retelling the story of Mr. Rees's First World War, plus his recent funeral, whilst they remade her bed with fresh linen and fixed the tea, keeping Muffin away from the considerable ambush skills of another old warrior, ginger-cat Amos.

'You know we used Mr. Rees's taxi as a hearse.'

'Your delphiniums look lovely, Mrs. Rees.'

'He would have liked that would have Mr. Rees.'

Finally, she rewarded Bronwyn and Laurel with two small lavender sachets, waving them goodbye standing stiffly at her front-room windows, calling after Amos not to get run over.

'Ah ha!' came the Aunt's quizzical inflection as they reached the village, a bus having just arrived from Pennorth with animated Bethan, Owen and Ollie tumbling out of it heady with discussion of the film they had seen at the Wednesday matinee.

'Do you know what flick they saw?' Bron asked. 'They invited you to join them, remember?' Laurel shook her head but from under her fringe of curls she observed a fickle Owen staring with Jersey cow eyes at every Olivia gesture and swirl, enchanting and flushed in her lace blouse and kilt.

Such amusement as all three tried to explain the plot of *Road to Utopia*; and such warmth of rekindled contact as Laurel linked arms with her best and most well-favoured friend, Olivia, and they walked home.

'You're getting better aren't you, Muff?' Laurel remarked, the evening sun still warm, her little dog yapping at a blackbird. Bronwyn stood at the kitchen sink unbraiding her hair. 'She's going to wash it. It must be Wednesday. Connor has gone so she's washing her hair for herself. It's the kind of hair you can sit on,' Laurel thought. 'I never saw anyone doing that, but Auntie can if she wants to. She'll rub oil in it first, a perfumed oil that reminds her of the East and she might even put on her long Egyptian skirt. How beautiful she looks, her hair gold-grey… and how sad.

CHAPTER 38

104 Welbeck Mansions
Wigmore Street
London W1
21st December 1961

Dear Laurel,

Denn eben, wo Begriffe fehlen,
Da stellt ein Wort zur rechen Zeit sich ein.

It was with deep regret that I said goodbye to you on Friday last week, knowing that I had not been able to furnish you with the information that you had sought with such assiduity, for you had finally managed to find me in this big city despite my semi-retirement and my tendency to reclusiveness. You make a good sleuth.

It was half-truths and half-lies that I told you because, true to form, as is the habit of the prevaricator (to which my dear, late wife would not infrequently take exception) I required time to reflect. For me it was important to understand the deep level of shock that this young woman was inflicting on me as she stood at the door in her red coat and leather boots, greeting me after all this time in informal German, then sitting in my office smiling the smile that had so beguiled the man I have never been able to dismiss from my mind. In spite of my half-expecting you to arrive here one day I had the picture in my head of a young girl with bare feet.

One piece of information that I could have shared with you to help us to feel a little more equal was the fact that the place you had chosen to study German after your sojourns in Belgium and France was the very place where my wife was completing her research shortly before the war, at just your age, some twenty-five years ago. By what strange reach of coincidence should you both have selected the once great city of Cologne.

Goethe is saying on my behalf in the quotation above, since I did not know how to write to apologise to you, and since I am always so devoid of ideas when I am required to act (I am not a psychiatrist for nothing): 'A word comes along to save the situation.' The word is *Veranwortung*. The situation is Tom and Laurel – a love story that continues to be written for it is more than an avocation, it lives and breathes in all that I recall of our exchanges then and it endures in your single-minded search for him now. Responsibility is an obvious translation of the word *veranwortung*, but there is a more literal way of interpreting it – answerability.

My loyalties of confidentiality in my profession, and of commitment to secrecy with the British Army who employed me, can perhaps in this case be overridden by a greater human good. I think so.

I shall tell you as much as I know about Tom's movements so that we can put as many pieces together as is possible. But firstly there is something that I should have disclosed to you when I saw you so recently. I heard from your Tom this year for the first time. He wrote me a letter from right out of the blue and although his precise address will always be censored, he still has found a way of leaving little clues. I feel sure that, with your tenacity, you will somehow manage to seek him out and appear before him suddenly as you did with me, and I take pleasure in imagining this event and the effect that it will have.

One fact firstly: he is not here in London as you had hoped, though it is good to think of you living and teaching here now.

Let us act. Please come to see me on the first Monday in the New Year, if you can. Come and drink coffee with me, as he did, or have lunch with me at my club so that I can be proud to show to my English acquaintances that the ageing Eastern European has a beautiful young woman at his table, and so that I can apologise properly and make amends.

I think it is going to snow in time for Christmas; I send my warmest wishes and respects.

Your obedient servant always,

Walter Solomon.

Postscript:

I attach his letter to me (to us.) It is full of intimation that has got past the censor. We will find him. What an excellent project.

ADDRESS CENSORED
July 1961
Dr. Walter Solomon,
104 Welbeck Mansions, Wigmore Street,
London W1
England

Dear Walter,

Are you still there? Do you remember me?

You gave me this private address ten years ago in the wood-panelled room of the big house, way, way out west – it seems like a lifetime – and I hope that this will still reach you now. You suggested that I give time for things to settle and then write to you as I would talk to a friend. I shall try, for it is a generous invitation and it has taken me an unconscionable time to lift the veil, to lift the pen.

Things have been a long while settling.

I want to tell you that after all your patient efforts to help me to remember, I am now in the position of being unable to forget. Rich irony.

Of course, it is Laurel I cannot forget and our time in the magic forest. I've forgotten all that earlier pain caused to me by those friends who became my enemies, and then inflicted by me on my beloved father when I betrayed his cause – by far the worse pain. You helped me with that one. But I fear that even you could not help me with this that will not go away.

I know that I must forget her. I know that she has a whole new young woman's journey ahead of her, perhaps a conventional journey for a change.

I only hope ours was a good start for her where men are concerned, that she was not too injured by the wounded wild beast I then was who took advantage of her weakness for wounded creatures, and worse, by the clumsiness and by the cruelty of my sudden departure. But now she is twenty-eight. Today she is twenty-eight. Today she might be thinking of me and the bird I made for her eighteenth birthday, with a measure of forgiveness and perhaps love, if my heart is to be trusted in what it says she feels.

Dear Solo man, as she would refer to you, I know I should be thinking the converse, but I don't. And although she might be in some exciting career by now, acting, perhaps, or even married to a good man with children and dogs and cats and a garden, I still want to get this letter and this confession through to you.

I miss you and am grateful to you. I miss her and feel guilty towards her. I remember you saying to me, gently prodding me, something like: 'Guilt is what we feel *instead* of what we feel…' love, Walter. I love her. She is in my marrow. Sweet Jesus.

I am starting to enjoy teaching literature again, though slow to respond to my newest false name in this latest hometown. And sometimes as I walk across the campus of this spacious southern capital, I imagine I catch a sight of her; or when I face my new year's intake of postgraduate students I have an absurd fantasy that she is there, sitting smiling amongst them in the back row. Although in this city I am as far away from the Welsh wood as it is possible to be. There are trees, oh yes; but with birds that do not seem to sing their own songs.

I wonder if you know this:

A mermaid found a swimming lad,
Picked him for her own,
Pressed her body to his body,
Laughed, and plunging down,
Forgot in cruel happiness
That even lovers drown.

Tom.

CHAPTER 39

Canberra is a strange construction, not quite as grandiose nor as beautiful and neglected as Brasilia but just as separated from reality. It was also created for political reasons and filled with diplomats and their entourages.

It had a new university, the National University of Australia, and an anonymous broad -streeted, Eucalyptus – lined suburb called Braddon where Tom could continue to live safely behind another new identity in a colonial bungalow with a shrub- filled garden on Lowanna Street.

His neighbours were friendly, the traffic minimal, so he could hear the calling of exotic birds and the scratching of marsupials who visited his garden especially since he'd managed to resist the temptation to buy himself a dog. He had stayed here longer than Darwin or Adelaide, or Uppsala or Kampala, and by now as the new academic year began, in the heat of late February and his first year literature students filed into his seminar room, a fondness for Australia was taking hold. With ten years gone, he was beginning to feel safe and almost to forget her.

Then there she was – Laurel.

Here she sat, behind others but clear to see, half smiling, with long hair and summer jacket and a tan.

She had the look of someone who has been on a long and amazing journey and is now ready to tell you about it.

Laurel!

He walked from his desk down the row to where she sat. Calm and slow. Nobody else, he hoped, could hear the noise made by his pounding heart.

He bent over her and said, 'The vice chancellor would like a word with you .

'With me?'

'Yes.'

'Do you know the way?'

'No.'

'Shall I show you?'

'Yes please, Doctor Lawton.'

She stood up, picking up her file and bag.

'Then walk this way.'

And she followed him, imitating him as he walked with a comic bowlegged stride out of the room.

He then began to run; down a corridor, across grass, jumping flowerbeds to his car. She kept up.

They drove away, and the university never saw them again.

'Do you want to know how I found you?' she asked.

'Do you want to know how I got here?' he asked.

'Not yet,' and, 'No!' they replied as they sped towards Kurrumpari and the coast with time to touch and to talk about love.

Printed in Great Britain
by Amazon